D0941712

THE STORY OF THE STONE

VOL. 4: The Debt of Tears

CHINESE LITERATURE IN TRANSLATION

Editors

Irving Yucheng Lo

Joseph S.M. Lau

Leo Ou-fan Lee

Eugene Chen Eoyang

THE STORY OF THE STONE

A Chinese Novel by
CAO XUEQIN
in Five Volumes

VOLUME 4
The Debt of Tears

EDITED BY
Gao E

TRANSLATED BY
John Minford

INDIANA UNIVERSITY PRESS
BLOOMINGTON

First Clothbound edition, 1982, by Indiana University

First published by Penguin Books Ltd 1982

Manufactured in the United States of America

Library of Congress Cataloging in Publication Data (Revised)
Ts'ao, Chan, 1717 (ca.)-1763.
The story of the stone.
(Chinese literature in translation)
Translation of Hung lou meng.
Vol. 4- translated by John Minford.
CONTENTS: v. 1. The golden days.—v. 2. The Crab-Flower Club.—[etc.]—v. 4. The debt of tears.
I. Hawkes, David. II. Title. III. Series.
PL2727.S2S713 1979 895.1'34 78-20279
ISBN 0-253-19261-7 (vol. 1)
0-253-19262-5 (vol. 2)
0-253-19263-3 (vol. 3)
0-253-19264-1 (vol. 4)
0-253-19265-X (vol. 5)
0-253-19266-8 (set)

1 2 3 4 5 86 85 84 83 82

FOR RACHEL

CONTENTS

NOTE ON SPELLING 11

PREFACE 15

CHAPTER 81
Four young ladies go fishing and divine the future; Bao-yu receives a homily and is re-enrolled in the Family School 31

CHAPTER 82
An old pedant tries to instil some Moral Philosophy into his incorrigible pupil; And the ailing Naiad, in a nightmare, confronts the spectres of her fevered mind 50

CHAPTER 83
An Indisposition in the Imperial Bedchamber calls for a Family Visitation; While insubordination in the inner apartments reveals Bao-chai's long-suffering nature 72

CHAPTER 84
Bao-yu is given an impromptu examination, and his betrothal is discussed for the first time; Jia Huan visits a convulsive child, and old hostilities are resumed 94

CHAPTER 85
It is announced that Jia Zheng has been promoted to the rank of Permanent Secretary; And it is discovered that Xue Pan has once more brought upon himself the threat of exile 115

CHAPTER 86
Bribery induces an old mandarin to tamper with the course of justice;
And a discourse on the Qin provides a young lady with a vehicle for romantic feelings 137

CHAPTER 87
Autumnal sounds combine with sad remembrances to inspire a composition on the Qin;
And a flood of passion allows evil spirits to disturb the serenity of Zen 158

CHAPTER 88
Bao-yu gratifies his grandmother by praising a fatherless child;
Cousin Zhen rectifies family discipline by chastising two unruly servants 178

CHAPTER 89
Our hero sees the handiwork of a departed love, and is moved to write an ode;
Frowner falls prey to hysterical fear and resolves to starve to death 195

CHAPTER 90
A poor girl loses a padded jacket and puts up with some obstreperous behaviour;
A young man accepts a tray of sweetmeats and is put out by some devious goings-on 212

CHAPTER 91
In the pursuance of lust, Moonbeam evolves an artful stratagem;
In a flight of Zen, Bao-yu makes an enigmatic confession 228

CHAPTER 92
Qiao-jie studies the Lives of Noble Women and

shows a precocious enthusiasm for Virtue;
Jia Zheng admires a Mother Pearl and reflects on the vicissitudes of Life 243

CHAPTER 93
A Zhen retainer seeks shelter in the Jia household;
And shady activities are revealed behind the Iron Threshold 262

CHAPTER 94
Grandmother Jia gives a crab-blossom party – a celebration of the ominous;
Bao-yu loses his Magic Jade – a strange disappearance of the numinous 280

CHAPTER 95
A rumour comes true and the Imperial Consort passes away;
A counterfeit is deceptively like the real thing, and Bao-yu loses his wits 303

CHAPTER 96
Xi-feng conceives an ingenious plan of deception;
And Frowner is deranged by an inadvertent disclosure 322

CHAPTER 97
Lin Dai-yu burns her poems to signal the end of her heart's folly;
And Xue Bao-chai leaves home take part in a solemn rite 340

CHAPTER 98
Crimson Pearl's suffering spirit returns to the Realm of Separation;
And the convalescent Stone-in-waiting weeps at the scene of past affection 368

APPENDIX I	*Prefaces to the first Cheng-Gao edition Joint Foreword to the subsequent Cheng-Gao edition*	
APPENDIX II	*The Octopartite Composition or 'bagu wenzhang'*	389
APPENDIX III	*The Qin or Chinese Lute, and Knowing the Sound*	391
APPENDIX IV	*Iron Threshold Temple and Water-moon Priory*	392
CHARACTERS IN VOLUME 4		393
GENEALOGICAL TABLES		399

NOTE ON SPELLING

Chinese proper names in this book are spelled in accordance with a system invented by the Chinese and used internationally, which is known by its Chinese name of *Pinyin*. A full explanation of this system will be found overleaf, but for the benefit of readers who find systems of spelling and pronunciation tedious and hard to follow a short list is given below of those letters whose Pinyin values are quite different from the sounds they normally represent in English, together with their approximate English equivalents. Mastery of this short list should ensure that names, even if mispronounced, are no longer unpronounceable.

c = *ts*
q = *ch*
x = *sh*
z = *dz*
zh = *j*

CHINESE SYLLABLES

The syllables of Chinese are made up of one or more of the following elements;

1. an initial consonant (b.c.ch.d.f.g.h.j.k.l.m.n.p.q.r. s.sh.t.w.x.y.z.zh)
2. a semivowel (i or u)
3. an open vowel (a.e.i.o.u.ü), *or*
a closed vowel (an.ang.en.eng.in.ing.ong.un), *or*
a diphthong (ai.ao.ei.ou)

The combinations found are:

3 on its own (e.g. *e, an, ai*)
1 + 3 (e.g. *ba, xing, hao*)
1 + 2 + 3 (e.g. *xue, qiang, biao*)

INITIAL CONSONANTS

Apart from c = *ts* and z = *dz* and r, which is the Southern English *r* with a slight buzz added, the only initial consonants likely to give an English speaker much trouble are the two groups

j q x and zh ch sh

Both groups sound somewhat like English *j ch sh*; but whereas j q x are articulated much farther *forward* in the mouth than our *j ch sh*, the sounds zh ch sh are made in a 'retroflexed' position much farther *back*. This means that to our ears j sounds halfway between our *j* and *dz*, q halfway between our *ch* and *ts*, and x halfway between our *sh* and *s*; whilst zh ch sh sound somewhat as *jr chr shr* would do if all three combinations and not only the last one were found in English.

SEMIVOWELS

The semivowel i 'palatalizes' the preceding consonant: i.e. it makes a *y* sound after it like the *i* in *onion* (e.g. Jia Lian)

The semivowel u 'labializes' the preceding consonant: i.e. it makes a *w* sound after it, like the *u* in assuages (e.g. Ning-**guo**)

VOWELS AND DIPHTHONGS

i. Open Vowels

- a — is a long *ah* like *a* in *father* (e.g. J**ia**)
- e — on its own or after any consonant other than y is like the sound in French *œuf* or the *er*, *ir*, *ur* sound of Southern English (e.g. Gao **E**, Jia Sh**e**)
- e — after y or a semivowel is like the *e* of *egg* (e.g. Qin Bang-**ye**, X**ue** Pan)
- i — after b.d.j.l.m.n.p.q.t.x.y is the long Italian *i* or English *ee* as in *see* (e.g. Nannie L**i**)
- i — after zh.ch.sh.z.c.s.r. is a strangled sound somewhere between the *u* of *suppose* and a vocalized *r* (e.g. Sh**i**-yin)
- i — after semivowel u is pronounced like *ay* in *sway* (e.g. Li G**ui**)
- o — is the *au* of *author* (e.g. D**uo**)
- u — after semivowel i and all consonants except j.q.x.y is pronounced like Italian *u* or English *oo* in *too* (e.g. Bu G**u**-x**iu**)
- u — after j.q.x.y and ü after l or n is the narrow French *u* or German *ü*, for which there is no English equivalent (e.g. Bao-y**u**, N**ü**-wa)

ii. Closed Vowels

- an — after semivowel u or any consonant other than y is like *an* in German *Mann* or *un* in Southern English *fun* (e.g. Yu**an**-chun, Sh**an** Ping-ren)
- an — after y or semivowel i is like *en* in *hen* (e.g. Zhi-**yan**-zhai, Jia L**ian**)
- ang — whatever it follows, invariably has the long *a* of *father* (e.g. Jia Q**iang**)

en, eng the e in these combinations is always a short, neutral sound like *a* in *ago* or the first *e* in *believe* (e.g. Cousin Zh**en**, Xi-f**eng**)

in, ing short *i* as in *sin, sing* (e.g. Shi-y**in**, Lady X**ing**)

ong the o is like the short *oo* of Southern English *book* (e.g. Jia C**ong**)

un the rule for the closed u is similar to the rule for the open one: after j.q.x.y it is the narrow French *u* of *rue*; after anything else it resembles the short *oo* of *book* (e.g. Jia Y**un**, Ying-ch**un**)

iii. Diphthongs

ai like the sound in English *lie, high, mine* (e.g. D**ai**-yu)

ao like the sound in *how* or *bough* (e.g. B**ao**-yu)

ei like the sound in *day* or *mate* (e.g. B**ei**-jing)

ou like the sound in *old* or *bowl* (e.g. G**ou**-er)

The syllable er is a sound on its own which does not fit into any of the above categories. It sounds somewhat like the word *err* pronounced with a strong English West Country accent, (e.g. Bao **Er**).

PREFACE

Mid-January in Peking should be bitterly cold. But this turned out a warm, sunny day, more like spring than winter. It was a Sunday, and families were walking in the streets, strolling through Beihai Park, skating on the lakes. North of the broad avenue running along the site of the old northern wall of the Imperial City is an area of small lanes, or *hutongs*, which still retains something of the atmosphere of seclusion it had during the Qing dynasty, when princes and wealthy Bannermen had their palaces here, and it was a 'poetical, cultivated, aristocratic, elegant, delectable, luxurious, opulent locality', a sort of Manchu Kensington.

Skirting the west bank of the lake called Shichahai, I came to a point where five or six of these lanes intersected, and stopped for a moment to try and get my bearings. In those mazes of bare, grey walls it is the easiest thing to get lost, even if you know exactly where you are going. And I only knew that I was looking for a palace, and that it lay vaguely somewhere in this north-west corner of the old Tartar City. A friend had, the previous evening, described the whole expedition as foolishly romantic, doomed to failure, in a country where everything happens either as the result of some elaborate bureaucratic procedure, or through some privately arranged back-door.

Squatting by one of the walls, I took a little book from my knapsack. This book, published recently, expounds the view of one of the most eminent Stone-scholars, Zhou Ruchang, that Cao Xueqin's Rong-guo Mansion and Prospect Garden were in some sense based on the site of the palace I was looking for. This palace at one time longed to Qianlong's favourite Heshen (1750–99). It was then bestowed in turn upon various princes, the most famous of whom was Prince Gong (1833–98), younger brother of the Xianfeng Emperor and doyen of Chinese foreign relations in the second half of the nineteenth century. In the 1930s, the palace was bought by Furen Catholic University. Studying the little sketch map at the front of Zhou's book, I found it hard to superimpose its eighteenth-century topography on to the crude tourist street-plan I had with me, and harder still to relate the two to the anonymous walls before me. I was just beginning to give up, when a voice shouted 'Firecrackers for sale!' about six inches from my ear. I looked up and saw an old man smiling down at me. 'Looking for Prince Gong's palace?' he asked, pointing at the cover of my book. 'It's right in front of you.' He gestured along one of the many walls. But I had just come from there, and remembered seeing nothing but a block of large institutional fifties-style buildings, and a forbidding gateway through which I had glimpsed only buses, a few limousines and a long red screen-wall with some faded revolutionary slogan peeling from it.

The old man ignored my doubtful reaction and started off in the direction in which he had just pointed, clearly intending me to follow him. Several firecracker-sales later, he deposited me at the very same forbidding gateway. This time I read the writing: 'Chinese Academy of Music', inscribed vertically on the right-hand side. I shook my head at the old man again in disbelief. This was not what I had come to find. He assured me that this was the place, made a vigorous gesture in the direction of the screen-wall, which seemed to mean 'on the other side of that', and set off at a great pace, to sell more firecrackers.

Half an hour later, having with great difficulty convinced an unsympathetic gateman that I was not a spy, and having left my bundle of books in his lodge, I was allowed to wander in on my own, in search of my palace.

Once I had negotiated the screen-wall, to my amazement I saw before me, set among utilitarian classroom buildings, 'two great stone lions, crouched one on each side of a gateway' Inside this outer gateway was indeed a 'raised stone walk running up to the main gate'. Here was the palace, embedded in its modern surroundings like a jewel set in concrete.

It took me only five minutes of exploration to understand why some scholars have been led to see a connection between this palace and the Jia mansion in *The Stone* (a connection denied with equal emphasis by another school of scholars). The lay-out is so similar ('Grandmother Jia's courtyard', for example, is exactly where it should be in relation to the rest of the buildings), the architectural style and scale are so exactly what one would have expected, grand but in exquisite taste. Does it ultimately matter whether Cao Xueqin 'in fact' modelled his fiction on this reality, or whether those who lived here modelled their 'reality' on Cao's fiction? After all, as Cao himself wrote:

> Truth becomes fiction when the fiction's true;
> Real becomes not-real where the unreal's real.

What struck still deeper than these resemblances was the discovery – which came soon afterwards – that this marvellous building was being lived in by the very same kind of people – musicians, artists, dreamers – as those whose aspirations were voiced in *The Stone*. As I emerged from one of the long passageways connecting different parts of the palace, the sound of the two-stringed fiddle, played with passion and melancholy, wafted into the sunlit courtyard in front of the Hall of Auspicious Joy. And later, the same young musician began to play on the piano, with feeling and lightness of touch, a set of Mozart piano variations. Just as *The Stone* has over the years miraculously survived the assaults of ideology and intellect, so this palace has come through two hundred of the most turbulent years in Chinese history unscathed, and is still very much a living place – though it seems ultimately destined to become a museum. Palace and novel still perpetuate the same dream.

The garden to the north of the palace is not accessible from the Academy of Music. To reach it, you have to walk out again into the street, turn left, and follow the wall round to another gateway belonging to another institution, to the north-east. It was late in the afternoon by the time I reached this gate. Anxious to see the garden before dark, and slightly inebriated by my success in entering the palace alone, I did not bother this time to make my presence known at the lodge, but walked boldly in. I could just see in the distance what looked like a tall rockery, and had quickened my step, when I was rudely arrested by a woman's voice. It was no fairy either, come to complain of the arrival of some disgusting creature to pollute her pure maidenly precincts, but an extremely aggressive old lady carrying a large green kettle, who informed me that I had no right to come poking my nose in there, that I had better get out at once, and who was I anyway? I said nothing in reply, but hurried back to the lodge. There I was lucky to find a smiling and rather sleepy old man on duty, who assured me that there was no harm in my going in, and that I should tell anyone who asked that I had his permission. He then withdrew into his cosy little room and went back to the afternoon's Peking Opera broadcast.

In mid-winter, the prince's garden has a desolate charm. Entering it, I felt, even more than with the palace, that I was entering a world of vanished romance, a lost domain. The past, the world of illusion and dreams, hung heavily, almost stiflingly, in the air. Finding a gap in the eastern end of the extended artificial mountain which runs all the way along its southern side, I clambered up through weirdly shaped stones to a vantage point from which the first buildings were visible. Directly below, a moon-window gave on to a little partly dilapidated courtyard, withered creepers rambling over its cloister. Over to the left, at the foot of the 'mountain range', stood a small octagonal pavilion, and beyond it a pond (drained of water). On the far side of the pond stretched more miniature mountains and buildings. Looking down, I estimated the total area of the garden at two or three acres – far smaller than I had imagined Prospect Garden to be. But a sense of great space was created by the subtle disposition of the landscape elements. It was a masterpiece of imaginative design.

Climbing down the hill again, I found a plump, red-cheeked boy (he must have been about nine years old) staring at me with friendly curiosity. I asked him if he lived in the garden, and when he replied that he did, I expressed my great envy. He seemed unaffected by this, and offering in a business-like fashion to carry my knapsack, led me off to inspect rocks, grottoes, inscriptions – all his favourite haunts. There had been no other outsiders in the garden that afternoon, he said. A little while later, as we walked along an intricately constructed covered-way that led to the foot of the 'master-mountain' behind the central pond, another (less ferocious-looking) old lady accosted us. She spoke first to the boy, and turned out to be his aunt. When he told her of the purpose of my visit, she laughed and said to me: 'That's our house up there.' She pointed along the covered way to the little house it led to, on the top of the hill, and went on excitedly: 'That's Green Delights, you know, where Master Jia Bao-yu used to live!' At that moment another old lady appeared as if from nowhere and laughingly chided her: 'Come on now, don't you go leading the young man astray with your tall tales!' I laughed too, and went on to explore the rear part of the garden, where the main path ran in front of several little 'lodges', boring its way at one point through the rocks behind the 'master-mountain'.

Returning at length to the southern end of the garden, I found my young companion with three of his friends, playing football in the open space between the pond and the octagonal pavilion. I watched them for a while, and reflected that if it was fitting for the 'Jia mansion' to be inhabited by artists, it was equally fitting that 'Prospect Garden' should be a playground for children – and that their games should be occasionally interrupted by the voices of old women, fretting or gossiping as they made their way from 'Green Delights' to the 'Naiad's House'.

It was growing late, and I had to leave. On my way out I stopped briefly again at the lodge, and inquired of the sleepy old man what institution it was that now occupied the garden. There had been no writing whatsoever on the gateway. He told me it was used as residential quarters by the Ministry of Public Security. As I walked away down the dark lane, I kept turning this last little piece of information over in my mind. That Prince Gong's garden – a sort of *doppelgänger* of Prospect Garden – should have become a home for security officials and a playground for their children, that the mansion should have been turned into dormitories and practice-rooms for musicians – this new metamorphosis said much of the complexity, the contradictions, the light and shade of Chinese culture. It also seemed to me to symbolize the indestructibility of imagination and innocence.

*

The reader who reaches Volume Four of *The Stone* may be surprised to see the name of Gao E on the title-page, side by side with that of Cao Xueqin, and will want to know who this Gao was, and precisely what part he played in the completion of Cao's unfinished masterpiece. The answer to the second question is still highly controversial; but we do know enough about Gao's life to be able to piece together a biography of sorts. He was a Chinese Bannerman of the Bordered Yellow Banner, whose family were originally from Tieling, north-east of Mukden (present-day Shenyang), in what is now Liaoning province.

Who his father was is still unknown (we only know that he died in 1781). There were many Chinese Bannermen of the Bordered Yellow Banner named Gao, and many of them achieved wealth and distinction during the eighteenth century. One, Gao Qipei (d. 1734), whose family also came from Tieling, was renowned for his finger-painting (a style of painting much practised by Bannermen); Wu Shichang, to whose pioneering work on Gao E I am greatly indebted, has speculated that there might be some connection between these two men. But unfortunately, although the past sixty years have seen exhaustive research done into Cao Xueqin's family background, nothing of the same nature has been done for Gao E. Perhaps the next decade will see work of this kind, based on the relevant archives, clan genealogical registers, etc., done in China.

Gao E was born around the year 1740, and probably died in 1815. He seems to have supported himself by tutoring, until he passed his examinations at a rather late age (in 1788 and 1795), and became a minor official in Peking, working in the Grand Secretariat and in the Censorate. The highest rank he ever reached (5A) was that of Junior Metropolitan Censor, in 1812. During his life he had something of a reputation as a writer of Octopartite Compositions[1] (as did his contemporary the poet Yuan Mei, whom Gao resembles in more ways than one). He was also an amateur poet, and two collections of his work have survived, a rough manuscript of early lyrics written between 1774 and 1788, entitled *Inkstone Fragrance*; and a collection of his regulated and examination-style verse, compiled and published by two former students in 1816, a year or so after his death. Gao was certainly not a distinguished poet, but his work, though lightweight, hardly deserves the vituperation that has been hurled at it. In fact, I find one or two of the pieces rather attractive. This lyric,

1. For these, see Appendix II, pp. 389–90

for example, to the tune *Qing-yu-an*, is contained in *Inkstone Fragrance*:

Threads of incense
Denser than mist;
A tapestry
Of green shadows and red rain.
A baby swallow flies past
The office curtain.
Catkins like snow,
Clouds of pear-blossom like a dream –
Another Qing Ming Festival evening.

The gravestone
Bars the road of love;
The cuckoo
Is sung out of voice.
Cut off like this,
With whom can I share this feeling?
The East Wind (that seems to care)?
The sentimental moon?
It's certainly all wasted
On the noble families
Gathered today.

And this quatrain is one of many pleasantly atmospheric pieces contained in the 1816 collection:

Taiping Hermitage

A slight breeze
Stirs the blinds and flags;
Now and again
The clear tinkle of windchimes.
From the inner sanctum
Of the Meditation Hall,
Listen to the orioles
Flitting in the cherry blossom.

When Gao and his friend Cheng Weiyuan brought out their complete printed editions of *The Stone* (1791–2), they wrote altogether two Prefaces (one each) and a joint

Foreword. I have included complete translations of these in Appendix I (see pp. 385–8). I myself believe that what they wrote was substantially the truth. The questions that I want to pose here are: why did Cheng ask Gao to undertake this particular task? Was he wise in his choice? In other words, did Gao's background enable him to enter fully into the world of Cao Xueqin's dream? Did he have the necessary editorial ability – an eye for detail, order and consistency? And did he have the right temperament, did he share Cao Xueqin's outlook on life?

Cheng Weiyuan himself used to be written off as a common bookseller with an eye for a quick profit. This was until half a dozen years ago, when new evidence came to light showing him to have been not a bookseller at all, but quite an accomplished painter (he practised finger-painting) and littérateur, whose only other venture into publishing was to edit a volume of poems written by his patron, the Manchu Military Governor of Mukden, Jinchang. Cheng earned his living as a private secretary – as did his contemporary Shen Fu, author of *Six Chapters of a Floating Life*. In fact, Shen Fu was secretary to a close friend of Gao E's brother-in-law, Zhang Wentao. All of them, Cheng Weiyuan, Gao E and Shen Fu, belonged to a generation that we might call late-Qianlong/Jiaqing. But Gao differed from the other two in that he was a Bannerman, and it was very probably because Cheng knew how close Gao's environment was to Cao Xueqin's that he turned to him for help in editing this fragmentary manuscript. Although not having the entrée to quite the same circle of princes and Imperial Clansmen as the one in which the Cao family had moved, Gao was certainly on calling terms with some of the leading figures in the Bannerman literary world of his (slightly later) day. One of these, the Mongol Fashishan, lived on the west bank of Shichahai, a stone's throw from the palace that was later occupied by Prince Gong. Another friend of Gao's was the Chinese Bannerman poet Wang Lengcun, for an anthology of whose poems Gao E wrote a Postscript in 1782. Gao, Wang and another friend went, one autumn day, to visit the Ji Gate Pavilion, a little to the north-west of Peking. The view from this pavilion (groves of trees as far as the eye could see) was famous as one of the Eight Views of Peking, and Qianlong personally wrote an inscription for a tablet that stood in the yellow-tiled building: 'Here stood one of the gates of the ancient city of Ji.'[2] Gao wrote a poem to celebrate their excursion which includes the lines:

> Hazy trees stretch beyond the cold walls,
> Autumn light bathes the Forbidden City.
> In stylish caps and climbing boots, Ji, Ruan and I
> Roam the high hills, expressing our delight in verse.

It is interesting that Gao should refer to his two friends as Ji (Ji Kang, 223–62) and Ruan (Ruan Ji, 210–63), two famous individualist poets of the Bamboo Grove côterie. Cao Xueqin used as one of his sobriquets the words 'Dreaming of Ruan (Ji)'. It was only natural that Bannermen of the late eighteenth century with literary aspirations should like to think of themselves as reincarnations of these earlier romantic figures, these 'literary rebels or eccentric aesthetes'.[3] And what was true of Bannermen in general was particularly true of Imperial Clansmen. As Arthur Waley remarked, 'these relations of the Emperor led a curious existence, locked away in the Forbidden City and intent upon proving, by a parade of unworldliness and exaggerated aestheticism, that they had no political aspirations'.[4]

Another Bannerman family which Gao E was connected with was that of the brilliant young Manchu Linqing (1791–1846). He wrote a Preface for an anthology of

2. For this, see Tun Li-ch'en (trans. Bodde), *Annual Customs and Festivals in Peking*, 2nd edn, Hong Kong, 1965, p. 69.

3. See Jia Yu-cun's list in ch. 2, *The Golden Days*, p. 79.

4. *Yuan Mei*, London, 1956, p. 187.

verse by Linqing's mother, and was a friend of Linqing's, in spite of the fifty-year difference between their ages. Linqing, as a young man, to judge from his autobiography, [5] was something of a latter-day Jia Bao-yu.

We know from his poems, and from the Prefaces and Prefatory Poems written by Gao's friends for his collections of Octopartite Compositions, that Gao knew a great many more eminent Bannermen of this period. He would in this respect have had little difficulty in recapturing some, if not all, of Cao Xueqin's world.

As for his editorial ability, Cheng Weiyuan probably felt that his craftsman-essayist friend would find this kind of work congenial – sorting out a patchwork manuscript and making some sort of consistent whole of it. In this respect too, I think his expectations were fulfilled. While not himself a creative or distinguished prose stylist, Gao was a literate, intelligent and conscientious editor (though not a perfect one – who could have been, in the circumstances?).

Gao's own temperament and philosophy can best be seen in his own poems. He certainly shared Cao's predilection for Zen (as did so many Bannermen of the time), and expressed his feelings on completing his work on *The Stone* in the following terms:

Gone are the days
When the sun would find me
Still in bed at noon,
Days of thoughtless pleasure
And delight.
Last night
I chanced to see
The Goddess of the Moon,
And glimpsed the brightness
Of Zen's unfettered light.

5. *Hong-xue yin-yuan tu-ji*. Extracts from this have recently been translated by T. C. Lai and published, together with some of the superb illustrations, under the title *A Wild Swan's Trail*, Hong Kong, 1978.

We can also find in the poems evidence of a similar aesthetic sensitivity, and a love of watching drama, that bring Gao close to Cao Xueqin. We find a strong sense of pathos, and a liking for the slightly salacious – both of which are present throughout *The Stone*. But side by side with all of these, we find in Gao's poems many instances of comfortable occasional versification, of a sort we could hardly imagine from our proud, impoverished and probably drunken Brother Stone. And when we turn to the last forty chapters of the novel, there are a few of the same telltale signs – passages that have seemed to generations of readers to betray a slacker personality, a less boldly individualistic outlook, a weakness for platitude and compromise. After all, Cao Xueqin died in poverty in the Western Hills, while Gao E lived on to a respectable old age, a minor civil servant.

If at the end he became rather an Establishment figure, the first fifty years of his life, if we read between the lines of his poems, and eke the picture out with the one or two other scraps of information that have been handed down, must have had their share of turmoil and insecurity. And it is my guess that one of the reasons for his partial success as a creative editor (for this is essentially how I see him, sometimes rearranging incoherent material, sometimes bridging gaps, sometimes trying to account for abrupt transitions or tying up loose ends) was his ability to transfuse at least part (the first part) of the edited ending with a measure of his own autobiographical experience. It is fascinating to watch scholars gradually pulling to bits the magnificent structure of *The Stone*, until we see no longer one man's autobiography, but a composite novel incorporating autobiographical elements from several individuals' lives.[6] Perhaps Gao E should be included as one

6. For an introduction to the latest controversy on the authorship of *The Stone*, see David Hawkes, 'The Translator, the Mirror and the Dream', in *Renditions*, no. 13, Spring 1980.

of these, and his achievement viewed in this light, rather than as the malicious tampering of an outsider.

To be more specific: the decade leading up to 1791 saw a sequence of events in Gao E's own life that would have made him feel particularly close to the mood of *The Debt of Tears*, especially if we bear in mind that during this time he had no permanent position, but was supporting himself probably by tutoring while continuing to sit unsuccessfully for the state examinations. In 1781, both his father and his first wife died; in 1785 he remarried, this time to the eighteen-year-old younger sister of the celebrated poet Zhang Wentao. Only two years later, at a tragically young age, his second wife Zhang Yun died. She was herself a talented poetess, as her brother informs us in a touching poem written in her memory:

> I still seem to hear
> your stifled sobbing at death's door,
> A life of twenty years
> about to end . . .
> Heaven begrudged you children
> to tend your grave;
> The shades should pity me, long absent,
> come to bid you farewell . . .
> 'Delicate clouds
> slowly bear the moon aloft' –
> (a line from my sister's poem *Viewing the Moon from the River*)
> I grieve to recall
> your verses of old . . .
> You died full of remorse,
> pining for home;
> Life brought you face to face with a raksha,
> taught you meek submission . . .

A Manchu historian, Zhenjun, writing at the beginning of this century, deduced from this that Zhang's sister died because of Gao E's harsh treatment of her – and this accusation has been frequently repeated since. But to blame her unhappiness and death wholly on Gao is somewhat arbitrary. The raksha referred to in the poem (which is the only source of information concerning Zhang Yun's death) could equally have been Gao's mother. After his father's death in 1781, Gao was responsible for looking after his mother, who lived on to a ripe old age (it was largely for this reason, perhaps, that he kept on trying to pass the exams). We know, besides, from various lyrics in *Inkstone Fragrance*, that Gao's mother was responsible for driving out of the household his concubine, a woman named Wan, who had borne him at least one child, and towards whom Gao seems to have felt a deep attachment. Wan took refuge in a nunnery, and it seems that Gao continued to visit her there occasionally. On one such visit, when they had talked together of the old days, he wrote the following lyric, to the tune *Xi yu chun man*:

Spring is waning;
The East Wind restless blows.
How can I bear to see my flower
Without her lord –
The Phoenix Hairpin broken,
The solitary Lyrebird in the glass?
Who paints
Those enticing eyebrows for you now,
In your boudoir?
We used to talk of Past and Future Lives;
Now in your life of chanted prayer and meditation,
Who can you chat with
In the old easy spirited way?
That grace and beauty
In the half-lit window,
A forlorn sight . . .
Don't rail at Heaven for being unfair.
Since time began
Rosy cheeks have turned to dust.
However hard you try
To pierce the Void,
Heaven will make you no reply.

Could the 'broken Phoenix Hairpin' be a reference to the famous story of the Song dynasty poet Lu You and his wife and cousin Tang Wan (even the name Wan is written in a similar fashion)? Lu You's mother took a dislike to the girl and she had to go, even though she and Lu loved each other. Years later, when they had both remarried, she and Lu met again by chance, and it is on this occasion that Lu is thought by some to have written one of his most famous lyrics, to the tune *The Phoenix Hairpin.*

Gao's work on *The Stone* was finished in 1791, only a few years after these events – the death of his young wife, and the expulsion of his concubine. Is it surprising that he was able to edit (and perhaps expand) so effectively a manuscript that dealt with the fates of characters like the Ailing Naiad, and Adamantina? This empathy of Gao's is most noticeable in *The Debt of Tears.* In the fifth and last volume, which I have entitled *The Dreamer Wakes*, the reader becomes more aware of 'something missing'. This is, I suspect, partly because there was probably less of the fragmentary original manuscript for Gao to work on in the first place, and partly because, although he had been able to follow through to the bitter end the tragic story of the love between Bao-yu and Dai-yu, and Dai-yu's death, he was unable to enter fully into the two other important elements of Cao Xueqin's grand theme, elements which take on a greater importance than ever after the death of Dai-yu: one of these is the thorough disenchantment and enlightenment of Bao-yu (his seeing through the Red Dust); the other is the ultimate débâcle of the Jia family fortunes. These were intense experiences, deep insights, of a sort that, so far as we know, Gao E did not share; perhaps it was for this reason that he was a less creative and less effective editor when he came to the very end of the novel.

But this is looking ahead. So far as *The Debt of Tears* is concerned, it can, I believe, stand side by side with the rest of the novel without shame. No amount of scholarly argument has succeeded in supplanting these last forty chapters as *the* ending, despite their shortcomings. They are here to stay, and indeed some of the scenes in them are deservedly among the most famous in the whole novel. As the mid-nineteenth-century commentator Yao Xie remarked of chapter 82:

> This is written with such feeling and truth! It says all there is to be said. Theirs was a love that would never change, not if the seas ran dry and rocks crumbled! If the author had not experienced this feeling at first-hand, he would never have been able to enter into their minds with such passionate intensity.

*

In translating this section of the novel, I am fortunate in having had help from many sources. I am grateful to the Australian National University; to Dr David Hawkes and Professor Liu Ts'un-yan for many hours of patiently given advice; to Professor Ting Su of Los Angeles for helping me with the fortune-telling (and telling my own son's fortune); to Professor Matsudaira Chiaki of Kyoto University, and Professor Kakei Fumio of Ritsumeidan University, Kyoto, for help with Gō terminology; to Dr Laurence Picken for help with musical terminology; to Mr Gao Mingjie of Tientsin for the calligraphy on page 301; and to Miss Ludmilla Panskaya, Dr Pierre Ryckmans, Mr Stephen Soong and many others for all their encouragement and moral support. Since my arrival in China, I have been greatly helped by Professors Yang Xianyi and Wu Shichang. I hope all these, and other kindly readers, will point out the many errors which, I am sure, still remain.

JOHN MINFORD

Tientsin,
ten days before the Spring Festival,
1981

CHAPTER 81

Four young ladies go fishing and divine the future
Bao-yu receives a homily
and is re-enrolled in the Family School

TO CONTINUE OUR STORY

After Ying-chun's departure, Lady Xing continued as though nothing had happened. It was Lady Wang who had gone out of her way to be kind, and her sympathy was genuine and deeply felt. In the morning, when Bao-yu came to her apartment to pay his respects, he found her alone, sighing pensively to herself. He thought he could see traces of tears on her cheeks, and not wanting to intrude, stood to one side. When she told him to sit down, he sidled up onto the kang and settled down next to her.

He lapsed at once into a silent stare, and she could tell that he had something on his mind.

'Well, and what are *you* looking so glum for?'

'Nothing really . . . I just can't stop thinking about Cousin Ying. It's so awful. I haven't mentioned it to Grannie, but I haven't been able to sleep properly for two nights now. How helpless and defenceless she must feel, especially after growing up in a family like ours! She's so weak too, and never could stand up for herself properly. Why should she of all people have to fall into the hands of such a bully, someone who'll never be able to give her the sort of tenderness and understanding she needs?'

He was on the verge of tears.

'It is hard, I know,' said Lady Wang. 'But as they say,

"marry a daughter, throw out the water". At this stage, what is there I could possibly do?'

'I've thought of something,' replied Bao-yu somewhat unexpectedly. 'It came to me last night. If we report the whole thing to Grannie, we can get her permission to fetch Ying and move her back to Amaryllis Eyot. Why not? She'll be able to lead her old carefree life, we'll all be together again, and that Mr Sun can go to hell and take his temper with him! If he dares to try and ask for her back, we'll simply refuse to let her go. He can come a hundred times, we'll never give in. We'll just say that it's Grannie's orders, and he won't be able to do a thing. Don't you think it's a brilliant plan?'

'My dear child!' exclaimed Lady Wang, her voice registering both amusement and motherly vexation at this effusion. 'There you go again, carried away by yet another of your silly ideas! How *can* you be so hopelessly naive? Can't you see that sooner or later every girl has to leave home, and that once she's married her own family has no business to interfere? She must look to her own future. If fate has been kind to her, well and good. If not, she must learn to live with it all the same. You must know the old rhyme:

> When rooster crows at break of day,
> All his hen-folk must obey.
> No choice for a dog's wife
> But to make the best of a dog's life.

Not all the girls can be called to court like your elder sister, you know. Besides, Ying is still an inexperienced wife, and her husband a young man. Their temperaments differ, and if at this early stage they don't get on very well together, that's only to be expected. Given time, when they've both learned to understand one another better and have a family of their own, things will sort themselves out, I'm sure they will. You're certainly not to breathe a word of this to your grandmother! If I discover that you have, I shall be extremely cross. Now, off you go, I've heard quite enough of your nonsense.'

Realizing that his mother was adamant, Bao-yu sat there a while longer in silence, then walked listlessly out of the room. Choking with frustration, he made his way back to the Garden and straight to the Naiad's House. The instant he entered the door, he let out a great wail and burst into tears.

Dai-yu, who had only just that minute finished washing and putting up her hair, was shocked to see the state he was in and asked in some alarm:

'Whatever's the matter? Who's upset you?'

Bao-yu, however, was already slumped over the table, sobbing his heart out and far too distraught to reply to her questions. From her chair Dai-yu studied him anxiously for a while, before asking again:

'Well, at least let me know if I'm the culprit or not . . .'

'That's not it! It's nothing like that!' he replied at last, with a despairing motion of his hand.

'Then why the tears and everything?'

'I just think the sooner we all die the better! There's no joy left in life!'

'What *do* you mean? Have you gone quite mad?'

'I'm not in the slightest mad. Let me explain and I'm sure you'll feel as I do. When Ying was here, you saw how she looked, you heard everything she said, didn't you? Why is it that the minute they're grown up, girls are married off and have to suffer so? When I think of the happy times we all had together when we first started the Crab-flower Club, always inviting each other round for parties and holding poetry contests – there seemed no end of wonderful things to do. And now? Bao-chai has already moved out, which means Caltrop can't come over either, and with Ying gone as well, our band of kindred spirits is being broken up, everything is being spoiled!

'I had thought of a plan, to get Grannie on our side and rescue Ying. But when I told Mother, she just called me naive and silly and wouldn't take me seriously. So I had to give up the idea.

'You only have to look around you! Our Garden's altered so much in such a short time. What could become of it in the next few years just doesn't bear thinking about. Now do you see what I mean, and why I can't help despairing?'

As she listened to all that he was saying, Dai-yu very slowly bowed her head and moved back almost imperceptibly onto the kang. She did not say a word, but only sighed and curled up facing the wall.

This was how Nightingale found them when she came in to serve tea. Her attempts to puzzle out what could have happened were cut short by the arrival of Aroma.

'So this is where you are!' she said as she came into the room. 'You're wanted at Her Old Ladyship's, Master Bao. I thought I'd find you here...'

Recognizing Aroma's voice, Dai-yu sat up a little and nodded to her to sit down. Bao-yu noticed that her eyes were red from crying.

'I got a bit carried away, coz,' he said. 'Please don't take it to heart so. What you must do is look after yourself properly and get fit and well. And when I say that, I mean it. So have a rest now. I'm wanted at Grannie's. I'll be back.'

With these words he set off.

'What's up with you two then?' whispered Aroma.

'Oh, he's upset about Miss Ying,' Dai-yu replied. 'I'm all right. My eyes have been itching and I've been rubbing them, that's all.'

Aroma said nothing and hurried out after Bao-yu. He reached Grandmother Jia's only to find that she had already retired for her midday nap, and was obliged to go back to Green Delights.

In the afternoon he woke from his sleep feeling very bored, and picked up a book to read. Aroma hurried off to make tea, eager to sustain him in his studies. He had chanced upon an anthology of early verse, and as he turned its pages found himself reading a stanza by Cao Cao:

> Come drink with me and sing,
> For life's a fleeting thing.
> Full many a day has fled
> Like the morning dew . . .

Far from distracting him, this only served to increase his ennui, and he put the book down and picked up another. This time it was '*The Gathering at Orchid Pavilion* and other Prose Selections from the Jin Dynasty'. After a page or two he suddenly closed it, and when Aroma returned with his tea, she found him sitting there, head propped on hand, looking his most dazed and distant.

'Why have you given up so soon?' she asked.

Bao-yu took his tea without a word of reply, drank a sip, then mechanically replaced the cup. Aroma was out of her depth and could do nothing but stand there dumbly looking on. Suddenly he stood up, and muttered sarcastically:

> '*Oh gemlike ecstasy . . .*'

Aroma half-wanted to laugh, but on reflection thought it safer not to probe too far.

'If you don't feel like reading,' she suggested tactfully, 'why not go for a walk in the Garden? There's no sense in sitting here and working yourself up into one of your states again.'

Bao-yu mumbled something in reply and walked abstractedly out of the room.

He soon came to Drenched Blossoms Pavilion, and gazed out over the lake. All around him he saw nothing but dereliction and decay. Walking on, he reached All Spice Court, which was locked and shuttered. Only its rockery was still tenanted by the familiar herbs and creepers. He was just turning to go on past the Lotus Pavilion, when something caught his eye. Looking across the water, he could just distinguish a small group of people leaning over the stone balustrade on Smartweed Bank, and some maids down below, squatting on their heels and apparently searching for something. He darted behind a large rock and crept up on them, listening all the while.

'Will it come up? Will it...'

He thought he recognized the voice of Li Wan's cousin, Li Wen. Then came a laugh:

'There! It's gone! You see, I told you it wouldn't bite!' (There was no mistaking Tan-chun's voice.)

'Of course it won't if you keep moving about like that, Wen!'

'Look! It's going to!'

The last two voices were those of Li Wen's younger sister Qi, and Lady Xing's niece Xiu-yan.

Such an opportunity was altogether too tempting. Picking a brickbat from the ground, Bao-yu lobbed it into the water right in front of the four girls. There was a resounding splash and they jumped for their lives, with cries of:

'What the... Who's that trying to give us a scare? Of all the mean...'

A beaming Bao-yu sprang from his hiding-place.

'Having a lovely time, are you? And why wasn't I invited, pray?'

It was Tan-chun who replied:

'Typical! I knew it! That had "Bao-yu" written all over it! Well I'm not going to waste my breath scolding you, just hurry up and catch us another fish to make up for that one. It was practically on the hook when you had to come along and scare it away.'

'Not likely!' said Bao-yu with a grin. 'Here you are on a fishing excursion and leaving me out – it's you who owe me a penalty!'

Everyone laughed.

'I know,' he went on. 'As we're all fishing today, why don't we try a round of "Fateful Fish"? It's very simple.

If you catch a fish it means a year of good luck, and if you don't a year of bad luck. Come on, who's going to have first go?'

Tan-chun offered the rod to Li Wen, but she declined.

'Oh well,' said Tan-chun, 'it looks as if I'll have to start.'

She turned to Bao-yu. 'If you scare mine away again, brother, you'll be for it.'

'I only wanted to make you all jump. You'll be perfectly safe this time, I promise.'

Tan-chun cast her line, and in just a few seconds a little 'leaf-wriggler' swallowed the hook and down went the float. She pulled in and landed her catch, alive and jumping. Scribe, after a lot of scrambling about, managed to get a grip on the thing, and carrying it over in both hands, placed it carefully in a little earthenware jar of fresh water. Tan-chun passed the rod on to Wen. She too felt a tug on the line almost immediately, and pulled in excitedly, only to find nothing on the hook. She cast out again, and this time stood there angling for ages. At last the line tautened and she pulled in again. Another false alarm. She picked up the hook to examine it, and discovered that it was buckled.

'No wonder I couldn't catch anything!'

She laughed and without more ado told Candida to straighten it out for her, put on some fresh bait and fasten on the reed-float securely. This time after only a few minutes, down went the float, in she pulled with great determination, and there it was – a little two-inch silver carp. Delighted, she turned to Bao-yu.

'You next.'

'Qi and Xiu-yan must go first,' replied Bao-yu. 'I insist.'

Xiu-yan was silent.

'You go first, Cousin Bao,' protested Qi. As she spoke a big bubble popped on the water.

'Come on!' cried Tan-chun. 'There's no need to overdo

it. Look, the fish are all over there by you, Qi. You have a go quickly!'

Qi took the rod with a giggle of embarrassment. Sure enough, down went her float and she had a catch first time. Xiu-yan was the last of the girls to have her turn. She caught one and passed the rod back to Tan-chun, who handed it on to Bao-yu.

'I shall follow in the footsteps of old Sire Jiang,' he declared.

'Straight was his hook,
  His bait a single grain:
Yet of their own accord
  The fish unto him came . . .'

Walking solemnly down the jetty, he sat at the water's edge in the pose of the Fisherman Sage. Unfortunately, at the approach of this human shadow, the fish took refuge in the far end of the pond, and for all his exertions in the higher art of angling, a long time seemed to pass without the slightest sign of a bite. When once a fish did venture near and deigned to blow a few bubbles near the bank, he jerked the rod and scared it away.

'Oh dear!' he sighed. 'It's no good. The trouble is that I'm so confoundedly impatient, and the fish are so slow on the uptake. We must be incompatible. I shall never catch anything at this rate. Come on now, help me! *Feel* yourself being drawn, there's my brave little fish!'

There was a peal of laughter from the girls. Then, before anyone could say a word, the line was seen to move a fraction. A bite at last! The sage yanked in for all he was worth. The rod crashed into a protruding rock and broke clean in two. The line snapped, and the hook (with whatever it may or may not have secured) sank without trace. This final stroke of virtuosity had his audience in stitches. Tan-chun called out:

'I've never seen such a clumsy fool!'

As she was speaking, who should come rushing up but Musk, in a state of great excitement.

'Master Bao, Her Old Ladyship has woken up and wants to see you at once!'

The five of them exchanged startled glances.

'But what about?' asked Tan-chun.

'I don't know,' replied Musk. 'All I heard was something about a "scandalous revelation" they want to question Master Bao about. They've asked Mrs Lian to come and answer questions as well.'

Bao-yu stood for a moment in stunned silence. Eventually he said:

'I wonder which poor maid is in for the high jump this time?'

'We've no idea what it's about,' said Tan-chun, 'so Bao, you'd better go straight away and as soon as you've any news, send Musk over to let us know.'

The four girls went their way, and Bao-yu set off for Grandmother Jia's apartment. He arrived to find her in the middle of a game of cards with Lady Wang, and realized to his relief that it could be nothing as serious as he had feared. Grandmother Jia saw him come in and asked him:

'Bao darling, do you remember last year, when you were so seriously ill , and those two holy men – that mad-looking monk and that lame Taoist – came and cured you, in the nick of time – what did the illness feel like?'

Bao-yu reflected for a moment.

'I can remember how it started. I was standing in my room when suddenly someone seemed to come from behind and ram something hard, like a wooden bar, up against the back of my head. It hurt like anything, my eyes started throbbing and everything went pitch-black. All I could see in the room was a mob of green-faced devils with huge fangs, carrying swords and cudgels. I went to lie down on the kang, but then it felt as if I had tight bands round my head and the pain became so excruciating that I no longer knew what was happening.

'I remember how I got better. There was a ray of golden light from the hall outside my room, that shone right onto my bed. The devils just took to their heels and vanished. They seemed scared of the light. My headache went away and I felt quite myself again.'

'You see!' exclaimed Grandmother Jia, turning to Lady Wang. 'It ties in perfectly.'

As she was speaking, Xi-feng entered the room and greeted first Grandmother Jia, then Lady Wang.

'What did you want to ask me about, Grannie?' she asked.

'Tell me,' replied Grandmother Jia, 'can you recall that nasty attack you had last year?'

Xi-feng laughed.

'Not very clearly. The main thing I remember about it is that I was possessed. There was someone manipulating me, filling my head with the most bloodthirsty intentions. I had a terrible urge to grab hold of everything in sight and kill it. I was exhausted, but I couldn't stop.'

'And then?' asked Grandmother Jia. 'When you were cured?'

'There was a voice,' replied Xi-feng, 'that seemed to speak to me from nowhere. But what it said I honestly can't remember.'

'That settles it!' exclaimed the old lady. 'That's exactly the sort of thing she got up to! So it *was* her doing, it must have been! Oh! How could the old woman sink so low – and Bao-yu's own godmother too! Gracious Lord, to think that if those two holy men had not arrived in time, he might easily have died! And we still have not repaid them . . .'

'But Grannie,' asked Xi-feng, 'what made you think of all this in the first place?'

'Ask your aunt,' replied Grandmother Jia. 'I've done enough of the talking.'

Lady Wang took over the story.

'Sir Zheng told us when he was here this morning. Apparently Bao-yu's godmother, Mother Ma, is an evil old woman and a practising witch. As the result of certain scandalous revelations, she's been arrested by the secret police and sent to the Central Jail. I should imagine she's been sentenced to death by now.

'The whole thing started the other day, when a Mr Pan San-bao informed against her. He had been trying to sell a property to a pawnbroker across the street. His price had already risen by several hundred per cent, and when he asked for more the pawnbroker backed out. So, in an attempt to salvage his sale, Mr Pan hired the services of our Mother Ma, whom he knew to be a regular visitor at the pawnshop and intimate with all the womenfolk there. She duly succeeded, by some evil means, in throwing the pawnbroker's wife into a convulsion. Then, waiting until the attack reached alarming proportions, she had the effrontery to arrive in person, claiming to possess a patent cure for the affliction. And sure enough, after a few burnt offerings of her paper charms, paper money and so forth, the wife recovered and the witch coolly demanded a dozen or so taels of silver for her services in exorcizing her own spell!

'But nothing escapes the watchful eye of the Good Lord Buddha,' continued Lady Wang. 'Her detection and downfall were already close at hand. That same day, in her haste to leave the pawnbroker's premises, she inadvertently dropped a silk bundle. The pawnbroker picked it up, took a look inside, and noticed a number of paper figures and four unusually potent cakes of incense. He became suspicious, and when the old woman returned to recover her bundle he seized her and subjected her to a quick search. He discovered hidden on her person a casket containing two ivory statuettes, a male and a female, both completely naked – you know those pocket-sized figures of the devil they use – and seven red embroidery needles.

'She was taken straight to the secret police, and when questioned revealed her intimate connections with the mistresses and young ladies of several eminent and wealthy families. The case was reported to the highest authorities, and her house was searched. They found quite a few clay figures of those horrible Spectral Furies and several boxes of narcotic incense; also, hanging in a hidden compartment behind the kang, a Seven Star Lamp with all kinds of straw effigies spread below it, some with bands round their heads, others with nails through their chests or padlocks round their necks. She had a whole cupboard full of spare paper figures, and there were account slips all over the floor, listing families dealt with and amounts outstanding, together with records of goodness knows how much money received for "oil and incense".'

'Our attacks were definitely her doing!' exclaimed Xi-feng. 'I remember now. It was after we recovered – when the old witch came to visit Aunt Zhao a couple of times to collect her "contributions" – something horrible seemed to come over her when she saw me; she went pale, and there was a nasty look in her eyes. I wondered what it meant at the time, but I just couldn't see any reason for her to cause trouble. After what you've just said, though, it all makes sense. With my responsibilities I can't help making enemies, and some of them are bound to try and get their own back somehow or other. But who could bear a grudge against Bao-yu? That must be pure malice.'

'Or jealousy,' suggested Grandmother Jia, 'because she knows I'm not as fond of Huan as I am of Bao-yu. Perhaps that's why she tried to harm you both.'

'Anyway,' said Lady Wang, 'as the old woman is already in prison, we won't be able to call on her to testify, and without her evidence we will never be able to make Aunt Zhao confess. Besides we simply can't have the family involved in a scandal of this sort. We must bide our time. She is certain to give herself away sooner or later.'

'You're quite right,' Grandmother Jia complimented Lady Wang. 'In cases like this it is so hard to prove anything without conclusive evidence. We must just be thankful that the all-seeing Lord Buddha and his bodhisattvas have kept our two from harm. There! It's all over! And please, Feng, don't ever bring the subject up again. You can both stay and have dinner with me.' She turned to Faithful and Amber. 'Tell them we are ready to be served.'

The old lady's parting shot did not go unnoticed by Xi-feng, who laughed and said:

'So now *I'm* the one that set *you* worrying, am I?'

Lady Wang laughed at them both. Meanwhile the waiting-women were standing expectantly outside the door, and Xi-feng told the junior maids that she and Lady Wang were staying to dinner and that they could commence service. As she was speaking, Silver came in with a message for Lady Wang from Sir Zheng. He had mislaid something, and would she go over after dinner and help him find it?

'You'd better go now,' said Grandmother Jia. 'You never know – it might be something important.'

'Yes, Mother.'

Leaving Xi-feng to hold the fort, Lady Wang walked over to her own apartment. A brief search soon revealed the missing item.

'Has Ying-chun gone back yet?' Jia Zheng asked her in the course of conversation. 'How is she getting on with the Suns?'

'The poor girl could do nothing but cry while she was here,' replied Lady Wang. 'She says her husband is an absolute monster.'

Jia Zheng sighed as she told him Ying-chun's sad tale.

'I knew they were unsuited,' he commented. 'But what could I do? Brother She insisted on going ahead with it. The child will have her share of suffering, I'm afraid.'

'They've not been married long, don't forget,' replied Lady Wang. 'We must hope that time will sort things out for them.'

She suddenly laughed.

'What's the joke?' asked Jia Zheng.

'Oh, I just remembered some nonsense of Bao-yu's. He came here first thing this morning specially to talk to me about Ying-chun.'

'Oh yes? What did he have to say?'

Lady Wang gave a humorous account of her early morning interview with Bao-yu and of his 'brilliant plan', which despite himself Jia Zheng found rather amusing.

'Speaking of Bao-yu,' he said, in a more serious tone, 'the boy spends all his time loafing about in the garden – it simply won't do. With one's daughters – well, one has one's disappointments, I realize, but in the long run girls get married and leave the family anyway. With a son, however, it is totally different. If *he* should fall by the wayside, the whole future of the family could be threatened.

'It so happens that only the other day a friend recommended a tutor, a widely-read scholar, a man of the highest principles, and what is more a southerner like ourselves. But I have come to the conclusion that southerners are altogether too easy-going for the boys up here in the capital, who misbehave themselves abominably and are most of them smart enough to get by without having to do a stroke of work. They're a bumptious breed to begin with, and if their teacher mollycoddles them and is not prepared to take them down a peg or two, it's a waste of everyone's time.

'That is why it has never been a family practice to engage outside tutors, and why we have always had a member of the clan, an older man, with a decent smattering of culture of course, to run the school. Dai-ru, the present preceptor, may be rather a mediocre scholar, but he's certainly an effective disciplinarian, and sees to it that the work gets done. Bao-yu's present state of idleness is thoroughly unsatisfactory, and in my opinion the best solution would be for him to resume his studies at the Family School.'

'I agree with you entirely,' said Lady Wang. 'Since your

last posting he has been constantly ill, and what with one thing and another has fallen a long way behind with his studies. I think the routine of going to school would do him good.'

Jia Zheng nodded, and they continued chatting for a while longer.

*

Little time was lost. The very next day, as soon as Bao-yu was up and had finished washing and combing his hair, a deputation of pages arrived and sent in the message: 'Sir Zheng wishes to see Master Bao.' Hurriedly tidying his clothes, Bao-yu went straight over to his father's study. He paid his morning respects and stood to attention.

'Tell me,' Jia Zheng began, 'what you have been doing recently in the way of work? A fair amount, were you going to say? A very *magnum opus* of your worthless doodling, no doubt... I have observed you of late. Your idleness goes from strength to strength. I am also constantly hearing of some new ailment of yours, or shall we rather say ingenious pretext to play truant. I trust I find you fully recovered?

'Another thing: I gather you spend the greater part of your time fooling around with your cousins in the garden, and that even the maidservants are permitted to participate in your infantile antics. Isn't it time you grew up and acquired a little self-esteem? You must understand that those verses you write are not going to impress anyone. The only thing the examiners are interested in is a well-written composition. And the effort you have expended in that direction has so far been non-existent.

'Now listen carefully to what I have to say. From today, I want you to forget all about your verses and couplets. You are to concentrate exclusively on Octopartite Compositions. I will give you twelve months' grace. If by the end of that time you are still in your present unregenerate state, you may as well give up altogether, and I for my part shall have to think again about owning a creature like you as my son.'

He summoned Li Gui.

'Inform Tealeaf that he is to take Bao-yu first thing tomorrow morning to collect the required textbooks, and then bring them here for my inspection. I shall be accompanying him to school myself.'

Turning to Bao-yu:

'Off with you!' he trumpeted. 'I shall expect you early tomorrow morning.'

Bao-yu returned to Green Delights, where Aroma was anxiously awaiting him. The pleasure with which she received the news of his renewed course of study contrasted strangely with the incredulous horror that had rendered him speechless while in Jia Zheng's presence, and that now prompted him to send an urgent message through to Grandmother Jia, begging her to intervene. She sent for him at once and said:

'You should give it a try, my darling. You don't want to anger your father. Don't worry. Remember I shall always be here if you need me.'

There was nothing for it but to go back and give the maids their instructions. 'Wake me at the crack of dawn, as Father will be waiting to take me to school.' Aroma and Musk took it in turns to stay awake that night.

In the morning Aroma woke Bao-yu punctually, helped him wash, comb his hair and dress, and sent a junior maid out with instructions for Tealeaf to wait with the books at the inner gate. She had to spur him on a couple of times before finally he left and made his way towards the study. On his way he stopped to inquire if Sir Zheng had arrived yet, and was informed by a page from the study that one of the literary gentlemen had just called, but had been kept waiting outside, as the Master was still in his dressing-room. This calmed Bao-yu's nerves a little, and he proceeded on to the inner sanctum. As luck would have it, a servant was at that very moment coming out on his way to fetch him, so he went straight in. After another brief homily, Jia Zheng led the way and father and son took a carriage to the school, Tealeaf following with the books.

A look-out had been posted, and Dai-ru had been alerted and was standing in readiness for the party's arrival. Before the old man could come forward to greet him, however, Jia Zheng walked into the schoolroom and paid his respects. Dai-ru took him by the hand and inquired politely after Lady Jia. Bao-yu then went up and paid his respects. Jia Zheng remained standing throughout, and insisted on waiting until Dai-ru was seated before sitting down himself.

'I have come here today,' he began, 'because I felt the need to entrust my son to you personally, and with a few words of instruction. He is no longer a child, and if he is to shoulder his responsibilities and earn a place in the world, it is high time he applied himself conscientiously to preparing for his exams. At home, unfortunately, he spends all his time idling about in the company of children. His verses, the only field in which he has acquired any competence, are for the most part turgid juvenilia, at their best romantic trifles devoid of substance.'

'And he looks such a fine lad,' interposed Dai-ru. 'He seems so intelligent. Why this refusal to study, this perverse streak of hedonism? Not that one should entirely neglect poetic composition. But there is surely time enough for that later on in one's career.'

'Precisely,' said Jia Zheng. 'For the present I would humbly suggest a course of reading and exegesis of primary scriptural texts, and plenty of compositions. If he should show the least sign of being a recalcitrant pupil, I earnestly beseech you to take him in hand, and in so doing to save him from a shallow and wasted life.'

On this note he rose, and with a bow and a few parting remarks took his leave. Dai-ru accompanied him to the door.

'Please convey my respects to Lady Jia.'

'I will,' said Jia Zheng, and climbed into his carriage.

When Dai-ru returned to the classroom, Bao-yu was already sitting at a small rosewood desk in the south-west corner of the room, by the window. He had two sets of texts and a meagre-looking volume of model compositions stacked in a pile on his right. Tealeaf was instructed to put his paper, ink, brush and inkstone away in the drawer of the desk.

'I understand you have been ill, Bao-yu,' said Dai-ru. 'I hope you are quite recovered?'

Bao-yu rose to his feet.

'Quite recovered, thank you sir.'

'We must see to it that you apply yourself with zeal from now on. Your father is most insistent that you should do well. Start by revising the texts you have already memorized.

'Your timetable will be as follows:

Pre-prandium – General Revision
Post-prandium – Calligraphy
Meridianum – Exegesis

And conclude the day's work by reciting quietly to yourself a few model compositions. That should do for the time being.'

'Yes sir.'

As Bao-yu sat down again, he glanced around him. Most of the old faces from the Jokey Jin days were gone, and in their place were quite a few new boys. He reflected on their exceptionally boorish appearance, and the face of Qin Zhong came suddenly into his mind. Since the death of his friend there had been no one to keep him company in his studies, no one to share his innermost thoughts. He was overwhelmed with a sense of grief and loneliness, and sat silently staring at his books.

Not long afterwards Dai-ru came over to say that as this was his first day he could leave early.

'Tomorrow,' he said, 'I shall go through a passage with

you. On second thoughts, to do justice to your natural intelligence, I should like you to expound a passage or two for me. That will give me a clearer idea of the sort of work you have been doing and the standard you have reached.'

Bao-yu's heart was already thumping. But to learn how he fared the following day, you must read the next chapter.

CHAPTER 82

An old pedant tries to instil some Moral Philosophy into his incorrigible pupil
And the ailing Naiad, in a nightmare, confronts the spectres of her fevered mind

'Bravo!' cried Grandmother Jia as Bao-yu came in from school. 'So they've finally broken in my frisky colt! Come along now, your father will be expecting to see you I'm sure. Then you must find something nice and relaxing to do.'

'Yes, Grannie.'

Bao-yu reported to the study.

'Back already?' said Jia Zheng. 'Well, has the Preceptor given you a scheme of work?'

Bao-yu rehearsed his timetable: '*Pre-prandium* – General Revision; *Post-prandium* – Calligraphy; *Meridianum* – Exegesis and reading of model compositions.'

'H'm...' Jia Zheng nodded. 'Fair enough. Off you go now and keep your grandmother company for a little while. Let's see if you can turn over a new leaf and behave seriously from now on. No more of the old childish nonsense, eh? Go to bed on time, rise early, and attend your classes regularly. Understood?'

With a string of fluent 'Yes Sirs', Bao-yu backed smartly out of the study. He hurried over to see his mother, put in another brief appearance at Grandmother Jia's – so brief that he hardly had time to turn around – then dashed off once more, impatient to reach the Naiad's House.

'I'm back!' he called from outside the doorway. The unexpectedness of his arrival, and the explosion of laughing and clapping that announced it, gave Dai-yu quite a turn. Nightingale drew aside the portière and he walked in and sat himself down.

'Does my memory fail me,' said Dai-yu, 'or didn't I hear something to the effect that you were going to school today? Haven't you been let off rather early?'

'Goodness!' exclaimed Bao-yu. 'I can hardly believe it! Yes, Father did banish me to *that place* – what an ordeal! I don't know how I stuck it out! I thought I'd never see you all again! But now, one glimpse of you has raised my spirit from the dead! How does the old Song go?

> 'Twas scarce a day we were apart –
> It seemed three autumns long!

That's just how I feel.'

'Have you been to see Grandmother and your parents?' asked Dai-yu.

'Yes, yes . . .'

'And the others?'

'Not yet.'

'Shouldn't you go and see them now?'

'But I don't feel like going anywhere. All I want to do is sit here and chat with you for a bit. Anyway Father says from now on it's "early to bed and early to rise" so the others will have to wait until tomorrow.'

'Very well then,' said Dai-yu. 'A short stay. Then you must be sensible and go and lie down.'

'But I'm not tired,' protested Bao-yu. 'Just fed up with all *that*. It's doing me a world of good in fact, being here with you, if you'd only stop thinking of all these things I should be doing.'

A faint smile crossed Dai-yu's face.

'Nightingale, would you make Master Bao a cup of Dragon Well tea? We must see that scholarship is suitably rewarded.'

Nightingale smiled and went to fetch the tea, which she entrusted to one of the junior maids. Bao-yu reacted smartly.

'Scholarship! Why, you're almost beginning to sound like one of *them*! I can't abide all that hypocritical moralizing. And those absurd Octopartite essays, which they have the nerve to call "Propagation of Holy Writ", are nothing more than a shoddy way of worming themselves into a job. The whole thing makes me sick! Not content with botching together a few classical tags, they try to hide the fact that they haven't got a single original idea of their own by churning out a lot of far-fetched purple passages – and then pride themselves on having been "subtle" and "profound". Urrghhh! Holy Writ! Holy Pretentious Humbug I'd call it! I know Father is forcing that sort of thing down my throat at present, and I just have to grin and bear it, but that's no reason for you to go on about it the moment I'm back.'

'I know girls don't have to read Octopartites,' replied Dai-yu. 'But when I was little and was having lessons with your cousin Yu-cun, I looked at a few and remember thinking that some were quite well thought out and sensibly written. One or two were even quite subtle, and had a certain delicate charm. They were rather above my head at the time, but I still enjoyed reading them. It's silly to run them all down. Anyway, I think if you want to get on in life, this is quite an admirable way of doing it.'

Bao-yu could hardly believe his ears. What had come over Dai-yu? She had never preached wordly wisdom at him like this before. Not wishing to provoke a full-scale argument, however, he restricted himself to a little snort of amazement.

Meanwhile, voices could be heard outside.

'Aroma sent me to Her Old Ladyship's to fetch Master Bao home from school.' It was Ripple. 'I've tracked him down at last!'

'Go on,' replied Nightingale. 'Let him drink his tea first. It's just this minute been made.'

The two maids came in together, and Bao-yu laughed:

'I was just on my way, Ripple; you shouldn't have bothered to come.'

'You'd best drink your tea and be off!' Nightingale chimed in, before Ripple could get a word in. 'Can't you see how they've been pining for you all day . . .'

'Pscht! You mean little fibber!' cried Ripple, rising perfectly to the bait. Everyone laughed. Bao-yu finally stood up to say goodbye, and Dai-yu saw him to the door. Nightingale stood at the foot of the steps till he was on his way, and then she too went back indoors.

When Bao-yu arrived at Green Delights, Aroma emerged from the inner room to greet him.

'Finished school then?' she asked.

'Oh, Master Bao's been back for ages,' Ripple answered for him. 'He's been at Miss Lin's.'

'Did anything happen while I was away?' asked Bao-yu.

'Oh, nothing much,' replied Aroma pointedly. 'Just a lecture from Faithful. Her Ladyship sent her to let us know that this time the Master is in deadly earnest about your studies, and if any of us dares to play the fool with you again, we'll be dealt with like Skybright and Chess.' She sighed. 'We do our very best to serve you, and that's all the thanks we get. It's all so pointless.'

Her evident distress brought a swift reply from Bao-yu. 'My poor Aroma! You've no need to worry. So long as I work hard, none of you need ever hear another word from Mother. I'm going to do some work this evening, as the Preceptor wants me to do some exposition tomorrow. If there's anything I need, Musk and Ripple can get it for me, so you go and have a rest.'

'If only you would work hard,' said Aroma, 'it would be a joy to serve you.'

Inspired by her words, Bao-yu bolted his supper, had his reading-lamp lit and sat down straight away to revise his basic texts, the Four Books of Confucian Scripture. One glance at the first page, however, with its columns of heavily annotated text, and he began to experience a familiar sinking feeling. He tried flicking through one volume, and the general drift seemed clear enough; but the moment he went into it in any detail, it seemed to slip from his grasp. He turned for help to the marginal commentaries, he read the expository essays, keeping up the struggle till late in the evening.

'Poems are easy,' he thought to himself. 'But I can't make head or tail of this stuff.'

He sat back, gazed at the ceiling and was soon lost in a daydream.

'Bedtime,' said Aroma firmly. 'You've done quite enough work for this evening.'

Bao-yu gave an inaudible reply. Musk and Aroma helped him into bed, and then went to sleep themselves.

During the night, they woke to hear him tossing and turning on the kang.

'Are you still awake?' said Aroma. 'You must stop fretting and have a good night's sleep. You can work hard again tomorrow.'

'I know,' replied Bao-yu. 'But I just can't get to sleep. Come and take off one of my covers.'

'It's a cold night. You'd better keep it on.'

'I feel so restless!' He threw back the top cover himself. Aroma immediately clambered over to tuck it in again, and put her hand to his brow. It felt slightly feverish.

'Lie still!' she said. 'You've a fever.'

'I know.'

'What's the matter?'

'It's nothing. I'm just nervous, that's all. Please don't make a thing of it. If Father finds out, he's bound to say I'm cooking up an excuse to miss school. It would seem too much of a coincidence. I'll feel better in the morning, and once I'm at school it'll go away.'

Aroma gave in.

'I'll sleep here by your side,' she said. She massaged his back a little and in no time they were both fast asleep. When they woke next morning the sun was already high in the sky.

'Help!' cried Bao-yu. 'I'm late!' He quickly washed and combed his hair, completed his round of morning duties and set off for school. The Preceptor's severe expression as he walked into the schoolroom did not bode well.

'Tardy, boy, tardy! What is the meaning of this? Small wonder that you have incurred your father's displeasure and caused him to call you his prodigal son, if this is the way you think you can behave on your second day.'

Bao-yu told him of his fever the night before, then crossed over to his desk and sat down to his work.

It was late in the afternoon when he was called forward.

'Bao-yu, step up here. Oral Exposition of this text.'

Bao-yu walked up. On inspection, he found to his relief that it was a rubric he knew. *Analects*, chapter IX, verse XXII: *Maxima Debetur Puero Reverentia* – RESPECT DUE TO YOUTH. 'What a stroke of luck!' he thought to himself. 'Thank goodness it's not from the *Mag** or the *Med*!'

'How do you wish me to begin, sir?'

'*Amplificatio Totius*, boy. Give the substance of the passage carefully in your own words.'

Bao-yu first recited the original chapter, in the prescribed sing-song intonation, and then began:

'In this verse we have the Sage's Exhortation to Youth to Seize the Hour and Strive with Zeal, lest they end up becoming...'

Bao-yu looked up at Dai-ru. The Preceptor sensed what was coming and tried to conceal his embarrassment with a short laugh:

'Come on boy, come on. What is holding you back? Are you afraid of using a *non-licet* expression up to books? Remember: Scriptural Exegesis is exempt from the normal rules of Verbal Prohibition. *Liber Rituum*, Book I: "*In Canonicorum Classicorumque Librorum Studiis Nomenclationum cessat Prohibitio.*" What may they end up becoming?'

* Young scholars of that time were wont to use these affectionate abbreviations to refer to those two other venerable texts of Scripture, the *Magna Scientia* or Great Learning and the *Medium Immutabile* or Doctrine of the Mean.

'Complete Failures, sir,' said Bao-yu, barely suppressing a mischievous smile. 'In the first Segment, *Sunt Verendi*, the Sage is Spurring Youth on to Moral Endeavour in the Present, while the last Segment, *Non Sunt Digni Quos Verearis*, contains his Caution for the Future.'

He looked up again at Dai-ru.

'That will do. *Interpretatio Partium.*'

Bao-yu began again:

'Confucius saith: "For the Duration of Youth, each Spiritual and Mental Talent must be held in Due Esteem. For how can we ever Predict with Certainty another's Ultimate Station in Life? But if a man, by Drifting and Wasting his Days, should reach the Age of Forty or Fifty and still be Unsuccessful and Obscure, then it can fairly be said that his Youthful Promise was an Empty One. He will have Forfeited For Ever the Esteem of his Fellow Men."'

'Your *Amplificatio Totius* was passably clear,' commented Dai-ru with a dry smile. 'But I am afraid your *Interpretatio Partium* showed a good deal of immaturity. In the phrase *sine Nomine, Nomen* refers not to Success in the Worldly Sense but rather to an Individual's Achievement in the Moral and Intellectual Spheres. In this sense it by no means implies Official Rank. On the contrary, many of the Great Sages of Antiquity were Obscure Figures who Withdrew from the World; and yet we hold them in the Highest Esteem, do we not? *Nonne sunt Digni quos Vereamur*?

'You construe the last sentence incorrectly,' he droned on. 'Here it is not the element of Esteem but the Irreconcilable Nature of the Judgement of his Fellow Men that is being contrasted with their Tentative Appraisal of him as a Youth (see second sentence of your text). This emphasis is central to a Correct Elucidation of the passage. Do you follow me?'

'Yes, sir.'

'Good. Here is another.'

Dai-ru turned back a few pages and pointed out a passage to Bao-yu. It was *Analects* again, this time chapter IX, verse XVIII: *Ego nondum vidi qui amet Virtutem sicut amat Pulchram Speciem* – THE RARITY OF A SINCERE LOVE OF VIRTUE. Bao-yu scented danger ahead and said with his most ingenuous smile:

'I'm afraid I can't think of anything to say, sir.'

'Nonsense, my boy! Is that what you would write if it turned up as a *Thema* in your paper?'

Reluctantly Bao-yu set the wheels in motion.

'Confucius saith: 'Men will not love Virtue, and yet they Fall Down and Worship Sensual Beauty at First Sight. The Reason for this Disaffection is that they are Blind to the Intrinsicality of Virtue. Beauty is an Intrinsic Quality too, and as such Loved by All, but it belongs to the Realm of Human Desire, whereas Virtue is a Natural Principle. How can Principle hope to Compete with Desire for the Affections of men? Confucius is both Lamenting the State of the World and Hoping for a Change of Heart. The Love of Virtue he has observed has been for the most part a Shallow and Short-lived Affair. How Fine it would be if only men would feel for Virtue the Devotion they feel towards Beauty . . .'

'Thank you, that will do,' said Dai-ru. 'I have but one question to put to you. If you understand the words of Confucius so well, why is it that you transgress these very two Precepts? I am only an outsider, but without need of explanation from your Father I can identify your Moral Shortcomings. One cannot hope to become a Man except by dint of Constant Self-Improvement. You are at present a Youth of Promise, or as our text has it *Puer Verendus*. Whether or not you Fulfil this Promise depends entirely on your own efforts. Are you to be a Man of Merit, *Vir Nominis*, or are you to be a Man No Longer Esteemed by his Fellow-Men, *Vir Non Iam Verendus*?

'I shall allow you an initial period of one month in

which to revise your old texts thoroughly, and a further month in which to study models of Octopartite Composition. At the end of the second month I intend to set you your Maiden Theme. If I detect any sign of slackness on your part, you need not expect me to be lenient. As the saying goes:

> Perfection comes through ceaseless effort;
> Effortless ease brings but perdition.

Be sure to bear in mind all that I have said.'

'Yes sir.'

*

And so we must leave Bao-yu for the present, submitting reluctantly to his daily lessons. During his absence at school, Green Delights became unrecognizably quiet and the days passed slowly and uneventfully. Aroma even found time to do some sewing. One day she sat down to finish a betel-nut 'refresher' bag she had been embroidering, and fell to thinking of the great change wrought in all their lives by Bao-yu's new routine. How easy life was for the maids now that he was away all day! If things had only been like this earlier, Skybright might never have come to such a wretched end. Poor Skybright! Aroma sighed; for does not the hare in the trap set the fox's heart a-beating? It was the shortest step from grieving for Skybright to brooding over her own future. What was to become of her? What sort of a life would she lead, as Bao-yu's concubine? Bao-yu himself was no problem. She knew how to handle him. But what if he were to marry someone like Mrs Lian or Mr Pan's new wife? Was she fated to be a second You Er-jie or Caltrop? To judge from Lady Jia and Lady Wang's attitude in the past, and from the frequent hints dropped by Mrs Lian, it seemed a foregone conclusion that he would marry Miss Lin. Now *there* was a complicated young lady . . .

With this new turn of thought Aroma's colour deepened, her heart beat faster and her aim with the needle became more and more erratic. Finally she abandoned her embroidery altogether and set off for the Naiad's House, determined to put Dai-yu's disposition towards her to the test.

Dai-yu was reading a book. When she saw Aroma come in, she moved over slightly and nodded to her to sit down.

'I hope you're feeling quite better, Miss,' began Aroma, anxious to create the right impression.

'Not really,' replied Dai-yu. 'I suppose I do feel a little less weak. What have you been doing at home?'

'Now that Master Bao's at school,' replied Aroma, 'it's very quiet at home, so I thought I'd come round for a chat.'

Nightingale came in with tea and Aroma rose promptly to her feet.

'Please sit down, Nightingale dear.' She laughed as she continued: 'You've been making fun of us, so Ripple was telling me the other day . . .'

'You don't take any notice of what *she* says, do you?' said Nightingale with a smile. 'All I meant was that with Master Bao away at school all day, and Miss Chai and Caltrop both living out, things must be dull for you.'

Aroma seized her opportunity:

'Caltrop, did I hear you say? Oh, that poor girl! I feel so sorry for her! This new wife of Mr Pan's is a Total Eclipse if ever there was one! She's even worse than *a certain person* . . .' Here Aroma held up two fingers, indicating the Second Young Lady of the household – Xi-feng. 'This Mrs Pan doesn't seem to care a bit what people think.'

'That *certain person* was bad enough,' said Dai-yu. 'To think that You Er-jie is dead!'

'I know,' said Aroma. 'They were both human beings,

after all. It was only their positions that were different. Why did she have to be so malicious? It hasn't done the family name any good.'

This was the first time Dai-yu had heard Aroma gossip like this, and she began to suspect what was at the back of it.

'It's hard to tell,' she said. 'In every family affair, one side or the other *has* to win. If it's not the East Wind it's the West.'

'A concubine should know her place,' said Aroma. 'She should be too scared to take advantage of the wife.'

At this point in the conversation an old woman's voice was heard in the outer courtyard.

'Is this where Miss Lin lives? Which maid is in charge here?' Snowgoose went out to see who it was, and vaguely recognized her as one of Aunt Xue's serving-women.

'What do you want?' she asked.

'I'm here on an errand for Miss Bao-chai,' replied the woman. 'Something for Miss Lin.'

'Wait here a minute.' Snowgoose went in to consult with Dai-yu, who told her to show the old woman in. Once inside the room, she curtseyed to Dai-yu, then screwed up her eyes and peered at her curiously. Not a word of her errand. Dai-yu began to feel rather embarrassed, and asked what it was that Bao-chai had sent over.

'A pot of honeyed lychees is what I've been instructed by Miss Bao-chai to bring to you, Miss Lin,' replied the old woman, her features relaxing into a smile. Then she spotted Aroma in the room. 'Why, if it isn't Master Bao's maid, Miss Hua!'

'That's right, nanny dear,' replied Aroma. 'And how did you come to know who I was?'

'Well, looking after Madam's room as we do, we hardly ever go out visiting with Madam and Miss Bao-chai, so *you* wouldn't recognize *us*. But *we* remember just about all the young ladies that come round *our* way.'

She handed the pot to Snowgoose, took another look at

Dai-yu, then turned back to Aroma and said with a confidential smile:

'No wonder our Madam says that Miss Lin and your Master Bao were made for one another! She really does look just like a fairy!'

Aroma made a valiant attempt to avert any further blunders.

'Come along, nanny, you must be tired. Why don't you sit down and have a cup of tea?'

'Oh no – we're much too busy at home today,' the old girl cackled on regardless. 'We've everything to prepare for Miss Bao-qin's Giving-away. And I've still two pots of lychees to deliver to Master Bao-yu from Miss Bao-chai.'

She took her leave and went waddling busily out of the room. Dai-yu, who for Bao-chai's sake had tried to disguise her annoyance at the way the old woman had come barging in, called out after her:

'Please thank Miss Bao-chai for her kind present.'

'La-di-da-di-da!' the old girl could still be heard burbling away to herself. 'Only Bao-yu would have the style to match such a fine lady . . .'

Dai-yu pretended not to hear.

'Really,' said Aroma, trying to laugh the whole thing off, 'when people reach her age they just talk utter nonsense. You don't know whether to scold or laugh.'

Snowgoose passed the lychees to Dai-yu.

'I couldn't; put them away, would you?'

They chatted a little longer and then Aroma left.

*

That evening, when Dai-yu went into her side-room to undress for the night, she caught sight of the lychees again. They reminded her of the old woman's visit, and revived the pain she had felt at her tactless gossiping. Dusk was falling, and in the stillness a thousand gloomy thoughts seemed to close in and oppress her mind.

'My health is so poor . . . And time's running out. I

know Bao-yu loves me more than anyone else. But Grannie and Aunt Wang still haven't mentioned it! If only my parents had settled it for us while they were still alive... But suppose they had? What if they had married me to someone else? Who could ever compare with Bao-yu? Perhaps I'm better off like this after all! At least I've still some hope.'

Like the rope on a pulley her secret hopes and fears spun up and down, tangling themselves tighter and tighter round her heart. Finally, with a sigh and a few tears, she lay down in her clothes, weary and depressed.

She became vaguely aware of one of the junior maids coming in and saying:

'Miss Lin, Mr Jia Yu-cun is outside and wants to see you.'

'What could he want?' thought Dai-yu to herself. 'I'm not a regular student of his. I'm not even a boy. He just happened to coach me when I was a little girl. Anyway, all the times he's come to see Uncle Zheng he's never once asked after me, so why should I have to see him now?'

She told the maid to convey her respects and thank Mr Yu-cun for calling, but to say that poor health obliged her to stay in bed.

'But Miss,' said the maid, 'I think he's come to congratulate you, and some people have come to take you to Nanking.'

As she was speaking, a group including Xi-feng, Lady Xing, Lady Wang and Bao-chai advanced into the room and announced cheerfully:

'Congratulations my dear! And bon voyage!'

'What do you mean?' asked Dai-yu in great confusion.

'Come on now.' It was Xi-feng who replied. 'You needn't try and pretend you haven't heard the news. Your father's been promoted to Grain Intendant for Hupeh Province and has made a second and highly satisfactory marriage. He doesn't think it right that you should be left here on your own, and has asked Yu-cun to act as go-between. You're engaged to be married to a relation of your new stepmother's, a widower himself I believe. They've sent some servants to fetch you home. You'll probably be married straight away. It's all your stepmother's idea. In case you're not properly taken care of on the voyage, she has asked your cousin Lian to accompany you.'

Xi-feng's words made Dai-yu break out in a cold sweat. She now had a feeling that her father was still alive. She began to panic, and said defiantly:

'It's not true! It's all a trick of Xi-feng's!'

She saw Lady Xing give Lady Wang a meaningful look:

'She won't believe us. Come, we are wasting our time.'

'Aunt Wang! Aunt Xing! Don't go!' Dai-yu begged them, fighting back her tears. But she received no reply. They all gave her a curious smile, and then left together.

As she stood there and watched them go, panic seized her. She tried to speak, but the only sound that came was a strangled sobbing from the back of her throat. Then she looked about her and saw that somehow she had been transported to Grandmother Jia's apartment. In that same instant she thought to herself: 'Grannie's the only one that can save me now!' and fell at the old lady's feet, hugging her by the knees.

'Save me Grannie, *please*! I'd rather die than go away with them! That stepmother's not my real mother anyway. I just want to stay here with you!'

Grandmother Jia's face only registered a cold smile.

'This has nothing to do with me.'

'But what's to become of me, Grannie?' she sobbed.

'Being a man's second wife has its advantages,' Grandmother Jia replied. 'Think of the double dowry you'll have.'

'If I stay, I won't cause you any extra expense, I promise I won't. Oh please save me!'

'It's no use,' said Grandmother Jia. 'All girls marry and leave home. You're a child and don't understand these things. You can't live here for ever, you know.'

'I'll do anything to stay – I'll work for my keep, be a

slave, anything! Only please don't let them take me away!'

This time Grandmother Jia made no reply. Dai-yu hugged her again and sobbed:

'Oh Grannie! You've always been so good to me, fussed over me so – how can you treat me like this in my hour of need? Don't you care about me any more? I may not be one of your real grandchildren, a true Jia like the others, but my mother was your own daughter, your own flesh and blood! For her sake have pity on me! Don't let me be taken away!'

With these last words she flung herself frantically upon Lady Jia, burying her head in her lap and sobbing violently.

'Faithful,' the old lady commanded, 'take Miss Dai-yu to her room to rest. She is wearing me out.'

There was no mistaking the finality in Grandmother Jia's voice. To Dai-yu, suicide now seemed the only course. She rose, and as she walked from the room her heart yearned for a mother of her own to turn to. All the affection shown her by grandmother, aunts and cousins alike, had now been exposed for what it was and had been all along – a sham. Suddenly she thought: 'Why haven't I seen Bao-yu today? *He* might still know of a way out.' And as the thought entered her mind, she looked up and sure enough, there, standing right in front of her, all laughter and smiles, was Bao-yu himself.

'My warmest congratulations, coz!'

This was too much for Dai-yu. Her last vestige of maidenly reserve vanished. She clutched hold of him and cried out:

'Now I know how heartless and cruel you really are, Bao-yu!'

'No, you are wrong,' he replied. 'But if you have a husband to go to, then we must go our separate ways.'

Dai-yu listened in despair as this, her very last hope, was taken from her. Clinging to him helplessly, she gave a feverish cry:

'Oh Bao! I've no separate way to go! How could you say such a thing!'

'If you don't want to go, then stay here,' he replied calmly. 'You were originally engaged to me. That's why you came to live here. Has it never occurred to you how specially I've always treated you? Haven't you noticed?'

Suddenly it all seemed clear. She really was engaged to Bao-yu after all. Of course she was! In an instant her despair changed to joy.

'*My* mind is made up once and for ever! But you must give me the word. Am I to go? Or am I to stay?'

'I've told you, stay here with me. If you still don't trust me, look at my heart.'

With these words he took out a small knife and brought it down across his chest. Blood came spurting out. Terrified out of her wits, Dai-yu tried to staunch the flow with her hand, crying out:

'How could you? You should have killed me first!'

'Don't worry,' said Bao-yu. 'I'm going to show you my heart.'

He fumbled about inside the gaping flesh, while Dai-yu, shaking convulsively, afraid someone might burst in on them at any moment, pressed him to her tightly and wept bitterly.

'Oh no!' said Bao-yu. 'It's not there any more! My time has come!'

His eyes flickered and he fell with a dull thud to the floor. Dai-yu let out a piercing scream. She heard Nightingale calling her:

'Miss Lin! Miss Lin! You're having a nightmare! Wake up! Come along now, you must get undressed and go to sleep properly.'

Dai-yu turned over in her bed. So it had all been a nightmare. But she could still feel her throat choking, her heart was still pounding, the top of her pillow was drenched in sweat, and a tingly, icy sensation ran down her back and chilled her to the core.

'Mother and father died long ago. Bao-yu and I have never been engaged,' she thought to herself. 'What ever could have made me have such a dream?'

The scenes of her dream passed before her eyes again. She was on her own in the world, she reflected. Supposing Bao-yu really died – what then? The thought was enough to bring back all the pain and confusion. She began to weep, and tiny beads of sweat broke out down the length of her body. Finally she struggled up, took off her outer robe and told Nightingale to make the bed. She lay down again, and began turning restlessly from side to side, unable to get to sleep. She could hear the gentle sighing of the wind outside her window – or was it the drizzle falling softly on the roof? Once, the sound died away and she thought she could hear someone calling in the distance. But it was only Nightingale, who had already fallen asleep and was snoring in a corner of the room. With a great effort, Dai-yu struggled out of bed, wrapped the quilt around her and sat up. An icy draught from a crack in the casement soon sent her shivering back under the covers again. She was just beginning to doze off when the sparrows struck up their dawn-chorus from their nests in the bamboos. First light was gradually beginning to show through the shutters and paper window-panes.

Dai-yu was now wide awake again and started coughing. Nightingale awoke at once.

'Still awake, Miss? Coughing too – it sounds as if you've caught a chill. Why, it's almost light, it'll soon be morning! Please try and stop thinking so much, and rest. You need to sleep.'

'I want to sleep,' replied Dai-yu. 'But what's the good? I just can't. You go back to sleep anyway.' These last words were interrupted by another fit of coughing.

Nightingale was already distressed at her mistress's condition and had no inclination to go back to sleep. When she heard her coughing again, she hurried over to hold up the spittoon. By now it was dawn outside.

'Haven't you gone to sleep?' asked Dai-yu.

'Sleep?' replied Nightingale cheerfully. 'It's already daylight.'

'In that case, could you change the spittoon?'

'Certainly Miss.'

Leaving the full spittoon on a table in the outer room, Nightingale went promptly to fetch a fresh one, which she placed at the foot of the kang. Then, closing the door of the inner room carefully behind her and letting down the flower-patterned portière, she went out to wake Snowgoose, taking the full spittoon with her. When she came to empty it in the courtyard, and looked closer, she noticed to her horror some specks of blood in the phlegm.

'Goodness!' she blurted out. 'How awful!'

'What's the matter?' Dai-yu called out at once from inside.

'Oh nothing, Miss!'

Nightingale tried her best to cover up her blunder. 'The spittoon slipped in my hand and I nearly dropped it.'

'You didn't find anything odd in the phlegm?'

'Oh no, Miss.' A lump came into Nightingale's throat, and she could say no more. Tears came streaming down her cheeks.

Dai-yu had already noticed a sickly taste in her mouth, and her earlier suspicions were strengthened first by Nightingale's cry of alarm, and now by the unmistakable note of dismay in her voice.

'Come in,' she told Nightingale. 'It must be cold outside.'

'I'm coming, Miss.' She sounded more disconsolate than ever. Her tragic snuffly tone set Dai-yu shivering. The door opened and she walked in, still dabbing her eyes with a handkerchief.

'Come along now,' said Dai-yu. 'Crying so early in the morning?'

'Who's crying?' said Nightingale, doing her best to smile. 'It's so early and my eyes are a bit itchy, that's all.

You were awake longer than ever last night, weren't you, Miss? I could hear you coughing half the night.'

'I know. The more I wanted to sleep, the wider awake I became.'

'You're not well, Miss. I think all this worrying is ruining your health. And good health is like the hill in the proverb:

> Keep the hill green, keep the hill green,
> And you'll never lack fuel for winter again.

Besides, everyone here cares for you so. Her Old Ladyship does, Her Ladyship does, *everyone* does!'

How could Nightingale know that the mere mention of these homely names, intended to reassure and comfort, was enough to conjure up again the horror of the nightmare? Dai-yu felt her heart thumping, everything went black before her eyes, and she seemed on the point of fainting altogether. Nightingale quickly held out the spittoon while Snowgoose patted her lightly on the back. After a long while she coughed up another mouthful of phlegm. In it was a thick wriggling strand of dark red blood. The two maids were pale with fright. They stood supporting her, one on each side, until finally she slumped back, scarcely conscious. Nightingale, aware of the critical nature of her condition, looked at Snowgoose and made an urgent movement with her lips that clearly meant: 'Go and fetch someone – quickly!'

Snowgoose was no sooner out of the door than she saw Kingfisher and Ebony coming towards the Naiad's House, smiling as they walked along.

'Isn't Miss Lin up yet?' inquired Kingfisher cheerfully. 'My mistress and Miss Tan-chun are both round at Miss Xi-chun's discussing her painting of the garden.'

Snowgoose hushed them both with a quick gesture.

'What's the matter?' they asked in alarm. Snowgoose told them all that had happened, and they shot out their tongues in horror.

'But that's serious! Why haven't you been to tell Her

Old Ladyship? What a terrible thing! How could you be so silly!'

'I was on my way when you two arrived,' replied Snowgoose.

'Who's that talking outside?' called Nightingale from the bedroom. 'Miss Lin wants to know.'

The three of them went in together, to find Dai-yu lying wrapped up in bed.

'What's all the excitement about?' she asked them. 'Who's been telling you tales?'

It was Ebony who replied:

'Miss Tan-chun and Miss Xiang-yun have just gone over to Miss Xi-chun's to discuss her landscape of the garden, and they sent us here to ask you to join them, Miss Lin. We're sorry to hear that you're not well.'

'It's nothing serious,' said Dai-yu. 'I'm just feeling a bit weak, that's all. I'll be up when I've had a little rest. Will you tell Miss Tan-chun and Miss Xiang-yun that I should like them to come here after lunch, if they're not too busy? I don't suppose Master Bao's been over there, has he?'

'No, Miss,' came the reply. 'Master Bao has been going to school the last few days,' continued Ebony, 'and the Master tests him every day, so he doesn't get a chance to romp around as he used to.'

Dai-yu was silent and thoughtful. The two maids stood around for a minute or two longer and then discreetly withdrew.

At the Lotus Pavilion, Xi-chun's painting of Prospect Garden was being subjected to an aesthetic appraisal by Tan-chun and Xiang-yun. Too much here, not enough there, a little too thin in one place, too crowded in another. They were thinking of adding a poetry inscription, and had sent to ask for Dai-yu's advice. They were busily talking when Kingfisher and Ebony came back, looking very flustered. Xiang-yun was the first to question them:

'Why hasn't Miss Lin come with you?'

'She had a bad relapse last night, Miss,' replied Kingfisher, 'and was up coughing most of the night. According to Snowgoose the phlegm in her spittoon was flecked with blood.'

'Are you sure?' asked Tan-chun, aghast.

'Quite sure,' replied Kingfisher.

'We've just been in to see her, Miss,' said Ebony. 'She looks dreadful, and hardly has the strength to speak.'

'If she's as sick as *that*, she's hardly likely to be able to speak,' said Xiang-yun bluntly.

'What nonsense, Yun! Why if she couldn't speak that would mean she was past . . .'

Tan-chun broke off in mid-sentence.

'Dai is a clever soul,' said Xi-chun. 'But she does have a tendency to take everything too seriously. If only she could see beyond it all.'

'We must go and see how she is, anyway,' said Tan-chun. 'If it *is* serious, we'd better tell Cousin Wan and let Grannie know, so they can send for a doctor and find out what to do.'

Xiang-yun agreed, and she and Tan-chun set off with a couple of junior maids for the Naiad's House. Xi-chun said she would follow later.

The sight of the girls coming into her room gave Dai-yu a queer feeling, and set her brooding once more over her dream. If Grandmother Jia had proved so cold in the dream, wouldn't Tan and Yun have been even more so? Would they even have bothered to come and see her now, she wondered, if she had not made a point of asking them to? Not allowing these doubts to show, she made a big effort and told Nightingale to prop her up, murmuring to the others to sit down. Tan-chun and Xiang-yun sat one at each end of the bed, deeply moved by the sight of Dai-yu in this condition.

'What do you think is the matter, Dai?' asked Tan-chun.

'Oh, it's nothing serious. I just feel so drained.'

Nightingale, who was standing on the other side of Dai-yu, secretly pointed to the spittoon, and Xiang-yun (the younger and by nature less circumspect of the two girls) picked it up and had a look. It was too late:

'Ith thith *yourth*, Dai?' she asked in a voice of horror. 'How awful!'

Earlier Dai-yu had been too faint and overwrought to examine the contents of her spittoon. But now Xiang-yun's question reawakened her suspicions. Her heart sank as she turned to look. Tan-chun tried to cover up for Xiang-yun:

'That only means you've got some inflammation on your lungs, and have brought a little up. It's quite common. Yun's so pathetic the way she goes on about the slightest thing!'

Xiang-yun blushed and wished she had never opened her mouth. Tan-chun could see how low Dai-yu's spirits were, and how tired she was. She rose to leave:

'You must rest and build up your strength. We'll leave you now and call back again later.'

'Thank you both for thinking of me.'

'Mind you look after Miss Lin properly now, Nightingale.'

'Yes, Miss Tan-chun.'

They were about to leave, when the hushed atmosphere was rudely disturbed by a voice shouting outside. But if you wish to learn whose voice it was, you must turn to the next chapter.

CHAPTER 83

An Indisposition in the Imperial Bedchamber calls for a Family Visitation While insubordination in the inner apartments reveals Bao-chai's long-suffering nature

It was told in our last chapter how Dai-yu's visitors, who were on the point of leaving, heard a voice outside the window crying:

'What's a little trouble-maker like you doing here in the garden anyway? You're nothing but a nuisance!'

Dai-yu immediately let out a great cry:

'I can't stay here any longer!'

She rolled her eyes and gestured with one hand in the direction of the window.

The truth is that after all this time, despite Grandmother Jia's constant love and protection, Dai-yu still suffered from an acute sense of insecurity, of being an 'outsider in the Garden'. On this occasion, incredible though it may seem, she had instinctively taken herself to be the target of the old woman's abuse (for the voice was that of an old serving-woman), and had immediately set about reconstructing the 'plot' in her mind: someone, taking advantage of the fact that she was an orphan, had sent this woman to insult her in public. She was being persecuted! The sense of injury, the unfairness of it, were more than she could bear. Another fit of sobbing left her unconscious.

'What's the matter, Miss?' Nightingale was in tears herself. 'Please wake up!'

Tan-chun also called out in an effort to rouse her, and eventually Dai-yu came round. She could not speak, and her only explanation was another gesture towards the window. Tan-chun understood. She opened the door and went outside, to discover the old woman, with a stick in her hand, chasing a scruffy little maid.

'I'm trying to get on with my gardening,' she was grumbling. 'You've no business to be here. Just wait till we get home and I get my hands on you! I'll learn you!'

The little girl merely cocked her head, stuck a finger in her mouth and stared at the old woman with a cheeky grin.

'Have you both taken leave of your senses?' exclaimed Tan-chun severely. 'How dare you use language like that here?'

When the old woman saw who it was, she pulled herself up smartly and answered with her most ingratiating smile:

'It's my daughter's girl here, Miss Tan-chun. She would follow me over you see, and I knew she'd only be a nuisance so I was shooing her along home. Dearie me, if I'd stopped to think where I was I'd never have dared raise my voice I'm sure.'

'That's quite enough,' said Tan-chun. 'Off you go both of you. Miss Lin is not feeling very well today – so hurry up and go!'

'Yes Miss! Straightaway Miss!' The old girl bustled off and her granddaughter went running after her.

Returning indoors, Tan-chun found Xiang-yun holding Dai-yu's hand and crying helplessly, while Nightingale was supporting her mistress with one hand and using her free hand to rub her chest. Slowly the life returned to Dai-yu's eyes and she looked up. Tan-chun smiled kindly:

'Did you take offence at what that old woman said?'

Dai-yu answered with a feeble shake of the head.

'It was her own granddaughter she was shouting at,' Tan-chun went on to explain. 'She told me all about it. People like her are the end. They never know when to hold their tongue.'

Dai-yu sighed and held Tan-chun's hand.

'Oh Tan . . .' she cried feebly, but could say no more.

'There, you mustn't start worrying,' said Tan-chun. 'We're cousins and cousins should stick by one another. That's why I came to see you. Besides, I know you're a bit short of help. Listen, all you have to do is take your medicine like a good girl and look on the bright side a bit, and you'll soon start to build up your strength. And then we can start having meetings of our poetry club again, and everything will be fine.'

'Tan's right,' echoed Xiang-yun. 'Won't that be fun!'

'Oh, if only you knew!' sobbed Dai-yu. 'I feel so weak. I don't think I'll ever pull through.'

'That's no way to talk,' said Tan-chun. 'We all fall ill, we all have our troubles. There's no cause for you to be so pessimistic. Be sensible and have a good rest now. Yun and I had better go over to Grannie's. We'll come and see you again later. If there's anything you need, tell Nightingale and I'll send it over for you.'

'Tan, when you see Grannie, you won't say I'm very ill, will you? Please!' Tears were streaming down Dai-yu's face as she spoke. 'Just curtsey for me and say I'm not feeling very well but it's nothing serious and she's not to worry.'

'Of course. Now don't fuss. Just rest and get better.'

Tan-chun and Xiang-yun went on their way.

*

When they had gone, Nightingale settled Dai-yu down once more. She left all the fetching and carrying to Snowgoose, and herself stayed constantly at Dai-yu's side, trying her best not to betray her own distress by shedding any more tears. Dai-yu closed her eyes and lay still for a while. But sleep would not come. The garden outside, which had always been such a haven of quiet and solitude, now seemed alive with sounds – the wind, insects buzzing, birds chattering, the fall of human footsteps, children crying faintly in the distance – all of which drifted in through the window and set her nerves on edge. She told Nightingale to let down the curtains around her bed.

Presently Snowgoose appeared, carrying before her in both hands a bowl of Bird's Nest Soup, which she gave to Nightingale, who whispered through the curtains:

'Would you like some soup, Miss?'

A faint 'yes' was heard from inside, and handing the soup back to Snowgoose for the moment, Nightingale climbed up and helped Dai-yu into a comfortable sitting position. Turning to take the bowl again, she first tasted the contents herself, then held it carefully to Dai-yu's lips, while supporting her firmly round the shoulder with one arm. Dai-yu opened her eyes feebly, took a couple of sips, then showed by a shake of her head that she could not manage any more. Nightingale handed the bowl back to Snowgoose and gently settled her down again.

For a few minutes all was quiet and Dai-yu seemed more peaceful. Then a whisper was heard from outside the window:

'Is Nightingale in?'

Snowgoose hurried out. It was Aroma.

'Come in,' she whispered.

'How's Miss Lin?' asked Aroma.

They walked together towards the doorway and Aroma listened aghast as Snowgoose described what had happened that morning and the preceding night.

'No wonder!' she exclaimed. 'Kingfisher said something of the sort just now and had Master Bao so worried that he sent me straight round to find out how she is.'

As they were talking, Nightingale lifted the portière and beckoned to Aroma, who tiptoed into the room:

'Is Miss Lin asleep?'

Nightingale nodded. 'Has Snowgoose told you?' she added.

Aroma nodded, then frowned and said:

'This is dreadful! Master Bao had me worried to death last night too!'

'What do you mean?' asked Nightingale. Aroma explained:

'When he went to sleep in the evening he seemed

perfectly all right. But in the middle of the night he started screaming his head off, first about a pain in his heart, and then about being stabbed by a knife – he was quite delirious, and didn't quieten down till after the dawn watch. Wouldn't you have been scared? He's not allowed to go to school today, and the doctor has been sent for to prescribe something for him.'

While they were talking, Dai-yu could be heard coughing again from inside the bed-curtains, and Nightingale hurried over to hold up the spittoon. Dai-yu opened her eyes feebly:

'Who's that you're talking to?'

'It's Aroma, Miss. She's come to ask how you are.'

Aroma was already standing close by the bed. Dai-yu told Nightingale to help her up and gestured to Aroma to sit down on the bed. Aroma perched on the edge and said in her best bedside manner:

'Are you sure you ought to be sitting up like this, Miss?'

'Why not?' replied Dai-yu. 'Stop behaving as if it's the end of the world, will you? Who was that you mentioned just now, with a pain in the heart during the night?'

'Oh that wasn't *real*!' said Aroma. 'That was just a nightmare Master Bao had.'

'It's very thoughtful of Aroma,' thought Dai-yu to herself. 'I know she's only trying to stop me from worrying. But I *must* know!' She tried again, more insistently this time:

'What sort of a nightmare? What did he say?'

'Oh, he didn't say anything,' lied Aroma.

Dai-yu nodded pensively and fell silent for a minute or two. Then she sighed again and said:

'You're none of you to mention my illness to Master Bao. It might affect his work and cause trouble with Sir Zheng.'

'Of course we won't, Miss,' Aroma reassured her. 'Now you lie down and rest.'

Dai-yu nodded and asked Nightingale to settle her down again. Aroma stayed a little longer by her bedside, said a few more comforting words and then left. When she arrived back at Green Delights she reported that Dai-yu was feeling a little uncomfortable but that her condition was not a serious one, and thereby succeeded in setting Bao-yu's mind at rest.

*

Tan-chun and Xiang-yun, on leaving the Naiad's House, made their way together to Grandmother Jia's apartment. As they went, Tan-chun warned Xiang-yun:

'When we see Grandmother, please be more careful what you say, will you?'

Xiang-yun nodded:

'I will. I'm afraid just now I was too shocked by Dai's state to think what I was doing.'

They arrived at Grandmother Jia's and Tan-chun mentioned Dai-yu's illness. As she had predicted, the old lady was somewhat ruffled:

'Dear oh dear! How illness and misfortune seem to pick on those two! Ever since Dai-yu was a little girl, it's been one thing after another. Now that she's grown up, it is time she learned to take better care of her health. She's too highly strung, that's her trouble.'

No one dared say anything. She turned to Faithful:

'The doctor's coming in the morning to see Bao-yu. Tell them he's to look in at Miss Lin's afterwards.'

'Yes, ma'am.'

Faithful went out to tell the serving-women, who passed on the instructions. Tan-chun and Xiang-yun stayed on at Grandmother Jia's for dinner, and then returned to the Garden together.

*

Next day the doctor came to see Bao-yu. He pronounced that a dietary imbalance had brought on a slight chill, which would soon be put right by a mild dispersant. Lady Wang and Xi-feng sent the prescription over for Grandmother Jia to inspect, and at the same time sent someone ahead to the Naiad's House to let them know the doctor was on his way. Nightingale tucked Dai-yu up in her quilt and let down the bed-curtains, while Snowgoose quickly tidied the room.

Presently Jia Lian arrived with the doctor, announcing that as it was their regular practitioner there was no need for the maids to disappear. An old serving-woman raised the portière, Jia Lian ushered the doctor into Dai-yu's room and the two men sat down. Jia Lian began:

'Nightingale dear, please tell Doctor Wang what you can about your mistress's illness.'

'Excuse me,' interposed the doctor. 'Please allow me to take her pulses and reach my own diagnosis first. Then the young ladies may judge for themselves and correct me if anything I say conflicts with what they already know of her condition.'

Nightingale arranged Dai-yu so that one of her hands was showing through the bed-curtains and resting on the diagnostic arm-rest, and gently slid back her bracelet and sleeve so as not to obstruct the pulse. The doctor sat for a long while feeling the pulses first of one hand, then of the other. When he had finished, he withdrew with Jia Lian to the outer room, where they both sat down.

'The six pulses have an extremely taut quality,' said the doctor, 'and indicate an advanced morbid obstruction.'

As he spoke, Nightingale appeared in the doorway. He turned towards her and said:

'This condition should manifest itself in the following ways: dizzy spells, loss of appetite, frequent dreams, and fitful sleeping in the early hours; during the daytime a tendency to take offence for no reason and a generally nervous and apprehensive attitude towards other people. Some might attribute all these to a peculiarity of temperament, but they would be mistaken. They are organically related to a deficiency of Yin in the liver, with a concomitant diminution of cardiac vitality. Does my diagnosis accord with what you have observed?'

Nightingale nodded, and turning to Jia Lian said: 'That is exactly how Miss Lin has been, sir.'

'Good,' said Doctor Wang, rising from his chair. 'We may proceed.'

Jia Lian escorted him out of the Garden and across to his study, where his pages had already laid out the requisite pink prescription form in readiness. Tea was served, then Doctor Wang took up the brush and wrote:

DIAGNOSIS
The six pulses are slow and taut. Prolonged morbid obstruction of the humoral flow.
Left distal pulse weak. Diminution of cardiac vitality.
Left median pulse strong and irregular. Hyperactivity of the liver (*Wood*).
The hepatic humour, unable to disperse naturally, has encroached upwards on the spleen (*Earth*), with consequent loss of appetite. The extreme distemper has also caused a reversal of the elemental sequence, and the lungs (*Metal*) have certainly been damaged.
Since humour cannot circulate, it has congealed into phlegm. Upsurge and expectoration of blood.

TREATMENT
1. Sedation of liver.
2. Restoration of lungs.
3. Fortification of both heart and spleen.

The usual tonics are too violent in their action. For the present, I suggest my own *Black Ethereal Essence*, to be taken with *Elixir Pneumoferriferum*. Prescriptions for both humbly appended for esteemed approval.

The doctor wrote out a prescription of seven items and an adjuvant to go with it. Jia Lian took the paper and glanced down the list.

'I see you include Hare's Ear in your prescription,' he said. 'Forgive me if I am wrong, but I thought that was ruled out in haematic eruptions?'

'You must be thinking,' replied Doctor Wang with a

knowledgeable smile, 'of its emetic properties, which, as is well known, contra-indicate this particular herb in cases of haemoptysis or epistaxis. But allow me to inform you that in preparation with Turtle's Blood (as in my prescription), Hare's Ear constitutes the only effective remedy we have for draining the humour of the Lesser Yang periphery of the gall-bladder. You see, the judicious admixture of Turtle's Blood has the remarkable effect of inhibiting the emetic properties of Hare's Ear, while enabling it to restore the hepatic Yin and check the phlogistic disturbance. In the words of the *Ars Medicandi: "Obstructa obstruit, aperitque aperta."* And the – at first sight – paradoxical inclusion of Hare's Ear is none other than the classic stratagem of the loyal counsellor befriending the usurper . . .'

'I see,' said Jia Lian, nodding appreciatively. 'Thank you for enlightening me, Doctor Wang.'

The doctor continued:

'I should like the young lady to take two doses of the decoction, and then we shall see whether to alter the prescription, or perhaps try a new one altogether. I have another appointment, so I hope you'll excuse me. I shall call again another day.'

As Jia Lian saw him out, he asked:

'And what have you prescribed for my cousin?'

'Oh there's very little the matter with *him*. Another dose of the dispersant I have prescribed should put him right.'

With these words Doctor Wang stepped into his carriage.

Jia Lian dispatched a servant to purchase the various drugs needed and went in to inform Xi-feng of Dai-yu's diagnosis. They had not been talking long when Zhou Rui's wife arrived to consult Xi-feng about a few trivial details of domestic management. After listening for a while, Jia Lian rose to leave.

'Carry on, Mrs Zhou, I must be going.'

With Jia Lian out of the room, and all remaining household business soon disposed of, Zhou Rui's wife was able to come to the real purpose of her visit.

'I've just come from Miss Lin's, ma'am. I don't like the look of it at all! There's not a spot of colour left in her cheeks, and to touch her she's nothing but skin and bones. I tried asking her what the matter was, but she wouldn't speak, just sat there crying. Before I left, Nightingale asked if you could advance them a couple of months' allowance. She said that with Miss Lin so ill, and her so proud anyway about not being beholden to a soul for anything, she'd made bold to ask about it herself. The medicine Miss Lin is taking goes on the general account of course, but she said they might be needing some extra money for incidental expenses. I said I'd mention it to you, ma'am.'

Xi-feng lowered her head for a moment, then replied:

'Oh very well, I'll send her a few taels to be going on with. There's no need to tell Miss Lin though. I'm against advances on principle. If one person starts we'll never hear the end of it. Do you remember the scene Mrs Zhao and Miss Tan-chun had about this very question? Besides, as you know, with so many expenses and so little coming in to pay for them, things are extremely tight at present.'

After a pause, she continued:

'Some people are under the illusion that it's all caused by bad management on my part. Some even have the nerve to suggest that I am lining the Wang nest at the Jia family's expense. But you know better, my dear Mrs Zhou. You've seen far too much of what really goes on to pay any attention to such gossip.'

'Why I never heard such downright wicked lies in all my days, ma'am,' said Zhou Rui's wife. 'Bless my soul! Where would this great rambling household be now, I should like to know, without you to keep everything running smoothly the way you do? I'd like to see any other lady try to take it on. Why, a grown man with six arms and three heads would crumple under the strain of what you have to bear, for certain sure! There's no justice left in this world!'

Suddenly she broke into a cackle of laughter.

'Mind you, Mrs Lian, the things people *will* say! The other day when Mr Zhou came home from town, he told me how people are all talking about us, trying to guess just how rich the family is. Take this for example: "The Jias have got rooms piled high with silver and gold! Every stick of furniture in the house is inlaid with gold and studded with precious stones!" Or sometimes they gossip about Her Grace: "That daughter of theirs at Court," they'll say, "you can bet your last buckle she's managed to smuggle home half the Emperor's things. That time she went on that grand visitation, we saw it with our own eyes – cartloads of gold and silver she brought along with her, had the old home twinkling away like a fairy palace... And when the family laid on that big do at the Temple (which must have cost them a fortune), they didn't bat an eyelid! Those lions outside the main gate are solid jade, and they've a golden kylin in the garden – used to be two, till one was stolen! You'd expect the ladies to be grand of course: but in that set-up the maids are quite as genteel and ladylike as the ladies themselves! They never do a hand's turn, just lounge around drinking wine, playing music or perhaps a little chess, or doing a spot of leisurely painting now and then... There's never any shortage of others to do their work. All they need fuss about is which silk gown to slip into next. If you could see the delicacies they eat or the clothes they wear, you wouldn't believe your eyes. And the children! So pampered, if they were to ask for a moonbeam someone would be off to fetch it down for the pretty little darlings to play with!" There's even a song about us:

Moneybags Ning
And Rolling Rong
Treat their cash
Like piles of dung.

It seems so fine,
But please beware!
If you look too . . .'

Mrs Zhou broke off in mid flow. The last two lines of her song were in fact:

If you look too close,
The cupboard's bare!

She had been so carried away with her rendition that she only stopped in the nick of time. Xi-feng could tell that the song carried a sting in its tail.

'I know the sort of thing,' she remarked casually. 'But what could have given rise to that story about the golden kylin?'

'They must mean the little one old Abbot Zhang gave Master Bao at the Temple,' replied Mrs Zhou. 'He lost it and then several days later young Miss Shi found it for him. A little thing like that is quite enough for those townfolk to spin one of their yarns around! They're so ridiculous, aren't they, Mrs Lian? The only thing one can do is laugh.'

'I can't say I find it particularly funny,' replied Xi-feng. 'It's actually rather frightening. The trouble is that behind our magnificent façade things are going from bad to worse. There's a popular saying:

Fattest pigs make choicest bacon;
Famous men are for the taking.

And our fame has been won under false pretences anyway. Sometimes I worry a great deal where all this will lead to.'

'I understand your concern, ma'am,' said Mrs Zhou. 'But talk like that has been going round town for over a year, in the teahouses and wineshops, in every alley-way. It's too late to stop it now, isn't it?'

Xi-feng nodded. She told Patience to weigh out a few taels of silver and gave them to Mrs Zhou.

'Take these to Nightingale. Say it's just a little extra

from me to help out. If she needs to make any purchases out of common funds, she mustn't be afraid to say so. No more talk of advances, though. I know Nightingale is a bright girl and will understand what I mean. Tell her that when I've a free moment I'll be over to see Miss Lin.'

Zhou Rui's wife took the money and departed to carry out these instructions.

*

No sooner had Jia Lian left Xi-feng closeted with Zhou Rui's wife than he was accosted by a page-boy with an urgent summons from his father, and was obliged to go straight over to Jia She's apartment.

'I've just got wind of the fact that someone at Court is ill,' Jia She explained. 'A senior consultant and two orderlies from the College of Physicians have been summoned to the palace, which indicates an illness in His Majesty's immediate entourage. Tell me, have we had any news of Her Grace the past few days?'

'None,' replied Lian.

'Go and ask your uncle, and check with Cousin Zhen,' said Jia She. 'See if they know any more about it. If not, then send someone to inquire at the College. We must find out what is going on.'

'Yes, father.'

Jia Lian pursued both lines of inquiry simultaneously, dispatching one of his men to the College, while he himself set off in haste to find Jia Zheng.

'Where did you hear of this?' asked Jia Zheng, after listening to Lian's account of the story.

'From father, just a minute ago.'

'Well, you and Cousin Zhen had better go straight to the Palace and see what information you can glean there.'

'I have already sent someone to the College,' replied Lian, 'to see if there is any news. I'll go to the Ning side and fetch Cousin Zhen.'

He had no need to go as far as Ning-guo House, however, since Cousin Zhen was already on his way over.

'Yes, I'd heard the same rumour myself,' remarked Zhen, as Lian told him the story and the two of them walked together towards Jia Zheng's study. 'I was just on my way to consult your father and Uncle Zheng about it.'

By the time they arrived, Jia Zheng's attitude had become somewhat more philosophical.

'If it *is* Her Grace,' he advised them, 'we are sure to be informed sooner or later.'

Meanwhile Jia She had joined the gathering.

At noon, the four of them were still waiting for Jia Lian's messenger to return with news from the College, when one of the janitors came in to report the arrival of two Palace Eunuchs, with an Imperial Communication for Sir She and Sir Zheng.

'Show them in,' ordered Jia She, and he and his brother went out to greet them at the inner gate. They knelt Manchu-style and did homage as 'Her Grace's most Humble Servants', before ushering the Imperial delegation through the gateway and across the courtyard to the main reception-hall, where they begged them both to be seated. One of the eunuchs rose to his feet and said:

'Your daughter, Her Grace the Imperial Concubine, having been somewhat indisposed of late, it is His Majesty's Pleasure that four ladies of her family should visit the Imperial Bedchamber tomorrow. Each lady is to be permitted a single maidservant in attendance. Male relatives are to proceed as far as the Inner Gate and present their cards. They may not proceed any further but are to do homage and await any further instructions outside the gate. Appointed time of arrival is nine a.m., departure to be completed by five p.m.'

Jia Zheng and Jia She and all the others present received this edict standing. When it was concluded, they sat down once more and offered the eunuchs tea, after which the

Imperial party took its leave. The two senior brothers saw them out as far as the main gate, and then went in to report to Grandmother Jia.

'*Four*?' queried the old lady. 'Your two ladies and myself makes three. Who can the fourth place be for?'

There was a momentary pause. No one dared make a suggestion, and after a moment's reflection Grandmother Jia continued: 'It must be meant for Feng. She knows how to cope with any situation. Well, you menfolk go off and make your arrangements.'

Leaving promptly, Jia She and Jia Zheng gave instructions that apart from Lian and Rong whose job it would be to stay and look after the two mansions, a full turn-out of junior and senior clan-members was expected. Next the servants were told to fit out four of the family's best green court-sedans, and a dozen carriages with blue canopies, and have them lined up before first light in the morning. The servants hurried about their business, while the two Masters returned for a final consultation with Lady Jia.

'We have to be there at nine o'clock, and leave at five, Mother. It seems advisable to retire rather earlier than usual tonight if we are to make a prompt start in the morning. We need to allow ourselves ample time to prepare for court.'

'Very well,' replied Grandmother Jia. 'You can go now.'

The brothers withdrew, leaving Grandmother Jia with her two daughters-in-law and Xi-feng. They talked for a while about Yuan-chun's illness, and then after a little more desultory chat, retired for the night.

Next morning, before dawn, maids lit the lamps in every apartment, and the ladies sat down to their toilet. At five o'clock, when the ladies were ready and the gentlemen had put the finishing touches to their ceremonial outfits, Steward Lin and Lai Da came to the Inner Gate to report that the chairs and carriages were all ready as ordered and had been drawn up outside. Jia She and Lady

Xing arrived, and the party was complete. After breakfast, which they all took together, Lady Jia led them out, leaning on Xi-feng's arm, and the household gathered round as the four ladies, each accompanied by a single maid, walked slowly out. An advance party, consisting of Li Gui and one other senior boy, went on horseback to make preliminary arrangements at the Outer Gate of the Palace. Three generations of Jias stepped into their carriages or mounted their horses. The procession fell into line and, with retainers swelling the train, set off through the streets. Jia Lian and Jia Rong remained behind to look after the two mansions.

The procession came to a halt under Westwall Gate, one of the outer gates of the Forbidden City, and shortly afterwards two eunuchs emerged to announce:

'By Imperial Dispensation! The ladies of the Jia family will now enter the Palace for their Personal Visitation. The gentlemen may also proceed but may not enter the Palace precincts. They will halt at the Inner Gate and do their homage from there.'

There was a cry of '*Forward*!' from the men on the gate, and a junior eunuch guided the four ladies' chairs onward, while the gentlemen followed on foot at a stately pace, leaving their servants at the Outer Gate. As they approached the Inner Gate, they could see several elderly eunuchs sitting there, who rose to their feet as the procession arrived and announced:

'Gentlemen of the Jia family! Halt here!'

Jia She and Jia Zheng lined their men up outside the Gate in order of seniority, while the ladies passed through in their chairs, halted under the Gate and dismounted. A new escort of junior eunuchs now presented itself, and the Jia ladies, each leaning on a maid's arm, continued on foot through the inner precincts of the Palace, until they saw before them the lavishly ornamented façade and brilliantly glazed roof-tiles of the Imperial Concubine's Bedchamber.

Two young ladies-in-waiting stepped forward to inform

them that the only formality required would be a curtsey. Expressing their humble appreciation for this favour, the visitors approached the bed and curtseyed in turn. Yuan-chun bade them be seated, which they did after a polite show of reluctance. She spoke first to Grandmother Jia:

'Have you been keeping well?'

Leaning on her maid, the old lady rose shakily to her feet and replied:

'Thanks to Your Grace's beneficent aura I am still in good health.'

Yuan-chun went on to speak to Lady Wang and Lady Xing, who both rose to answer in similar fashion. Then she turned to Xi-feng:

'How are things at home?'

Xi-feng rose to her feet.

'We manage to get by, Your Grace,' she replied, and sat down.

'I appreciate,' said Yuan-chun, 'that it has not been easy for you these past few years.'

Xi-feng was about to rise again and reply when a lady-in-waiting entered with a lot of official cards for Her Grace's inspection. As she recognized the familiar names, Yuan-chun felt a bitter pang of grief and tears began to flow down her cheeks. The lady-in-waiting proferred a silk handkerchief, which she used to wipe away her tears, saying:

'I am a little better today, please tell them. And bid them wait outside.'

The Jia ladies were once more on their feet and expressing their gratitude. Yuan-chun's eyes were still wet with tears.

'Humble families are so much luckier than we are! At least they can be together!'

Lady Jia and the others were also on the brink of tears.

'We beseech Your Grace not to be sad. Your exalted blessings have already made themselves felt a thousandfold at home.'

'How is Bao-yu coming along?' asked Yuan-chun.

'He is taking his studies more seriously now,' replied Lady Jia. 'His father has been extremely strict with him, and he is turning into quite a little scholar.'

'I am so glad to hear that.'

Yuan-chun gave orders for their luncheon to be served in the outer reception-hall, and two ladies-in-waiting, assisted by four junior eunuchs, escorted them out. The seating had been arranged in accordance with Jia family precedence, and the ladies sat down to an immaculately presented meal, details of which our narrative omits.

When luncheon was over, the four ladies returned to give thanks. After further desultory chat, they saw that it was nearly five o'clock, and anxious not to overstep their limit, took their leave. Yuan-chun sent one of her ladies-in-waiting to accompany them as far as the Inner Gate, where the same four eunuchs were waiting to guide them out. Lady Jia and company stepped into their chairs and were carried to the Outer Gate, where they were joined by Jia She and the menfolk. The whole family returned in procession together.

The Visitation was repeated the following day and the day after, and as the arrangements made were identical to the last detail, we need not elaborate any further here.

*

Meanwhile, in the Xue household, things were going from bad to worse. Ever since Xue Pan's disappearance, Jin-gui had felt the lack of a sparring partner. Caltrop (Lily) had moved out to live with Bao-chai, and the only person left within range was Moonbeam. But since her promotion to the Master's bed, Moonbeam had acquired a new self-assurance, and Jin-gui soon observed that her stratagem in giving Moonbeam to Pan had misfired. Her maid had indeed become her strongest rival. 'Very well,' she thought to herself one day, when she had been drinking heavily and was lying on her kang in a maudlin frame of mind, 'let's see what she's worth...' A round or two with Moonbeam might be just the seltzer she needed.

'Come on!' she taunted her. 'Where's our precious Lord and Master disappeared to, eh? Where's he hiding? You do know, of course, don't you?'

'I've not the least idea,' replied Moonbeam coolly. 'If he wouldn't tell you, Mrs Pan, no one else is likely to know.'

'Spare me the "Mrs", will you!' said Jin-gui with a malicious smile. 'You and that Lily think you run the place, don't you? I can't get near that little Miss Unmolestable, with all her friends in high places to take care of her – all right! I won't stick my neck out in that direction! But you're still my maid, I don't have to take cheek from *you*! If you're so sure of yourself, why not get on with it and strangle me? Then you and Lily can have the field to yourselves. I'm just in your way – go on, say it!'

Moonbeam wasn't taking this lying down. She looked Jin-gui straight in the eye:

'Mrs Pan, you have no right to accuse me like that! When have I ever said a word against you? Just because you can't do anything to *her*, there's no need to take it out on *me*! You're just being a bully! You know what the real trouble is, so why pretend you don't?'

She burst into floods of tears and Jin-gui, who was now back in her element, clambered fuming down from the kang and went after her. Moonbeam had learned a thing or two in the Xia household and fought back every inch of the way. Jin-gui, ignoring her cries and protestations of innocence, attacked her with whatever she could lay hands on, and chairs, tables, cups and bowls were soon flying in every direction.

Aunt Xue happened to be in Bao-chai's room and heard the terrible racket they were making.

'Caltrop,' she ordered without thinking, 'go over and see what's going on, will you? Try and get them to quieten down.'

'You can't possibly send Caltrop,' Bao-chai reminded her. 'That would only make things worse.'

'Very well then, I shall go myself,' declared Aunt Xue.

'I don't think you should, Mama,' advised Bao-chai. 'We shall have to let them fight it out. There's nothing we can do, I'm afraid.'

'What an intolerable state of affairs!' cried Aunt Xue, and leaning on one of her maids she set off in the direction of Jin-gui's apartment. Bao-chai followed reluctantly, giving Caltrop strict instructions to stay behind. As they approached Jin-gui's apartment, they could hear the storm continuing unabated inside.

'What's the meaning of this?' cried Aunt Xue. 'Look at the state things are in! What a disgraceful way to behave! Other people can hear what goes on, you know. Aren't you ashamed of what our relatives will think? Aren't you afraid of being made a laughing-stock?'

'Me a laughing-stock – that's rich!' Jin-gui yelled from inside. 'It's this topsy-turvy family of yours that's a laughing-stock. There's no respect, no proper order, not a single thing right in this godforsaken dump! I was brought up differently, I can tell you! In my home people knew their place. I've had as much from your family as I can take!'

'Sister-in-law,' pleaded Bao-chai, 'Mother only came because she heard the two of you fighting. If she seemed to be blaming you, and didn't distinguish between you and Moonbeam, it's only because she was upset. I'm sure she didn't mean anything by it. Wouldn't it be better to explain whatever it is that's troubling you, and all of us try to get along peaceably together? Poor Mother, we're worrying her to death.'

'Yes,' added Aunt Xue, 'before you start accusing me, kindly explain what the trouble is.'

'You're such a saint, aren't you!' said Jin-gui, addressing herself to Bao-chai. 'I'm sure a fine lady like you will marry a gentleman and live in a nice home – not like me, stranded here, trampled under foot, taken advantage of by all and sundry! I might as well be a widow! What a fool I am! Don't judge me too harshly. I'm only a poor fatherless creature that's never been taught any better. And I'm sure you'd rather I spared you the sordid details of what goes on in here between my husband and his various womenfolk!'

Only the thought of what her mother must be suffering enabled Bao-chai to contain her intense anger and shame at these words.

'Sister-in-law,' she pleaded, 'please don't say any more. No one is judging you, no one is taking advantage of you – we never did with Lily and of course we don't with you.'

At this Jin-gui started whacking the side of the kang and shrieked at the top of her voice:

'Lily! How could I ever compare with her? I'm not worth the ground she treads on, am I? She's been here longer than I have, she understands you and knows how to butter you up, and I don't, I'm just a newcomer! I know! There's no need to remind me of it! But remember, we can't all be Imperial Concubines; you'd better watch your step and make sure you don't end up like me, married to a great half-baked booby, left in the lurch for all the world to mock at!'

Aunt Xue could contain herself no longer and rose to her feet:

'I am not just defending her because she is my daughter; she has tried her best to make peace with you but you seem quite determined to provoke her. Whatever your trouble is, leave the poor girl alone! If you have to punish someone, why not strangle me instead?'

'Please don't you get angry too, Mama,' begged Bao-chai. 'We only came to try and help. If all we're going to do is make things worse, I honestly think we should go. Let's give her time to think it all over. And don't *you* go causing any more trouble either!' This last remark was addressed to Moonbeam.

And so the two of them left and returned to their own apartment. As they crossed the courtyard, they saw one of

Lady Jia's personal maids coming out to greet them with Caltrop.

'Which way did you come?' asked Aunt Xue, adding: 'I hope Lady Jia is well.'

'Very well, thank you ma'am,' replied the maid. 'Her Old Ladyship asked me to send you her best regards, to thank you for the lychees you sent the other day, and to congratulate Miss Qin on her engagement.'

'How long have you been here?' asked Bao-chai.

'Quite a time,' was her reply. The colour rose in Aunt Xue's cheeks when she realized how much the maid must have overheard.

'I'm afraid we've been having some dreadful scenes here recently,' she said. 'We must be a laughing-stock over on your side.'

'Oh ma'am, it's nothing serious,' said the maid. 'Every family has its little troubles. That's as natural as plates clinking in a picnic-hamper. You're worrying too much.'

She went inside with them and sat for a while before returning to Grandmother Jia's.

A moment or two later, Bao-chai was busy giving Caltrop some instructions when suddenly Aunt Xue cried out:

'Ai! My chest!'

She lay down on the kang, sending Bao-chai and Caltrop into a great state of panic. But if you wish to know the outcome, you must turn to the next chapter.

CHAPTER 84

Bao-yu is given an impromptu examination,
and his betrothal is discussed for the first time
Jia Huan visits a convulsive child,
and old hostilities are resumed

Bao-chai diagnosed her mother's sudden pain as an upward movement of humour from the liver into the chest, brought on by the recent scene with Jin-gui. Without waiting for a doctor, she sent a servant out instantly to buy a few drams of Woody Vine Hooks, and made a strong brew for Aunt Xue to drink. Then Caltrop helped administer a leg-pummelling and chest-massage. The pain eased a little; but Aunt Xue's anger at Jin-gui's outrageous behaviour, and her distress that Bao-chai should have had to submit to such humiliation, continued unabated.

Eventually, after another dose of daughterly reasoning, she fell asleep, and the humour was given a chance to subside.

'Now please don't worry any more, Mama,' pleaded Bao-chai, when she awoke. 'In a day or two, when you feel up to it, why not go over and see Lady Jia and Aunt Wang? It would do you a world of good. Caltrop and I can take care of things here while you're away. And I'm sure there will be no more trouble from *her*.'

Aunt Xue nodded.

'Perhaps I will in a couple of days.'

*

The news finally arrived that Yuan-chun had recovered, and everyone in the Jia family was greatly relieved. A day or two later a party of eunuchs arrived from the palace with a consignment of presents and parcels of money.

They announced that it was Her Grace's wish to reward the family for the diligence they had shown in visiting her during her Indisposition. The eunuchs handed over the carefully labelled gifts one by one. Jia She, Jia Zheng and the other menfolk went in to report to Grandmother Jia, and then all returned to express their thanks for the largesse. When the eunuchs had drunk their tea and gone, there was a family gathering in Grandmother Jia's apartment. After a few minutes, while they were still chatting, an old serving-woman came in with a message:

'The pages have reported that there's a visitor at the other side on important business for Sir She, milady.'

With Grandmother Jia's permission, Jia She left to see to his own affairs. When he had gone, she suddenly thought of something and her face lit up with a smile.

'It's so touching,' she said, turning to Jia Zheng, 'the way Her Grace remembers Bao-yu! The other day she made a point of asking about him.'

'Her solicitude,' replied Jia Zheng with a sarcastic smile, 'is as generous as it is undeserved. Increasing idleness is the only fruit *that* young tree will ever bear.'

'But I gave him a glowing report!' protested Grandmother Jia. 'I said how well he was doing at his compositions.'

'I only wish it were the truth,' said Jia Zheng with a crushing smile.

'But you and your friends are always asking him to write verses and things for you – I'm sure he's making progress, whatever you say. He's still young, be patient with him. "A single spoonful never made a bouncing babe," as the saying goes.'

Jia Zheng affected a dutiful smile.

'Yes, Mother.'

'Which brings me,' the old lady continued, 'to the other thing I want to talk about. Now that Bao-yu is growing up, it's time you and his mother started thinking seriously of choosing a nice wife for him. Marriage is going to be a most important step in his life. We needn't worry too much how closely related to us she is, or how much money they've got; but we must be sure that she's sweet-natured, and a pretty sort of girl.'

'Thank you for reminding me, Mother,' replied Jia Zheng rather stiffly. 'But although of course I appreciate the importance of choosing a suitable bride, the first step, as I see it, must lie with Bao-yu himself. Without a marked improvement on his part, any alliance we might hope to arrange would be doomed, and would certainly be a regrettable error for the young lady concerned. His present shiftless attitude can only spell matrimonial disaster.'

His response did not please Grandmother Jia.

'I know that it's your decision!' she replied testily, 'and that I'm an interfering old busybody! But let me say just this: even if I *did* rather spoil him when he was little, and even if he *isn't* quite as grown-up and responsible as you think he ought to be, I still think he has always been a nice, well-mannered, honest boy. I think you're quite wrong to treat him as a ne'er-do-well, or as some sort of threat to a young girl's happiness. He's not like that at all. Oh perhaps I *am* prejudiced! He's preferable to young Huan, anyway. Or would you like to correct me there as well?'

Jia Zheng was by now feeling extremely uncomfortable. 'You are of course by far the more experienced judge of character, Mother,' he replied swiftly. 'You may be right in thinking that fate has favoured him. Perhaps it is my own – how shall I put it? – impatience to detect a sense of *purpose* in the lad that has made of me a crabbed old father, and of Bao-yu the – eh – "crab-apple of my eye"?'

The labour required on his part in the manufacture of this sparkling piece of verbal merriment did not quite nullify its object, viz. the humouring of the old lady, and she smiled, whereupon the other ladies contributed a polite round of laughter.

'Yes,' said Grandmother Jia, 'and don't forget how

much older you are. It's that and your experience as a civil servant that have made you so mellow and wise.'

She turned to Lady Xing and Lady Wang with a formidable glance and went on mischievously:

'If you could have seen *him* when *he* was a boy! He was quite impossible! *Far* worse than Bao-yu! It was only marriage that taught him a thing or two about life. And now he won't stop complaining about poor Bao. If anything, the boy is more mature for his age than his father was.'

The ladies thought this assault on the bastion of Jia Zheng's dignity a great joke, and started laughing and calling Grandmother Jia a tease. Then the junior maids came in and informed Faithful that lunch was ready to be served.

'Speak up!' called out Grandmother Jia, her good humour quite restored. 'Let me in on the secret!'

Faithful smiled and passed on the message.

'Well in that case,' said Grandmother Jia, 'everyone can go home for lunch, except Feng and Cousin Zhen's wife. I'd like them to stay and keep me company.'

Jia Zheng, Lady Wang and Lady Xing waited until lunch was served and then, after a few more prods from the old lady, they left and went their separate ways.

*

On their return, Jia Zheng, in the course of conversation with Lady Wang, brought up the subject of his recent contretemps with Grandmother Jia:

'How Mother idolizes that boy! If only he can do well enough to scrape through his exam, then she will have something to feel proud of, a return for all her love, and he will have something to offer in the event of his marriage.'

'How true!' concurred Lady Wang.

Jia Zheng sent a maid out at once with the following orders for Li Gui:

'Tell Bao-yu I wish to see him this evening. Instead of

coming to see me after school, he is to have his dinner first and come straight to my study afterwards. There are some questions I wish to put to him.'

Li Gui intercepted Bao-yu on his way home from school that afternoon, just as he was about to go in and pay his respects to his father. Bao-yu seemed thunder-struck by the ominous summons; he went to see Grand-mother Jia, hurried back to Green Delights, ate a scanty meal, quickly rinsed his mouth and set off again for his father's apartment.

Jia Zheng was waiting for him in the inner study. Bao-yu entered, made his bow and stood attentively to one side.

'As you know,' Jia Zheng began, 'I have been rather preoccupied recently and have not had an opportunity to question you on the progress of your studies. Let me see, I recall that the Preceptor had set you a month for revision, after which time he was to give you your Maiden Theme. That must have been at least two months ago. You should have made a start by now, I think.'

'I have, sir,' replied Bao-yu. 'I have written three compositions. I have been waiting for my work to improve before venturing to trouble you with any specimens of it. Those were the Preceptor's instructions, sir.'

'What were your first three Themes?'

'The first was from Analects, sir, Book Two,' replied Bao-yu. '"*Annos Quindecim natus*: The Sage Bent upon Learning in his Fifteenth Year." The second was also from Analects, Book One: "*Obscuritatem Aequo Animo Toleratam*: Lack of Acclaim Borne with Equanimity." And the third was from Mencius, Book Three, Part Two: "*Tunc Accedunt Micium*: They Succumb to the Mician Heresy."'

'And have you kept your draft versions?' asked Jia Zheng.

'I have fair copies of all three, sir, with the Preceptor's emendations.'

'Are they at home, or in the schoolroom?'

'In the schoolroom, sir.'

'Then have someone go and fetch them at once. I should like to see them.'

Bao-yu sent an 'express' message through to Tealeaf: 'Go to the schoolroom; in the drawer of my desk is a thin bamboo-paper copybook with *Tasks* written on the cover. Bring it here, quickly!'

In a short while Tealeaf returned with the book, which he handed to Bao-yu who presented it to his father. Jia Zheng opened it at the first page and began reading the first of the eight 'legs' of Bao-yu's Maiden Task.

AMPLICATIO PRIMA
THEMA: ANNOS QUINDECIM NATUS
CRUS PRIMUM: APERTURA
Sapiens perfectusque Vir
a puero quidem
se ad Philosophiam applicavit.

Jia Zheng glanced at the emendation and asked Bao-yu to construe his Apertura orally. Bao-yu began:

'The Sage, while still a boy . . . forsooth . . . was wholly Bent upon Learning.'

Jia Zheng looked up.

'Your use of *puer* betrays an inadequate comprehension of the Theme. I see the Preceptor has substituted the *annos quindecim natus* of the original. Good. *Pueritia*, you see, covers the whole span of boyhood up to and including the age of sixteen, whereas here the Sage is alluding to specific milestones in his own life. We must echo the numbers he uses, if we are to preserve the correct sequence of his moral and intellectual development.'

Jia Zheng continued with the second 'leg'.

CRUS SECUNDUM: CONTINUATIO
Tantam autem Applicationem
Rarissimam esse confiteor.

'And what,' he asked with a shake of the head, 'do you mean by this?'

'That the Sage's application,' replied Bao-yu, 'is a thing ordinary mortals scarcely ever achieve.'

'Childish nonsense, my boy! It only shows what a creature of indolence you are. I am glad to see that the Preceptor has rewritten the entire *Continuatio* for you. Kindly construe, from "*omnibus enim*".'

Bao-yu obliged:

'For many are those who aspire to Learning. But how few alas possess the application necessary for the fulfilment of this Aspiration. Does not the Sage's achievement testify to the strength of his Moral Convictions in his Fifteenth Year?'

'I thank you. I trust you understand the emendation?'

'Yes sir.'

Jia Zheng passed on to the second Theme:* 'Lack of Acclaim Borne with Equanimity.' Jia Zheng read the Preceptor's emended version, translating to himself as he went along:

'If a man is able to view Worldly Acclaim with Equanimity, nothing can affect his Pleasure and Delight'.

He screwed up his eyes to decipher Bao-yu's original:

'What's all this? "Equanimity is the Essence of Scholarship." You have completely failed to treat the first element in your Theme, *Obscuritas*, and have embarked prematurely on a discussion of *Nobilitas* which should be kept for a later section. Your Preceptor's emendation shows a correct *Dispositio*. I hope you notice the way in which he uses *Amoenitatem Delectationemque Animi* to

* It may be helpful at this point to provide some idea of the pedagogic principles that guided Dai-ru in his selection of Themes for his young pupil. His plan was roughly speaking as follows:
First Theme – reiterate need for Youthful Zeal.
Second Theme – clarify point raised during second day's oral exegesis, viz. Worldly Success versus Moral Achievement.
Third Theme – Orthodoxy versus Heresy.

allude to the passage in Analects immediately preceding the rubric? Do you recall? *Nonne quidem amoenum? Nonne quidem delectabile*? You must study this sort of thing carefully.'

'Yes sir.'

Jia Zheng went on to read Bao-yu's *Continuatio*. There was another reference here to the Essence of Scholarship, which had once again been emended by the Preceptor to Pleasure and Delight.

'The same fault as in your *Apertura*,' commented Jia Zheng. 'The emendation is tolerable. Not particularly stylish, but clear.'

He moved on to the third and last Theme: 'The Mician Heresy'. As he recollected the provenance of the quotation, he looked up in surprise and after a moment's thought asked Bao-yu:

'Have you reached this far in Mencius?'

'Yes sir,' Bao-yu hastened to assure him. 'The Preceptor decided to go through Mencius with me first, as it is the easiest of the Four Books. We finished the whole of Mencius three days ago, and now we are doing Analects Part One.'

Jia Zheng continued reading. By the time Bao-yu had come to write this third composition, he had more or less mastered the 'ignoble art of the Octopartite', and had learned to handle the necessary rhetorical constructions with a certain glib dexterity. Jia Zheng studied the first two 'legs', and observed that in this case the Preceptor had paid the young essayist the compliment of a total suspension of the corrective brush. The *Apertura* lamented the fact that those who rejected the Hedonist Doctrine of Yanxius (*Yanxianam illam Voluptatis Doctrinam*) were still unable to find the True Path of Confucian Orthodoxy (*Orthodoxiae Confucianae Veram Viam*), but were instead blindly drawn into the fold of that prevalent (and deplorable) Mician Heresy of Universal Love (*Micianam illam Caritatis Universae Heterodoxiam*).

'Nicely put,' Jia Zheng commented, and continued reading. A little further on he paused. 'Tell me,' he asked, evidently impressed by what he read, 'did you write this unaided?'

'Yes sir.'

He nodded pensively.

'Nothing brilliant about it of course, but for a first attempt not at all bad, I must say. Ah, Mencius! I recall how during my tour of duty as an examiner I had occasion to set as one of my Themes "*Soli Nobilitatis Sapientiaeque Alumni sunt potis*". All the first-degree candidates, I regret to say, had their heads crammed full of the standard compositions on the Theme, and not a single one of them could come up with anything original. All plagiarisms. Are you familiar with the quotation?'

'Yes sir. Mencius, Book One, Part Two: "Only Good Breeding and a Heritage of Culture have the power to sustain a man in the face of Adversity".'

'Good,' replied Jia Zheng. 'I should like you to show me what you can do. Something of your own, please, not another feat of memorization. An *Apertura* will do.'

Bao-yu lowered his head in concentration and began racking his brains for a pithy opening phrase, while Jia Zheng stood thoughtfully in the doorway, hands clasped behind his back. Just at that moment, a diminutive page-boy went flashing past. As he caught sight of the Master in the doorway, he froze, his body slightly inclined, his arms hanging limp at his side.

'What is your errand, boy?' asked Jia Zheng brusquely.

'Please, sir, Mrs Xue has just arrived at Her Old Ladyship's and Mrs Lian has sent me with special instructions to the kitchen, sir,' jabbered the unfortunate boy. Jia Zheng made no reply, and he fled.

Now Bao-yu assumed that if Aunt Xue had come over for a visit, then Bao-chai (whom he had greatly missed since her departure from the Garden) was sure to have come with her. His excitement at the thought of seeing her again spurred him on.

'Sir,' he ventured, 'I have a draft *Apertura* for your approval.'

'Go ahead.'

Bao-yu intoned his opening sentence:

'Non omnes Sapientiae Alumni sunt, neque possunt carere Stabili Patrimonio.'

Jia Zheng nodded.

'Thank you. That will do for today. In future, please bear in mind these two Golden Rules for Composition. Before raising your brush, always be certain of the sequence of your *Dispositio* and the clarity of your *Inventio*. Tell me, was your grandmother aware that I sent for you?'

'Yes sir.'

'Off you go then. You had better go over and see her now.'

'Sir!'

Bao-yu manoeuvred his way backwards out of the study and set off along the covered way, imitating to perfection the scholar's leisurely gait. As soon as he reached the moon-gate, however, and had placed its large protective screen between himself and the study, he broke into a run and raced ahead towards Grandmother Jia's apartment.

'Careful you don't trip!' Tealeaf shouted after him. 'The Master's coming.'

Bao-yu was much too excited to pay any attention. As he neared the entrance to Grandmother Jia's apartment, he could hear the sounds of conversation and laughter coming from within. He could make out, among others, the voices of Lady Wang, Xi-feng and Tan-chun.

When the maids saw him coming, they quickly drew aside the portière and whispered in his ear as he passed through:

'Mrs Xue is here, you know.'

Bao-yu hurried in to greet his aunt, and then paid his respects to Grandmother Jia. He gave her a full account of his interview with Jia Zheng, and her face radiated pride and delight.

'Where's Cousin Chai?' he asked, turning to the assembled company.

'She couldn't come with me today,' said Aunt Xue, with a rather unconvincing smile. 'She and Caltrop have a lot of sewing to catch up on at home.'

Bao-yu was very disappointed, and only a sense of duty kept him from leaving at once. Dinner was served and Grandmother Jia and Aunt Xue sat up at the table of honour, while Tan-chun and the others took their places down below.

'Where will Bao-yu be sitting?' asked Aunt Xue.

'Up here with me,' said Grandmother Jia with a smile.

'Li Gui told me to have my dinner before seeing Father,' Bao-yu hastily informed her. 'So I asked for a quick meal when I got in from school. I had a dish of something and a bowl of rice steeped in tea. You all go ahead, please.'

'In that case,' said Grandmother Jia, 'Feng can come and sit with us. Your mother says it's one of her vegetarian days today, so she can eat alone.'

'That's right,' said Lady Wang to Xi-feng. 'You eat with them. Don't wait for me. I shall be having my vegetables at home.'

Xi-feng politely took her seat and the maids put out the wine cups and chopsticks. Then Xi-feng went round with the wine kettle, and, when everyone's cup was filled, returned to her seat.

After they had all had a drink of wine, Grandmother Jia asked Aunt Xue:

'Didn't I hear you say Caltrop just then? That's funny. One of my maids was talking only the other day about someone called Lily, and I couldn't for the life of me think who she meant. When I asked her, she told me it was Caltrop's new name. Do tell me what she wants to go and change her name for?'

The colour rose in Aunt Xue's cheeks and she sighed:

'Please don't ever mention it again. Since the day Pan married that wretched wife we haven't had a moment's peace. The bickering, the nastiness, it's been too awful. I've tried talking to her several times, but she is quite impervious to reason. And I can't bear quarrelling with them all the time, so I just end up trying to turn a blind eye. Yes, she decided to change Caltrop's name because she said she didn't like it.'

'Oh well,' said Grandmother Jia, 'what's in a name when all's said and done?'

'I shall die for shame!' cried Aunt Xue. 'I'm sure all of you know the *real* reason. It wasn't the name. It was the fact that Bao-chai had thought of it in the first place. *That's* what she *really* objected to.'

'What *do* you mean?' asked Grandmother Jia.

Aunt Xue had been dabbing at her eyes all the while with her handkerchief. She heaved another deep sigh before she was able to continue.

'Surely you must know? Every single thing my daughter-in-law does is aimed at provoking Bao-chai. She won't leave her alone. The other day, when you sent someone round to see me, we were in the middle of one of our scenes!'

'That must have been the day I heard you had a little bit of a liver upset,' said Grandmother Jia tactfully. 'I was going to send someone over to see how you were, but then I heard that you were feeling better so I thought no more about it. You should take my advice, dear, and stop worrying. They're a newly married couple and you must give them time to settle down. And you're so lucky to have Chai. She is such a gentle, unflappable girl. She may be young, but my word, she has the aplomb of someone twice her age! When my maid came back and told us what had happened that day, and the way she coped with it, we were all singing her praises. Such a wonderful disposition! She's a girl in a million. When *she* gets married, if you don't mind my saying so, her mother-in-law will take her to her bosom and the whole household will be devoted to her, I am certain of it.'

Earlier, Bao-yu had found the general tenor of the

conversation rather distasteful, and was just saying something about having to leave when his grandmother embarked upon this eulogy of Bao-chai, and he found himself listening with rapt attention.

'What's the use?' said Aunt Xue. 'Whatever her qualities, she is still only a daughter. With a son as hopeless as Pan, I can have no peace; I never stop worrying in case he has gone off to one of his haunts, had too much to drink again and landed himself in another brawl. In fact the only time I ever feel at all reassured is when he's over here with his cousins Zhen and Lian.'

At this, Bao-yu chirped up:

'There's really nothing to fear, Auntie. I can vouch for Cousin Pan's friends. They are all serious businessmen and far too respectable to get into trouble.'

'In that case,' said Aunt Xue with a smile, 'perhaps I shouldn't worry.'

Supper was over by now, and Bao-yu excused himself, saying he still had some preparation to do that evening. The maids were serving tea, when Amber came into the room and whispered something in Grandmother Jia's ear. She turned to Xi-feng:

'You'd better go quickly, my dear. It's Qiao-jie.'

Xi-feng had no idea what the matter could be and the others were as puzzled as she was.

'Patience sent one of the younger maids round with a message for you, Mrs Lian,' explained Amber, crossing over to where Xi-feng sat. 'Miss Qiao-jie does not seem at all well and would you please go over as soon as possible.'

'You'd better go straight away,' said Grandmother Jia. 'You don't have to stand on ceremony for your Aunt Xue.'

'Yes Grannie,' said Xi-feng, and she took her leave of Aunt Xue. As she was on her way out she heard Lady Wang say:

'You go ahead. I'll be along shortly. Tell the maids to be quiet and not to make a lot of fuss. Little ones get so easily unsettled. And make sure that kitten and puppy are kept well out of the way. Poor child! I suppose little upsets are to be expected in a family as greatly blessed as ours.'

Xi-feng promised Lady Wang to carry out her instructions and left with her maid. After her departure, Aunt Xue went on to inquire after Dai-yu's health.

'Miss Lin is all right,' replied Grandmother Jia. 'She just takes everything too seriously. That's what is undermining her health, if you ask me. She may be as clever as Bao-chai, but she lacks your daughter's easy way with people. Chai is so responsible and considerate.'

The conversation continued a little longer, and then Aunt Xue said she must be going.

'I'll leave you in peace now. I'd better see how Chai and Caltrop are getting on at home. I'll go along with Aunt Wang and have a look at Qiao-jie on my way.'

'What a good idea,' said Grandmother Jia. 'With your experience you will be able to give them some helpful advice, I'm sure.'

Aunt Xue took her leave and went with Aunt Wang to Xi-feng's apartment.

To return to Jia Zheng: he had been pleasantly surprised by Bao-yu's performance that evening, and mentioned it later in the course of conversation with his literary friends in the outer study. A newcomer among them, an excellent Go-player by the name of Wang Er-tiao (also called Go-between Wang), remarked:

'I think we have all noticed a marked progress in Master Bao, sir. He is becoming quite a cultured young fellow.'

'I hardly think so,' replied Jia Zheng. 'His powers of comprehension have improved, I grant you. But culture? No, he has a long way to go yet.'

'Come come, Sir Zheng!' said Zhan Guang. 'You are being too modest. Friend Wang's opinion is one we all share. Master Bao will surely go far.'

'I'm afraid you are allowing your partiality for the boy

to sway your judgement,' was their patron's reply, but he was visibly pleased.

'With your leave, sir,' continued Wang, 'there is another matter in this connection that I should like to broach if I may.'

'By all means.'

Wang gave a smarmy smile.

'An acquaintance of mine, Excellency Zhang, who used to be Taotai of the Nanshao Circuit, has a daughter, sir, a most attractive, industrious and generally commendable child, so I am told, and as yet unbetrothed. Excellency Zhang has no sons of his own and is, I should add, a man of enormous wealth. He is most particular in this matter, and stipulates that his son-in-law must come from an eminent and prosperous family, and must be a young man of distinguished character himself. In the two months I have been here, sir, I have become aware of the moral and intellectual calibre of young Master Bao, the promise of great things to come. If the proposal were known to come from a family as illustrious as your own, sir, it would I am sure need but a single visit from me for the betrothal to be as good as settled.'

'It is true that Bao-yu has reached a marriageable age,' replied Jia Zheng. 'Lady Jia has reminded me of it more than once. But who is this Excellency Zhang? I'm afraid I don't know him.'

'Allow me to clarify, if I may,' ventured Zhan. 'I am acquainted with the Zhang family friend Wang refers to. They are related to Sir She's family, in point of fact, and it should be easy enough to elicit more information from them.'

'Really?' said Jia Zheng thoughtfully. 'I can't say I have ever heard the name of any such relation mentioned at my brother's.'

'Well, strictly speaking, sir,' explained Zhan, 'they are related by marriage to Lady Xing's elder brother.'

'So, that's where the relationship lies,' thought Jia Zheng.

A little later he went in, with the intention of talking this new proposal over with Lady Wang and asking her to sound out Lady Xing about the Zhang family. He found, however, that his wife was out, visiting Qiao-jie with Aunt Xue. At lighting-up time, when Aunt Xue went home and Lady Wang returned, Jia Zheng discussed the proposal with her. He also asked after Qiao-jie.

'We think it's convulsions,' she said.

'Nothing serious, I hope?'

'It's too early to tell. The fits have still not passed.'

Jia Zheng sighed but said no more, and they retired for the night.

*

Next day, when Lady Xing came to pay her morning respects to Grandmother Jia, Lady Wang mentioned the marriage proposal and took the opportunity of asking Lady Xing about the Zhang family.

'Yes, they are relations of ours,' divulged Lady Xing. 'But we've had no contact with them for years now, so I've no notion what this Miss Zhang is like. Now that you mention it, Ying's mother-in-law, Mrs Sun, sent one of her women to call on me a day or two ago, and she mentioned the Zhangs. She told me they had a daughter and had asked the Suns to look out for a suitable husband for her. Apparently she is an only child and rather delicate. She has had a little education and sounds a quiet, shy sort of girl, used to staying at home. As she is an only child, her father won't contemplate her leaving home. He is afraid the severity of a mother-in-law might be too much of a strain for her and insists on her husband coming to live with them and taking on his share of their family responsibilities.'

'Out of the question!' exclaimed Grandmother Jia. 'Bao-yu is difficult enough for us to look after as it is. Can you imagine sending him out to be the head of some strange family?'

'You are absolutely right of course,' said Lady Xing.

Grandmother Jia turned to Lady Wang.

'Be sure to tell Zheng when you go home that I say this match is definitely off.'

'Yes Mother.'

'Tell me,' the old lady continued, 'how was Qiao-jie when you went to see her yesterday? Patience gave me the impression earlier on that it was something serious. I should like to go and see her myself.'

The two ladies thanked Grandmother Jia for the kind thought, but begged her not to trouble herself for Qiao-jie's sake.

'It's not only for her sake. It's the exercise. I'd like to stretch my legs a bit,' said the old lady. 'You two have your lunch and then we can all go over together.'

Lady Wang and Lady Xing went home for lunch. Afterwards they collected Grandmother Jia and escorted her to Xi-feng's apartment. Xi-feng greeted them at the door and conducted them inside.

'How is she?' asked Grandmother Jia.

'It seems to be an attack of convulsions,' Xi-feng informed her.

'Hadn't you better call the doctor straight away?'

'We already have, Grannie dear.'

Grandmother Jia went in with Lady Wang and Lady Xing and found Qiao-jie in the arms of her nurse, wrapped in a little padded quilt of pink damask-silk, her face deathly white, her eyebrows and nostrils quivering slightly. After a brief inspection, they withdrew to the outer room, and sat down to talk. Presently a junior maid from Lady Wang's apartment came in with a message for Xi-feng:

'The Master has sent to inquire how Qiao-jie is, Mrs Lian.'

'Tell him we have sent for the doctor,' replied Xi-feng, 'and that I will report as soon as he has made out his prescription.'

The maid's arrival reminded Grandmother Jia of the recently aired marriage proposal. She turned to Lady Wang:

'You ought to go and tell Zheng straight away about that business, dear. If we put a stop to it now, before someone talks to the Zhang family, we will save ourselves the trouble of having to say no to them later.'

She turned to Lady Xing.

'Why is it you haven't seen much of the Zhangs lately, anyway?'

'As a matter of fact,' replied Lady Xing, 'they're very mean and not the right sort of family for us at all. It would have been a needless humiliation for Bao-yu.'

'That must be Bao-yu's betrothal you are talking about, Mother?' said Xi-feng, who had already formed a shrewd idea of what was going on.

'Why yes, we are actually,' said Lady Xing.

Grandmother Jia told Xi-feng about the Zhang proposal. Xi-feng laughed:

'I hope you'll excuse me, Grannie, Mother, Auntie Wang, for speaking out of turn, but what need is there to go looking for a wife for Bao-yu, when we have a "predestined affinity" here before our very eyes?'

'What *do* you mean?' asked Grandmother Jia, intrigued.

'Surely, Grannie, you can't have forgotten Bao's Magic Jade and Chai's Golden Locket?'

Grandmother Jia laughed.

'Of course! But why on earth didn't you mention it while Aunt Xue was here yesterday?'

'It would hardly have been right for me to speak up in the presence of my elders and betters,' replied Xi-feng. 'Besides, Aunt Xue had come on a social call and it would have been out of place. If we are to do the thing properly, Mother and Aunt Wang must go over and ask Aunt Xue formally for Bao-chai's hand.'

They all laughed at her.

'Bless you, Fengie,' said Grandmother Jia. 'I really *must* be going gaga.'

Meanwhile the doctor was announced and Grandmother Jia took a seat in the outer room, while the two ladies discreetly withdrew. The doctor entered with Jia Lian and paid his respects to Grandmother Jia before proceeding into Qiao-jie's room. When he returned, he bowed to Grandmother Jia and pronounced his diagnosis.

'The little girl is suffering from a convulsive attack complicated by an internal fever. She must first take a single dose of a combined anti-spasmodic and expectorant, and then I want you to give her a course of Four Prodigies Powders. It is quite a serious attack.

'You will notice Cow's Bezoar-stone in my prescription. I should mention that a lot of the Bezoars sold by the apothecaries nowadays are not genuine. It is important that you procure the real thing.'

Grandmother Jia thanked him for coming, and the doctor went out with Jia Lian, wrote out his prescription and left.

'There's always Ginseng in the house,' said Xi-feng, 'but I don't think we've any Bezoar. We'll have to buy some and make sure it's genuine.'

'Wait until I've sent someone round to my sister's,' said Lady Wang. 'I know Pan has often done business with merchants from overseas. They might easily have some real Bezoar.'

As she was speaking, several of the girls arrived to see Qiao-jie. They stayed for a short while, and then left with Grandmother Jia and the others.

Qiao-jie's expectorant was now prepared and poured down her throat. There was a retching sound and up it came, medicine, phlegm and all, much to Xi-feng's relief. One of Lady Wang's junior maids arrived with a little red paper packet.

'We found some Bezoar, ma'am. Her Ladyship says you're to weigh out the correct amount and take as much as you need.'

Xi-feng asked the maid to convey her thanks to Lady

Wang, took the package and told Patience to mix Pulverized Pearl, Baros Camphor and Cinnabar in the prescribed proportions and bring them to the boil. She herself weighed out the correct amount of powdered Bezoar on the scales and added it to the mixture. She waited for Qiao-jie to wake again before administering the potion.

Who should lift the door-blind and walk in at this very moment but Jia Huan.

'How's Qiao-jie, Cousin Feng? Mother sent me to inquire.'

The sight of either Aunt Zhao or her son invariably made Xi-feng's hackles rise.

'She's a little better,' she replied in rather a caustic tone. 'When you go back, please tell your mother I'm sorry to have caused her so much trouble.'

Jia Huan mumbled something about going, but started nosing round the room.

'I say,' he said after a while. 'I heard you had some of that Bezoar stuff in here. I've never seen any before. Let's have a look.'

'Qiao-jie is only just on the mend,' said Xi-feng, 'so do you mind not crashing around in here? The Bezoar has all been used for her potion anyway.'

Hearing this, Jia Huan reached out clumsily for the chafing-skillet to have a look. He lost his grip, and there was a great hiss as the skillet tipped over and the precious medicine spilled into the brazier, half extinguishing the fire. Jia Huan could see he was in for trouble and beat a hasty retreat. Xi-feng was so furious she seemed to emit sparks of rage.

'You vile harpy's brat!' she screamed after him. 'Bane of my life! What can I have done in a past life to deserve such spite? Your mother tried to do *me* in, now it's Qiao-jie's turn! How many generations must this feud go on for?'

Patience had her share of the blame too, for not being more careful. While Xi-feng was in full spate, a maid came in to fetch Jia Huan home.

'Go and tell Mrs Zhao,' ordered Xi-feng, 'that she is putting herself to too much trouble. Qiao-jie is as good as dead already, so she needn't go to such lengths!'

The maid, nonplussed by Xi-feng's remarks, went over to Patience, who was busy mixing up another dose of medicine, and asked her in a whisper:

'What's made Mrs Lian so angry?'

Patience told her about Jia Huan's disastrous episode.

'No wonder he ran away and didn't dare come home!' exclaimed the maid. 'Goodness knows how that Huan will turn out! Can I help you tidy up, Patience?'

'Don't worry. Luckily we had a little Bezoar left and it's all mixed now, so you might as well go.'

'I'll certainly tell Mrs Zhao the minute I get back. Perhaps that will stop her bragging about him all the time.'

The maid returned and, true to her word, gave Aunt Zhao a detailed account of Jia Huan's débâcle.

'Bring him to me!' cried Aunt Zhao in an agitated tone.

After a brief search, the maid discovered him skulking in the adjoining room, and Aunt Zhao immediately began discharging a volley of abuse in his direction:

'You miserable little runt! What did you have to go and get yourself into trouble for, spilling their medicine all over the place? I said go and ask how she was, not go barging in! But you had to, didn't you? And when you were in, you had to stay and goad the dragon on. You must have known you were playing with fire! You wait till I tell your father about this! He'll give you the thrashing you deserve!'

Even stronger words had already been let loose in reply from the other room. But to hear for yourself, please turn to the next chapter.

CHAPTER 85

It is announced that Jia Zheng has been promoted to the rank of Permanent Secretary
And it is discovered that Xue Pan has once more brought upon himself the threat of exile

'All I did was knock a skillet over and spill a bit of medicine!' yelled Jia Huan before his mother could finish. 'That measly little brat of hers is still alive, isn't she? Anyone would think I'd done her in, the way you two are going on at me about it, slandering me and dragging my name in the mud! One day I really will finish her off! That would teach you all a lesson! You'd better tell them to look out!'

Aunt Zhao came hurtling in and clapped a hand over his mouth.

'You're asking for it, saying such dreadful things! They'll have your neck first, my boy, see if they don't!'

They kept it up like this for some time. Jia Huan slipped in Xi-feng's barbed little message, which made his mother more implacable than ever. There was now no question of her sending anyone over to Xi-feng's with an apology, and although Qiao-jie made a complete recovery a few days later, the episode had deepened the feud between the two sections of the family.

*

One day Steward Lin came in to report to Jia Zheng that it was the Prince of Bei-jing's birthday.

'Are there any special instructions, sir?'

'Send whatever we usually send,' replied Jia Zheng. 'Report to Sir She first, before delivering the presents.'

'Very good sir,' said Lin, and went to make the necessary arrangements. A little later, Jia She arrived himself, to discuss with his brother the details of the visit. They decided to take Cousin Zhen, Jia Lian and Bao-yu along with them. If for the four older men it was merely another social engagement, for Bao-yu it was an opportunity long awaited. He had been a fervent admirer of the Prince's handsome looks and graceful bearing ever since their memorable first encounter at the roadside halt. He changed eagerly into his smartest clothes and went to join the others.

On arrival at the Palace, Jia She and Jia Zheng presented their cards and before long a Eunuch Chamberlain of the Household emerged, fingering his beads, and greeted them with a little peal of falsetto laughter:

'I hope you are both keeping well?'

They reciprocated the inquiry and the three younger Jias came forward to make their greeting.

'His Imperial Highness will be pleased to receive you now.' The eunuch led the five of them in, through two further gateways and past a large state-room, to the Inner Gate of the Prince's personal residence. Here they halted once more, while the eunuch went in to announce their arrival, leaving them to be entertained by the various junior eunuchs in attendance at the gate.

After a brief interval their original escort returned.

'This way, please.'

They all stepped solemnly forward again. The Prince, dressed in full robe of state, had paid them the compliment of coming out to receive them in one of the covered walks by the entrance to the main hall. The two brothers advanced first and did homage, followed in order of seniority by Cousin Zhen, Jia Lian and Bao-yu. The Prince took Bao-yu by the hand.

'It has been a long while since we last met. You have been much in my thoughts.'

He smiled:

'Tell me, how fares it with that stone of yours?'

Bao-yu dropped to a half-kneeling position and with head bowed replied:

'Your Highness's beneficent aura has preserved us from misfortune.'

'There is nothing very special to eat today,' continued the Prince pleasantly. 'But at least we shall be able to spend a little time talking together.'

Eunuchs lifted the portière, and the Prince made a charming gesture of yielding the *pas* to his guests before leading the way in. The Jias followed, walking with a deferential stoop, and once inside Jia She was the first to offer his birthday felicitations. These the Prince accepted modestly, while Jia She sank to his knees. The others followed suit.

Once these formalities (a detailed description of which our narrative omits) were over, the Jias began discreetly to take their leave. The Prince turned to his eunuchs and gave instructions that they were to be escorted to the reception which was being given for his own family and a few other distinguished guests and that they were to be attended to with the utmost care. He asked Bao-yu to stay behind for a chat.

'Do sit down,' he began, when the others had left. Bao-yu made his kotow of thanks for this honour, and perching delicately on a covered porcelain tabouret near the door, talked for a while of his studies and compositions and other things. The Prince seemed fonder than ever of his young protégé, and offered him some tea – a still greater honour. He went on to say:

'Excellency Governor Wu was in town yesterday for an audience with His Majesty. He told me that your father, in his last posting as Commissioner of Education, showed the most scrupulous impartiality and gained the respect of all the candidates he examined. At the audience, when H.M. inquired, Wu gave your father the highest recommendation. Clearly a favourable omen . . .'

Bao-yu had risen swiftly to his feet when the Prince began speaking, and when he finished replied:

'You have shown us a great favour, Your Highness, and Governor Wu has done us a great kindness.'

As he was speaking, a junior eunuch returned from the reception in the front state-room to convey a message of thanks from the various Lords and Gentlemen for their banquet, and to present their cards of appreciation and midday greeting to the Prince, who glanced through them and handed them back with a gracious smile and a brief word of acknowledgement.

'And, if it please Your Highness,' the eunuch continued, 'the repast you ordered specially for Master Jia Bao-yu is now ready.'

The Prince gave him a few further words of instruction, and the eunuch led Bao-yu out to an exquisitely appointed suite of rooms facing a small courtyard, where he ordered another attendant to wait upon him during the meal. Afterwards, Bao-yu returned to give thanks and the Prince continued chatting in the same complimentary vein. Suddenly he laughed:

'When I first saw that stone of yours, I was so taken with it, you know, that on my return I gave my jade-workers a description of it and asked them to make me one like it. I am so glad you have come today. I can give it to you to take home. It might amuse you to keep it.'

One of the junior eunuchs was ordered to bring the jade in, and the Prince himself handed it to Bao-yu, who received it humbly in both hands, gave thanks and then took his leave. The Prince told two more junior eunuchs to accompany him out, he rejoined the other members of the family, and they all returned home.

On arrival, Jia She paid his respects to Grandmother Jia and left for his own apartment. Jia Zheng and the others also paid their respects and gave her a full account of the reception. Bao-yu communicated to his father the news he had received about Governor Wu's sponsorial activities.

'Governor Wu,' commented Jia Zheng drily, 'is an old friend, and a man after my own heart. He is also, I might add, a statesman of the highest integrity.'

After a little more chat, Grandmother Jia gave permission for them all to disperse. Jia Zheng took his leave, and was followed by Cousin Zhen, Jia Lian and Bao-yu as far as the door.

With a parting injunction to the three of them to stay and keep Grandmother Jia company a little longer, Jia Zheng returned to his apartment. He had not been there long when a maid came in to announce that Steward Lin was waiting outside with something to report. She also handed him a red visiting card with Governor Wu's name on it. Jia Zheng told her to admit Lin, and went out to speak to him on the verandah.

'Excellency Governor Wu called to see you today, sir,' reported Lin. 'I informed him that you were out. And another thing, sir; I have heard that a Permanent Secretary's position has become vacant in the Ministry of Works. According to various people, including officials in the Ministry, you are to be given the post as confirmation of your present rank.'

'H'm . . .' said Jia Zheng. 'We shall see.'

Lin conferred with his master on one or two other matters and then left.

*

After Jia Zheng's departure, Cousin Zhen and Jia Lian returned to their separate apartments, while Bao-yu went back to Grandmother Jia's. He was now able to tell her all about *his* day at the Palace. He described how kindly the Prince had treated him, and took out the jade he had been given, which was passed round and commented on with some amusement. Grandmother Jia told a maid to put it safely away.

'And don't whatever you do take your *own* off,' she said to Bao-yu. 'You don't want to go getting them mixed up.'

Bao-yu promptly untied his original from around his neck.

'But look,' he said, 'they're so different, how could I ever get them mixed up? That reminds me, Grannie, of something that happened the other night, as I was going to bed. I had just taken my jade off and hung it inside the bed-curtains, when I noticed a halo around it, and the whole inside of my bed was lit up with a rosy glow.'

'You silly boy!' exclaimed Grandmother Jia. 'There's red thread in your pelmet. That must have been the lamp-light showing through.'

'But it couldn't have been. The lamps were all out and it was pitch-black in my room, and I *still* saw it glowing.'

Lady Xing and Lady Wang exchanged a meaningful smile. A certain 'rosy' event had been much in the fore-front of their minds recently. Xi-feng too could not re-strain herself from remarking cryptically:

'No doubt this heralds the Big Event...'

'What big event?' asked Bao-yu.

'Nothing you would understand,' put in Grandmother Jia promptly. 'Now come along. It's been a hectic day for you, and you ought to go and rest, and not waste any more time here telling tall stories.'

Bao-yu stayed a minute or two longer and then re-turned to the Garden. When he was out of the room, Grandmother Jia turned to Lady Wang:

'Well, have you been to see Mrs Xue, and put it to her yet?'

'Yes Mother, we have,' replied Lady Wang. 'Feng has been so busy with little Qiao-jie the last few days, and we just haven't had a chance to go until today. Anyway, my sister seems very happy with the idea, but she says she will have to wait until Pan comes home before saying any-thing final. She must consult him first, as the eldest man in the family.'

'Quite right,' said Grandmother Jia. 'We shall have to bide our time until they have had a chance to talk it over. In the meantime, not a word of this to anyone.'

*

We must leave these matrimonial confabulations and accompany the unwitting subject of them, who on his arrival at Green Delights confided to Aroma:

'Grannie and Feng were being most mysterious about something just now. I don't know what's going on.'

Aroma looked thoughtful for a moment.

'I've no idea either,' she finally returned, with a peculiar smile, adding (as if it were an afterthought): 'I wonder, was Miss Lin there when they were talking?'

'Of course not! You know she's been ill and has to stay in.'

Their conversation was interrupted by the sound of Musk and Ripple having a tiff in the next room.

'What *is* the matter with you two?' Aroma called out.

'It's all Ripple's fault!' replied Musk. 'She's been cheating at cards! She took my money fast enough when *she* won, but now that *I*'ve won she won't let go of a penny. And now I'm cleaned right out!'

'Oh come on!' Bao-yu chided them with a laugh. 'Stop being so stupid! Who wants to quarrel over a few coins?' They both pouted and went off in high dudgeon, leaving Aroma to settle Bao-yu down for the night.

Now Aroma was sure that the mysterious conversation Bao-yu had referred to in some way concerned his betrothal. She had only feigned ignorance for fear that in his present mood, mention of such a touchy subject might provoke another of his fits. She herself was most anxious to know the latest news, and while she lay awake that night she decided to go and see Nightingale first thing in the morning. Nightingale would be sure to know, and would be able to tell her what was going on.

And so the next day she rose early, and after seeing Bao-yu off to school, completed her own toilet and strolled through the Garden to the Naiad's House. Nightingale was out in the front courtyard picking flowers, and greeted her with a smile:

'Hello, Aroma. Do come in and sit down.'

'Thank you. Busy with your flowers, I see . . . How is Miss Lin?'

'She has just finished her toilet. She's waiting for her medicine to be warmed up.'

Nightingale took Aroma inside. Dai-yu was reading a book, which provided Aroma with a ready-made topic of conversation. She gave an ingratiating smile:

'It'd be a wonder if you *didn't* feel tired sometimes, Miss, reading at such an early hour. If Master Bao would only follow your good example!'

Dai-yu smiled wanly and put her book down. Meanwhile Snowgoose had come in with a small tray containing two cups, one of medicine and one of water. She was followed by a junior maid bearing spittoon and bowl.

Aroma's intention in coming had been to sound them out; but somehow amid all these medical ministrations an easy opening failed to present itself, and she reckoned that it was not worth running the risk of offending the prickly Miss Lin on the offchance of obtaining the information she wanted. So, after sitting there a little longer and making a little desultory chat, she said goodbye and set off back home.

She was approaching Green Delights, when she saw to her considerable surprise two male figures standing a little way off, and thought it more discreet not to proceed any further. One of them had already spotted her, however, and came running up. It turned out to be Ploughboy, one of Bao-yu's pages.

'What do you think you're doing here?' she asked him.

'Master Yun's just come with a letter for Master Bao, and he's waiting for a reply.'

'But you know perfectly well that Master Bao goes to school every day, so what's the point of waiting?'

'That's what I told him,' said Ploughboy, grinning sheepishly. 'But he just said that I was to tell *you* and he'd wait for your reply instead.'

A suitable retort was already on Aroma's lips when she noticed that the other man had started slinking towards them. A closer inspection confirmed that the stealthy intruder was indeed Jia Yun. She turned to Ploughboy and said briskly:

'Tell him his letter will be delivered to Master Bao in due course.'

Jia Yun's slow and sinuous progress had been designed to camouflage his true aim, which was to achieve a tête-à-tête with the delectable Miss Aroma. His dismissal (which he heard only too clearly), when almost within reach of his goal, obliged him to abandon these plans and come to a premature standstill. Aroma turned smartly on her heel and walked on into Green Delights, leaving Ploughboy to escort the crestfallen Jia Yun from the Garden.

Aroma related the incident that evening to Bao-yu, on his return from school:

'That Master Yun from West Lane was here today,' she said briefly.

'What did he want?'

'He left a note for you.'

'Where is it? I'd better see what it says.'

Musk went to fetch Yun's note from the bookshelf in the inner room, and handed it to Bao-yu. The envelope bore the inscription: 'To My Honoured Uncle'.

'Funny,' said Bao-yu. 'I thought I was supposed to be his father!'

'What?' retorted Aroma.

'Don't you remember, the year before last when he sent me that white Autumn Crab-blossom, he signed himself my "Dutiful and Affectionate Son"? It seems I've been demoted to plain Uncle...'

'Honestly!' exclaimed Aroma. 'The pair of you should be thoroughly ashamed of yourselves! Fancy a grown man like him passing himself off as your son! He ought to know better! And as for you . . . Father Bao indeed! Why you're not even . . .'

Aroma stopped short. She blushed and gave a little smile. Bao-yu knew what she meant.

'Who knows?' he quipped. 'Perhaps he thought of me as his Spiritual Father, like that

> celebrated celibate of yore
> whose children could be numbered by the score . . .

I only agreed to it because I thought he was quite clever and a likeable sort of fellow; if he's changed his mind, I really couldn't care less.'

'If you want to know, he gives me the creeps,' Aroma continued, as Bao-yu opened the letter. 'He's for ever trying to worm his way in, and looks so shifty about it. I wouldn't trust him an inch.'

Bao-yu was too absorbed in examining the contents of the letter to take any notice of what she was saying. She studied his face as he read. A frown, then a smile, which soon gave way to a shake of the head, and finally an expression of impatience. When he seemed to have finished, she asked:

'What's it all about then?'

By way of response Bao-yu tore the letter into shreds. Aroma thought it wiser to change the subject.

'Are you planning to do some work after dinner or not?'

'What a cad!'

She smiled at this capricious reply:

'Well, what was it about?'

'Oh who cares! Let's have dinner. Then I'm going straight to bed. I feel quite sick!'

He told one of the junior maids to light a fire and threw the remains of Yun's letter into it.

Supper was soon served, but Bao-yu was in no mood for it and only sat there staring glumly in front of him.

After trying every form of pressure and persuasion Aroma finally succeeded in making him swallow a mouthful, only to see him put his bowl down once more and flop listlessly onto his bed. Suddenly he began to cry.

Neither she nor Musk had the slightest idea what was the matter.

'Come on, you've got to tell us,' protested Musk. 'It's all this Yun's fault, or whatever his wretched name is. I can't imagine what his stupid letter was all about, to have such a queer effect on you, laughing one minute, crying your heart out the next. If you carry on in this strange way much longer, you'll worry us to death, indeed you will!'

She was on the verge of tears herself. Aroma could not help smiling:

'Musky dear, don't you go making things worse, *please*. He's got quite enough on his mind as it is. Unless of course you want people to think the letter had something to do with you . . .'

'Well, *that*'s a stupid remark I must say!' replied Musk. '*You* don't know what it said, anyway. It might have been anything. Why drag *me* into it? Unless of course it's got something to do with you . . .'

Before Aroma could reply there was a splutter of laughter from the bed and Bao-yu sat up, gave his clothes a shake and said to them both:

'Come on, that's enough. Let's go to sleep. I've got to work early in the morning.' With these words he settled himself down and went to sleep.

The night passed uneventfully, and next morning, after completing his toilet, he set off for school. He had just walked out of the doorway when he remembered something and, calling to Tealeaf to wait, turned back.

'Musk!'

She came hurrying out.

'What's the matter?'

'If Yun comes today, tell him not to make a nuisance of

himself here again or I'll report him to Her Old Ladyship and Sir Zheng.'

'I will.'

Bao-yu set off once more, and was on his way out when who should come bustling in but Jia Yun himself. When he saw Bao-yu he promptly saluted and said:

'My heartiest congratulations, Uncle!'

Bao-yu took this as a reference to the business contained in the previous day's letter and replied curtly:

'You tactless meddling fool! It makes no difference to you if there are things people care about...'

'But Uncle!' protested Yun with a smug smile. 'If you don't believe me, take a look for yourself. The crowds are outside the gate.'

'What are you talking about?' snapped Bao-yu, the anger rising in his voice.

At that moment a wave of shouting and cheering came wafting in from the street outside.

'Hear that!' exclaimed Jia Yun. '*Now* will you believe me?'

Bao-yu was more perplexed than ever. He could distinguish a few words above the general din:

'Have you people no manners? What do you mean by coming here and making this racket?'

Another voice replied:

'The hand that raised Sir Jia has given us the privilege of bearing tidings other houses would be only too glad of receiving!'

Bao-yu understood at last that his father's promotion had been officially announced, and that the din outside the gates was coming from a crowd of professional well-wishers (their joy made the more vocal by the expectation of a tip). He was delighted and hurried on out of the Garden, only to be cornered again by Jia Yun.

'Happy Uncle? Needless to say the joy would be doubled if we could only announce your betrothal as well...'

Bao-yu blushed fiercely and spat in Jia Yun's face:

'Ugh! Why don't you clear off? You make me sick!'

Jia Yun blushed too.

'What's this? I can see you're a little . . .'

'A little what?' asked Bao-yu angrily.

But Jia Yun's nerve failed him and he left his remark unfinished.

Bao-yu hurried off to school, where Dai-ru greeted him with a smile:

'I have just heard the good news, my boy. I must say, I am somewhat surprised to see you here at all today.'

'I thought I should report to you first, sir, before going to offer my congratulations,' replied Bao-yu with a polite smile.

'I see. Well, no need to attend class today. Take a day's grace. But please try not to fritter it away in that garden of yours. At your age, though you may not be able to take an active part in family affairs, I am sure you would benefit greatly from the company of your older cousins.'

'Yes, sir.'

Bao-yu returned home. As he was approaching the inner gate of Grandmother Jia's apartment, he encountered Li Gui coming in the opposite direction.

'I'm glad you're back,' said Li Gui, halting by his side with a smile. 'I was on my way to school to fetch you.'

'Who told you to?' asked Bao-yu.

'Her Old Ladyship sent someone round to your place,' replied Li Gui, 'but the maids said you had already gone to school, so she sent someone with instructions for me to arrange a few days off school for you. I hear they are having players over for the festivities. Anyway, thanks, you've saved me a journey.'

Bao-yu went in, to find Grandmother Jia's front courtyard overflowing with maids and serving-women, their loyal faces beaming with pleasure and excitement:

'You're late, Master Bao! You'd better hurry on in and congratulate Her Old Ladyship!'

Bao-yu's face lit up. When he entered the room, he

found Grandmother Jia with Dai-yu and Xiang-yun sitting to her left and right up on the kang, while assembled down below were Ladies Xing and Wang, Tan-chun, Xi-chun, Li Wan, Xi-feng, Li Wan's two cousins Wen and Qi, and Lady Xing's niece Xing Xiu-yan. He noticed that Bao-chai, Bao-qin and Ying-chun were not there.

Overjoyed to see such a gathering, Bao-yu offered his congratulations first to Grandmother Jia, then to his mother and Lady Xing, and then greeted the rest of the family. He turned to Dai-yu with a smile and said:

'Are you quite recovered now, coz?'

'Yes, thank you,' replied Dai-yu, with a hint of a smile. 'And you? I heard that you were not very well yourself.'

'Yes, I had a sudden pain in my heart that night. It's been better for quite a while, but I've been having to go to school every day, so I haven't been able to come over and see you.'

Before he had even finished speaking, Dai-yu turned away to talk to Tan-chun. Xi-feng was standing near them and observed sarcastically:

'I thought you two were meant to be inseparable? The way you *talk* anyone would think you were strangers. Still, I suppose

His to honour,
Hers to obey . . .'

Everyone laughed. The colour flew into Dai-yu's face and at first she was quite speechless with embarrassment. But thinking that some sort of reply was expected of her, she finally came out with:

'Who'd expect *you* to understand . . .'

which seemed to amuse everyone even more.

After a moment's reflection Xi-feng realized that her joke had been in rather poor taste, and she was about to introduce a fresh topic of conversation, in an attempt to clear the air a little, when Bao-yu suddenly turned to Dai-yu and said:

'Coz, do you know what that tactless, blundering fool Yun tried to . . .' But whatever it was he had been going to say, he thought better of it. There was a puzzled laugh from the others. Someone said:

'What are you talking about?'

Dai-yu was as much in the dark as they were and smiled awkwardly. Bao-yu extricated himself by launching off at another tangent:

'I heard just now that someone is planning to send over some players. When are they coming, does anyone know?'

They all stared at him in amazement and laughed. It was Xi-feng who replied:

'You're the one who's heard. Why ask us?'

'I'd better go and check,' he said promptly.

'Now don't go getting into mischief out there,' warned his grandmother. 'You don't want the crowd to make fun of you, do you? And remember, this is a very special day for your father, and if he comes home and finds you gadding about, there's sure to be trouble.'

'Yes, Grannie,' replied Bao-yu, and effected his escape.

When he had gone, Grandmother Jia asked Xi-feng:

'What's all this about sending players?'

'Uncle Wang Zi-sheng's family,' replied Xi-feng, 'want to do something to congratulate you and Uncle Zheng and Auntie. They've hired a new troupe of young actors specially, and they say that the day after tomorrow is a lucky one.'

Xi-feng laughed:

'And it is too, in more ways than one.'

She looked at Dai-yu and smiled. Dai-yu smiled shyly back.

'Of course!' exclaimed Lady Wang. 'It's our niece's birthday!'

When Grandmother Jia had taken in what they were saying she laughed out loud:

'It just goes to show how absent-minded I'm getting in

my old age! It's a good thing I've Secretary Feng here to keep me organized. Well, what could be better: they can celebrate your Uncle Zheng's promotion, and we can celebrate your birthday at the same time!'

This had everyone laughing, and it was proposed and carried unanimously that with such an apt way of putting things, the old lady positively had a right to enjoy such prodigious good fortune.

Bao-yu had returned in time to hear about the party and was beside himself with joy. They all sat down to lunch in an atmosphere of great excitement. After lunch, Jia Zheng returned from giving thanks at court, and having performed his ceremonial prostrations in the family shrine, came in to kotow before Grandmother Jia. He rose to his feet and said a few words before leaving to pay various official calls.

Over the next day or two there was constant bustle and confusion, as a stream of relatives besieged Rong-guo House. Horses and carriages thronged the main entrance, and in every corner important-looking gentlemen in starched official hats trimmed with sable sat waiting their turn. Truly:

Where flowers bloom,
    Bees and butterflies abound;
Skies and oceans swell
    When the moon is round.

*

Two days later, the players, on the instructions of Wang Zi-sheng and other relations, arrived early in the morning to set up their mobile stage in Grandmother Jia's courtyard, facing the main hall. The Jia menfolk, in full dress, entertained their relatives in the open courtyard, where more than ten tables had been laid. A special glass play-viewing screen had been put up between the courtyard and the gallery overlooking it from the north side, and four tables had been laid in the enclosed space, to give the ladies a chance of seeing the plays, and particularly for Grandmother Jia's benefit (as she was more enthusiastic about the whole venture than anyone else). Aunt Xue was installed at the head of the table of honour, with her sister Lady Wang and her niece Bao-qin, while Grandmother Jia sat at the head of the table opposite with Lady Xing and her niece Xiu-yan. The two remaining tables were still empty, and Grandmother Jia sent word for the girls to hurry up.

Presently Dai-yu arrived, ushered in by Xi-feng and a convoy of maids. She had chosen one or two of her newer things to wear, and as she came into the enclosure she looked exactly like the Goddess of the Moon descending to Earth. She greeted Grandmother Jia and her aunts with a shy smile, and Xiang-yun and the two Li sisters asked her to sit at the head of their table. Her polite refusals were soon over-ruled by Grandmother Jia:

'Go on, you *must*, dear. After all, this is *your* day too!'

'Really?' exclaimed Aunt Xue, rising to her feet. 'Is Miss Lin celebrating something today as well?'

Grandmother Jia laughed:

'It's her birthday!'

'Oh goodness, I quite forgot! How awful of me!' Aunt Xue went up to Dai-yu: 'I'm *so* sorry. I hope you'll forgive me for being so forgetful. I must ask Bao-qin to call on you later and wish you happy returns properly.'

'Please don't go to such trouble on my account,' murmured Dai-yu with a smile. She looked around her as they all sat down, and noticed that Bao-chai had not come.

'I hope Cousin Chai isn't ill or anything. Why couldn't she come today?'

'She was going to,' replied Aunt Xue. 'But we needed someone to look after things at home, so in the end she had to stay behind.'

Dai-yu flushed and said with a slightly puzzled smile:

'Surely now that Cousin Pan's married there's no need for her to stay at home? She probably didn't feel in the mood for all the noise and excitement. I'm sorry she didn't come. I miss her such a lot.'

Aunt Xue smiled:

'How very sweet of you, dear. She thinks of you all a great deal too. In a day or two I must tell her to come over and have a chat.'

The maids were already pouring wine and setting out dishes on the tables, while outside in the courtyard the show had begun. It opened, predictably enough, with a couple of festive pieces. The third selection, however, turned out to be something of a novelty. A chorus of Golden Pages and Jade Maidens came onto the stage, fairy streamers fluttering and flags aloft, to reveal in their midst a gorgeously attired lady, her head draped in black, her costume shimmering with the celestial hues of the Rainbow Skirt and Feathered Jacket. She (or rather he, for the part was played by a female impersonator) sang a short aria and then left the stage.

None of the family could identify the piece at all, but they overheard one of the guests saying:

'That was "The Transfiguration", from one of their latest productions, "*The Palace of Pearls*". It tells the story of Chang E, who comes down to earth from her palace in the moon and is about to give her hand to her mortal lover when the Goddess of Mercy opens her eyes to the truth, and she dies before the marriage can take place. In that scene, she is being wafted up to the moon. Didn't you catch the words of her aria?

'Tis Love that rules the minds of men,
And of this Truth Eternal
Obscures all trace:
That even harvest moons must wane
And purest beauty vernal
Fade from grace.
Alas, 'twas Mortal Love
That veiled my sight,
And all but stole me
From my Orb of Light.'

Next on the programme was 'A Wife Eats Husks', from '*The Story of the Lute*', followed by 'Bodhidharma and his Disciple Crossing the River', from '*The Pilgrim's Path*'. This last scene was full of the most spectacular feats of acrobatic mime and other phantasmagorical effects. The excitement had just reached its height when one of the Xue family's servants, his face dripping with sweat, burst into the courtyard auditorium and hurried over to Xue Ke's table:

'Master Ke! Come home quickly! And send word in to Madam that she must come too. It's very urgent!'

'What's happened?' asked Xue Ke.

'I'll tell you when we get home, sir!' panted the boy.

Without even stopping to thank his hosts, Xue Ke followed the boy out of the courtyard, sending one of the Jia maids in with a message to the ladies' enclosure. When Aunt Xue heard the news, she went white in the face. Taking Bao-qin with her, she made a distracted farewell and went straight out to her carriage, leaving the whole assembly in a state of high alarm.

'We had better send someone over with them,' said Grandmother Jia. 'I am sure everyone is most anxious to learn what this is all about.'

They all agreed.

*

The players continued with their programme. But we must leave them and follow Aunt Xue, who on her arrival at home saw two yamen runners waiting in the inner gateway. With them were some employees from the family pawnshop.

'When Mrs Xue arrives,' they were saying, 'she'll be able to explain everything.'

When the yamen runners saw this elderly lady sweeping up to the gate with her large retinue of male and female attendants, and realized the distinguished position of the person they were dealing with, they stood to attention and let her pass. Aunt Xue went on through the reception hall and could already hear the sound of heavy wailing coming from her daughter-in-law's apartment. She quickened her step. Bao-chai came out to meet her, her face wet with tears.

'Have you heard, Mama? Please don't panic! We must try to *do* something!'

They went inside together. Aunt Xue had already been told the main facts by one of the servants on her way in, and was still sobbing and trembling from the shock.

'But *who? Who* was it?' she asked agitatedly.

'Madam,' said one of the servants, 'details like that are not going to make much difference at present. The law says "a life for a life". So we must think what to do.'

'Think!' cried Aunt Xue hysterically. 'What's the earthly good of thinking at a time like this?'

'The best thing as we see it,' continued the servant, 'is this. First, send young Master Ke with some money tonight to visit Mr Pan in prison. Then, first thing tomorrow, Master Ke must get himself a good scrivener, someone well-versed in legal terminology. He must offer him a good fee to make sure this death-sentence is quashed. Then, when that's been done, we must ask one of the Jia gentlemen here to pull a few strings. But first of all, we must tip the yamen runners outside a few taels. Then we can get on with the rest of the plan.'

Aunt Xue was not convinced.

'Just find the man's family,' she said. 'Give them whatever they want for funeral expenses and compensation. If they don't press the charge, surely he'll be let off lightly?'

Bao-chai's voice could be heard through the door-curtain:

'No, Mama, that will never do. The more money we hand out the more trouble we'll cause in the long run. We should do as the boy says.'

'What have I left to live for?' sobbed Aunt Xue. 'Let me

go there and see him once! Then the two of us can die together!'

Bao-chai begged her to take heart, and at the same time called out for the boy to set off with Xue Ke at once. The maids helped Aunt Xue indoors again. Xue Ke came by on his way out.

'Send someone home with a letter as soon as you have any news,' Bao-chai instructed him. 'You must stay there. We're counting on you.'

Xue Ke promised to do his utmost and left.

While Bao-chai applied herself once more to the task of soothing her agitated mother, Xia Jin-gui took the opportunity of launching an undisturbed attack on Caltrop:

'So a murder was nothing to *this* family, was it?' she screamed at her. 'You all came straight up to town afterwards as if nothing had happened, did you? Well it looks as if spoke once too often, Miss Swanky Panky! Because this time it's the real thing, and look at you! Where's all your money and all your fine friends and posh relatives *now*? You're all so scared you don't know if you're coming or going! And in a few days, when they put Pan away, then I suppose you'll bugger off and leave me here to carry the can single-handed!'

She broke into one of her dramatic wails. Aunt Xue heard every word and was so furious that she fainted. Bao-chai was at her wits' end. And in the midst of this pandemonium one of Lady Wang's senior maids arrived, to ask 'if there was any news'. This presented Bao-chai with an additional problem. She was fully aware of her delicate position since the official betrothal visit a few days previously, and knew that strictly speaking she should shun all contact with her future bridegroom's family (including the domestic staff). However, the fact that the betrothal was still not finally settled, and the nature of the present emergency, seemed to justify a temporary waiving of the rules.

'We don't know the full story yet,' she said to the maid. 'All we've heard is that my brother has killed someone and that he has been arrested by the local magistrate. We don't know exactly what kind of homicide he has been found guilty of, but Master Ke has gone to find out. We should have more definite news in a day or two and will let Her Ladyship know straight away. Please thank her for her kind inquiry and say that at a later stage we'll be sure to need all the support Sir She and Sir Zheng can give us.'

The maid returned with this message.

The next two days were spent by Aunt Xue and Bao-chai waiting in unbearable suspense. At last on the third day a boy came back with a letter from Xue Ke, which he gave to a maid to hand to the ladies. Bao-chai opened it, and this is what she read:

'Pan's case is "fatal bodily harm by mischance", *not* "intentional homicide". I lodged an appeal in my own name first thing this morning and am still waiting for the magistrate's rescript. Pan bungled his original statement, and once the appeal has been approved, we must change his plea at the rehearing. We should be able to get him off.

'I urgently need Tls. 500. Have the pawnshop forward it *without delay.* Tell Aunt not to worry. The boy can tell you the rest.'

When Bao-chai had finished reading the letter aloud to her, Aunt Xue wiped her eyes and said:

'His life hangs in the balance, doesn't it?'

'Before you go upsetting yourself all over again, Mama,' said Bao-chai, 'let's send for the boy and ask him what *he* knows.'

A maid was sent to fetch the boy. When he came in, Aunt Xue told him to give them a full account of everything he had heard.

'The evening we arrived,' he began, 'when I heard what Mr Pan told Master Ke, I nearly died of fright . . .'

But for the rest of the account, please turn to the next chapter.

CHAPTER 86

Bribery induces an old mandarin to tamper with the course of justice
And a discourse on the Qin provides a young lady with a vehicle for romantic feelings

It was told in the last chapter how Bao-chai read Xue Ke's letter aloud to her mother, who then summoned the boy and told him to repeat whatever Xue Pan had said about his misadventure.

'I couldn't make out every word, ma'am,' he began, 'but I did hear Mr Pan tell Master Ke that...'

He glanced quickly round the room, and having satisfied himself that there was no one else present, continued:

'... that he couldn't stand any more of the terrible scenes at home, and had decided to go on a business trip in the South. He knew someone in this town about seventy miles south of the capital, and was thinking of asking him along on his travels. On his way to this man's house, who should he meet but that fellow Jiang Yu-han he used to be friendly with, on his way to the capital with some young actors. The two of them went into a bar for a jug of wine and a bite to eat, and that's when things started to go wrong. The waiter kept making eyes at Jiang, which made Mr Pan angry. Well, Jiang left that same day. But the next day, Mr Pan took this other man – the one he was planning to travel with – to the same bar for a drink. After a few rounds he remembered the waiter's cheeky behaviour and made a point of complaining about the wine. The waiter took a long time coming with a fresh jug; Mr Pan picked up his cup and aimed it at the waiter's face. Well, the waiter turned out to be a daring sort of rogue himself;

he stuck his head out and challenged Mr Pan to hit him. Next thing, wham! Mr Pan smashed the cup right down on top of his head. Blood came spurting out, and the waiter went down, cursing and swearing. Then he came over all quiet . . .'

'But why on earth did nobody try to stop them?' asked Aunt Xue.

'I didn't hear Mr Pan say anything about that, ma'am. That's all I know.'

'All right. You may go and rest now.'

'Thank you ma'am.'

So saying, the boy went out.

Aunt Xue went first to her sister and entrusted her with the task of enlisting Jia Zheng's support. When Lady Wang brought the matter up and gave Jia Zheng a detailed account of what had happened, he hummed and hawed and said that he could do nothing until Xue Ke's appeal had gone through the normal channels and the judge had issued his rescript.

Aunt Xue had the five hundred taels weighed out in the family pawnshop and gave it to the boy to deliver post-haste to Xue Ke.

Three days later, the letter they were waiting for arrived. It was handed to Aunt Xue, who sent a junior maid at once to fetch Bao-chai. She hurried over, and this is what she read:

'Dear Aunt. Tls. 500 received and distributed as tips among the yamen staff. Pan is being reasonably treated in jail, so please don't worry.

'Our problem is that the people here are being very awkward. Neither the dead man's family nor the eye-witnesses will cooperate. Even Pan's so-called friend – the one he invited to travel with him – is on their side. It's especially hard for Li Xiang and myself, as strangers, but luckily we have managed to find a good scrivener who has agreed to help us – for a pretty stiff fee. His advice was that we should get to work on Wu Liang (that's the "friend"). First, since he was being held in custody as a primary witness, we should get someone to stand bail for him; then offer him money to corroborate *our* plea of death by mischance. If Wu refused to cooperate we were to try accusing *him* of being the murderer himself and of using an outsider as a scapegoat. He'd be too scared then not to play along.

'So far so good. We got Wu out on bail, bribed the family and various other witnesses, and lodged our appeal the day before yesterday. The rescript was issued today. It speaks for itself.'

Bao-chai went on to read out the copy of the appeal and appended rescript.

APPEAL

brought by *Xue Ke*, younger cousin of and proxy for the defendant, *Xue Pan*, wrongfully convicted of the Intentional Homicide by Blows of *Zhang San*, late of this county.

STATEMENT OF FACTS: The defendant, registered domicile Nanking, at present resident in the capital, on the ____ of the ____ month, left home intending to do business in the Southern Provinces. Not many days later, his servant returned home with the news that the defendant had been involved in an incident in which another party had lost his life. The appellant came hither in all haste, to discover that the above-mentioned Mr *Zhang* had indeed met his death at the hand of the defendant, but that it was a case of Fatal Bodily Harm by Mischance and not of Intentional Homicide by Blows, as previously alleged.

PLEA: On arrival at the County Jail, the appellant was a witness to the most earnest protestations of innocence on the part of the defendant, and hearty denial of any previous animosity towards *Zhang*, with whom indeed he had not been in the slightest degree acquainted before the incident in question, which had occurred solely as the result of a trivial disagreement over a jug of wine. The defendant, by way of complaint, emptied the contents of his cup onto the floor. At precisely the same instant, the deceased bent down to retrieve some object from an adjacent spot, slipping as he did so, with the unfortunate, but *entirely accidental* consequence that a fatal collision occurred between the defendant's cup and the deceased's *os bregmatis*.

When Your Honour saw fit to apprehend the defendant and subject him to judicial interrogation, his terror of the rack was so extreme that he rashly admitted the charge of Homicide by Blows, thus bringing upon himself the sentence of Strangulation, with possibility of Commutation to Exile. Your Honour, in your great Wisdom and Clemency, aware no doubt of some latent injustice, has delayed passing sentence until the present time. The defendant, being in custody, is prevented by law from appealing *pro sua parte*. The appellant has therefore been emboldened by considerations of family loyalty to act on his behalf, most humbly and earnestly beseeching Your Honour to reopen the case and subject all parties concerned to a second examination. This would be a magnanimous course of action, and one that would earn the never-ending gratitude and lifelong devotion of the appellant and his entire family.

Bao-chai now came to the judge's rescript, which read as follows:

RESCRIPT

An inquest was held at the scene of the crime, and the evidence heard was conclusive. No torture of any kind was applied to the defendant, who freely admitted the charge, *viz*. Homicide by Blows. His admission of guilt has now been officially entered in the records.

You, the appellant, an outsider with no first-hand knowledge of the case, in presuming to fabricate this unfounded appeal are guilty of contempt of court. In view of the mitigating circumstances of family loyalty, your offence will be overlooked in this instance.

APPEAL REJECTED

'There's no hope left then!' cried Aunt Xue. 'What can we do now?'

'That isn't all,' said Bao-chai. 'There's a P.S.'

She read on:

'For confidential instructions, ask the boy – *urgent*.'

Aunt Xue immediately questioned the boy, who supplied the following information:

'The people at the yamen know how rich we are, ma'am, and Master Ke says we'll have to use family connections here in the capital, and send another large bribe, if we're to get a rehearing and a lighter sentence. He says you must act quickly, ma'am, as delay now could mean hardship for Mr Pan.'

Aunt Xue dismissed the boy and went at once to see her sister again. Lady Wang pleaded strenuously with Jia Zheng, but the most he was prepared to do was send someone to 'have a word' with the judge. He refused to contemplate the use of 'pecuniary considerations'. Aunt Xue, fearing that this gesture would prove ineffective, begged Xi-feng to speak to Jia Lian. The judge's price was high – the figure ran into several thousands of taels; but in the end an agreement was reached, and the way was clear for Xue Ke to proceed with his plan.

The case was officially re-opened, and all the parties concerned were summoned once more to the district yamen – the beadle, eye-witnesses, relatives of the deceased, etc. Xue Pan was brought out from the cells. The clerk of the court called the roll, and the judge ordered the chief beadle to verify the original depositions. Then Mrs Zhang (née Wang) and Zhang Er, the deceased's mother and uncle, were called to give evidence.

'May't please Yeronner,' began Mrs Zhang, punctuating her delivery with sobs, 'we Zhangs are country folk and live to the south of town. Papa Zhang's been gone these eighteen years. We had the three boys, but our eldest and second have both passed away. The only one as I had left was our third, and now he's gone too!' (More sobs.)

'Twenty-three this year he'd've been, anitplease Yeronner, and still a single lad. He'd took this job at Li's Bar by way o' helpin' me out, seein' as we'd so little comin' in. It'd've been 'bout midday when this man come to the door – I can see 'im now – "There's been a fight at Li's Bar!" says he, "And your boy's been killed!" My poor heart, Yeronner! I was took that bad! I runned to Li's and there was my boy lyin' on the ground, the blood runnin' out 'is poor 'ead! I tried askin' 'im what 'ad 'appened, but 'e couldn't say nothing, 'e was 'ardly breathin', and then . . . well, then 'e was gone! If I could only get my hands on that wickedevilmurderin' . . .'

A growl of disapproval rippled through the ranks of the court underlings. Mrs Zhang rapidly kotowed to the bench:

'All I'm askin' for is reglar justice Yeronner! He was all I 'ad left in the world!'

'Next witness – Gaffer Li!' called the judge peremptorily.

Gaffer Li, proprietor of Li's Bar, came forward and knelt before the bench.

'Was this fellow Zhang employed for casual work on your premises?' asked the judge.

'He was a regular waiter,' replied Li.

'I see here that in your original deposition, as recorded at the Inquest, you state that Xue Pan dealt Zhang San a fatal blow on the head. Tell me, did you personally observe this blow?'

'No, Your Honour. I was behind the counter at the time, in the tap-room. I heard that one of the customers in a private room had ordered some wine. Then a little later I heard that someone had been hurt. I ran in and saw Zhang San lying on the floor. He couldn't speak. I informed the beadle, and sent someone to tell Mrs Zhang. I have no idea how the fight started. There was a gentleman sitting at Mr Xue's table, Your Honour. Perhaps he could supply the necessary information . . .'

'*What*!' thundered the judge impressively. 'In your original deposition it says quite plainly that you *saw* the incident with your own eyes. Are you now trying to tell me that you saw nothing?'

'When I made that first statement, Your Honour, I was in such a fluster that I must have got my facts a bit muddled . . .'

Another growl through the ranks.

'Next witness!' ordered the judge.

The next witness was Wu Liang, Xue Pan's 'friend'.

'Tell me,' said the judge, 'were you sitting drinking with the defendant at the time of the crime? Exactly how did the fatal blow occur? Be sure to speak the truth.'

'On the day in question, Your Honour,' replied Wu, 'Mr Xue called at my house and kindly invited me out for a drink. As he was dissatisfied with the quality of the wine, he ordered a fresh jug to be brought. But the waiter, Zhang San, refused to oblige. This annoyed Mr Xue, and by way of protest he threw the contents of his cup in the waiter's face. It all happened very fast, and somehow the cup must have slipped from Xue's hand and collided with Zhang's head. This is a true account of the incident as I saw it with my own eyes.'

'*Nonsense*!' cried the judge. 'Why, at the Inquest the defendant himself admitted to "assaulting Zhang and dealing the fatal blow with the cup", and you verified the admission yourself. This is perjury! Slap his face!'

An answering cry came from the appropriate section of the court, and the punishment was about to be administered, when Wu protested:

'Mr Xue never started a fight, sir! The cup slipped from his hand and collided with Zhang's head! It was all an accident! Question the defendant himself! Have mercy!'

The judge summoned Xue Pan.

'Now, Xue, for the last time, tell me: what was your grudge against Zhang San? And how did he meet with his death? I want the whole truth!'

'Your Honour, be merciful I beseech you!' pleaded Xue Pan. 'I never raised a hand to strike the man. All I did was empty my cup on the floor because he refused to bring the wine I had ordered. Before I knew it, the cup slipped from my hand and struck him on the head. I did all I could to staunch the wound, but it was hopeless. The loss of blood was so great that he died in a matter of minutes. At the Inquest I was in such fear of torture that I made a false confession of assault. I beg Your Honour to show mercy accordingly!'

'*Miserable wretch*!' bellowed the judge. 'You have already pleaded guilty to intentional assault. Are you now trying to say that it was no more than an *accidental collision*?'

He went on in this fashion, making a series of suitably august noises, threatening Pan with the rod one minute and the rack the next, if he would not confess. This time, however, Pan persisted in his denial.

The coroner was now called upon to make public the results of his post-mortem.

'May it please Your Honour, I have duly examined the corpse of Zhang San, and find no trace of injury but a single scalp-wound, caused by a porcelain artifact. The wound is approximately one and three-quarter inches in length, penetrating to a depth of half an inch. The bregmatic bone has sustained a fracture approximately one third of an inch in length. The type of wound points unmistakably to a collision of an accidental nature.'

The judge checked the coroner's certificate, which (as he knew quite well) had been altered by his clerk, and without raising any objections casually asked all concerned to sign their statements.

'*But Yeronner*!' wailed Mrs Zhang. 'What about all them other wounds? Ever so many there was! Coronary said so himself last time, I remember! Where've they all got to now?'

'Foolish woman!' exclaimed the judge. 'Here is the certificate, duly signed – see for yourself.'

He called the dead man's uncle forward (a more cooperative witness):

'Zhang Er, will you tell the court how many wounds there were on your nephew's corpse?'

'Just the one on his skull, sir,' replied Zhang.

The judge turned to Mrs Zhang:

'What further need have you of proof!'

He told the clerk of the court to hand Mrs Zhang the certificate, and instructed the chief beadle and Zhang Er to explain it to her. The other documents in the case were now collated – the proceedings of the inquest, duly authenticated with the signatures of those present at the time, and the depositions of the witnesses, which were now unanimous in stating that there had been no quarrel, *ergo* no assault, *ergo* Xue Pan was only guilty of 'causing fatal bodily harm by mischance', a lesser degree of manslaughter redeemable by payment of a fine. The parties were now required to affix their signature or mark to the document, Xue Pan was detained until confirmation of his sentence was received, and Wu Liang and his guarantor were released. The court was adjourned.

As the judge was leaving, Mrs Zhang broke into another untimely bout of wailing and sobbing, and he ordered the court lictors to send her packing. Uncle Zhang also did what he could to bring her to her senses:

'It really was an accident,' he said, 'so why hold an innocent man guilty? His Honour has passed sentence now, so for goodness' sake pipe down.'

Xue Ke had been waiting outside, and was greatly relieved to hear that all had gone according to plan. He sent a letter home, saying that he planned to stay on until the confirmation came through, when he would pay Xue Pan's fine.

Walking through the town later that day, he became aware of a buzz of excited conversation in the street:

'Have you heard? One of the Imperial Concubines has passed away, and there's to be a three-day Recess at Court . . .'

Since the Imperial Mausoleum was not far from the town, Xue Ke thought to himself, the judge would now be busy preparing for the funeral and repairing the road with yellow earth for the procession. He would hardly have time to think about routine legal matters, and consequently he himself would achieve little by hanging around. So he went to the jail and explained to Pan that he was going home for a few days. Pan was glad for his mother's sake, and sent a brief note to reassure her. 'I'm fine,' he wrote. 'A few more taels in the right pockets and I'll be home! But be sure to keep the cash flowing!' Xue Ke left the boy Li Xiang behind just in case, and set off home straight away.

On arrival, he gave Aunt Xue a full account of how the judge had managed the transition from 'assault' to 'mischance'.

'All that's left now,' he finished by saying, 'is to give the Zhangs a bit more money. Then, when the commutation is confirmed, it will all be over.'

Aunt Xue breathed a sigh of relief.

'I was hoping you would be able to come home,' she said. 'I have been wanting to go over and thank the Jias for all that they've done, and I thought it would be nice if I could go and keep an eye on things for Aunt Wang and spend some time with the girls. With the death of the Zhou Concubine the family is away every day and they must be rather lonely at home. But I couldn't go until now because there was no one here to take charge.'

'The funny thing is that on my way here I heard it was the Jia Concubine that had died,' said Xue Ke. 'That's why I came back in such a hurry – though I must say I found it hard to credit.'

'She was ill a while ago,' replied Aunt Xue. 'But she recovered, and I have heard nothing about her being ill since. It's odd, though: Lady Jia was not feeling well a few days ago, and whenever she closed her eyes she had a vision of Her Grace. Everyone was most concerned at first, and they even sent someone to Court to inquire, but were told that Her Grace was in good health. Then, three days ago, in the evening, Lady Jia suddenly said out loud: "Why have you come all this way on your own to see me, Your Grace?" This time they put it down to her illness and didn't take it seriously. "If you don't believe me," said Lady Jia, "let me tell you what Her Grace said: Prosperity may all too soon be spent; draw back, draw back before it is too late." They thought she was imagining it all – it was just the sort of thing a lady of her years would be preoccupied with, after all – and paid no attention. So can you imagine the panic the next morning, when somehow they heard from Court that one of the Concubines was critically ill, and that all members of the family with titles were to proceed to the Palace! They were in the most dreadful state when they set off! But before they had even left the palace, we heard that it was the Zhou Concubine. It is odd, don't you agree, that the rumour you heard should have tallied so exactly with Lady Jia's premonitions?'

'The public always gets its facts mixed up,' commented Bao-chai, 'and the Jias are so sensitive about the whole thing that they've only to hear the words "Her Grace" mentioned to start jumping to the most dire conclusions. It nearly always turns out to be a false alarm. During this latest excitement, I was chatting to one or two of their maids and older serving-women, and they told me they'd known all along that it couldn't possibly have been Her Grace. I asked one of them how they could be so sure, and she told me of something that happened several years ago.

'It was the first month of the year, and there was a fortune-teller from one of the provinces here in the capital, who had been recommended to the family for his great accuracy. Lady Jia gave instructions to slip Her Grace's Eight Stems and Branches in with some of the maids', and to ask this man to tell their fortunes. He singled hers out at once. "There must be some mistake here", he said. "I see that this young lady was born on the first of the first month. If the Stem and Branch of her natal hour were correct, she would have to be a person of high estate, and not a servant in this household." Sir Zheng and the others urged him to cast the horoscope anyway, so he went on:

"The Cyclical Year *Jia Shen* (Wood + Metal), the Prime Month *Bing Yin* (Fire + Wood). Both Failure and Decline are present. Although the Year Branch *Shen* shows Rank and Wealth, as it is not her fate to be raised within the household, the aspect of this Branch is not particularly favourable. The Day *Yi Mao* (Wood + Wood), commencement of Spring, Wood at its zenith. We have here a conflict, a Configuration of Peers. In this case it enhances the subject, just as fine timber is only fashioned into an instrument of true greatness when it encounters the axe. The Hour Stem *Xin* (Metal) indicates Nobility, while the Hour Branch *Si* (Fire) indicates Rank and Fortune again, this time the High Degree known as *Lucky Horse Rides the Sky.* The Day Conjunction shows Supreme Rank and the Forces of Heaven and the Moon presiding over her fate. She will be favoured with residence in the Imperial Bedchamber. If the Hour Stem and Branch are correct, this subject must be an Imperial Concubine."

'As the maid said,' Bao-chai continued, 'the horoscope fitted Her Grace perfectly. They remembered the end part, too. "Alas!" he said, "such Glory cannot endure. When Hare meets Tiger, and Wood meets Wood, in a *Mao* Month of a *Yin* Year, her Peers will outshine her, the Decline will reach its nadir, and the fine wood, through being too prettily carved, will lose its heart and strength." Although the family in their panic forgot all about this final prediction, the maid remembered. As she said to Cousin Wan, "this is a *Yin* Year, and we've already passed the *Mao* Month, so it couldn't be Her Grace!"

Bao-chai had hardly finished when Xue Ke exclaimed:

'Forget about the Jias for a minute; if there is such a good fortune-teller around, why not ask him about Pan? Perhaps he could tell us what evil force has crossed his path and brought him such bad luck this year? Give me Pan's Stems and Branches, and I'll go and find out if the future holds any more upsets in store for him.'

'The fortune-teller was from one of the provinces. Who knows where he is now?' replied Bao-chai.

During this conversation, they had already started to pack Aunt Xue's things. She went over to the main mansion, to find that, as she had supposed, Li Wan, Tan-chun and the girls had been left on their own. They welcomed her and asked after Xue Pan. They were greatly relieved when she told them that he was out of danger and only waiting for confirmation of his sentence.

'Mother was saying only yesterday,' said Tan-chun, 'that she'd always relied on you in the past, Auntie, whenever there was any sort of crisis, to come over and keep an eye on things. But this time she felt she could hardly ask you, as you had enough to cope with. She was rather uneasy about leaving us here on our own, all the same.'

'I've been worrying about you myself,' replied Aunt Xue. 'But you know how it's been this last week or two. Your Cousin Ke has been away trying to sort out Pan's affairs, and really I couldn't leave Bao-chai on her own, she'd never be able to manage. Especially as Pan's young wife is so incompetent. What with one thing and another, I simply haven't been able to get away. The only reason Ke has been able to come home and relieve me now is that the judge in charge of the case is going to be tied up with the Zhou Concubine's funeral arrangements for a few days'.

'We'd be so pleased if you could stay for a day or two,' said Li Wan.

Aunt Xue nodded.

'I should very much like to be here and keep you girls company. The only thing is, I am a little worried that Bao-chai may feel lonely without me.'

'Well why not ask her to come over as well?' suggested Xi-chun.

Aunt Xue gave a little laugh.

'Oh, I couldn't do that.'

'But why not? She used to live here, didn't she?'

Li Wan replied for Aunt Xue.

'You don't understand. It's not the same now. They're very busy at present, so she can't possibly come.'

Xi-chun supposed that this was the real reason for Bao-chai's absence, and dropped the matter.

As they were talking, Grandmother Jia and the rest of the family arrived back from their visit of condolence. When they saw that Aunt Xue was there, preliminary courtesies were dropped for once and everyone wanted to know the latest in the Pan affair. Aunt Xue told them the whole story. Bao-yu was present, and pricked up his ears when he heard Jiang Yu-han's name mentioned. Although he thought it inadvisable to show much interest in front of the others, secretly he asked himself why his old actor-friend had not been to look him up, if he was back in town. Then, noticing that Bao-chai had not accompanied her mother, and trying to imagine what could be keeping her at home, he began to drift into one of his brown studies, and was only aroused and restored to a more cheerful frame of mind by the unexpected arrival of Dai-yu. He stayed for dinner with the others at Grandmother Jia's. After dinner everyone retired to their respective apartments, except for Aunt Xue, who stayed the night in Grandmother Jia's guest-room.

Bao-yu returned to Green Delights, and was divesting himself of his going-out clothes, when suddenly he remembered the cummerbund Jiang Yu-han had once given him as a first-meeting present.

'Do you remember that crimson cummerbund I gave you?' he asked Aroma. 'The one you wouldn't wear? Have you still got it?'

'I've put it away somewhere. Why do you ask?'

'Oh, I just wondered.'

'Didn't you hear what terrible trouble Mr Pan got into, all because he made friends with such riffraff! Will you never learn? Haven't you more sense than to go bringing up a thing like that? Instead of filling your head with such stuff, what you should be doing is quietly concentrating on your studies.'

'Oh for goodness' sake! I'm not the one that's got into trouble! I just happened to think of it, that's all. I couldn't care less whether you've still got it or not. If I'd known you were going to start giving me a lecture . . .'

Aroma smiled.

'I'm not giving you a lecture. It's just that you know what people say about actors. Now that you're studying the classics and learning all the proper rules of behaviour, you should try to conform and get on in the world. When your sweetheart comes along, surely you'll want to make a good impression then?'

'Goodness!' exclaimed Bao-yu, aroused by the mention of the word sweetheart, 'that reminds me! There was such a crowd at Grannie's, I didn't have a chance to speak to Cousin Lin, and she didn't speak to me either. She left before I did, so she's probably home by now. I'll be back in a minute.'

He was gone.

'Don't stay too long!' Aroma called after him. 'Now I've done it! I should never have opened my mouth!'

Bao-yu did not reply, but made his way directly to the Naiad's House, head bowed in thought. On arrival there, he found Dai-yu at her table, poring over a book.

'Have you been back long, coz?' he asked, walking over and standing by her side.

'As you were ignoring me,' she said, returning his smile, 'there was little point in my staying . . .'

He laughed.

'Everyone was talking at once, and I couldn't get a word in.'

Looking down at the page open in front of her, Bao-yu found that he couldn't understand a single character on it. Some of them seemed familiar, like the characters for

Peony and *Vast*; but on closer inspection he saw that even they had been in some way changed. There was the character for *Hook*, with a *Five* inside it, and a *Nine* and *Big* on top; and there was a *Five* next to a *Six*, with *Wood* below and another *Five* at the very bottom. It was all very puzzling.

'You must be very advanced, to be able to decipher this esoteric script!' he said.

Dai-yu gave a little 'chee!'

'Not much of a scholar really are you! Fancy never having seen a Qin tablature before!'

'It's music! Of course! But why don't I know any of the characters? Do *you* know what they mean?'

'No, of course not; that's why I'm reading it . . .'

'Do you *really*? I never knew you could play. Did you know about the Qins hanging on the wall in the main library? There are quite a few. I remember the year before last Father had a friend who was a Qin player – Antiquarian Ji I think he was called. Father asked him to play a piece, but when he tried the instruments he said they were none of them fit to play. He said that if Father really wanted to hear him play, he would come back another day with his own instrument. But he never did. I think he must have decided Father was tone-deaf. Well! So all this time you've been hiding your light under a bushel!'

'Oh no,' replied Dai-yu. 'I'm no good. It just happened that a day or two ago, when I was feeling a little better, I was looking through my bookcase and came across an old Qin Handbook. It seemed such a fine thing, and made such fascinating reading. It began with a preface on the general philosophy of the Qin, which I found most profound, and then it explained the technical side in great detail. I realized that playing the Qin is a form of meditation and spiritual discipline handed down to us from the ancients.

'I had a few lessons when we lived in Yangchow, and made some progress. But since then I've become so out of practice, and now my fingers are all "overgrown with brambles", as they say! The first Qin Handbook I found only had the names of the Airs, it didn't have the words and music. But now I've found another with the Airs written out in full. It's so interesting! Of course, I realize that I shall never be able to do justice to the score. To think what the great Master Musicians of the past could do – like Master Kuang, whose playing could summon wind and thunder, dragon and phoenix! And to think that Confucius could tell from his Music Master Xiang's first notes that he was listening to a musical portrait of King Wen! To play a Rhapsody of Hills and Streams and share its inner meaning with a fellow music-lover . . .'

Dai-yu fluttered her eyelids and slowly bowed her head.

Bao-yu was completely carried away:

'Oh coz! How wonderful it all sounds! But I'm afraid I still don't understand these peculiar characters. Please teach me how to read some of them.'

'I don't need to teach you. It's easy.'

'But I'm such a fool! Please help me! Take that one there – all I can make out is *Hook*, with *Big* on top and *Five* in the middle.'

Dai-yu laughed at him.

'The *Big* and *Nine* on top mean you stop the string with the thumb of your left hand at the *ninth* fret. The *Hook* and *Five* mean you *hook* the middle finger of your right hand slightly and pull the *fifth* string towards you. So you see, it's not what we would call a character, it's more a cluster of signs telling you what the next note is and how to play it. It's very easy. Then there are signs for all the graces – the narrow and the wide *vibrato*, the rising and the falling *glissando*, the mordent, the *tremulo*, the falling *glissando* with open-string drone . . .'

Bao-yu was beside himself with joy.

'As you understand it so perfectly, coz, why don't we start studying the Qin together?'

'The essence of the Qin,' replied Dai-yu, 'is restraint. It was created in ancient times to help man purify himself and lead a gentle and sober life, to quell all wayward passions and to curb every riotous impulse. If you wish to play, then you must first

> seek out a quiet chamber,
> a studio with distant view,
> or upper room;
> or some secluded nook
> 'mong rocks and trees,
> on craggy mountain-top,
> by water's edge . . .

Let the weather be clear and calm, a gentle breeze, a moonlit night. Light some incense, and sit in silent meditation. Empty the mind of outward thoughts. Poise Breath and Blood in Perfect Harmony. Your Soul may now commune with the Divine, and enter into that mysterious Union with the Way.

'As the ancients said, true music-lovers have always been few. If there is no one able to share your music's true delight, then sit alone, and

> serenade the breeze and moonlight,
> hymn the ancient pines
> and weather-worn rocks;
> let wild monkeys and venerable cranes
> hear your song,

rather than the vulgar mob, whose dull ears would only sully the precious virtue of the Qin.

'So much for the setting. The next two essentials are finger-technique and touch. And before you think of playing, be sure to dress in a suitable style – preferably in a swansdown cape or other antique robe. Assume the dignified manner of the ancients, a manner in keeping with the chosen instrument of the sages. Wash your hands. Light the incense. Sit on the edge of your couch. Place the Qin on the table before you, and sit with your chest opposite the fifth fret. Raise both hands slowly and gracefully. You are now ready, in body and mind, to begin.

'You must while playing observe carefully the dynamic markings – *piano, forte, allegro, adagio* – and maintain a relaxed but serious manner at all times.'

'Goodness me!' cried Bao-yu. 'I was thinking we could do it for fun! If it's as complicated as that, I'm not sure I'd be up to it!'

While they were talking Nightingale came in, and on seeing Bao-yu in the room, inquired with a smile:

'To what are we to attribute this joyful event, Master Bao?'

'Cousin Dai has just been teaching me about the Qin. It's as though scales had fallen from my eyes! I could go on listening for ever!'

'I didn't mean that,' said Nightingale. 'What I meant was, it's so rarely that we see you at all nowadays, I wondered if something out of the ordinary had happened to bring you here today?'

'I suppose it must seem like that,' replied Bao-yu. 'But the only reason I've not been round more often is that I know Cousin Dai has not been well, and thought it best not to trouble her. And then I've been having to go to school . . .'

'Well,' interrupted Nightingale, 'Miss Lin has only just started to feel better, so don't you think you should let her rest now, and not wear her out giving you lessons?'

'Why yes! How thoughtless of me!' he exclaimed with a laugh. 'I was so absorbed in what she was saying, that it never entered my head she might be tiring herself.'

'I wasn't,' said Dai-yu, smiling. 'Talking about music doesn't tire one, on the contrary, it raises one's spirits. *I* only wonder if what I was saying wasn't beyond you . . .'

'It doesn't matter,' said Bao-yu. 'I'm sure if we take it slowly I'll be able to understand.'

He stood up.

'But seriously, I think I should leave you in peace now. Tomorrow I'll ask Tan and Xi if they'll come over with me. You three can learn together. I think I'll just sit in . . .'

'Why, you lazy thing!' laughed Dai-yu. 'Imagine if we three *did* learn to play, and you were as ignorant as ever; wouldn't we then be casting our . . .'

She felt she was allowing herself to become too intimate, and suddenly stopped short. Bao-yu only laughed:

'I'd be happy just to hear you play. I'd do anything for that – even be your swine!'

Dai-yu blushed, but laughed nonetheless. Nightingale and Snowgoose laughed too.

Bao-yu took his leave, and had reached the door, when Ripple appeared, followed by a junior maid bearing a small pot of orchid-plants.

'Her Ladyship has been given four pots of these orchids,' said Ripple, 'and she thought that, as she was so busy at the palace and wouldn't have time to appreciate them, she would give one to you, Master Bao, and one to you, Miss Lin.'

Dai-yu looked at the orchids. Among them were some of the double-headed kind, and looking at these, she had a strange sensation that they *meant* something. Whether it was joy or sorrow that they portended, she could not tell. But it was something of importance. She stood staring at them, lost in thought.

Bao-yu's mind, by contrast, was still full of *vibratos* and *glissandos*, and as he left he said gaily:

'Now that you have these orchids, coz, you'll be able to compose your own *Lonely Orchid Pavan*. And I'm sure it will be just as good as the one Confucius wrote!'

Dai-yu's heart was too troubled to respond to this parting jest. She walked indoors, and staring once more at her orchids, thought to herself:

'Flowers have their spring-time, a time for fresh blossoms and young leaves. I am young, but frail as the willow that dreads the first breath of autumn . . . If all turns out for the best, I may grow stronger yet. But if not, my fate will be like that of the fallen petals at spring's end, driven by the rain and tossed in the wind...'

These sombre reflections brought tears to her eyes. Nightingale was puzzled to see her cry. 'Just now,' she thought to herself, 'when Master Bao was here, they were both in such high spirits; and now look at her! And all she's done is look at those flowers!'

She was still trying in vain to think of some consolation to offer, when one of Bao-chai's serving-women came into the room. But if you wish to know the purpose of her visit, you must read the next chapter.

CHAPTER 87

Autumnal sounds combine with sad remembrances
to inspire a composition on the Qin
And a flood of passion allows evil spirits
to disturb the serenity of Zen

The serving-woman was shown into the Naiad's House. After paying her respects, she delivered a letter for Dai-yu and was taken off to drink tea with the maids. Dai-yu opened her letter. It was from Bao-chai, and began:

'Dear Cousin,

Some malign star must surely have ruled the day of my birth! Misfortune pursues the family at every turn! Cousin Qin and I both fatherless; Mother advanced in years; to which add the sounds of bestial ululation that now emanate from our inner apartments at every hour of the day and night; and, to complete this recital of family woes, Brother Pan's recent and most cruel blow! Alas! We are indeed beset with howling winds and torrential rains! As I lie awake at night, tossing on my bed, unable to master this grief, my only consolation is the thought of a kindred spirit such as yours. Ah, dear Cousin! You, I know, have the heart to share my present trials, as once you shared the joys of that golden autumn, when harmony and conviviality prevailed. Then, united beneath the aegis of the Crab-flower Club, we tasted crustacean delicacies and contemplated chrysanthemums. Once, I recall, you questioned the flowers thus:

> "Who world disdainer, shares your hiding-place?
> Of all the flowers, why do yours bloom so late?"

The lines never fail to rive my heart. For are not you and I late blooms, that tremble at the approaching chill?

'I have endeavoured to compose a lament in four stanzas, to express these feelings of mine. I beg you, read it not as a piece of literary art, but as a simple vessel for my tears.

Your Affectionate Cousin,
Bao-chai.'

The poem was attached.

Alas! the seasons turn,
  and turning bring once more
The chill of autumn
  to our joy-forsaken door.
We have a flower,
  flos matris is its name,
  Heartsease . . .
Poor Mother! What art
  can heal thy grief,
  or ease thy heart?
My soul aches for thee.

The scudding clouds
  by biting autumn winds are blown;
The courtyard-walk
  with withered leaves is thickly strewn.
Whither shall I go?
  To whom shall I turn?
  My love is gone,
And only an anguish
  too deep for words
  remains.
My heart is desolate.

The mighty sturgeon
  has his pool;
The stork upon the dam
  makes his habitation.
Fish in scaly armour,
Birds in serried plumes,
  find protection.
In my distress
I question
  that inscrutable expanse:

O bowels of earth!
O boundless sky!
Will ye not hearken to my cry?

Above, the twinkling Milky Way;
The air cold,
Slanting moonlight,
The water-clock
sunk past midnight.
My restless heart
grieves still;
I read once more this sad lament,
Before entrusting it to you,
My kindred soul and friend!

Dai-yu was deeply moved. 'She knew I'd be able to understand!' she thought to herself. 'That's why she wrote to me rather than anyone else.' She was lost in thought, when a voice called from outside:

'Is Cousin Lin at home?'

Refolding the letter, she replied in a somewhat distant tone:

'Who's that?'

Her visitors were already on their way into the room – Tan-chun, Shi Xiang-yun and the two Li sisters. The girls exchanged greetings, and Snowgoose served them with tea. During the conversation that followed, Dai-yu found her thoughts turning back to the gathering, two years earlier, at which they had written the chrysanthemum poems:

'Don't you think it's strange?' she remarked to the others. 'Since Cousin Chai moved out of the Garden, she's only been to see us a couple of times all together. And now it seems as though nothing will induce her to come. I'm beginning to wonder if she'll ever visit us again.'

Tan-chun smiled.

'Of course she will! It's just that at the moment things are a bit difficult: Cousin Pan's wife is rather a tricky sort of person, Aunt Xue is getting on in years, and with this latest trouble of Pan's on top of everything else, Chai really is needed to look after things at home. It's not like the old days, when she was free to do as she pleased.'

As she spoke, they heard a sudden gust of wind outside, and a patter of falling leaves against the paper-covered window. A faint scent drifted into the room. They all tried to guess what flower it could be coming from.

'It's very like cassia-blossom,' suggested Dai-yu.

Tan-chun laughed.

'Still a southerner at heart! It's the ninth month, long past cassia-time.'

Dai-yu smiled.

'You're right. But then I didn't say it *was*, only very *like*...'

'Anyway, Tan,' Xiang-yun butted in, 'you can't talk. Don't you know the lines:

> The lotus fragrance drifts for miles,
> The cassia blooms till autumn's end?

In the South, the late-flowering cassia is at its best now. It's just that you've never seen it. If you ever have a chance to go to the South, you'll be able to see it for yourself.'

'And what should I be doing in the South?' retorted Tan-chun with a crushing smile. 'Anyway, I knew all that *ages* ago, thanks very much...'

The Li sisters grinned at each other.

'You never know, Tan,' said Dai-yu. 'We are "fairy earthlings, fleet of foot", that's what the old proverb says. Here today, who knows where tomorrow. Take me, for example. I was born a southerner, but here I am living in the North.'

Xiang-yun clapped her hands.

'Well said! Dai's got you there, Tan! And she's not the only one to have had such an experience. Look at the rest of us. Some of us are northerners, born and bred. Some were born in the South but grew up in the North. And some grew up in the South and then moved here later. And yet here we all are together. It's our fate, you see. People and places have an affinity. Their karma brings them together.'

They all nodded at Xiang-yun's little discourse, except for Tan-chun who just smiled. After chatting for a while longer, they got up to go. Dai-yu walked with them as far as the door, and would have gone out, but they dissuaded her:

'You've only just started to feel better. If you come out now, you might catch a chill.'

So she stood in the doorway, said a few parting words, and watched the four of them walk out of the courtyard gate.

When they had gone, she went indoors again and sat down. The birds were returning to their nests; the sun was setting. With Xiang-yun's words about the South still ringing in her ears, Dai-yu drifted into a daydream. If her parents were still alive... If she still lived in the South, that gentle land of spring flowers and autumn moonlight, of limpid waters and luminous hills... How she would love to be there again, to visit the Twenty Four Bridges in Yangchow and all the famous historical sites of Nanking! In the South she would have plenty of servants of her own to wait on her. She could do and speak as she pleased, sail in painted pleasure-boats and ride in perfumed carriages, watch the fields of red apricot-blossom go by, spot the inn-signs through the trees... She would be a young lady in her own right, not an outsider, dependent on others for everything. However much the Jias did for her, she always felt the need to be on her best behaviour. What wrong had she done in a previous incarnation to deserve this lonely existence? Those words written in captivity by the last emperor of Southern Tang –

> Here, all day long, I bathe my face in tears –

how well they expressed her own feelings! Her soul seemed transported to some distant region.

When Nightingale came in, a single glance sufficed to

tell her the cause of Dai-yu's 'absence'. She had been in the room when Xiang-yun was talking, and knew how easily Dai-yu was upset by the slightest reference to the South.

'I thought you might feel tired again, Miss,' she said, 'after all your visitors and such a lot of talking, so I've just sent Snowgoose to the kitchen for a bowl of ham and cabbage broth, cooked with dried shrimps, dried seaweed and bamboo-shoots. Doesn't that sound good?'

'I suppose so.'

'And some congee?'

Dai-yu nodded.

'I'd rather you and Snowgoose made the congee yourselves. Don't have it done in the kitchen.'

'No Miss. You can never be sure how clean things are in the kitchen. We'll cook the congee ourselves. I asked Snowgoose to tell Cook Liu in the kitchen to take special care with the soup. Cook Liu said we were not to worry, she'd see to it personally and prepare it in her own room. Her daughter Fivey is going to keep an eye on it while it simmers.'

'That's not what I meant,' replied Dai-yu. 'I wasn't complaining that the kitchen was dirty. It's just that I've been imposing on people for so long, and this illness of mine has caused quite enough extra trouble as it is. With all these special orders for soup and congee, I'm afraid I shall make myself unpopular.'

Her eyes were a tell-tale red.

'Oh Miss! You're imagining things!' protested Nightingale. 'You're Her Old Ladyship's own granddaughter, the apple of her eye. A chance to serve you is something people compete for, not grumble about.'

Dai-yu nodded thoughtfully.

'By the way,' she asked, 'is that Fivey you mentioned the one who used to be friendly with Parfumée when she was at Master Bao's place?'

'That's right.'

'Didn't I hear that she might be going into service at Master Bao's herself?'

'Yes, she was. Then she fell ill, and by the time she was better again and ready to start, there was all that trouble over Skybright, and it had to be put off.'

'I've always liked the look of her,' said Dai-yu.

Meanwhile a serving-woman had arrived with the soup, and Snowgoose went out to fetch it.

'Cook Liu says to tell Miss Lin this one's been specially cooked in her room by her Fivey,' said the old woman, 'so she won't need to fuss about its not being clean.'

Snowgoose said she would relay this message and carried the soup into the room. Dai-yu, however, had already heard their conversation, and told Snowgoose to go back at once and ask the woman to thank Mrs Liu on her return. Snowgoose did this, and the old woman went on her way.

Snowgoose now laid out Dai-yu's bowl and chopsticks on the table.

'Would you like some of that dried turnip slaw we brought with us from the South, Miss, if I mix a little sesame-oil and vinegar dressing with it?'

'If you like. But don't go to too much trouble.'

Snowgoose filled her bowl with congee. Dai-yu ate half and drank a couple of spoonfuls of the soup. She put down her spoon, and the two maids cleared away the things and cleaned the little table, which they then removed and replaced with the one that usually stood there. Dai-yu rinsed her mouth and washed her hands.

'Nightingale, have you put some incense on the brazier?'

'I was just going to, Miss.'

'You and Snowgoose have some of the soup and congee. They're good and wholesome. I'll see to the incense.'

The maids went into the outer room to eat. Dai-yu put some more incense on the brazier and sat down again. She was about to pick up a book to read when her attention was caught by the melancholy soughing of the wind through the trees outside. A long sigh swept from one end of the Garden to the other. The metal wind-chimes started jangling under the eaves.

Snowgoose was the first to finish her soup, and came in to see if there was anything Dai-yu needed.

'It's turning colder,' said Dai-yu. 'Have those fur clothes had a proper airing yet – the ones I asked you to take out the other day?'

'Yes, Miss.'

'Bring them here, will you? I'd like something warm to put over my shoulders.'

Snowgoose went out and returned with a bundle of fur-lined clothes, wrapped in a piece of felt. She undid the wrapper and held the clothes out for Dai-yu to choose from. Dai-yu noticed among the clothes another smaller bundle wrapped in silk. She reached out a hand to pick it up, and untied the wrapper. Inside she found a pair of silk handkerchiefs. She recognized them at once as the ones Bao-yu had secretly sent her during his convalescence! There were the verses she had written on them! Even the tear-stains could still be seen! And next to them in the little bundle were the perfumed sachet she had embroidered for him (and half-demolished in a fit of pique), the torn fan-case, and the snipped remains of the silken cord she had made for his Magic Jade. Nightingale, in sorting out the clothes for airing, must have come across these mementos in one of the chests, and slipped them into this bundle for safety. Dai-yu seemed to have forgotten Snowgoose and the clothes entirely. She stood with the handkerchiefs in her hands and stared at them as though entranced. As she read the verses tears began to stream down her cheeks.

Nightingale came in, to find Snowgoose standing there dumbly, with the felt-wrapped bundle of clothes still held out in front of her, while spread on the little table at Dai-yu's side were the sachet, fan-case and cord . Dai-yu was holding two faded handkerchiefs with some writing on them, and was gazing at them in tears. As the poet says:

> Tokens of past estrangement
> Catch the lover's eye;
> Fresh tears fall
> On tears of days gone by.

Nightingale knew only too well the tender memories attached to each one of those objects. She thought that sympathy would have little chance of success as a remedy, and decided instead to administer a cheerful rebuke.

'Come along now, Miss, what's the sense in looking at things like that? They belong to the past. You and Master Bao were children then. Goodness knows how many silly tiffs you had! All smiles one minute, crying your hearts out the next. Thank goodness you're both older and have learned to take life a bit more seriously. You wouldn't dream of spoiling pretty things like these *now* would you?'

She had meant well. But her words only reminded Dai-yu of the old days with Bao-yu, and released a fresh flood of tears. Nightingale tried again to cheer her up:

'Come on now, Miss. Snowgoose is waiting. Please choose something to wear.'

Dai-yu let the handkerchiefs drop. Nightingale swiftly retrieved them, wrapped them up again with the sachet and the other things, and put them away.

Finally Dai-yu draped one of the fur-lined jackets over her shoulders and walked listlessly to the outer-room. She sat down, and looking round saw Bao-chai's poem and letter still lying on the table. She picked them up and reread them a couple of times.

'The *feeling*'s the same,' she said to herself with a sigh, 'even if our circumstances are different. I should write something in reply. I'll write four stanzas and set them to an air for the Qin. Then tomorrow I can make a copy and send it to Chai.'

She told Snowgoose to bring in her brush and inkstone, which were on the table outside, and moistening the ink, began to write. When she had completed four stanzas, she took a Qin Handbook from her shelf and looked through it. She decided to make a suite out of the two old melodies, *Lonely Orchid Pavan* and *Saintly Virtue.* Having done the pointing, she wrote out a copy of the words there and then to send to Bao-chai, and asked Snowgoose to fetch the three-quarter size Qin she had brought from home, which was stored in a trunk. She tuned the strings and did a few preliminary finger-exercises. Her natural aptitude compensated for her lack of practice, and it was not long before all that she had learnt as a child came back to her. After playing for a while, seeing that it was already late in the night, she told Snowgoose to put away the Qin, and went to bed. And so we must leave her.

*

One day Bao-yu, after completing his toilet, set off as usual with Tealeaf to go to school. On their way they encountered Inky, another of his page-boys, who came bounding up to them with a broad grin on his face and announced:

'Good news, Master Bao! The Preceptor's not at school today, and you've all been given the day off!'

'Are you being serious?' asked Bao-yu.

'If you don't believe me, take a look: isn't that Master Huan and Young Master Lan on their way back now?'

Bao-yu looked and sure enough there were his half-brother and young nephew coming towards him with their contingent of pages, chatting away and giggling, though he could not catch what it was they were saying. When they saw him, they halted and stood with their arms respectfully at their sides.

'Why have you come back from school so soon?' Bao-yu asked them.

'The Preceptor is busy today,' replied Huan, 'and says we can all have the day off. We're to attend as usual tomorrow.'

Hearing this, Bao-yu turned about and, having reported the news to Grandmother Jia and his father, returned to Green Delights.

'Why are you back?' asked Aroma.

He told her what had happened, and after sitting with her for a minute or two made a move to go out again.

'Where are you off to in such a hurry?' she asked. 'If you've been given the day off school, that doesn't mean you have to go charging about. You ought to make it a day of rest.'

Bao-yu stopped in his tracks and hung his head.

'I know you're right. But when will I next have a chance to get out and have some fun? Be a sport...'

He said this in such an appealing tone of voice that Aroma relented.

'All right,' she said with a smile.

Meanwhile lunch had been brought in, and he had to stay and eat it. He bolted it down, rinsed his mouth and was off. Fast as a puff of smoke he sped to the Naiad's House. He found Nightingale in the courtyard hanging handkerchiefs out to dry.

'Has Miss Lin had her lunch yet?' he asked.

'She had half a bowl of congee earlier on,' replied Nightingale, 'but wasn't feeling very hungry. She's sleeping at the moment. You'd better go somewhere else just now, Master Bao, and come back a bit later.'

He left reluctantly, not knowing quite where to go. Suddenly it occurred to him that he had not seen Xi-chun for several days, and he began strolling in the direction of Smartweed Loggia. When he reached the courtyard and stood by one of the windows, it all seemed very quiet and deserted. She too, he concluded, was having her nap and not to be disturbed. He was about to leave when he heard a faint sound coming from inside, too faint to identify. He stood still and listened again, in the hope of hearing it more clearly. There it was! A distinct little tap! He was still trying to think what it could be, when a voice said:

'Why have you made that move, and not countered there?'

It was a game of Go! But Bao-yu did not have time to recognize the voice of the speaker. He heard Xi-chun reply:

'Why should I bother? If you take me there, I shall simply counter here, and if you take me again I shall take you again. I shall still be one move ahead, and in the end I shall be able to connect.'

'And what if I take you here?'

'Aiyo!' exclaimed Xi-chun. 'You had an inside counter-attack up your sleeve. I'm defenceless.'

That other girl's voice was so familiar! But he still couldn't quite place it. It wasn't one of his cousins, he was sure of that. And yet Xi-chun was unlikely to be entertaining an outsider. Lifting the door-curtain very gently aside, he peeped in. The Go-partner was none other than the nun from Green Bower Hermitage, the Dweller Beyond The Threshold, Adamantina. He dared not intrude any further. The girls were totally absorbed in their game, and had neither of them noticed that they were being spied upon. Bao-yu continued to stand there and watch. Adamantina leant low over the board and said to Xi-chun:

'Do you *want* to lose that whole corner?'

'Of course not! It's perfectly safe. All those pieces of yours are "dead", aren't they?'

'Are you sure? Go ahead and try.'

'All right. There's my move. Now let's see what you can do.'

A smile crossed Adamantina's face. She placed her next piece to link up with one she already had on the edge of the board, and then pounced on one of Xi-chun's pieces and annihilated her entire corner. She laughed:

'That's called "Pulling Your Boots Off Upside Down"!'

Before Xi-chun had time to reply, their unobserved

observer, unable to contain himself any longer, burst out laughing. The two girls were startled out of their wits.

'What do you mean by sneaking in here without saying a word?' exclaimed Xi-chun. 'What an ill-mannered way to behave, honestly! How long have you been there?'

'I came in just as you started to play for that corner. I had to watch it out.'

He bowed to Adamantina.

'Greetings, Reverend Sister!' he said with a smile. 'Wherefore this rare excursion from the mystic portals of Zen? What karma brings thee to Maya's dusty realm?'

She blushed from ear to ear, said nothing, lowered her head and stared at the Go-board. Bao-yu could see that he had embarrassed her, and tried to make up for it.

'Seriously,' he said, with a charming smile, 'how can common mortals compare with those who, like you, have renounced the world? In the first place, you have achieved inner peace. And with that peace comes a deep spirituality. And with that spirituality a clear insight . . .'

As he was speaking, Adamantina lifted her eyes a fraction and glanced at him. She looked down again at once, and a deep flush spread slowly across her face. Bao-yu realized that she was deliberately trying to ignore him, and sat down awkwardly beside the table. Xi-chun wanted to continue the game, but after a silence Adamantina said:

'Let's play another day.'

Having said this, she stood up, straightened out her dress and sat down again. Then, turning to Bao-yu, she asked, in a zany tone of voice:

'Where have you come from?'

It came as a great relief to Bao-yu that she should speak to him at all, and he was grateful of the chance to remedy his earlier blunder. But then it suddenly struck him that her question might not be as straightforward as it sounded. Was this one of her Zen subtleties? He sat there tongue-tied and red in the face. Adamantina smiled and turned to talk to Xi-chun. Xi-chun smiled too.

'Cousin Bao,' she said, 'what's so hard about that? Haven't you heard the saying "I come from whence I come"? To judge by the colour of your face anyone would think you were among strangers. Don't be shy!'

Adamantina seemed to take this banter personally. She experienced a strange stirring of emotion, and her face grew hot. She knew she must be blushing again, and became extremely flustered. Rising to her feet, she said:

'I've been here a long time. I think I should be making my way back to the Hermitage.'

Xi-chun knew the peculiarity of Adamantina's temperament and did not press her to stay. She was showing her out, when Adamantina gave a little laugh and said:

'It's so long since I've been to see you, and the way home is so full of twists and turns. I'm afraid of losing my way.'

'Pray allow me to be your guide!' volunteered Bao-yu promptly.

'I would be greatly honoured,' she replied. 'Please go ahead, Master Bao.'

The two of them said goodbye to Xi-chun and walked out of Smartweed Loggia. Their winding path led them near the Naiad's House, and as they approached they heard strains of music in the air.

'That's a Qin,' said Adamantina. 'Where could it be coming from, I wonder?'

'It must be Cousin Lin playing in her room,' replied Bao-yu.

'Really? Is that another of her accomplishments? I've never heard her mention it.'

Bao-yu repeated what Dai-yu had told him.

'Shall we go and watch?' he suggested.

'You mean listen, I suppose?' said Adamantina. 'One listens to the Qin. One never watches.'

'There you are!' said Bao-yu with a grin. 'I said I was a common sort of mortal.'

They had now reached a rockery close to the Naiad's

House. They sat down and listened in silence, touched by the poignancy of the melody. Then a murmuring voice began to chant:

> 'Autumn deepens, and with it
>   the wind's bitter moan.
> My love is far away;
>   I mourn alone.
> Gazing in vain
> For a glimpse of home,
> I stand at my balcony.
> Tears bedew my gown.'

After a brief pause, the chant began again:

> 'Hills and lakes melt
>   into distant night.
> Through my casement shines
>   the clear light
> Of the moon
> And the sleepless Milky Way.
> My thin robe trembles
> As wind and dew alight.'

There was another brief pause. Adamantina said to Bao-yu:

'The first stanza rhymed on "moan", the second on "night". I wonder how the next will rhyme?'

The chant began again from within:

> 'Fate denies you freedom,
>   holds you bound;
> Inflicting on me too
>   a heavy wound.
> In closest harmony
> Our hearts resound;
> In contemplation of the Ancients
> Is solace to be found.'

'That must be the end of the third stanza,' said Adamantina. 'How tragic it is!'

'I don't know anything about music,' said Bao-yu. 'But just from the way she sang, I found it terribly sad.'

There was another pause, and they heard Dai-yu tuning her Qin.

'That tonic B-flat of hers is too sharp for the scale,' commented Adamantina.

The chanting began again:

> 'Alas! this particle of dust,
> the human soul,
> Is only playing out
> a predetermined role.
> Why grieve to watch
> The Wheel of Karma turn?
> A moonlike purity remains
> My constant goal.'

As she listened, Adamantina turned pale with horror.

'Just listen to the way she suddenly uses a sharpened fourth there! Her intonation is enough to shatter bronze and stone! It's much too sharp!'

'What do you mean, too sharp?' asked Bao-yu.

'It will never take the strain.'

As they were talking, they heard a sudden twang and the tonic string snapped. Adamantina stood up at once and began to walk away.

'What's the matter?' asked Bao-yu.

'You will find out in time. Please don't say anything about this.'

She walked off, leaving Bao-yu in a state of great confusion. Eventually he too made his way dejectedly home. And there our narrative leaves him.

*

Adamantina arrived back at Green Bower Hermitage to find the old lay-sisters waiting for her return. They closed the gate after her and she sat with them for a while, intoning her Zen breviary. They had dinner, and after dinner the incense braziers were replenished. They all bowed before the shrine of the Bodhisattva and the women went off duty, leaving Adamantina alone. Her couch and back-rest were set out for her. Sitting cross-legged, she first regulated her breathing and closed her eyes. Then, cleansed of all wayward thoughts, her mind began to soar towards the realm of higher truth. She sat in meditation until well after midnight, when she was disturbed by a sudden clattering sound on the roof. Afraid there might be burglars about, she rose from her couch and went into the front hall. Looking out, all she could see were long clouds that stretched across the sky, and the moon shining through a watery haze. It was a mild night, and she stayed there for a while, leaning over the balustrade.

Suddenly two cats started wailing to each other on the roof above her head. The words Bao-yu had spoken to her that afternoon came flashing into her mind. She felt an involuntary racing of the heart, her ears burned. Making a determined effort to compose herself, she went back into her meditation room and sat down again on her couch. Her efforts were in vain. Something was overpowering her. She felt ten thousand horses stampeding through her head. The couch itself seemed to start swaying, and her body seemed to leave the Hermitage. She was surrounded by handsome young noblemen, all asking for her hand in marriage. There were matchmakers hustling her towards a bridal carriage against her will. Then the scene changed again. Now she was being kidnapped. A gang of ruffians with swords and clubs was threatening her, mauling her. She started screaming for help.

By now the old nuns and lay-sisters were wide awake, and had come hurrying into the hall with candles to discover the cause of the disturbance. They found her lying on the ground, with her arms outstretched, frothing at the mouth. She was woken from this apparent coma, only to fix her eyes into a rigid stare and cry out, her cheeks burning a fierce crimson:

'Buddha is my Protector! Don't touch me, you ruffians!'

The women were too scared to do anything but call out:

'Wake up! Wake up! We're here now!'

'I want to go home!' replied Adamantina. 'Who'll be my friend and take me home?'

'But this *is* your home!'

While the others stayed talking to her, one of the nuns was sent to pray at the shrine of the Goddess of Mercy. She shook the bamboo-box of tallies kept by the altar, and on consulting the relevant passage in the divination-book read that the Yin spirit of the south-west corner had been offended.

'Of course!' exclaimed one of the others, when she reported back. 'The south-west corner of the Garden was originally uninhabited, so it would be sure to contain a high concentration of Yin essence.'

Some busied themselves making soup, others brought water. One of the nuns, who had come with Adamantina from the South and was for that reason closer and more devoted to her than the others, sat next to her on the couch and put her arms protectively round her. Adamantina turned her head:

'Who's that?'

'It's only me.'

Adamantina looked at her curiously for a minute.

'Oh it really *is*!' she cried, and flung her arms round the nun, sobbing hysterically. 'Oh Mother, save me, or I'm going to die!'

The nun called out to her in an attempt to bring her to her senses, and began to massage her gently. The old women brought in tea, and they sat up together till dawn when finally Adamantina dozed off. The nun sent for the doctor, and several doctors came and took her pulses. There were as many differing diagnoses as there were doctors. Excessive worry damaging the spleen; phlogistic intrusion into the haematic system; offence caused to an evil spirit; a combination of internal and external chill. None of these seemed conclusive. Finally a doctor came whose first question after reading her pulses was:

'Did the young lady practise meditation?'

The women informed him that it was a regular thing with her.

'And did this illness develop quite suddenly last night?'

'Yes, it did.'

'Indubitably a case of heat in the cardiac orb affording entrance to a vagrant evil spirit.'

'Will she be all right?'

'Luckily the meditation does not seem to have been too far advanced and the spirit was therefore not able to penetrate too deeply. She will most probably recover.'

He wrote out a prescription for the Dephlogistication of the Cardiac Orb, after one dose of which Adamantina began to show signs of improvement.

News of her attack soon spread, and it became a subject of gossip for the lads in town. 'All that chastity and religion was bound to be too much for a girl of her age. Especially such an attractive, lively thing . . . Sooner or later she'll get soft on some lucky fellow and run away.'

A few days later Adamantina was slightly better. But her concentration seemed to have gone and she often found herself drifting off into a dreamlike state.

The news did not reach Xi-chun for a few days. She was sitting in her room when Landscape came hurrying in.

'Miss, have you heard what's happened to Sister Adamantina?'

'No – what is it?'

'I heard Miss Xing and Mrs Zhu talking about it yesterday. Remember that day she was here playing Go? Apparently that very night she had a fit. She was talking about bandits trying to carry her away and all sorts of other strange things. She still hasn't quite recovered. Don't you think it's peculiar?'

Xi-chun thought silently to herself:

'So for all her fastidious purity, Addie's worldly karma is still not complete. If only I had been born into a different family! If only I were free to become a nun! I would never be tempted by evil spirits. I know I would be able to subdue every unholy thought and achieve total detachment from the world and all its entanglements.'

With this thought she experienced a sudden sense of illumination, which she tried to express in the following gātha:

> Since at first there was no space,
> Things can have no proper place.
> From Void all comes;
> To Void must all return.

She told a maid to light some incense, and meditated for a while. Then she took down her Go Handbook and began looking through it, studying the tactics of such famous Go Masters of old as Kong Rong and Wang Ji-xin. There was 'Crab Wrapped in Lotus Leaves', and 'Golden Oriole Strikes Hare'; but she found neither of these very impressive, and 'Corner Kill in Thirty Six Moves' she found too hard to understand and harder still to remember. It was 'Dragon-chain of Ten Galloping Horses' that really caught her fancy. She was still working it out, when she heard someone come into the courtyard and call out:

'Landscape!'

But to know who this visitor was, you must turn to the next chapter.

CHAPTER 88

Bao-yu gratifies his grandmother
by praising a fatherless child
Cousin Zhen rectifies family discipline
by chastising two unruly servants

Xi-chun was puzzling over her Go Handbook when she heard someone calling outside:

'Landscape!'

She recognized the voice as Faithful's. Landscape went out into the courtyard, and reappeared with Faithful, followed by a younger maid carrying a small parcel wrapped in yellow silk.

'What's that?' asked Xi-chun, her curiosity aroused. Faithful explained.

'Next year is Her Old Ladyship's eighty-first birthday, and since eighty-one is nine times nine, she has pledged herself to hold a nine-day mass, and to have three thousand six hundred and fifty-one copies made of the *Sutra of the Immaculate Diamond*. That has all been handed out to copyists. But there is a popular saying: "If the *Diamond Sutra* is the outer shell of the magic, its core is the *Sutra of the Heart of Wisdom*." In other words, to enhance one's merit, one should slip in a *Heart Sutra* too. So now Her Old Ladyship wants copies of that as well, and because of its greater importance as scripture and its connection with Our Lady of Mercy, she wants three hundred and sixty-five copies to be done by the young ladies and young mistresses of the family. Apart from Mrs Lian, who's too busy running the household, and can't write anyway, all the ladies that can write at all are being given a share in this act of piety and devotion, even Mrs Zhen and Mr Zhen's other ladies in the Eastern Mansion. Of course, everyone in the inner family will be expected to take part.'

Xi-chun nodded.

'Sutra-copying is one thing I can do with conviction. Leave it there, will you? Would you like some tea?' Faithful deposited the little package on the table, and sat down with Xi-chun, while Landscape poured her a cup of tea.

'Will you be doing some copying too?' asked Xi-chun with a smile.

'Don't tease, Miss!' answered Faithful. 'Three or four years ago I might have, perhaps. But I'm so out of practice now. When did you last see me with a brush in my hand?'

'But think of the merit you'd acquire.'

'I've already seen to that,' replied Faithful. 'Every day, after settling Her Old Ladyship down to sleep, I've been saying Lord Buddha's name and counting my "Buddha Rice". I've been collecting the rice-grains for more than three years and putting them by for just such an occasion as this, to dedicate them to Buddha and add my contribution, my little act of charity and devotion, to Her Old Ladyship's.'

'It sounds as if when Lady Jia becomes Our Lady of Mercy,' said Xi-chun, 'you'll have to be her inseparable companion, the Dragon King's daughter!'

'Oh no, Miss!' protested Faithful. 'That's too grand for me. It is true though, I could never serve anyone but Her Old Ladyship. I must be bound to her by some karma from a past life.'

With these words Faithful rose to leave, bidding the younger maid untie the little parcel, and exhibiting its contents to Xi-chun.

'This roll of plain paper is to be used for the sutra. And while you write,' she went on, handing her a bundle of Tibetan incense-sticks, 'you are to light one of these.'

Xi-chun nodded, and Faithful returned with the other maid to Grandmother Jia's apartment, where she reported on her errand and stood watching the game of backgammon that was in progress between the old lady and Li Wan. Li Wan with her next throw removed several of Grandmother Jia's pins to the bar, and Faithful had difficulty in keeping a straight face.

They were presently distracted from their game by the arrival of Bao-yu, carrying in each hand a little bamboo-splint cage containing crickets.

'I heard you weren't sleeping very well, Grannie,' he said, 'so I brought you these to help you relax.'

Grandmother Jia laughed.

'You naughty boy! Just because your father's not at home...'

When he protested his innocence, Grandmother Jia asked:

'Why aren't you at school then? What are you up to with those things anyway?'

'They weren't my idea, Grannie,' explained Bao-yu. 'What happened was that a day or two ago Huan and Lan each had a couplet to complete in class, and as Huan got stuck, I whispered something to help him out. When he recited it, the Preceptor was impressed and praised him highly for it. Huan bought me the crickets as a thank-you present. I should like to give them to you.'

'Hasn't that boy been doing any work, for heaven's sake!' exclaimed Grandmother Jia. 'Surely he can manage a couplet on his own? If not, then he deserves a good spanking from the Preceptor. It might teach him a thing or two. As for you, have you forgotten the state you got into when your father was at home and asked you for a few lines of verse? Don't you go getting too full of yourself now. What a little rascal that Huan is! To go begging for help, and then look around for a nice present to butter you up with! He certainly seems precocious enough when it comes to cheating – he should be ashamed of himself! Heaven alone knows how he'll turn out when he grows up...'

A ripple of laughter spread through the room.

'But tell me about young Lan,' went on Grandmother Jia. 'How did he manage? As the youngest, strictly speaking he should have been helped by Huan . . .'

Bao-yu detected the note of sarcasm in her voice and laughed.

'Oh no! He didn't need any help. He could manage on his own.'

'I don't believe you!' said Grandmother Jia. 'It was you at your tricks again, I'll be bound. Hark at you! A camel among sheep! Just because you're so grown-up now, and so good at your compositions . . .'

Bao-yu smiled.

'No, seriously, Lan managed perfectly well on his own. The Preceptor was very pleased and said he had a brilliant future ahead of him. If you don't believe me, Grannie, send for him and test him yourself.'

'If that *is* the truth,' said Grandmother Jia, 'then I am overjoyed to hear it. But I have a feeling that you are making it all up. If he really can do such things at his age, he may well distinguish himself when he grows up.'

She looked at Li Wan, and thought of Lan's father Jia Zhu.

'What a consolation that would be for your elder brother's death,' she went on, addressing Bao-yu again. 'And what a well-earned reward for all his mother's efforts in bringing him up! In time he will be a pillar of support to the family, as his father would have been!'

The thought brought tears to her eyes. Li Wan was also moved, but seeing the old lady becoming somewhat emotional, she checked her own tears and said with a brave smile:

'Whatever good fortune we may enjoy, Grannie, we owe it all to you. I only pray that Lan will live up to your expectations and bring fortune to the whole family. His progress should be a source of joy. Please don't go upsetting yourself.'

She turned to Bao-yu.

'And please don't you go giving him exaggerated ideas of his achievements, Bao. He is only a child, remember. He may take you seriously and not realize that you are only trying to encourage him; and then he will become proud and conceited and *never* do well.'

'Well said, my dear,' commented Grandmother Jia. 'But remember too that he is still very young and should not be driven too hard. Children only have a certain amount of strength. Push them too soon and you can ruin them. Then they may never be able to study properly, and all your efforts will have been in vain.'

Li Wan could contain herself no longer and burst into floods of tears. As she was hurriedly drying her eyes, Jia Huan and Jia Lan came into the room to pay their evening respects to Grandmother Jia. Lan then greeted his mother and returned to stand respectfully at his great-grandmother's side.

'I have just been hearing from your uncle Bao,' said Grandmother Jia, 'how well you did with your couplet, and what praises you won from the Preceptor.'

Lan smiled modestly. Faithful now came over to say that dinner was ready.

'I want to invite Mrs Xue,' said Grandmother Jia, and Amber promptly sent a maid over to Lady Wang's apartment. Bao-yu and Jia Huan withdrew from the room, while Li Wan's maid Candida and the younger maids came forward to clear away the backgammon pieces. Li Wan stayed to wait on Grandmother Jia, and Jia Lan stood at his mother's side.

'The two of you can stay to dinner with me,' said Grandmother Jia.

'Yes Grandmother,' replied Li Wan. A minute or two later dinner was brought in, and the maid returned from Lady Wang's apartment with the following message:

'Her Ladyship says that Mrs Xue will not be able to come. She was only over on a short visit and went home after lunch.'

Grandmother Jia told Jia Lan to occupy the seat next to her. Our narrative omits any further details of that evening's meal. After dinner, when she had washed her hands and rinsed her mouth, Grandmother Jia reclined on her couch and chatted idly with her granddaughter-in-law and great-grandson. A junior maid came in and asked Amber to say that Mr Zhen (who, in the temporary absence of Jia Zheng and Jia Lian, had that day been supervising business at Rong-guo House) was waiting outside to pay his evening respects.

'Tell him that I have been informed,' said Grandmother Jia, 'but that he need not bother to come in. He can go home and rest. He must be tired after the day's work.'

The maid relayed this to the old women outside, Cousin Zhen was informed, and returned to Ning-guo House.

*

The following day he came over again to Rong-guo House, to see to the day's business. After the pages on the gate had produced a series of miscellaneous matters for his attention, it was reported by another page that the farm-bailiff had arrived with the seasonal produce. Cousin Zhen asked to see the inventory, which was presented to him by the page, and he proceeded to read through the various items, mostly fresh fruit, with some game and vegetables.

'Who usually looks after this department?' asked Cousin Zhen.

'Zhou Rui, sir.'

Zhou Rui was summoned and Cousin Zhen instructed him:

'Check through all the items on this list and have them delivered. Have a copy made for my reference. And tell the kitchen to cook some extra dishes when they are preparing lunch for the servants. The bailiff is to have something to eat before he goes, and the usual tip.'

'Yes sir.'

Zhou Rui told the servants to carry the goods into Xi-feng's courtyard, and gave instructions for them to be checked against the inventory. Then he went off, only to reappear shortly afterwards before Cousin Zhen:

'Excuse me sir, have you checked the entries yet?'

'Do you think I have time to do that?' replied Cousin Zhen impatiently. 'I have given you the list and leave the matter entirely in your hands.'

'I have checked all the items through to the best of my ability sir, and everything seems in order. But perhaps you would like to send for the bailiff, as you have a copy yourself, to make sure the list is genuine . . .'

'What a lot of fuss over a bit of fruit!' exclaimed Cousin Zhen. 'It's really not that important. I take your word for it.'

At this moment Bao Er came into the room and kotowed to Cousin Zhen. (This Bao Er, it may be remembered, was the servant who had in the past been useful to both Cousin Zhen and Jia Lian. On this occasion he had come over for the day to assist Cousin Zhen.)

'I beg to be released, sir,' he said, 'and put back on external duties.'

'What is the meaning of this?' asked Cousin Zhen, addressing Bao Er and Zhou Rui simultaneously.

'What's the point of my being here if no one listens to my opinion?' replied Bao Er.

'Who asked for your opinion?' said Cousin Zhen brusquely.

'I'm tired of spying for other people!' muttered Bao Er to himself.

'Sir,' put in Zhou Rui promptly, 'I have been in charge of farm rents and income here for years, and on average I should say around four hundred thousand taels' worth passes through my hands each year, and I have never had a word of complaint from the Master or their Ladyships or the young mistresses about anything, let alone such a small matter as this. According to him, we are supposed to have made off with the family's entire property and estates!'

'It looks as if Bao Er has started some sort of quarrel,' thought Cousin Zhen to himself. 'Better get rid of him.'

'Out of my sight!' he barked. Then turning from Bao Er to Zhou Rui:

'That is all. Carry on with your work.'

The two servants left.

Not long afterwards Cousin Zhen was resting in the study when he heard the most terrific din break out in the direction of the main gate. He sent a servant to inquire, who came back to report that a fight had started between Bao Er and an adopted son of Zhou Rui's.

'Who is this adopted son?' asked Cousin Zhen.

'He San is his name, sir,' replied the servant. 'A worthless fellow who spends most of his time drinking and causing trouble. He sometimes comes round here and hangs about in the porter's lodge. Apparently he got involved in the argument between Bao Er and Zhou Rui.'

'This is the limit!' exclaimed Cousin Zhen. 'Have Bao Er and this He San character bound immediately! What about Zhou Rui?'

'He disappeared when the fighting started, sir.'

'Find him at once! This is preposterous!'

'Yes, sir!'

In the midst of this commotion, Jia Lian returned and Cousin Zhen told him what had happened in his absence.

'What next!' cried Lian. He sent an extra servant to help apprehend Zhou Rui, who soon realized that escape was impossible, gave himself up and was led before the masters.

'Tie him up as well!' ordered Cousin Zhen, and Jia Lian added, addressing himself principally to Zhou Rui:

'Mr Zhen settled your petty differences once and for all. Why go out and start fighting all over again? And as if that wasn't bad enough, you have to drag in this brat of yours, He San! And when you should have been bringing them to heel, you disappear and leave them to it!'

He dealt Zhou Rui a few hefty kicks.

'It's no good punishing only him,' said Cousin Zhen

grimly, and ordered his men to give Bao Er and He San fifty lashes each and send them packing. This done, he and Jia Lian sat down to discuss family business.

In the servants' quarters this incident became the subject of many a private exchange of opinions. Some saw it as an attempt on Cousin Zhen's part to cover up for incompetence; others said he was just inept at handling people; while others saw it as yet another instance of his unpleasant character. 'Wasn't it he who recommended Bao Er to Mr Lian in that sordid business with the You sisters? What's probably happened is that Bao Er's wife won't oblige Mr Zhen as she did Mr Lian, so now he's taken it out on the husband...' There were many differing interpretations.

Meanwhile the Jia clan lost no time in turning Jia Zheng's promotion at the Ministry of Works to their financial advantage. Jia Yun was certainly not going to be left out, but went around promising work to contractors (and negotiating percentages for himself), and having bought a quantity of fashionable embroideries, made his way to the apartment of his erstwhile patroness.

Xi-feng, who had just learnt from one of her maids that 'Mr Zhen and Mr Lian were in a temper and beating the servants', was on the point of sending someone to discover the details when she saw Jia Lian himself walk in, and was able to hear the full story from him.

'It may all have been over a trifle,' she commented, 'but we must put a stop to such behaviour at all costs. If they think they can get away with it now, when the family fortunes are supposed to be flourishing, what is going to happen when the younger generation takes over? They'll have a mutiny on their hands. I remember a year or so ago witnessing the most appalling scene at Ning-guo House – Big Jiao sprawled all over the steps, blind drunk and swearing sixteen to the dozen. None of us was spared. I don't care if he has rendered distinguished services in the past. Servants should know their place, and show a proper sense of respect. The trouble with Cousin Zhen's wife – please don't misunderstand me – is that she is much too unsuspecting and lets her staff get away with anything. This Bao Er of theirs – or whatever his name is – is typical. Come to think of it, hasn't he been rather useful to you and Zhen in the past? Aren't you being a bit ungrateful to start flogging him now?'

Stung to the quick, Jia Lian sheepishly tried to change the subject. Presently he remembered a pressing engagement and left.

Crimson now came in to report the arrival of Jia Yun.

'I wonder what he's after this time?' mused Xi-feng to herself. Then aloud to Crimson:

'You'd better show him in.'

Crimson went out. She looked Jia Yun in the face and gave him a cheeky smile. He (swift on the uptake as ever) advanced towards her and said:

'Did you tell Mrs Lian that I was here, Miss Crimson?'

She blushed.

'I suppose you have a lot of important business, Mr Yun . . .'

'On the contrary, I only wish I had had cause to come here and trouble you more often, Miss Crimson . . . I remember last year when you were employed at Uncle Bao's . . .'

He was about to say more but Crimson, who was afraid someone might interrupt them, asked in haste:

'Did you ever get my handkerchief?'

Her words provoked Jia Yun to such a pitch of excitement that he was ready to burst. But before he could say a word a maid came out from Xi-feng's room, and he and Crimson were obliged to go in together at once. They walked side by side, close enough for him to whisper:

'When I leave, be sure to see me out. I've something to tell you that might amuse you . . .'

She blushed fiercely and flashed her eyes at him without

a word. Going ahead to inform Xi-feng of his approach, she returned to usher him in, lifting the door-curtain and beckoning to him, while announcing in her most formal tone of voice:

'Madam will be pleased to see you now, sir.'

With a smile Jia Yun advanced with her into the room and greeted Xi-feng. He conveyed his mother's regards, which Xi-feng returned politely before asking:

'And what brings you here today?'

Jia Yun embarked upon his speech:

'Auntie's great kindness to me in the past has been ever present in my mind and a source of endless gratification. I have been awaiting an opportunity to present a token of my esteem and have only held back for fear that you might consider such a gesture inappropriate. The forthcoming Double Ninth Festival finally seemed sufficient justification for my purchasing a little something which, though I know you have more than enough of everything here already, I humbly pray you to do me the honour of accepting as an earnest of my humble devotion.'

Xi-feng laughed.

'Come on. Cut the cackle. What's it all about? Sit down and tell me.'

Jia Yun took a perch and deposited his offering gingerly with both hands on the surface of an adjacent table.

'I know you're pretty hard up,' Xi-feng went on, 'so why go spending money like this? I have no need of such things and don't expect them. Come on now, tell me what you have really come for.'

'Truly for no other reason than my deep and hitherto unexpressed sense of gratitude . . .'

There was however by now a trace of a smile.

'Come off it,' said Xi-feng. 'I am perfectly familiar with the state of your finances. Don't expect me to go taking things from you for nothing. If you want me to accept your present then tell me the truth. If you carry on beating about the bush like this, I shall certainly not accept anything from you.'

Jia Yun was forced to come to the point. He rose to his feet and donned his most obsequious smile.

'I did entertain one modest and I trust not altogether unreasonable hope. It reached my ears a few days ago that Sir Zheng had been given the overall supervision of mausoleum construction at the Ministry, and as I have one or two friends with considerable experience in that line – extremely competent people, I might add – I would just like to ask if it would be at all possible for you to put in a word for them with Sir Zheng. If a job or two were to come their way I should be indebted to you for eternity. And need I add that my own services are always at your disposal should anything materialize in the way of work here at the mansion.'

'In most matters I know I have a certain amount of influence,' replied Xi-feng. 'But when it comes to this sort of thing, the major contracts are completely in the pockets of the President and other senior officials, while the smaller jobs are handed out by the clerks and runners. No one else gets so much as a look in, I'm afraid. Our own people can only work for Sir Zheng as his personal staff. Even your uncle Lian only goes in when there's something directly connected with the family. He has nothing to do with official business. At home, as soon as things are patched up in one place they break out in another – even Mr Zhen can't keep order properly. A junior like you would never be able to cope. No, I'm afraid whatever jobs there might have been at the Ministry have nearly all gone. People are desperate for work. Surely there's something you can turn your hand to at home, to keep body and soul together? I'm being serious. Go home and think it over. As for your gratitude, consider it expressed. And take these things back to wherever they came from.'

While she was speaking, a group of nannies had come into the room with little Qiao-jie, dressed in a colourfully embroidered smock and clutching an armful of toys. She went running over to her mother, laughing and prattling away, and Jia Yun stood up once more and swiftly transferred his attentions and unctuous smiles from Xi-feng to her daughter.

'So this is my respected cousin? Now is there any little present you would like me to get you, dearie?'

A loud *Waaah!* burst from Qiao-jie's lips and Jia Yun retreated hastily.

'There, there, my darling! Come here!' Xi-feng held the child closely to her. 'This is your cousin Yun. Don't be shy.'

Jia Yun tried again.

'What a sweet little girl! Such a pretty face promises a lifetime of happiness.'

Qiao-jie turned her little head to take another peep at him and immediately burst out crying again. Jia Yun sensed that he was no longer welcome and rose to leave.

'Don't forget your things,' insisted Xi-feng.

'Oh please, Aunt Feng! Do me this one favour...'

'If you don't take them yourself, I shall send someone after you with them. Honestly Yun, this is not the way to go about things. You are not a stranger here. If something crops up I will certainly let you know. Until then there is nothing I can do, and there is nothing to be gained by wasting your time and money like this.'

Jia Yun could see that she was not going to relent. His face flushed as he took his leave.

'I shall nevertheless continue to search for an acceptable present.'

'Crimson, carry these things to the hall for Mr Yun,' said Xi-feng curtly, 'and see him out.'

'People are right,' thought Yun to himself on his way out. 'She's a real tyrant! Won't budge an inch! Hard as nails! Serves her right if she can't produce an heir. That little girl of hers gave me a queer feeling too... She seemed to take against me, almost as if we had some feud from a past life. What damnable luck! All that work for nothing!'

His rebuff came as a disappointment to Crimson too,

who picked up the parcel and followed him out. He took it from her and, when no one was looking, undid the wrapping, took out a couple of pieces of embroidery and gave them to her. At first she would not accept them and protested under her breath:

'You shouldn't, Mr Yun. Think how dreadful it would look for both of us if Mrs Lian found out.'

'Don't be silly. Keep them. She'll never know. If you don't, I'll take it as a personal insult.'

Crimson smiled vainly and took them from him.

'If you insist. But I don't want them. I really don't know *what* to think . . .'

Her face was burning again. Jia Yun laughed, and said:

'It's the thought that counts . . .'

By now they had reached the inner gate and Jia Yun concealed the remaining gifts inside his gown while Crimson urged him on his way.

'You must go now,' she said. 'If ever you want anything here, contact me. Now that I'm in service with Mrs Lian, you can approach me directly.'

Yun shook his head bitterly.

'She's too much of a tyrant. I shan't be coming back in a hurry. Don't forget what I said just now though. If I do have a chance to see you again, I've more to tell you.'

Crimson blushed from ear to ear.

'You'd really better go now. Come again as often as you like. If you've become distant from Mrs Lian, you've only yourself to blame.

'All right, I understand.'

Jia Yun went on his way and Crimson stood in the gateway, following him into the distance with a thoughtful gaze. Then she turned and went inside again.

Xi-feng meanwhile was giving instructions for her dinner, and asked the maids if they had cooked her congee. They hurried off to inquire, and returned after a short while to report that the congee was ready.

'I should like a couple of dishes of those pickled vegetables that have just come up from the South, to go with it,' Xi-feng said. Autumn took charge of this and detailed the other maids to proceed with service. Patience came in and said with a smile:

'There's something I forgot to mention earlier, ma'am. At midday, while you were over at Her Old Ladyship's, one of the prioress's women from Water-moon Priory came to see you, to ask for a couple of jars of southern pickle and for an advance of a few months' allowance. The prioress has been in poor health, she told me. I asked what the matter was, and she said it had all started four or five days ago. She had been having trouble with some of the Buddhist and Taoist novices at the Priory, who despite several warnings kept leaving their lights on at night. Then one night she noticed the lamps still burning at midnight, and called to them several times. Hearing no reply and thinking that they must have fallen asleep with their lights on, she went herself to put them out. When she came back to her room, the strangest thing happened: she saw a man and a woman sitting together on the kang, and when she asked them who they were, had a noose slipped round her neck by way of reply. Her cries for help aroused the other sisters, who lit their lamps and came hurrying to the scene to find her prostrate on the floor and foaming at the mouth. Thank heavens they managed to bring her round. She still cannot eat proper meals, which is why she thought of asking for some pickles. Since you were not in, I felt I could hardly give her any on my own authority, so I explained where you were, said that I would mention it to you later, and sent her back to the Priory. I should have forgotten all about it if I hadn't heard you asking for pickles just now yourself.'

Xi-feng stared thoughtfully for a moment.

'There's no shortage of pickles,' she said at last. 'Send her some by all means. You can see Mr Qin in a day or two about the money.'

As she was speaking, Crimson came in to report the

arrival of a messenger from Jia Lian. Business had detained him out of town, and he would not be back that night. This had received a perfunctory acknowledgement from Xi-feng, when suddenly there was a burst of crying from the back of the house and one of the junior maids came running breathlessly into the courtyard. Patience was already there and now several of the other maids gathered round and began whispering among themselves.

'What's going on out there?' asked Xi-feng.

'One of the maids has had a bit of a fright,' replied Patience. 'She says she's seen a ghost or something...'

'Which maid?' asked Xi-feng sharply. The maid in question entered the room.

'What's all this nonsense about ghosts?' asked Xi-feng.

'I was out at the back just now, ma'am,' replied the maid, 'asking one of the women for more charcoal to put on the braziers, when I heard this eerie noise coming from that small empty building. At first I thought it was just a cat chasing a mouse, but then I heard it go *whee* like somebody sighing. I was very frightened and came running back.'

'Stupid creature!' snapped Xi-feng. 'I won't have people talking such superstitious nonsense in my presence! I've never believed in such things. Go on – get out of my sight!'

The maid fled. Xi-feng sent for Sunshine and checked through the day's remaining accounts. It was nearly nine o'clock by the time they finished. She and the others sat for a while chatting, and then she sent the servants off duty for the night and went to bed herself. Just before eleven o'clock she was lying in bed still half-asleep, when suddenly her flesh begin to creep and she awoke with a start. She lay there trembling in ever-increasing terror until she could bear it no longer, and called Patience and Autumn to come over and keep her company. Neither of them could understand the strange state she was in.

Autumn had originally been rather hostile to Xi-feng,

but she had fallen from favour with Jia Lian because of the part she played in the persecution of You Er-jie and had subsequently been drawn into Xi-feng's camp, though her loyalty remained a matter of convenience and did not compare with the devotion of Patience. On this occasion, seeing her mistress in such a troubled state, she stood dutifully by the bedside and served her with tea. Xi-feng took a sip and said:

'Thank you. You can go back to sleep now. I shall be quite all right with Patience here.'

But Autumn was eager to please, and protested:

'Surely ma'am, if you can't get to sleep, it would be best if we took it in turns to sit up with you?'

Xi-feng had already dozed off. The maids heard a distant cockcrow and, seeing that Xi-feng was now fast asleep, both lay down fully dressed until daybreak, when they rose and busily began making preparations for her morning toilet. When she awoke, Xi-feng's mind was still haunted by the terrors of the night. Despite her shaky state, her habitual determination to keep going at all costs prevailed, and with a great effort she struggled up. She was sitting rapt in thought when she heard a maid in the courtyard calling:

'Is Patience in?'

Patience called out in reply, and the maid lifted the door-curtain and came in. It turned out that she had been sent by Lady Wang to summon Jia Lian.

'There's a messenger from the yamen on urgent business,' she said, 'and as the Master has just gone out, Her Ladyship sent me to ask for Mr Lian to come over.'

Xi-feng caught her breath in alarm. To ascertain the nature of this urgent business, please turn to the next chapter.

CHAPTER 89

Our hero sees the handiwork of a departed love,
and is moved to write an ode
Frowner falls prey to hysterical fear
and resolves to starve to death

We have seen in the last chapter how Xi-feng forced herself to get up, and was sitting brooding in her apartment, when suddenly a maid arrived with news of some fresh crisis.

'What has happened?' she asked in alarm.

'I don't know, ma'am,' replied the maid. 'A messenger has come from the Ministry for the Master. One of the pages on the inner gate reported to Her Ladyship, and Her Ladyship sent me here to ask for Mr Lian.'

Xi-feng became slightly calmer when she realized that it was only a Ministry affair.

'Will you tell Her Ladyship,' she said, 'that Mr Lian was away last night on business and has not yet returned. She had better send round for Mr Zhen at the other mansion.'

'Yes ma'am.' The maid departed.

Presently Cousin Zhen came over to Rong-guo House to receive the messenger from the Ministry. Having ascertained the facts, he went in to report to Lady Wang.

'The messenger says that yesterday the President of the Yellow River Conservancy Board presented a memorial, describing the bursting of dykes throughout Honan Province and the flooding of several prefectures, departments and districts. They are allocating funds for reconstruction of city walls. This is going to mean a lot of extra administrative work for the senior officials at the Ministry, and they wished to inform Sir Zheng at once.'

Having said this, Cousin Zhen withdrew. Jia Zheng was informed directly upon his return, and for most of the winter he was kept very busy and spent nearly all of his time at the Ministry. Although for Bao-yu this meant a period of less intensive studying, fear of being detected by his father still caused him to keep up his attendance at school, and inhibited him from spending much time with Dai-yu.

One morning in the middle of the tenth month, Bao-yu rose and prepared to set off as usual for school. The weather had suddenly turned chilly, and he saw Aroma come in with a bundle of winter clothes.

'It's very cold today,' she said. 'You'll need to wrap up well.'

She chose a garment for him to wear and wrapped up another, which she entrusted to one of the younger maids. The maid went out and gave it to Tealeaf, saying:

'As it's so cold today, you are to have this ready in case Master Bao wants to change.'

Tealeaf acknowledged these instructions, and followed Bao-yu to school with the felt-wrapped bundle in his arms.

On arrival, Bao-yu sat down to work. He was soon distracted from his books by the sound of the paper casements vibrating in the wind.

'The weather seems to have taken a turn for the worse,' observed the Preceptor, opening a touch-hole in one of the windows and looking out. A great bank of dark clouds in the north-west was surging steadily across the sky. Tealeaf came into the classroom.

'It's getting colder, Master Bao. You had better put something warmer on.'

Bao-yu nodded, and Tealeaf walked across the room. The sight of the garment he was carrying had a most curious effect on Bao-yu, who gazed at it as if in a trance. The other boys watched with fascination.

'Why did you have to bring this?' asked Bao-yu. 'Who gave it to you?'

He had recognized it at once as the Peacock Gold snow-cape, the one that Skybright had so bravely mended for him during her last illness.

'The maids wrapped it up and told me to bring it,' replied Tealeaf.

'Well, I'm not feeling particularly cold,' said Bao-yu. 'I don't think I'll wear it just now. You may as well wrap it up again.'

The Preceptor supposed that Bao-yu was reluctant to spoil so fine a garment, and noted with gratification this evidence of thrift.

'Please put it on, Master Bao!' pleaded Tealeaf. 'For my sake! You know I'll get the blame if you catch a cold.'

With extreme reluctance Bao-yu put it on, sat down again and stared glumly at his books. The Preceptor presumed that he was concentrating once more on his studies and gave the incident no further thought.

That afternoon, when the day's lessons were over, Bao-yu said that he felt unwell and asked to be excused from school the next day. Dai-ru had, of late, come to view his students in a more lenient light, more as companions with whom to while away his old age. His own health was poor, and he was glad to lessen his burden of work by the judicious dispensation of sick-leave. Besides, he knew that Sir Zheng had more important matters on his mind, and that Grandmother Jia always indulged her favourite grandson. With a nod he indicated to Bao-yu that his request was granted.

Bao-yu went straight home. After calling briefly on his mother and grandmother, neither of whom questioned his plea of illness, he returned to the Garden. He was not at all his usual smiling talkative self, in fact he hardly said a word to Aroma and the others, but lay down dressed as he was on the kang.

'Dinner's ready,' said Aroma. 'Do you want it now, or will you wait till later?'

Bao-yu: 'I won't have anything to eat. I'm not feeling well. You just have yours.'

Aroma: 'Well, you might at least take off that lovely cape. You'll crumple it and ruin it.'

Bao-yu: 'I want to keep it on.'

Aroma: 'It's not just the cape that I'm worried about. Look how carefully it's been darned. You'll spoil the stitching.'

This touched Bao-yu to the quick. He heaved a deep sigh.

'Oh all right! Put it away then. Wrap it up carefully. I shall never wear it again.'

He stood up to take it off. Aroma came over to take it from him, but he had already begun to fold it himself.

'Why are you being so industrious today?' she asked in surprise.

He made no reply but went on folding.

'Where's the wrapper?' he asked when he had finished.

Musk handed it to him, and as he carefully wrapped the cape, she turned to give Aroma a wink. Bao-yu took no notice of them but sat down, looking thoroughly dejected. The clock on the shelf chimed, and he glanced down at his watch. It was already half-past five. Shortly afterwards a junior maid came in to light the lamps.

'If you won't have a proper meal, at least have a little hot congee,' pleaded Aroma. 'If you go to bed on an empty stomach you could easily catch a fever. And then think of all the trouble we'll have.'

He shook his head.

'I'm not hungry. I'd only feel worse if I tried to force something down.'

'Well in that case,' said Aroma, 'you should at least have an early night.'

She and Musk made his bed and Bao-yu lay down. He tossed and turned, but found it quite impossible to get to sleep. Finally, just before dawn, he dozed off, only to awake again half an hour later. Aroma and Musk were already up and about.

'I heard you tossing and turning till the early hours,' said

Aroma. 'I didn't dare disturb you. Then I fell asleep myself. Did you manage to sleep in the end?'

'A bit. But I woke up again almost at once.'

'Have you got a pain anywhere?'

'No. I just feel depressed.'

'Will you be going to school today?'

'No. I asked for the day off yesterday. I thought I might go for a walk in the Garden to try and throw off this depression. But I think it will be too cold. Will you tell them to clear a room for me and put an incense burner and my writing things in it? I won't need you today. I just want to sit quietly on my own for a while. Tell the others I don't want to be disturbed.'

'Of course no one will disturb you if you want to study quietly,' said Musk as soon as she heard this.

'I think it's an excellent idea,' said Aroma. 'You will be able to keep warm, and a day of studying on your own will help you to feel more settled.' She added: 'But please, if you don't feel like eating a proper meal, have *something*. What would you like? Tell me now, and I can get them to prepare it in the kitchen.'

'Whatever's easiest,' replied Bao-yu. 'Don't go to a lot of fuss. It would be nice to have some fruit in the room, for the scent.'

'Which room would you prefer?' asked Aroma. 'They are all rather cluttered, except Skybright's old room, which has been empty for quite a while. That might be a bit cold and lonely though.'

'That doesn't matter,' said Bao-yu. 'Have the charcoal brazier moved in there.'

Aroma gave instructions for this to be done, and as she was speaking a maid came in carrying a tray with a bowl and a pair of ivory chopsticks, which she handed to Musk, saying:

'Here's the soup Miss Hua ordered from the kitchen.'

Musk took the tray and saw that the bowl contained Bird's Nest Soup.

'Is this what you ordered?' she asked Aroma.

'Yes,' replied Aroma with a smile. 'I thought that as Master Bao had nothing to eat last night and as he spent most of the night tossing in bed, he'd feel rather empty this morning, so I sent the younger maids to order this specially from the kitchen.'

She told the maid to bring up a table, and Musk served Bao-yu with the soup. When he had drunk it and rinsed his mouth, Ripple came in:

'The room's ready,' she said. 'We're waiting for the fire to get going properly and the air to clear, and then you can go in, Master Bao.'

He nodded, but was too lost in thought to reply. Shortly afterwards a maid came in to report that his writing things had been laid out. She received a perfunctory acknowledgement from Bao-yu and was immediately followed by another maid, who announced that breakfast was ready and asked where he wanted it served.

'Oh, just bring it in here,' said Bao-yu. 'There's no need to make all this fuss.'

The maid went out and returned with his breakfast. Bao-yu laughed and turning to Musk and Aroma said:

'I feel so depressed. I honestly don't think I could manage this on my own. Why don't you two join me? That might make the food taste sweeter, and then perhaps I might be able to eat more of it...'

Musk smiled.

'That's just a whim of yours, Master Bao. You know it wouldn't be right for us to eat with you.'

'I don't agree,' said Aroma. 'We've often drunk wine together in the past. I think it can be allowed as an exception, to cheer him up. Though of course as a regular practice it would be quite out of the question.'

So the three of them sat down, Bao-yu at the head and the two maids at either side of the table. After breakfast, one of the junior maids brought in the 'rinsing' tea, and Musk and Aroma supervised the clearing of the table. The tea was served and Bao-yu sat in gloomy silence again.

'Is the room ready yet?' he asked eventually.

'Ripple came in earlier on to tell you,' said Musk. 'What a silly question!'

After sitting there a moment longer, he made his way over to Skybright's old room. Having lit a stick of incense and arranged the fruit on the table, he dismissed all the maids and closed the door. Aroma and the others stood outside with bated breath.

He selected a length of pink paper with a gold-splash on it and flower patterns in the corners, said a short prayer, raised his brush and began to write:

FROM
GREEN BOY
TO
SISTER SKYBRIGHT
MAY THIS ODE
OFFERED
WITH
LIBATION OF TEA
AND
BURNING OF PRECIOUS INCENSE
FIND
ACCEPTANCE
IN YOUR SIGHT

O Sweetest and most
Inseparable friend!
Alas! that in so cruel a storm
Your life should end!
Your voice is gone, its tender
Music none can learn.
Forever eastward flows the stream,
Never to return.
Though dreams may never show
Your face to me again,
I see the Peacock Cape and feel
A haunting pain.

When he had finished writing, Bao-yu took a burning joss-stick, held the paper to it and set the ode alight. He sat in silence until the bundle of incense-sticks had burned to the end, then opened the door and walked out.

'Why are you coming out again so soon?' inquired Aroma. 'Are you feeling low again?'

He feigned a laugh.

'I was rather depressed earlier on. I needed to be on my own for a bit in a quiet place. I feel better now. I think I shall take a stroll.'

He walked straight out into the Garden. When he reached the Naiad's House, he called from the courtyard:

'Is Cousin Lin at home?'

'Who's that?' replied Nightingale.

She raised the door-curtain and saw him standing there.

'Oh it's you, Master Bao,' she said with a smile. 'Miss Lin is inside. Please come in and sit down.'

As Bao-yu went in with her, Dai-yu's voice could be heard from the inner room:

'Nightingale, please ask Master Bao to come in and wait a moment.'

Bao-yu, walking towards the inner room, stopped to admire the pair of calligraphic scrolls that hung one on either side of the doorway. The calligraphy looked recent and had been done on strips of dark purple paper, splashed with gold and decorated with a pattern of clouds and dragons. The two lines ran:

> Through casement green the moon shines brightly still;
> In bamboo chronicles the ancients are but empty words.

Bao-yu read them with an appreciative smile and passed through into the inner room.

'What are you doing, coz?' he inquired with a smile.

Dai-yu stood up, took a couple of steps towards him, smiled and said:

'Please sit down. I'm copying out part of this sutra. I

only have two lines left to do. I'll just finish and then we can sit and chat.'

She told Snowgoose to pour him some tea.

'Please carry on writing,' said Bao-yu. 'Don't take any notice of me.'

His attention had been caught by a painting hanging on the centre wall of the room. It was a vertical scroll showing Chang E, the Moon Goddess, with one of her attendants, and another fairy, also with an attendant who was carrying what seemed to be a long bag containing clothes. Apart from the clouds that surrounded the figures, there were no background details of any kind. The linear style of the picture was reminiscent of the Song master Li Long-mian. It bore the title 'The Contest in the Cold', written in the antique *ba-fen* style.

'Have you hung this picture of the Contest in the Cold here recently, coz?' asked Bao-yu.

'Yes. I remembered it yesterday while they were tidying the room, and so I brought it out and told them to hang it up.'

'What's the allusion in the title?'

Dai-yu laughed.

'Surely you know! It's such a well-known poem . . .'

'I can't quite recall it at present,' confessed Bao-yu, smiling rather sheepishly. 'Please tell me.'

'Don't you remember Li Shang-yin's lines:

> Braving the cold,
> Fairy Frost and Lady Moon
> Parade their rival charms . . .'?

'Of course!' exclaimed Bao-yu. 'How exquisite! And what an unusual subject! This is the perfect time of year to have it up too.'

He continued to amble round the room, inspecting it in a leisurely fashion, and Snowgoose brought him a cup of tea. He drank his tea, and in a few minutes Dai-yu finished the section of the sutra she was copying, and stood up.

'Forgive me,' she said.

'You know you don't have to stand on ceremony with me,' he replied with a smile.

He observed that she was wearing a little pale blue fur-lined dress embroidered with flowers, and an ermine-lined sleeveless jacket, while her hair was coiled up in her every-day style and had no flowers in it but only a flat hairpin of purest gold. Her padded underskirt was pink, and embroidered with flowers. How graceful she seemed, as a jade tree leaning in the wind; how gentle, as a fragrant lotus whose petals are moist with dew!

'Have you been playing your Qin at all these last few days?' he inquired.

'Not for a day or two. This sutra-copying makes my hands too cold.'

'Maybe it's just as well,' said Bao-yu. 'I know the Qin is a fine thing in its way, but I can't see that it does any real good. I have never heard of it bringing prosperity or long life; it only seems to cause sorrow and distress. And it must be such a labour to memorize those tablatures. I think, coz, that with your delicate constitution you should avoid anything so strenuous.'

Dai-yu smiled somewhat scornfully.

'Is that the Qin you play?' Bao-yu went on, pointing to one hanging on the wall. 'Isn't it rather short?'

'Not really,' explained Dai-yu. 'When I was a little girl and first started learning, I couldn't reach on an ordinary Qin, so we had this one specially made. It's not a collector's piece of course, made with wood 'saved from the flames' – but it has a Crane Fairy and a Phoenix Tail, and the Dragon's Pool sound-hole and Goose Foot tuning-pegs are all in the correct proportions. And look at the crackling on the varnish. Doesn't that look just like Cow Hair crackle to you? The fine workmanship gives it a beautiful tone.'

'Have you been writing any poetry recently, coz?' Bao-yu went on to inquire.

'Not much, not since the last meeting of the club.'

He laughed. 'You can't fool me. I heard you chanting. How did it go now?

> Why grieve to watch
> The wheel of Karma turn?
> A moonlike purity remains
> My constant goal . . .

I found your setting very striking. You did write it didn't you?'

Dai-yu: 'How did you come to hear it?'

Bao-yu: 'I heard you playing when I was walking back from Smartweed Loggia a few days ago. The music was so lovely and I didn't want to interrupt you, so I just listened quietly for a while and then went on my way. There is one thing I've been meaning to ask you. I noticed that in the first part you use a level-tone rhyme, but suddenly change to an oblique tone at the end. Why is that?'

Dai-yu: 'That is free composition. One doesn't have to abide by any rules. One just goes wherever the inspiration takes one.'

Bao-yu: 'I see! I'm afraid such subtleties were lost on my untrained ears.'

Dai-yu: 'True lovers of music have always been few.'

Bao-yu realized that without meaning to he had said the wrong thing, and was afraid that he had alienated Dai-yu. He sat there for a while. There was so much he wanted to say, but he was now too nervous to open his mouth again. Dai-yu had also spoken without thinking, and on reflection she wished that she had not been so scathing, and withdrew silently into her shell. Her silence only increased Bao-yu's own misgivings, and finally in some embarrassment he stood up and said:

'I must be on my way to see Tan. Please don't get up.'

'Give her my regards when you see her, will you?' said Dai-yu.

'I will,' he replied, and departed. Dai-yu saw him to the door, then returned to her chair and sat brooding to herself.

'Bao-yu's been so odd recently. He doesn't seem to say what he's thinking. He's friendly one minute and distant the next. I wonder what it means?'

Nightingale came in.

'Have you finished copying for today, Miss? Shall I put your writing things away now?'

'I shan't be doing any more,' replied Dai-yu. 'You can clear them away.'

Dai-yu went into the inner room and lay down on her bed, slowly turning all these things over in her mind. Nightingale came in to ask if she would like some tea.

'No, thank you. I just want to be alone and lie down for a bit.'

'Very well, Miss.'

Nightingale went out, to find Snowgoose standing in the doorway, staring oddly in front of her. She went up to her and said:

'What's the matter with you?'

Snowgoose was lost in thought, and the question gave her quite a turn.

'Sh! Don't say a word! I've heard something very strange. If I tell you, you must promise not to breathe a word to anyone.'

As she said this Snowgoose shot her lips out in the direction of Dai-yu's bedroom, then began walking away, nodding to Nightingale to follow her. They reached the foot of the terrace and she began again in a whisper:

'Have you heard that Bao-yu's engaged to be married?'

Nightingale gave a start.

'I don't believe you! It can't be true!'

'It is! Nearly everyone knows except us '

'Who told you?'

'Scribe. His fiancée is a prefect's daughter. She's very good-looking and comes from a wealthy family.'

As Snowgoose was speaking, Nightingale heard Dai-yu cough and thought she could hear her getting up again. Worried that she might come out and overhear them, she took Snowgoose by the hand and motioned to her to be silent. She looked inside, but all seemed quiet. She asked Snowgoose in a low whisper:

'What exactly did Scribe say?'

'Do you remember,' replied Snowgoose, 'a day or two ago you sent me to Miss Tan's to thank her for something? Well, she wasn't home, but Scribe was. We started chatting, and one of us happened to mention Master Bao and his naughty ways. Scribe said: "When will Master Bao ever grow up? He doesn't take anything seriously. And to think that he's engaged to be married now – and still as silly as ever!" I asked her if the engagement had been settled, and she said that it had and that the go-between was a Mr Wang, a close relation on the Ning-guo side, so the whole thing was a foregone conclusion.'

Nightingale put her head thoughtfully to one side. 'How very strange!' she thought to herself.

'Why has no one in the family mentioned it?' she asked Snowgoose.

'That's Her Old Ladyship's idea – so Scribe said. It's in case Bao-yu finds out and is distracted from his studies. She made me promise not to tell a soul, and said she would blame *me* if word got around.'

Snowgoose pointed towards the house.

'That's why I haven't mentioned it in front of *her*. But today when you asked, I thought I could tell you the truth.'

As she was speaking there was a loud squawk from the parrot:

'Miss Lin's back! Put the kettle on!'

The two maids had the fright of their lives and turned round expecting to see Dai-yu. But seeing no one, and realizing their mistake, they scolded the bird and went inside. They found Dai-yu at her chair. She was out of breath and had clearly only just sat down. Nightingale asked rather awkwardly if she wanted any tea or water.

'Where have you two been all this time?' asked Dai-yu. 'No one came when I called.'

She walked back to the kang and lay down once more facing the wall, telling them to let down the bed-curtains. They did so and left the room, each secretly thinking to herself that she had overheard them, but neither daring to say so.

Dai-yu, brooding on her bed, *had* heard them whispering outside and had crept to the door to eavesdrop. Details of their conversation eluded her but the main substance was clear. She felt as though plunged into a great ocean. The prophecy contained in her nightmare was to be fulfilled after all. Bitterness and grief overwhelmed her. There was only one way of escape left. She must die. She must not live to see this dreaded thing take place. Without Bao-yu what would life be worth anyway? She had no parents of her own to turn to. Surely if she neglected herself daily from now on, in a few months she would be able to undermine her health and leave this world and all its troubles behind her?

Having formed this resolution, without bothering to pull up her quilt or put on any extra clothes she closed her eyes and pretended to be asleep. Nightingale and Snowgoose came in several times to wait on her, but seeing no sign of movement did not dare disturb her, even for dinner. Later, when the lamps were lit, Nightingale peeped through the curtains and saw that she had fallen asleep with her covers in a crumpled heap at her feet. Afraid she might catch cold, Nightingale gently pulled them over her. Dai-yu lay still until she had gone, then pushed them back again.

Meanwhile Nightingale questioned Snowgoose again:

'Are you sure you weren't making it up?'

'Of course I wasn't!' replied Snowgoose rather indignantly.

Nightingale: 'But how did Scribe come to know?'

Snowgoose: 'It was Crimson that heard it first at Mrs Lian's.'

Nightingale: 'I think Miss Lin must have overheard us. I can tell that something has upset her greatly. We must be careful never to mention it again.'

The two maids tidied up and made themselves ready for bed. Nightingale went in to see how Dai-yu was and found the quilt in the same crumpled heap as before. She pulled it lightly back. That night passed without further event.

The next morning Dai-yu rose early without waking either of the maids, and sat up on her own, lost in thought. Nightingale awoke to find her already up and said in surprise:

'You're up very early this morning, Miss!'

'I know I am,' replied Dai-yu rather curtly. 'It's because I went to sleep so early last night.'

Nightingale quickly dressed and woke Snowgoose, and the two of them waited on Dai-yu at her toilet. She sat staring into the mirror. Tears began to stream down her face, and her silk scarf was soon wet through. In the poet's words:

> A wasted face
>   reflected in the spring stream;
> And pity flows
>   from face to mirror'd face
>   and back again.

Nightingale stood by, not daring to utter a single comforting word, for fear that she would say the wrong thing and cause further anguish. Dai-yu sat motionless for a considerable while, then finally began her morning toilet, negligently, her eyes still brimming with tears. When it was done, she remained sitting where she was for a few minutes, then asked Nightingale to light some of the Tibetan incense.

'But Miss,' protested Nightingale, 'you've hardly had any sleep. What do you want to go lighting incense for? You're surely not going to start copying the sutra again are you?'

Dai-yu nodded.

'But you woke so early, Miss. If you start writing now you'll exhaust yourself.'

'What does that matter? The sooner it's finished the better. I only want to do it to keep myself occupied anyway. And in days to come you will have my writing to remember me by.'

As she said this tears began to pour down her cheeks, and Nightingale was no longer able to offer consolation but burst into tears herself.

Dai-yu was resolved that from this day forward she would deliberately destroy her health. She soon lost her appetite, and gradually began to waste away. Bao-yu visited her whenever he could after school, but although there were a million things she wanted to tell him, her consciousness that they were no longer children inhibited her from showing her affection by teasing him in the old way, and rendered her powerless to express what was preying on her mind. Bao-yu for his part would have liked to talk with her sincerely and offer her some genuine comfort; but he was afraid of aggravating her illness by offending her in some way, and so when he did see her, he merely inquired politely how she was feeling and added a few words of encouragement. Theirs was a true case of estrangement in the very extremity of love.

Grandmother Jia and Lady Wang showed a motherly concern for Dai-yu, which however went no further than calling in the doctor. Not knowing the inner source of her illness, they put it down to her sickly constitution, and Nightingale and Snowgoose were much too afraid to tell them the truth. Dai-yu weakened day by day. After a fortnight her stomach had shrunk to the point where she could no longer bring herself to eat even gruel. Every conversation she overheard during the day seemed to her to be connected in some way with Bao-yu's marriage. Every servant she saw from Green Delights seemed to be involved in the preparations. When Aunt Xue came to visit her, Bao-chai's absence confirmed her suspicions. She began to hope that no one would come to see her. She refused to take her medicine. Her only remaining wish was to be left alone, and to die as quickly as possible. In her dreams she constantly heard people addressing the new 'Mrs Bao', and her mind grew totally obsessed with the idea, like the proverbial drinker who, seeing a curved bow reflected in his cup, is convinced that he has swallowed a snake.

A few weeks of this self-imposed starvation and it seemed as if she must soon die. Even the thinnest of gruels was now an impossibility. Her breathing was scarcely perceptible. She was hanging on by the slenderest thread. To learn whether she was to survive this crisis or not, please turn to the next chapter.

CHAPTER 90

A poor girl loses a padded jacket and puts up with some obstreperous behaviour
A young man accepts a tray of sweetmeats and is put out by some devious goings-on

During the first week or so of Dai-yu's decline, when Grandmother Jia and her aunts had taken it in turns to visit her, she had still possessed strength enough to make an occasional response to their inquiries. But now she would eat nothing whatsoever, and for several days had hardly said a word. The strange thing was that although at times she seemed unconscious, there were periods when she was perfectly lucid. They began to suspect something, and interrogated Nightingale and Snowgoose more than once. But the maids were too scared to say what they knew. Nightingale for her part, while she would have liked to discover the latest news from Scribe, feared that the truth would only provide a further shock and hasten the hour of Dai-yu's death, and so when she saw Scribe, she avoided the subject completely. Snowgoose, as the transmitter of the news, felt responsible for Dai-yu's condition and longed for a hundred tongues to cry out 'I never said a word!' She too, when questioned, maintained a close silence.

Nightingale, seeing that Dai-yu would eat nothing, and judging that all hope was now gone, stood by her bedside crying for a while, then went outside and whispered to Snowgoose:

'Go in and watch her carefully. I'm going straight over to tell Her Old Ladyship, Her Ladyship and Mrs Lian. She has definitely taken a turn for the worse today.'

She departed, and Snowgoose went in to take her place.

She found Dai-yu lying very still, as if in a deep sleep. Being only a child with no experience of such things, she took this state for death itself, and began to feel both tearful and frightened. If only Nightingale would hurry up and come back! At that very moment she heard footsteps outside the window. That must be Nightingale now! Breathing a sigh of relief, she stood up at once and went to the doorway of the inner chamber, lifting the door-curtain in expectation. She heard the swish of the outer door-curtain, and in came not Nightingale but Scribe, sent by Tan-chun to inquire how Dai-yu was. Seeing Snowgoose standing in the inner doorway, she asked:

'How is Miss Lin?'

Snowgoose nodded to her to come in and Scribe entered the inner room with her. She noticed that Nightingale was not there, and when she looked at Dai-yu and saw how feebly she was breathing, a look of horror came over her face.

'Where's Nightingale gone?' she asked.

'To tell their Ladyships,' replied Snowgoose.

Certain that Dai-yu, if not actually dead, was by this time at any rate 'dead to the world', Snowgoose decided to take advantage of Nightingale's absence to question Scribe. Taking her by the hand, she asked in a whisper:

'Did you really mean what you said the other day – about Mr Wang, and Master Bao's betrothal?'

'Of course I did!' replied Scribe.

'When was it settled?'

'I never said it was! What I told you was just what I'd heard from Crimson. Later I was at Mrs Lian's myself, and heard her say to Patience that the whole thing was something the Master's literary gentlemen had thought up, to please him and provide themselves with a connection. As it happened Lady Xing didn't even think it a good match. But even if she had approved, everyone knows how unreliable her judgement is. Besides, Her Old Ladyship already has someone else in mind for Master

Bao, someone here in the Garden. Lady Xing had no idea of that, of course, and Her Old Ladyship only allowed them to go ahead with the normal inquiries for the Master's sake. Mrs Lian said Her Old Ladyship wants Bao-yu to marry one of his cousins, and her mind is quite made up, so any other proposals are a waste of time.'

Snowgoose was beside herself.

'Then our mistress is dying for nothing!' she exclaimed.

'What *do* you mean?' asked Scribe.

'Don't you know? The other day Miss Lin overheard me telling Nightingale about the betrothal – that's why she has brought herself to this terrible state now.'

'Sh!' whispered Scribe. 'She might hear you!'

'She's completely dead to the world,' replied Snowgoose. 'Look – she can't last more than a day or two now.'

As she was speaking, the door-curtain was drawn aside and in came Nightingale.

'For goodness' sake!' she exclaimed. 'Can't you two do your gossiping somewhere else? You might as well *drive* her to her death!'

'I simply cannot believe such strange goings-on,' muttered Scribe.

'My dear Scribe,' retorted Nightingale, 'don't misunderstand me please. I didn't mean to offend you, But you must be so stupid to gossip like that.'

The three of them were interrupted by a sudden cough from Dai-yu's bed on the kang. Nightingale hurried to the bedside, while Snowgoose and Scribe stood in silence. Nightingale bent down and whispered to Dai-yu, who was lying with her face to the wall:

'Would you like some water, Miss?'

There was a barely audible 'yes' and Snowgoose promptly filled a cup half-full with hot water and handed it to Nightingale, who held it in the palm of her hand. Scribe meanwhile had moved towards the kang and was about to speak to Dai-yu when Nightingale motioned to her not to say anything and she checked herself. They stood waiting. After a short interval Dai-yu coughed again and Nightingale inquired at once:

'Would you like the water now, Miss?'

There was another faint 'yes' and Dai-yu seemed to want to lift her head, but was too feeble to do so. Nightingale climbed up onto the kang by her side and, holding the cup in her hand, first tested the water to make sure it was not too hot, then raised it to Dai-yu's mouth, supporting her head until the rim of the cup reached her lips. Dai-yu took a sip, and Nightingale was about to remove the cup when she saw that Dai-yu wanted some more. She held the cup where it was. Dai-yu drank again, shook her head to show that it was enough, took a deep breath and lay down once more. After a pause she opened her eyes a fraction and asked:

'Was that Scribe I heard talking just now?'

'Yes, Miss,' replied Nightingale.

Scribe was still in the room and came up to the kang at once to convey Tan-chun's message. Dai-yu stared at her for a minute and nodded. After a pause she said:

'When you go home, give Miss Tan my regards will you?'

Scribe took this to mean that Dai-yu wanted her to leave and made her way quietly out of the room.

Now although Dai-yu's condition was extremely grave, her power of reason was unimpaired. She was aware of Scribe's arrival and vaguely heard the first words she exchanged with Snowgoose. She felt too exhausted to cope with a visitor, and so pretended to be asleep. But as the conversation progressed, it became clear to her that what she had taken to be a fact had never been more than a proposal. And then she heard Scribe repeat Xi-feng's words, that Grandmother Jia intended to marry Bao-yu to one of his cousins, to one that lived in the Garden; and who could that be but herself? Just as at the winter solstice Yin gives birth to Yang, so now in her mind darkness gave way to light. She suddenly felt much clearer within herself, decided to drink some water and even spoke to Scribe.

It was at this moment that Grandmother Jia, Lady Wang, Li Wan and Xi-feng arrived on the scene, in response to Nightingale's urgent summons. Now that Dai-yu's inner doubts had been so dramatically dissipated, she no longer presented the spectacle of the dying maiden that Nightingale had led them to expect. She was still weak and low in spirits, but was able with an effort to say a few words in reply to their inquiries. Xi-feng called Nightingale over and questioned her:

'Miss Lin is not nearly as ill as you made out. Why did you exaggerate so? We were most alarmed.'

'Honestly, ma'am,' replied Nightingale, 'only a while ago she was in a bad way. That's why I came over. I would never have dared to bother you otherwise. She does seem a lot better now. It's most strange.'

Grandmother Jia said to Xi-feng with a smile:

'You shouldn't take what she says so seriously, my dear. She doesn't understand such things. Mind you she was quite right to speak up if she noticed anything the matter. I've no time for young people who never say a word or do anything for fear of appearing foolish.'

The ladies stayed for a few minutes chatting, then, deciding that all was well, returned to their apartments.

Truly:

> No remedy but love
> Can make the lovesick well;
> Only the hand that tied the knot
> Can loose the tiger's bell.

After this Dai-yu's condition continued to improve steadily, and Snowgoose and Nightingale offered many a secret prayer of thanks to the Lord Buddha.

'Thank goodness she's better!' said Snowgoose to

Nightingale. 'But what an odd illness! And what an odd way to get better!'

'We know what caused it,' said Nightingale. 'It's this sudden recovery that's puzzling. I think Bao-yu and Miss Lin must be destined to be married after all. 'The course of true love never did run smooth', but 'Marriages made in heaven can never be broken' either! You can tell they are destined to be together. That's what they both want in their hearts, and that must be what Heaven has decreed for them. Remember what happened to Bao-yu last year, when I told him Miss Lin was going home to the South? He nearly died of shock, and made the most terrible scene. And now that one remark of ours has nearly been the death of her. Theirs must be a bond from some previous life, made a century ago at the Rock of Rebirth!'

They exchanged a secret smile at this romantic theory, and Snowgoose exclaimed:

'Thank goodness she's better anyway! We must never mention it again! Even if Bao-yu were to marry another lady and I witnessed the wedding with my own eyes, I swear I wouldn't breathe a word of it to anyone.'

Nightingale laughed.

'Well said!'

Theirs were not the only secret discussions on this subject. Dai-yu's strange illness and stranger recovery gave rise to a great deal of whispering and speculation in the household, which soon reached the ears of Xi-feng. Lady Wang and Lady Xing vaguely suspected something, and Grandmother Jia herself had a shrewd idea what was at the bottom of it all. The four ladies were gathered one day in Grandmother Jia's apartment, and in the course of their conversation the subject of Dai-yu's illness came up.

'There is something I want to say to you all,' said Grandmother Jia. 'Bao-yu and Miss Lin have been together ever since they were little, and this has never troubled me, as I have always thought of them as children.

But of late I have noticed how frequent these illnesses of hers are becoming – how suddenly they come, and how suddenly they go – a sure sign that she is growing up. It really won't do to allow them to stay together indefinitely. What do you all think?'

After a thoughtful silence Lady Wang replied, choosing her words with care:

'Miss Lin reads such a lot into things. And Bao-yu's childish manner is deceptive: he can be extremely stupid and tactless. If we remove either one of them from the Garden, won't it be too obvious? It has always been said that every boy becomes a groom and every girl becomes a bride. Don't you think, Mother, that a better solution would be to go ahead as quickly as possible and get them both married?'

Grandmother Jia frowned.

'I know that Miss Lin's peculiar temperament is in some ways attractive. But I don't think we could possibly have her as a wife for Bao-yu. Besides, I'm afraid that with such a delicate constitution she is unlikely to live to any age. I'm sure Bao-chai is in every respect the more suitable choice.'

'Of course we all agree with you there, Mother,' said Lady Wang. 'But we must find a husband for Miss Lin too. If we do not, and if she has taken a fancy to Bao-yu – after all, it is only natural for a girl to have such feelings as she grows up – it might make things very difficult if she were then to discover that he was already betrothed to Bao-chai.'

'There can be no question,' replied Grandmother Jia, 'of marrying an outsider before one of the family. The order must be: first to marry Bao-yu, then to have Miss Lin betrothed. Besides Miss Lin is two years younger than Bao-yu anyway. If I understand you correctly, we shall have to conceal Bao-yu's betrothal from her ...'

Xi-feng turned at once to the various maids present:

'Is that clear? Not a *word* of Master Bao's betrothal to

anyone! If I catch one of you talking about it I shall show no mercy.'

'Feng dear,' continued Grandmother Jia, 'I have noticed that since your illness you have taken less interest in what happens in the Garden. You really must give it more of your attention. It's not just the sort of thing we have been talking about. Any repetition of that disgraceful drinking and gambling that was discovered among the servants last year must be prevented at all costs. Be rather more particular, will you, and keep a watchful eye on what goes on. They need to be disciplined, and you seem to be the one they respect most.'

'Yes, Grannie,' said Xi-feng.

The ladies sat talking for a while longer, then left to go their separate ways.

*

From now on Xi-feng began to inspect the Garden on a more regular basis. One day, in the course of one of her tours of inspection, she was walking along the bank by Amaryllis Eyot when she heard an old woman shouting outside the courtyard and went to investigate. As she drew near the old serving-woman caught sight of her, dropped her hands to her side and stood to attention, mumbling a confused 'Good morning, ma'am.'

'Why are you making such a racket out here?' asked Xi-feng.

'You and Mrs Zhu have given me a job to do here, ma'am,' replied the woman, 'looking after the flowerbeds and fruit-trees. I'd done nothing wrong, and Miss Xing's maid accused us of stealing...'

'And why should she do that?' asked Xi-feng.

'Yesterday our Blackie came with me here to play,' replied the woman. 'She didn't know any better and went inside Miss Xing's apartment to have a look around. I sent her home straight away. Then early this morning I heard one of the maids say they'd lost something. When I asked what it was, she started questioning *me* all about it...'

'That's no cause for you to lose your temper,' retorted Xi-feng.

'This Garden belongs to Mrs Zhu's family not hers!' protested the old woman. 'We work for Mrs Zhu and I won't be called a thief!'

Xi-feng spat straight in the old woman's face and said harshly:

'Hold your tongue! That's quite enough! You're responsible for things here and if something is lost the maids are quite right to hold you accountable for it. How dare you talk such nonsense! Call Steward Lin and have her dismissed!'

The maids were carrying out her orders when Xing Xiu-yan came hurrying out. She greeted Xi-feng and said with an anxious smile:

'You mustn't do that! It was nothing really. And it's all over now.'

'My dear girl,' said Xi-feng, 'that is not the right attitude to take. It's the principle I'm concerned with. The servants must learn to know their place.'

Xiu-yan saw that the woman was on her knees begging for mercy, and asked Xi-feng at once to go inside with her and sit down.

'I know her sort,' said Xi-feng. 'They think they can get away with anything – except when I'm around.'

When Xiu-yan continued to plead for the woman, however, and insisted on putting the blame on her own maid, she relented.

'Out of consideration for Miss Xing,' she announced, 'I shall let you off this once.'

The old woman came forward to kotow first to Xi-feng then to Xiu-yan, and left.

Once she had gone, Xiu-yan asked Xi-feng to be seated.

'What was it that you lost?' inquired Xi-feng pleasantly.

'Nothing of any importance,' replied Xiu-yan with a smile. 'Just an old red padded jacket of mine. I told them to look for it and when it didn't turn up thought no more about it. My maid was silly to question that woman. She was bound to take offence. My maid was very thoughtless and I've already given her a good talking to. The whole affair is over and best forgotten.'

While she was speaking, Xi-feng had been inspecting Xiu-yan's clothes and the general appearance of her apartment. Her few padded or fur-lined clothes looked rather worn and ineffective as protection against the cold. Most of her quilted bedding looked on the thin side too. She glanced at the furniture and the ornaments on her table, all of them provided by Grandmother Jia, and noticed how immaculately clean and tidy they had been kept. Xi-feng felt a warm respect towards her.

'I know a jacket is nothing to fuss over,' she said. 'But the weather is growing cold, and you need it to keep you warm. Of course you were right to question her. Honestly! The insolent way these servants carry on!'

She sat talking with Xiu-yan for a while and then left to continue her tour of inspection, stopping off in all the various residences before returning to her own apartment. There she instructed Patience to make up a parcel of her clothes to be sent over to Xiu-yan: it was to contain two padded jackets, one of dark-red imported silk, the other of viridian damask-silk lined with pearly lambswool, a long turquoise worsted skirt with brocade appliqué panels and an embroidered border, and a deep-blue ermine-lined jacket.

Despite Xi-feng's intervention on her behalf, Xiu-yan was still most mortified by the woman's rudeness. 'Of all the girls who live here,' she thought to herself, 'I'm the only one the servants would dare to offend in that way. They say things about me all the time. And now Feng has seen it for herself!'

The more she thought about it the more depressing her position seemed. And yet it was impossible for her to confide in anyone. Bowing to her fate, she was just beginning to weep when she saw Xi-feng's maid Felicity come in carrying a bundle of clothes. Soon realizing whose they were, she absolutely refused to accept them.

'But Miss,' protested Felicity, 'Mrs Lian says that if you think they are too old she will change them for newer ones.'

Xiu-yan smiled politely.

'It's very thoughtful of her. But I can't possibly let her give me some of her clothes just because I've lost one of mine. Please take them back and thank her most kindly for me. I do appreciate the thought.'

She gave her a little purse, and Felicity departed with some reluctance, carrying the bundle. Minutes later she was back, this time accompanied by Patience. Xiu-yan hurried out to greet them and asked them both to be seated. Patience smiled and said:

'Mrs Lian says you should accept them as one of the family and not be so polite.'

'But I'm not being polite,' replied Xiu-yan. 'Honestly. I'd be embarrassed to take them.'

'Mrs Lian says,' persisted Patience, 'that if you won't take them it must either be because they're too old or because you don't like the idea of wearing her things. She says that if I take them back she'll be cross with me.'

Xiu-yan blushed and smiled gratefully:

'Well, in that case, how can I possibly refuse? Please convey my thanks to Mrs Lian.'

She served them both tea, after which Felicity and Patience left. They were almost home again when they met one of Aunt Xue's women. She greeted them, and Patience asked her where she was going.

'Mrs Xue and our young lady sent me over to convey their regards to all their Ladyships and young madams and young ladies. I was at Mrs Lian's just now asking for you, and she told me you'd gone into the Garden. Have you just been to Miss Xing's by any chance?'

'Why, how did you know that?' asked Patience.

'Oh, a little birdie told me... It's most generous I think, what you and your mistress are doing...'

Patience gave a little laugh.

'Won't you come in and have a chat later on?'

'I still have things to do. Another day,' replied the old woman and went on her way, while Patience went in to report to Xi-feng.

*

When the serving-woman returned to the Xue household, which was in its usual state of upheaval, thanks to the disruptive behaviour of Xia Jin-gui, she recounted the story of Xing Xiu-yan's humiliation, and both Aunt Xue and Bao-chai began to weep.

'It's only because Pan's away,' said Bao-chai, 'that she has to go on suffering like this. We are lucky that Feng has been looking after her. In future we must keep more of an eye on her ourselves. She is after all practically one of the family now.'

As she was speaking Xue Ke came in.

'In all the years he's spent here Pan hasn't made a single decent friend!' he said. 'They're a pack of rogues the lot of them! I'm sure they don't care in the slightest what happens to him. They're only curious to know the latest news. This last couple of days I've told them all to go away, and I've given the janitors instructions not to let any of them in.'

'Is it that actor Jiang and his friends again?' asked Aunt Xue.

'No, as a matter of fact he hasn't been here at all. It's a different crowd.'

Xue Ke's words intensified Aunt Xue's anxiety.

'Though I have a son,' she said, 'it is as though I had none. Even if Pan wins this reprieve, his life is ruined. You are only my nephew, Ke, but you show much more sense than Pan. I can see that from now on I shall have to depend on you. Be sure to work hard and make the most of your life. And think of your bride-to-be, who comes from a family that has fallen on hard times. It is always hard when a daughter goes out into the world and gets married. One can only pray that her husband will turn out well and be capable of providing for her. Imagine if Xiu-yan were to turn out like this creature here . . .'

Gesturing in the direction of Xia Jin-gui's room Aunt Xue continued:

'But I don't want to talk about her. I know Xiu-yan to be an honest and thoughtful girl, thrifty and unspoilt. The sooner Pan's business is settled, the sooner we can get the two of you married and set my poor heart at rest.'

'Don't forget that Bao-qin is still waiting to be married,' Xue Ke reminded his aunt. 'I know how concerned you are about that. Don't worry on our account.'

They stayed chatting together for a few minutes longer and then Xue Ke returned to his room. He ate his dinner and began to think about Xiu-yan in the Garden, forced by poverty to be so utterly dependent on the Jias. The two of them had travelled by the same boat on their original journey to the capital, and he had been able to see for himself that she was a pretty, good-natured girl. How unjust of destiny to give a creature like Xia Jin-gui a life of wealth and luxury and turn her into a spoilt shrew, while for a girl like Xiu-yan there was nothing but hardship! What was in the mind of the Great Arbiter Yama when he made such a dispensation?

These gloomy thoughts stirred Xue Ke to express his sense of injustice in poetic form. His was an untutored pen, but he did as best he could.

> As the flood-dragon flounders on the shore,
> So our two hearts languish under like privations.
> When will we drink this bitter cup no more
> And soar unfettered through the constellations?

He read the lines through and thought of sticking them up on his wall. He felt a little self-conscious however, and thought to himself:

'What if someone sees them and makes fun of me . . .'

He read them through again.

'Oh who cares! I *will* put them up. I can read them anyway, to cheer myself up.'

A final reading made him change his mind yet again, however, and he slipped them between the pages of a book.

'I'm old enough for us to be married now,' he mused to himself. 'But who could have foreseen this family crisis, and who knows when it will ever end? What an ordeal for a gentle girl like Xiu-yan! How lonely and wretched she must feel!'

At that moment the door was pushed open and Moonbeam came in carrying a round covered-tray and a jug of wine, which she deposited with a simpering smile on the table. He rose and asked her to be seated. Still smiling she said:

'Four plates of sweetmeats and a small jug of wine, with Mrs Pan's compliments, Master Ke.'

'It's most kind of her,' replied Ke, 'but surely she could have sent one of the younger maids? She didn't need to bother you, Miss Moonbeam.'

'Oh Master Ke, there's no need to be so polite. It's all in the family after all . . . Mrs Pan knows what trouble you've been put to on account of Mr Pan, and she's been meaning for a long time to thank you herself but was afraid the others might take it the wrong way. In this household, as I think you know, sir, there's a lot goes on beneath the surface. People are only waiting to pounce on a little thing like a present, and then they start inventing all kinds of stories. That's why she's been ever so slightly discreet and asked me to come over personally with these few things today when no one was looking . . .'

She gave Xue Ke a saucy smile and continued:

'And please, no more of that 'Miss' Moonbeam – it makes me feel most uncomfortable. We are only here to serve, and if we can serve Mr Pan, then why not you as well?'

Xue Ke was young and had a trusting nature. It *was* odd that Pan's womenfolk should suddenly start treating him like this; but Moonbeam's explanation was a plausible one, he reflected.

'You can leave the sweetmeats,' he said. 'But take the wine back with you. I've never been much of a drinker. Occasionally if pushed to it I can manage a cup, but usually I don't drink at all. Surely you and Mrs Pan knew that?'

'Ask anything else of me!' pleaded Moonbeam. 'But I wouldn't dare take it back – you know Mrs Pan's temper. If I tell her you don't drink, she'll never believe me; she'll say I've failed in my duty.'

Reluctantly Xue Ke allowed her to leave the wine too. Moonbeam began to leave, but on reaching the doorway she took a quick look outside and glanced back at Xue Ke with a smile. Pointing in the direction of Xia Jin-gui's apartment she said:

'I think she might even come over herself to thank you for all you've done . . .'

Xue Ke was not sure how to take this, and began to feel rather nervous.

'Please convey my thanks to Mrs Pan will you? The weather is cold, and she must be careful not to catch a chill. Besides she is my cousin's wife and there's no need for her to go to such lengths.'

Moonbeam said nothing but tittered and went on her way.

At first Xue Ke had been prepared to accept the offering as a genuine expression of gratitude on Jin-gui's part. But now Moonbeam's suggestive behaviour had aroused his suspicions, and he began to think there was something fishy going on.

'But surely Jin-gui would never think of such a thing?' he argued with himself. 'She *is* my sister-in-law . . . Perhaps it's Moonbeam up to no good. She can't very well act on her own initiative. Maybe she is using Jin-gui as a cover . . . But then she's Pan's chamber-wife so that's hardly very . . .'

Suddenly it occurred to him:

'Of course! Jin-gui's no lady! Sometimes when she's in the mood, she gets herself up like a regular harlot – she obviously fancies herself as some sort of man-killer! Another possibility is that she's fallen out with Bao-qin and this is a plot to disgrace me and drag the family name in the mud . . .'

Xue Ke could not help finding all this rather daunting, and was racking his brains for some means of dealing with the situation, when to his great alarm he heard a splutter of laughter outside the window. But to discover who was laughing, you must turn to the next chapter.

CHAPTER 91

In the pursuance of lust,
Moonbeam evolves an artful stratagem
In a flight of Zen,
Bao-yu makes an enigmatic confession

We saw in our last chapter how Xue Ke was startled from his troubled reflections by a sudden splutter of laughter from outside his window.

'Moonbeam again! Or Jin-gui!' he thought to himself. 'I shall ignore them and see what happens.'

He listened for a while but there was no further sound. Not daring to touch the wine and sweetmeats, he closed the door and was about to undress when he heard a faint tap at the paper casement. He was already rattled by Moonbeam's behaviour and beginning to feel out of his depth. Hearing the tapping and yet unable to detect a presence outside the window, he didn't know what to think. He did up his gown again and sat down abstractedly by the lamp. He took a sweetmeat from the table and turned it over restlessly in his hand, studying it from every angle. Suddenly something made him look round. A small peephole (of the lick-and-spittle variety) had appeared in the window. Going across and putting his eye to the hole, he squinted through and received a blast of air in the face that quite startled the wits out of him. It was followed by another splutter of laughter. Rushing back, he blew out the lamp and lay down in the darkness, holding his breath.

A voice came from outside:

'Are you going to sleep without trying the wine and sweetmeats?'

Xue Ke recognized it as Moonbeam's voice but said nothing and lay there pretending to be asleep.

A few seconds later, in a disgruntled tone:

'Miserable spoilsport! You don't know what you're missing!'

This time he could not identify the voice with any certainty. It sounded like Moonbeam, but there was something of Xia Jin-gui's expression in it too. Whoever it was, there was no longer any doubt in his mind as to their intentions. He tossed and turned for most of that night, and it was not until after five o'clock that he finally fell asleep.

Shortly after dawn someone knocked at the door.

'Who's there?' Xue Ke called out.

No answer. He got out of bed to open the door and saw Moonbeam, her hair combed simply back, wearing a tight little sleeveless jacket, its gold-striped neck-line cut in the shape of a guitar, its buttons seductively undone. She had a new-looking viridian scarf around her neck and instead of a skirt was sporting pomegranate-red lined-pantaloons of a flowery design, and a pair of smart red embroided slippers. She had come before doing her morning toilet, to remove the sweetmeats before the rest of the household arose. Though rather taken aback to see her advancing into his room *en négligé*, he asked politely:

'Why are you up so early this morning?'

Moonbeam blushed in reply, piled the sweetmeats onto one plate and went out holding it in both hands. Xue Ke interpreted this as pique at her failure to seduce him the previous evening.

'Oh well,' he thought to himself, 'it's too bad if I've annoyed them. At least they'll lose interest and leave me alone.'

He decided that he could forget about the whole business, and called for water to wash his face. It would be wise, he decided, to stay at home and take a couple of days rest, for his own health and peace of mind, and also to avoid the unwelcome attentions of Xue Pan's so-called friends, who seeing the Xue family deprived of its head and observing his own youth and inexperience, had caught the scent of money in the air. Some of them would have been content to act as messengers; some professed a knowledge of legal phraseology or claimed contacts behind the scenes and offered to deliver bribes to the officials and minions involved in the case; others advised him to make some money out of it for himself, while a few even tried scaring him with false rumours. Since he first encountered them, Xue Ke had done his utmost to avoid these unsavoury elements, but was aware that by openly rebuffing them he might create further trouble for himself. The only safe course, he concluded, was to lie low at home and await the confirmation of Pan's sentence.

*

To return to Xia Jin-gui. She had sent Moonbeam over on the previous night with the wine and sweetmeats in order to explore Xue Ke's susceptibility to her charms. When Moonbeam returned and described in detail what had happened, Jin-gui realized that she had miscalculated and that by pursuing such a strategy she would cause herself much pointless trouble and forfeit Moonbeam's respect. If she were to disguise her disappointment with a few words of feigned indifference, that would do nothing to relieve her own hankering after Xue Ke. Unable for the present to think of any other means of achieving her ends, she sat in moody silence.

She was unaware that Moonbeam had been thinking along exactly the same lines as herself. Moonbeam too reckoned that Xue Pan might not be back for some time and felt in dire need of a substitute. She had only been held back from procuring one by the fear of being caught at it by Jin-gui. Now that Jin-gui had made the first move, however, Moonbeam was only too glad to cruise along in her wake. She would step in first and become

Xue Ke's mistress, and Jin-gui would have no choice but to accept the *fait accompli*. Such was the reasoning behind her provocative behaviour.

Her first impression had been that the young master showed promise. True, he was not exactly leaping into her arms. She would have to play him slowly, which is precisely what she was doing when, to her intense disappointment, he blew out the lamp and went to bed. She reported back to Jin-gui, anxious to see what new course of action she might suggest. As nothing was forthcoming from her mistress however but this moody silence, she helped her prepare for the night and herself went to bed.

She had a sleepless night. As she lay tossing and turning, a new plan began to take shape in her mind. She would rise early and go to Xue Ke's apartment at once to collect the tray; she would slip on a couple of the more alluring items in her wardrobe, but otherwise not bother with her morning toilet, in order to look as sleepy and seductive as possible, straight from the boudoir... She would observe what effect this had on Xue Ke, while maintaining a show of annoyance and indifference towards him. This surely would be his chance to repent of his folly. She could help him aboard and pip Jin-gui at the post.

In the event Xue Ke the morning after proved as totally incorruptible as he had been the evening before, and Moonbeam found herself obliged to go through in earnest with her charade of walking out in a huff. She did however still keep her wits sufficiently about her to leave behind the wine-jug, as a pretext for one final manoeuvre.

'Did anyone see you when you fetched the things?' Jin-gui asked her on her return.

'Not a soul.'

'What about Master Ke? Did he have anything to say?'

'No.'

Jin-gui too had spent a sleepless night, without having thought of any alternative plan of campaign.

'If I am to go ahead with things,' she thought to herself, 'I can hardly hope to keep Moonbeam in the dark much longer. I shall have to bring her in on it. I'm sure she won't say anything then. Besides I need her to act as a go-between. I can't go myself. I'd better talk to her and see if we can't think of a good plan between us.'

She smiled at Moonbeam and asked:

'What do you make of Master Ke anyway?'

'He seems rather a fool...'

Jin-gui laughed.

'How dare you insult one of the masters like that...'

Moonbeam laughed.

'He's asking for it, giving *you* the bird like that...'

'And just what do you mean by that?'

'Oh, only the way he wouldn't touch any of the sweet-meats you sent of course... What else?'

She said this with a smirk and a meaningful look at Jin-gui, who replied:

'That's quite enough of your insinuations! I sent those things to thank him for all that he's done for Mr Pan, and I only asked you what had happened in case people had been gossiping. I have no idea what you are trying to suggest.'

'There's no need to worry, ma'am,' said Moonbeam coolly. 'I'm on your side, you can count on me. But we must be very discreet. It would be serious if word got around.'

Jin-gui felt her face burning.

'You little whore! So you've fallen for him have you, and think you can use me as a cover for your goings-on, is that it?'

'Think so if you like, ma'am. I was only trying to help. If you really fancy him, I think I have a plan. "Every mouse will steal oil if he can." He's just scared of being found out, and wants to keep out of trouble. You must be patient, ma'am. Find as many little ways as you can of making yourself helpful. He is Mr Pan's younger cousin, after all, and doesn't have a wife. If you set your mind to it, I am sure you can get yourself into his good books, and no one will be able to say a word against you for it. In a few days he'll be ready to show *his* gratitude by paying you a return visit. You lay on a little party here – I'll help you get him drunk – and he's yours! If he won't play, we'll create a scene and accuse him of making a pass – that should clinch it. He'll be too scared to say no then! If he still holds out, why then we'll know that he's just a sissy and not worth wasting time over anyway. What do you think?'

Jin-gui was puce in the face.

'Why you little strumpet! I can see you've had a few in your time! No wonder Pan couldn't let you out of his sight!'

Moonbeam pulled a face and laughed.

'Is that all the thanks I get for helping to bring the two of you together?'

From now on Jin-gui's only thought was the conquest of Xue Ke. And as she wished to accomplish this without attracting attention, the Xue compound enjoyed a brief respite from its usual alarms and excursions.

Later that same day Moonbeam went to collect the wine-jug. She was as scrupulously well-behaved as she had been in the morning, and caused Xue Ke, who watched her out of the corner of his eye, a certain amount of remorse and self-doubt.

'Perhaps I was wrong,' he thought to himself. 'Perhaps I've been imagining the whole thing, and they really meant well. In which case my ingratitude may have offended her and who knows what trouble this may lead to. And it will all have been my own fault . . .'

A couple of days went by and all was quiet. Whenever he saw Moonbeam, she lowered her head and walked away without so much as a glance in his direction. Jin-gui, on the other hand, pursued him with an eagerness that made him feel most uncomfortable. But of all this more later.

*

Aunt Xue and Bao-chai noticed how quiet Jin-gui had become all of a sudden, and how charming she was being to everyone. The change came as a great surprise, but nothing could have pleased Aunt Xue more, and she reasoned to herself about it thus:

'At the time of his marriage Pan must have crossed some unlucky star, which is what has caused all his subsequent misfortune. Thanks to our financial resources and the efforts of the Jias we have managed to avert disaster in this court-case, and perhaps this sudden change on Jin-gui's part is a sign that his luck has turned for the good...'

It was in fact not far short of a miracle. One day after lunch Aunt Xue thought she would pay Jin-gui a visit, and set off supported by Prosper. She reached the courtyard in front of Jin-gui's apartment, when she heard a man's voice engaged in conversation with Jin-gui outside. Prosper called ahead diplomatically:

'Mrs Pan, Mrs Xue is here to see you!'

They were already in the doorway. As they advanced the figure of a man could be dimly seen escaping behind the door. Aunt Xue recoiled in alarm.

'Do please come in and sit down, Mother,' said Jin-gui. 'That's only my adopted brother Xia San. He's from the country and not used to company. This is the first time he has been here and he has never been introduced. He was intending to call on you to pay his respects.'

'If he is your brother, then I should be glad to meet him,' said Aunt Xue.

Jin-gui called her brother out from his hiding-place, and he made a bow and paid his respects. Aunt Xue replied politely and sat down.

'How long have you been in the capital?' she asked by way of conversation.

'I was only adopted into the family two months ago. Mother needed someone to look after household business. I arrived the day before yesterday, and came here today to see my new sister.'

Aunt Xue could see that he was rather an uncouth sort of fellow, and did not like to stay long.

'I must be going,' she said. 'Don't get up.'

Then turning to Jin-gui:

'As this is your brother's first visit, please invite him to stay for dinner.'

'Yes, Mother.'

Aunt Xue took her leave.

When she was out of the room, Jin-gui turned to Xia San.

'Sit down. I've kept our connection open and above board on purpose, so as to avoid suspicion from young Master Ke. I've some things I want you to buy for me in town, and I don't want anyone to know about them.'

'Of course, sis. Leave it to me. Give me the cash and I'll guarantee to deliver the goods.'

'Not so fast: you'd better be careful not to be swindled, or I might not accept delivery . . .'

After a little more banter of this kind, Jin-gui had dinner with Xia San, after which she specified her commissions, gave him certain other instructions and he went on his way. From that day on he became a frequent visitor at Jin-gui's apartment. The old janitor usually let him through without going through the proper procedure of making an announcement, knowing him to be Mrs Pan's brother. His visits provided the wherewithal for many a plot. But we anticipate.

*

One day a letter arrived from Xue Pan. Aunt Xue opened it and sent for Bao-chai to read it to her. This is what it said:

'Dear Mother,

I am being reasonably treated here in prison, so please set your mind at rest. I had some bad news yesterday however, from the clerk of the court. My sentence was approved at the prefectural level – I presume the family had been in touch with the prefect. But when the case came up before the circuit court, the Taotai rejected the judgement. The secretary here at the yamen has been very helpful and has sent an immediate petition in defence of the original judgement. But the Taotai has issued an official statement reprimanding the local mandarin for malpractice. He wants me to appear before the circuit court. If I do, I could be in trouble again. We can't have approached the Taotai yet. Please send someone to do this as soon as my letter reaches you. And send Cousin Ke here at once. Any delay may result in my being sent under escort to the circuit court. On no account stint the money! *Extremely urgent!*'

This sent Aunt Xue into floods of tears. Bao-chai and Xue Ke did their best to calm her down, while at the same time impressing upon her the need to act swiftly. Once again she was obliged to part with her nephew – bags were packed, money weighed out, and Xue Ke prepared to set off that same night with one of the family shop-assistants. It was a night of feverish activity, and Bao-chai herself stayed up till the early hours, helping and making sure that nothing was overlooked by the servants. The combination of nervous strain and physical exhaustion proved too much for a girl of her gentle nature and refined upbringing, and the next morning she went down with a fever and was unable to swallow water or medicine.

Oriole reported this at once to Aunt Xue, who came hurrying over. Finding Bao-chai unable to speak, her face bright red, her body burning hot to the touch, she immediately panicked and burst into tears. Bao-qin tried to comfort and support her aunt, while Caltrop was so affected by Bao-chai's appearance that she could only stand by the bedside calling her name and weeping. Bao-chai was too weak to speak or move her hands. Her eyes were dry, her nose blocked. They sent for the doctor, whose prescription gradually brought her round and to the family's intense relief the immediate crisis seemed to have been averted. The news had already reached the various inner apartments of the Rong-guo and Ning-guo mansions, and a maid soon arrived from Xi-feng's with one of her Ten Fragrances Revivifying Pills, followed by a maid with one of Lady Wang's Most Precious Pills. Grandmother Jia, Lady Xing, Lady Wang and all the ladies from both mansions including You-shi all sent maids to inquire how she was getting on, but all agreed that her illness should be kept a secret from Bao-yu. She went on taking various remedies for seven or eight days with no real improvement; it was only when she remembered her own Cold Fragrance Pills and took three of these that she began to recover. By the time Bao-yu learnt of her illness, she was already better and he did not go to visit her.

A letter arrived from Xue Ke, which Aunt Xue did not show to Bao-chai, for fear of upsetting her. She read it herself and went straight to Lady Wang to beg for her help, at the same time giving her an account of Bao-chai's condition. After Aunt Xue had gone to bed, Lady Wang went in to plead with Jia Zheng.

'With the higher-ranking officials a word is usually sufficient; but these provincials clearly need a more tangible incentive,' he said somewhat grimly. 'We shall have to dip into our pockets.'

Lady Wang went on to talk of Bao-chai:

'The poor girl! I feel responsible for her: she is almost one of the family. The sooner she and Bao-yu are married the better. It is ruining her health the way things are.'

'I agree,' replied Jia Zheng. 'But her family are very disorganized at present. And besides, it is midwinter. New Year will soon be upon us, and we shall all be busy putting our affairs in order. I propose the following timetable: the betrothal can take place sometime during the winter; early next year they can exchange presents; and the ceremony itself should be fixed for sometime after Mother's birthday. I should like you to put this to your sister.'

'I will,' replied Lady Wang.

The next day she told Aunt Xue, who thought the proposal a good one. After lunch the two of them went to see Grandmother Jia.

'Have you just come over, my dear?' inquired Grandmother Jia of Aunt Xue, after the usual courtesies had been exchanged.

'No, I was here yesterday,' replied Aunt Xue. 'But as it was rather late, I was not able to come and pay my respects.'

Lady Wang repeated Jia Zheng's proposal to Grandmother Jia, who seemed very happy with it. While they were talking, Bao-yu came into the room.

'Have you had your lunch yet?' asked his grandmother.

'I've been home for lunch,' he replied, 'and now I'm on my way back to school. I called in to see you, Grannie, and also I heard that Aunt Xue was here and wanted to pay my respects.'

Turning to Aunt Xue he continued:

'Is Cousin Chai quite better now?'

Aunt Xue smiled.

'Yes she is.'

Bao-yu noticed that his arrival had caused a sudden lull in the conversation. After sitting with them for a few minutes, he also noticed that Aunt Xue was not being as affectionate towards him as usual, and mused to himself:

'Even if she's not in a good mood, I don't see why they have to stop talking to me altogether . . .'

He set off for school greatly perplexed by what had happened.

That evening on his return he paid his usual evening calls and made his way to the Naiad's House. Lifting the door-curtain, he went in and was received by Nightingale. Seeing that there was no one in the inner room, he asked Nightingale where Dai-yu had gone, and was informed that she had gone to call on Grandmother Jia.

'Miss Lin heard that Mrs Xue was there,' said Nightingale, 'and wanted to pay her respects. Haven't you been there this evening, Master Bao?'

'Yes, I've just come from there, but I didn't see Miss Lin.'

'Wasn't she there?'

'No. Where could she have gone?'

'I'm not sure.'

Bao-yu was about to set off again when he caught sight of the graceful figure of Dai-yu walking slowly towards the door with Snowgoose.

'You're back, coz!' he exclaimed, stepping aside to let her pass, and then following her inside. She walked into the inner room.

'Do come in and sit down,' she said to Bao-yu. Nightingale fetched another jacket and helped her into it. She sat down and asked him:

'Did you see Mrs Xue at Grandmother's?'

'Yes, I did,' replied Bao-yu.

'Did she mention me at all?'

'No. And she didn't seem as friendly as usual towards me either. When I asked after Cousin Chai she just smiled and hardly said anything. I hope I haven't offended her by not going over to visit Chai this last couple of days.'

Dai-yu gave a short laugh.

'Have you been to see her?'

'I didn't know she was ill at first,' protested Bao-yu, 'I only heard a day or two ago, and I still haven't been . . .'

'Well that's certain to be the reason . . .'

'The truth is that neither Grandmother, Mother nor Father would let me go, and how could I without their permission? I used to be able to drop round and see her ten times a day if I felt like it; but now they've closed the little side-gate and I have to go round by the front, which is such a performance.'

'But how's she supposed to know all that?'

'You know Chai: she's sure to make allowances for me.'

'You shouldn't take it for granted,' retorted Dai-yu.

'Perhaps she won't. It's not as if it's her mother who's been ill: it's Chai herself. Think of all the poetry contests, all the pleasures you've shared with her in the past – the flowers, the wine, the parties. Now she's separated from us, and you know the troubles her family are having, yet when she falls seriously ill you behave with complete indifference. She's bound to be offended.'

Bao-yu: 'Surely you don't mean she doesn't like me any more?'

Dai-yu: 'I have no idea. I can only surmise how she might reasonably be expected to feel.'

Bao-yu stared in silence. Dai-yu ignored him, told one of her maids to put some more incense on the brazier, took out a book and began reading it. After a minute or two Bao-yu frowned and stamped his foot fretfully.

'What's the point in my being alive? The world would be an altogether better place without this thing called "me".'

'Can't you see?' said Dai-yu. 'It's the illusion of "me" that creates the illusion of "others", and a life lived under these twin illusions is bound to be beset with frustrations, fears, confusion, foolish dreams and a host of other obstacles and entanglements. I wasn't speaking in earnest earlier on. Mrs Xue was just in low spirits when you saw her. There was no need for you to bring Cousin Chai into it. Mrs Xue came over because of Cousin Pan's court-case. She was worried, and it's hardly surprising she wasn't in the mood to entertain you. You just allowed your imagination to run away with you and lead you astray.'

Her words brought Bao-yu a sudden sense of enlightenment.

'Of course!' he exclaimed with a laugh. 'That's exactly it! You're so much more perceptive than I am! No wonder you defeated me with that koan last year, when I was so wrought up. For all my pretensions, I need you to guide me to the truth. This bumptious Buddha bows to your Single Flower!'

'In that case,' said Dai-yu, seeing her opportunity, 'prepare yourself for another inquisition.'

Bao-yu crossed his legs, brought the palms of his hands together, closed his eyes, pursed his lips and said:

'Pray begin.'

Dai-yu: 'Now, let the First of my Propositions be that Cousin Chai likes you. Proposition the Second: she likes you not. The Third: she liked you a few days ago, but does no more. The Fourth: she does today, but will not do tomorrow. The Fifth: you like her, but she likes you not. The Sixth and last: she likes you, but you like her not. Consider these Six Propositions well.'

For several minutes Bao-yu was completely silent. Then suddenly he burst out laughing and cried:

'If all the Seas of Paradise were mine, with my simple gourd I'd be content.'

Dai-yu: 'What if your gourd is carried away by the stream?'

Bao-yu: 'Never! Wherever the stream flows, the gourd will always hold its own course.'

Dai-yu: 'What if the flow comes to an end and your Pearl sinks?'

Bao-yu: '"Like a catkin held fast in a puddle,
This Zen Mind:
Not a partridge, gaily cavorting
In the spring wind."'

Dai-yu: 'The first rule of Zen is not to tell lies.'

Bao-yu: 'But it's the truth, so help me Buddha, the Dharma and the Holy Brotherhood.'

Dai-yu lowered her head in silence. She heard a 'caw-caw' outside the window, and a crow flew up into the sky, wheeling towards the south-east.

Bao-yu: 'What sort of an omen is that?'

Dai-yu: 'Our fates cannot be learned from the cries of birds.'

Before Bao-yu could think of a reply, Ripple came into the room and said: 'Master Bao, please hurry! The Master sent someone to the Garden to ask if you were home from school yet. Aroma said you were, so you'd better be quick!'

Bao-yu jumped to his feet and hurried out in alarm. Dai-yu did not try to detain him. For the outcome, please read the next chapter.

CHAPTER 92

Qiao-jie studies the Lives of Noble Women
and shows a precocious enthusiasm for Virtue
Jia Zheng admires a Mother Pearl
and reflects on the vicissitudes of Life

'What does Father want me for?' asked Bao-yu in some alarm, as they left the Naiad's House. Ripple smiled.

'He doesn't. Aroma told me to fetch you, and I was afraid you wouldn't come, so I made it up . . .'

Bao-yu was greatly relieved.

'I would have come. There's really no need to scare me like that.'

He arrived back at Green Delights, to be interrogated by Aroma:

'Where have you been all this time?'

'At Miss Lin's. I got delayed. We were chatting about Aunt Xue and Cousin Chai's illness.'

'What were you saying?' asked Aroma inquisitively.

Bao-yu described his Zen dialogue with Dai-yu.

'You two are so silly,' was Aroma's comment. 'Why can't you have a normal conversation about ordinary things, or discuss something nice like poetry? What do you have to go talking about Zen for? You're not a monk!'

'You don't understand,' replied Bao-yu. 'We have our Zen secrets. No one else could join in our conversations.'

'I dare say,' returned Aroma, with a scornful sniff. 'I'm sure that if you two went on Zennifying at each other till you were both blue in the face, we should still be standing here quite as much in the dark as ever.'

'When I was younger,' said Bao-yu, ignoring her jibes, 'and Dai-yu was rather more childish in her ways, somehow I always managed to upset her by saying the wrong thing. Nowadays I think more about what I say, and she takes offence less easily. But all the same I have noticed that when we meet, which is not very often, as she seldom visits me and I have to spend so much time studying, we almost seem to have grown apart in some way.'

'I should hope so too,' said Aroma. 'Now that the two of you are older, of course you must learn to be more discreet.'

Bao-yu nodded his head irritably.

'I know – let's not talk any more about that now. What I want to know is, has anyone come over from Grandmother's with a message?'

'No.'

'Then she must have forgotten!' said Bao-yu. 'Tomorrow's the First of the Eleventh, isn't it? Every year Grannie has a party and invites the whole family over to celebrate the beginning of the Lessening Cold season, when the days start to get longer. I've already asked for the day off school, in fact. What am I to do? Should I go to school or not? If I do, that will be my day-off wasted. If I don't, and Father finds out, he'll scold me for playing truant.'

'I think you should go,' replied Aroma. 'You've just started to make progress with your studies, and this is no time to be thinking of letting up. You should be working as hard as you can. Only yesterday I heard Her Ladyship say how well young Lan is doing at his studies. When he gets back from school he settles straight down to his texts and compositions all on his own, and never goes to bed till the small hours. You're his uncle, and several years older than him. If you let him overtake you Her Old Ladyship will be very displeased. So I say, off to school early in the morning.'

Musk did not agree, however.

'In this cold weather?' she objected. 'If you go now, they'll wonder why you asked for the day off in the first place. It will look as though you were inventing an excuse to get off school. I think you should make the most of it and have a day's rest. If Her Old Ladyship has forgotten to have a party, we can always have one here instead...'

'Now he'll never go, and it will all be your fault,' complained Aroma.

'I believe in taking each day as it comes and having fun whenever you can,' said Musk defiantly. 'I don't believe in sucking up to people and working myself to death for a two-tael bonus every month like you do, Aroma dear...'

Aroma spat at her:

'You little hussy! Interfering in a serious discussion in such a silly manner...'

'On the contrary, I was saying it for your sake, dear...'

'For my sake?'

'Yes. As soon as Master Bao's gone to school, you'll sit around mooning and moaning again, longing for him to come home and bring the sunshine back into your life. Don't think you can fool me with that holier-than-thou attitude of yours...'

Aroma was on the point of giving Musk a large piece of her mind when one of Grandmother Jia's maids arrived and said:

'Her Old Ladyship says Master Bao's not to go to school tomorrow. Mrs Xue's been invited round to spend the day, and all the young ladies will probably be coming too. Miss Shi, Miss Xing and Mrs Zhu's cousins have all been invited. It's to celebrate the "lessening cold" or some such thing...'

'I told you so!' cried Bao-yu with glee before she could finish. 'It's always been one of Grannie's favourite occasions. Now I can have the day off *and* a clear conscience!'

Aroma said nothing, and Grandmother Jia's maid returned.

Bao-yu's recent stint of self-application had in fact left him more or less gasping for a respite of this sort. He was also delighted to hear that Aunt Xue was coming, as that would surely mean a chance to see Bao-chai.

'Let's have an early night,' he said. 'I want to be up first thing tomorrow.'

The night passed uneventfully, and early next morning, true to his resolution, Bao-yu went to pay his respects to Grandmother Jia and then to his father and mother, to whom he reported that 'Grannie had given him the day off school'. Jia Zheng raised no objection and Bao-yu withdrew from his presence at a snail's pace, waiting till he was a few yards from the study before breaking into a run and racing to Grandmother Jia's apartment. The other guests had not yet arrived, but he saw a nurse and a few younger maids enter the room with Xi-feng's little girl Qiao-jie, who walked up to her great-grandmother, paid her respects and said:

'Mama told me to come and say my good-morning and sit with you first, Great-grannie. She says she'll be here by and by.'

The old lady laughed.

'Bless you child! Here I've been sitting since cockcrow, and none of my guests has turned up, except your Uncle Bao.'

Qiao-jie's nurse did some discreet prompting:

'Say good morning to your uncle, Miss.'

Qiao-jie did so, and Bao-yu returned the greeting.

'My Mama wants to see you, Uncle Bao,' said Qiao-jie. 'She said so yesterday.'

'What about?' asked Bao-yu.

'She says she wants to find out if I've learnt my characters properly after all my lessons with Nannie Li. I promised her I had and offered to read them out for her. But she thought I was guessing and didn't believe me. She said I couldn't have learnt them because all I do all day long is play. But I don't think learning characters is hard. I can even read my *Girl's Classic of Filial Piety* – it's ever so easy. Mama thinks I'm making it up, so she wants you to go over it with me when you've got the time.'

Grandmother Jia laughed.

'Bless you darling! Your mother can't read a word, that's why she couldn't tell if you were cheating her or not. Tomorrow your uncle Bao will go over it with you, and she can listen in. Then she'll have to believe you.'

'How many characters do you know by now?' asked Bao-yu.

'Over three thousand,' replied Qiao-jie. 'I've finished the *Girl's Classic*, and a fortnight ago I started on *Lives of Noble Women Present and Past*.'

'Do you understand it all?' asked Bao-yu. 'If there's anything you're not clear about, you must tell me and I'll try and explain it for you.'

'What a nice idea,' commented Grandmother Jia. 'As her uncle, you should help her with her studies.'

Bao-yu cleared his throat.

'Let us leave aside,' he began, 'such household names as the worthy queen and consorts of Good King Wen, and pass on to those two other Models of Queenly Capability: Queen Jiang, who in order to rebuke her sovereign for his excessive attentions removed all her ornaments and stood like a prisoner awaiting sentence; and the Lady Hunchback of Wu-yan, whose earnest remonstrations restored order in the kingdom of Qi.'

'Yes,' said Qiao-jie, and Bao-yu went on:

'For Talent, we have the lady-historian Ban Zhao, Ban Jie-yu literary concubine of Emperor Cheng-di of Han, and the two poetesses Cai Wen-ji and Xie Dao-yun.'

'What about Paragons of Virtue?' asked Qiao-jie.

'Now let me see,' replied Bao-yu, 'for Virtue we have Meng Guang, the wife who wore a wooden hairpin and cotton skirts; we have Bao Xuan's wife, who drew her own water from the well, and Tao Kan's mother, who cut off her hair to buy wine for her son's guests. Their Virtue lay in their Acceptance of Poverty.'

Qiao-jie nodded her head enthusiastically.

'Then we have the famous cases of Hardship Endured,' continued Bao-yu. 'Princess Le-chang, who after a cruel separation was reunited with her husband by the stratagem of the broken mirror; and Su Hui, who embroidered a lengthy palindrome to send to her husband exiled in the wastes of Tartary. Then come the Paragons of Filial Piety: Mu Lan marching to war in her ailing father's place, Cao E throwing herself into the river after a fruitless search for her father's corpse – and many others besides . . .'

Qiao-jie had become very quiet and thoughtful, and when Bao-yu went on to recount the tale of Lady Cao who after her husband's death cut off her nose to deter any further suitors, and other tales of Widowed Virtue, her little face became more serious than ever. Thinking this might all be making her feel uncomfortable, Bao-yu introduced an apocryphal category of his own invention:

'Then of course we have the Famous Beauties, romantic ladies such as Wang Zhao-jun, Xi-shi, Cherry Lips, Willow Waist, Crimson Fairy, Zhuo Wen-jun, Red Duster – all of these were . . .'

'Enough!' interrupted Grandmother Jia, seeing the blank look on Qiao-jie's face. 'No more! You've filled the poor child's head to overflowing. How can she possibly remember all those names?'

'I recognize *some* of the names Uncle Bao mentioned,' said Qiao-jie. 'And his talk has certainly helped me to understand the ones I know.'

'I don't think we need bother going over the written characters for all those names,' said Bao-yu. 'I'm sure you know them.'

'Mama said that our Crimson used to be one of your maids,' said Qiao-jie out of the blue. 'And she says she still hasn't found you anyone to replace her. She's thinking of giving you Mrs Liu's daughter, Fivey I think her name is, if you're happy about it . . .'

Bao-yu was delighted to hear this and said with a grin:

'Your mother doesn't have to ask me about things like that. She makes all the decisions.'

He turned with a smile to Grandmother Jia.

'My young niece shows every sign of growing up to be a second Cousin Feng. Only I think she may be even cleverer, and will have the added advantage of being able to read.'

'I've no objection to girls learning their letters,' commented Grandmother Jia. 'But needlework must always come first.'

'Nannie Liu teaches me embroidery,' said Qiao-jie. 'I can do flowers and chain-patterns. I'm not very good yet, but I'm learning.'

'In a family like ours,' said Grandmother Jia, 'we never *need* to do our own sewing, I know. But it's as well to know how. Then you will never be at the mercy of others.'

'Yes, Great-grannie,' Qiao-jie smilingly replied. She would have welcomed some more Paragons of Virtue, but thought Bao-yu looked a little preoccupied and did not venture to ask.

What was preoccupying Bao-yu? The answer lies in Qiao-jie's mention of Fivey. This attractive girl had been originally designated for Green Delights, but one obstacle after another had so far prevented her from entering service there. First it had been illness; then they had been wary of choosing a good-looking maid for Bao-yu in the puritanical phase that followed on Lady Wang's expulsion of Skybright. A further opportunity of seeing her had presented itself when she and her mother had arrived with gifts during his secret visit to Skybright at her cousin's house – and his earlier favourable impression of her had been confirmed. She really was extremely pretty. What marvellous luck that Xi-feng should have remembered her now, and was arranging for her to take Crimson's place!

While Bao-yu was day-dreaming, Grandmother Jia was becoming more and more impatient at the lateness of her guests and sent word to hurry them along. A few minutes later the first contingent arrived: Li Wan and her two cousins Wen and Qi, Tan-chun, Xi-chun, Shi Xiang-yun and Lin Dai-yu. They all paid their respects to Grandmother Jia and greeted one another. Aunt Xue had still not come, and Grandmother Jia sent for her. Finally she arrived, accompanied by Bao-qin. Bao-yu paid his respects, and said hello to Bao-qin, wondering why it was that neither Bao-chai nor Xing Xiu-yan had come. When Dai-yu asked outright, 'Why couldn't Cousin Chai come today?', Aunt Xue pretended that she was not feeling well. Xiu-yan had stayed away because she knew that Aunt Xue (her future mother-in-law) would be there. Bao-chai's absence caused a momentary depression in Bao-yu's spirits, which was however soon dispelled by the presence of Dai-yu.

Lady Xing and Lady Wang arrived shortly afterwards. Xi-feng, who heard that they were there before her and was embarrassed at the thought of being late, sent Patience ahead to apologize for her.

'Mrs Lian was meaning to come, but she has had a bit of a fever and won't be coming till later,' said Patience.

'If she's not feeling well, she needn't bother to come at all,' said Grandmother Jia. 'We ought to start our lunch now.'

The maids moved the charcoal brazier to the back of the room and placed two tables in front of Grandmother Jia's couch, at which the party now arranged itself for lunch. After lunch they sat once more round the brazier chatting pleasantly, and there for the present we must leave them.

*

What was really detaining Xi-feng? It had at first been no more than her embarrassment at being later than Ladies Xing and Wang. But this had been further complicated by the arrival of Brightie's wife, who informed her that one of Ying-chun's women-servants had come to pay her respects. The woman had come straight to Xi-feng's apartment and had not notified the main mansion of her presence. Xi-feng was puzzled, and summoned her into the room.

'Is your mistress well?' she asked.

'Anything but well,' replied the woman. 'But that's not what I've come about, ma'am. Really it was Chess's mother who begged me to come and ask you for a favour.'

'But Chess has been dismissed,' said Xi-feng. 'What have her affairs to do with me now?'

'It's a long story, ma'am. From the day she was dismissed Chess did nothing but cry her heart out. Then one day that cousin of hers, her boy-friend Pan You-an, turned up again. Her mother was terribly rude to him when she saw him, swearing that he'd been her daughter's ruin. She took hold of him and tried to hit him, while he stood there meek and mild not saying a word. Chess heard what was going on and came rushing out and cried defiantly: "It was because of him I was dismissed – I don't need reminding! I know he acted wrong! But now that he's come back, why start hitting him? You may as well strangle me instead..." "You shameless slut!" cries the mother, "what do you want then?" "A girl can only marry once," replies Chess defiantly. "It was my mistake, I let him take me, and right or wrong I'm his now and no one else shall have me. If he could only have shown a little more courage then and stood by me instead of running away! But I'd wait for him now even if I had to die waiting. I'd rather die than let you marry me to someone else. Now that he's here, ask him if he'll take me for his wife. If he still wants me, I'll make you my farewell kotow and you can forget that I ever existed. I'll follow him to the ends of the earth. I'll beg in the streets if need be!" This put her mother in a terrible rage. Weeping and cursing she cried: "You're my daughter and if I say you can't marry him then you can't, and that's that!" But Chess was an obstinate creature. No sooner had her mother said this than she took a run at the wall and dashed her head against it. She split her skull open, the blood came pouring out and in a moment she was dead! Her mother began howling, but it was too late. Next she started screaming at him that he'd have to pay with his life. He replied – and this is the strangest part of the story – "Don't worry. I'm a wealthy man now. I never forgot your daughter, and came back today to find her. I have always been true to her. To prove that I'm telling no lie . . ." As he said this he brought out a casket from inside his gown, full of gold and precious stones. One look at them and Chess's mother changed her tune. "Why oh why didn't you say all this earlier?" she asked. "I know the ways of women," he replied, "how easily swayed they are by the idea of wealth. Now at least I know for sure that she was a girl in a million. These are yours," he added, handing her the casket. "I will go and buy the coffin now, and see to it that she is buried properly." The mother took the casket and left all the arrangements to her nephew. She seemed to have quite forgotten about Chess. When he returned, she saw to her astonishment that the bearers he had employed were bringing not one but two coffins. She asked him what he needed two coffins for, and he replied with a strange laugh that one would not be enough. He showed not the least sign of crying, and the mother decided his mind must have been deranged by the shock of his grief. For a while he was busy preparing Chess's corpse, dry-eyed and silent, when all of a sudden before anyone had time to take in what was happening he pulled out a knife and slit his throat and that was the end of him. The mother realized too late what a terrible thing she had done, and broke down in floods of tears. The whole neighbourhood knows, and they want to report the case to the magistrate. In her distress she begged me to ask you to use your influence to help her, ma'am, and said she would come herself and kotow to you in gratitude.'

'What a story!' exclaimed Xi-feng, aghast at this recital. 'That fate should have brought two such examples of folly together! Now I understand that look of calm indifference on her face when she was caught during the search of the Garden. What a determined young thing she must have been at heart. I don't really have time to meddle in such things, but your story has touched my heart! Tell her mother that I will speak to Mr Lian and send Brightie to sort the thing out for her.'

Xi-feng sent the woman on her way and herself departed to join the gathering at Grandmother Jia's.

*

One day, Jia Zheng was engrossed in a game of Go with one of his literary gentlemen, Zhan Guang. It had been quite a level game, and the outcome now hung on a *ko* that was in progress on one corner of the board. As they were playing, a page from the gate came in to report that Mr Feng had arrived and was waiting outside to see Sir Zheng.

'See him in,' instructed Jia Zheng.

The page did as bidden and Feng Zi-ying was shortly to be observed walking in through the inner gateway. Jia Zheng hurried out to receive him and conducted him through to the study. As he sat down, Feng noticed that they were playing Go.

'Please carry on with your game,' he said. 'I shall be very happy to watch.'

'My poor play is hardly a worthy spectacle for so distinguished an observer,' protested Zhan Guang with an obsequious smile.

'You are too modest,' said Feng. 'Carry on please.'

'What brings you here today?' inquired Jia Zheng.

'Oh, nothing of any importance,' replied Feng. 'Carry on, sir. I shall benefit greatly from watching your play.'

Jia Zheng turned to his partner.

'As Feng is an old friend and has not come on any pressing business, we may as well finish our game first. He can sit and watch.'

'Are you playing for stakes?' asked Feng.

'We are,' replied Zhan Guang.

'Then silence! On with the game!'

'I don't think we need be too strict about that,' said Jia Zheng. 'I may be a dozen taels up by the end, but I doubt very much if I shall see the colour of my money. I think friend Zhan will have to stand us a few drinks instead.'

'An excellent idea,' said Zhan with a laugh.

'Are you and friend Zhan on a par, sir?' inquired Feng.

Jia Zheng laughed.

'We used to play level, but he always lost, so I gave him a handicap of two. He still loses. And the trouble is, he thinks he can take his moves back all the time, and gets quite upset when I wave the rules at him.'

Zhan laughed.

'You exaggerate, Sir Zheng . . .'

'Well, we shall see . . .'

On this note of light-hearted banter, they continued their game. When it was finished and they counted up the pieces, Zhan was seven down.

'It all depended on that last *ko*,' commented Feng. 'You gained the advantage, sir, because you were less vulnerable to a *ko* threat.'

Jia Zheng turned to Feng.

'Please forgive us. How are you keeping?'

'It has been a long while since we last met,' said Feng. 'My visit today is partly of a social nature, and partly occasioned by the presence in the capital of a deputy-prefect from Kwangsi province, who is here for an audience with His Majesty and has brought with him four curios, some of them imported, that would make excellent palace-offerings. The first is a folding screen of twenty-four panels, carved of pure blackwood. Though the stone used for the carved inlay – landscapes, figures, buildings, birds and flowers – is not jade, it is a high quality serpentine. Each panel has a palace scene, with fifty or sixty palace-ladies. It is called "Spring Morning in the Han Palace". The features, gestures and costumes are rendered with great clarity. The finish is quite exquisite, the detail and composition of the highest order. It would be perfect for the main hall of Prospect Garden, sir. The second item is a large wall-clock over three feet high. This is a most unusual item. It has a little figure of a boy on the face that indicates the hour with a pointer, and inside it has a little mechanical orchestra. Those two heavier articles I was not able to bring with me. I have however brought the other two, which I think you will find quite fascinating.'

Feng produced an embroidered casket wrapped in several layers of white damask-silk. Unwrapping it, he raised the lid, removed the protective pad of silk-wool beneath it and displayed its contents. In the top compartment of the casket lay a little glass container with a fitted lid. In this container, on a piece of crimson silk that lined its inner casing of gold, lay a magnificent lustrous pearl, as large as a longan.

'This,' announced Feng, 'is known as a Mother Pearl.'

He asked for a tray and Zhang Guang handed him a tea-tray of black lacquer, asking:

'Will this do?'

'Perfectly,' replied Feng, taking from the inner pocket of his gown a white silk bundle. This too contained pearls, of an ordinary size, which he tipped out onto the tray. He then placed the 'Mother Pearl' in their midst and put the tray down on the table. Like so many perfect drops of water the smaller pearls rolled across the tray towards the large central pearl. And when Feng lifted the 'Mother', all the little ones clung to her. Not a single one was left on the tray.

'Amazing!' exclaimed Zhan Guang.

'An interesting phenomenon,' observed Jia Zheng. 'And most appropriately named.'

'Where is the other casket?' asked Feng turning to his page, who promptly came forward with a rosewood casket held aloft in both hands. The three men gathered round as it was opened. On its lining of tiger-brocade lay a length of blue gauze-like material, many times folded.

'And what is this?' asked Zhan Guang.

'This,' replied Feng, 'is called Byssus Net.'

He took it from the casket and laid it on the table. Folded as it was, it occupied a space no more than five inches long and less than half an inch thick. Feng began to unfold it. When he had done so a dozen times, it extended over the edge of the table.

'There are still two folds to come,' he explained. 'To unfold it to its full extent we would need to hang it in a room with a high ceiling. This fabric is woven from the Byssus, the so-called Mermaid's Tears. In extreme heat it would make a perfect fly and mosquito-net for use in a large reception hall. As you can see, it is extremely light and transparent.'

'Please do not unfold it fully,' said Jia Zheng. 'It might prove hard to fold again.'

Feng and Zhan Guang carefully folded the net and replaced it in its casket.

'The price being asked for these four curios is really very reasonable,' said Feng. 'I think he would be willing to part with the four for twenty thousand taels. Ten thousand for the Mother Pearl, five thousand for the Byssus Net and two thousand five hundred each for the screen and striking clock.'

'We could not possibly buy them, I'm afraid,' said Jia Zheng.

'But with your connections in the palace,' said Feng, 'surely they would make an ideal presentation.'

'I dare say they would,' replied Jia Zheng. 'I dare say all sorts of things would. But we simply haven't the money. I would like Lady Jia to see them, all the same.'

'By all means.'

Jia Zheng sent a page to fetch Jia Lian, who was instructed to take the pearl and the precious net through to Grandmother Jia's apartment. He also sent a servant to invite Lady Xing, Lady Wang and Xi-feng to come and view them.

'There are two other items,' Jia Lian explained to the ladies. 'A folding screen and a musical clock. The whole lot is going for twenty thousand taels.'

'What!' said Xi-feng sharply. 'I grant you they're fine pieces. But we definitely haven't the cash to spare. Besides we're not like provincial viceroys and governors, who are expected to make such offerings. No; over the years I've come to the conclusion that the most sensible way to secure our financial future is to invest in land and property – trust-land for provision of sacrificial funds, and free burial-grounds for the clan with permanent caretakers' quarters. Such things would be there for the family to fall back on in hard times, an insurance against ruin. I don't know if Grannie, Father and Mother agree with me or not? Of course, if Sir Zheng and Father want to buy these things, it's entirely their decision.'

Grandmother Jia led the chorus in Xi-feng's support.

'You're absolutely right, my dear.'

'Give them back to me then,' said Jia Lian grumpily. 'Sir Zheng only sent me to show them to Grandmother as a possible palace-offering. No one said anything about buying them for ourselves. Trust you to pour cold water on the whole idea before Grandmother has even had a chance to speak!'

Jia Lian returned to the study with the curios, and reported that Grandmother Jia did not wish to buy them.

'No one denies their quality,' he said to Feng Zi-ying. 'But we just can't afford them. I'll keep my eyes open though, and if I come across a likely buyer I'll definitely let you know.'

Feng packed them away again, evidently disappointed. He sat and chatted for a while without much enthusiasm, and soon made motions of leaving.

'Won't you stay to dinner?' asked Jia Zheng.

'I have already taken up too much of your time . . .'

'Not at all. We should be delighted.'

As they were speaking Jia She was announced. He was already in the room, and after greeting Feng engaged him in conversation for a few minutes. Presently wine was served and various delicacies were set on the table. After the fourth or fifth round of wine, the subject of the curios came up again.

'Actually it's rather hard to sell stuff like this,' confessed Feng. 'The market is restricted to the few illustrious families such as yours.'

'Oh come, I am sure you will find someone,' Jia Zheng consoled him.

'Besides,' observed Jia She in a rather maudlin tone, 'we are not exactly the great and glorious house we once were, you know. Nothing but a hollow facade . . .'

'How is Mr Zhen over at Ning-guo House by the way?' asked Feng. 'I saw him the other day and in the course of conversation he mentioned this new wife of his son's. Not a patch on his first, so he was saying. Who is she anyway? I never did ask her name.'

'She's a Hu–they're an old local family. Her father was once Taotai of the Metropolitan Circuit,' Jia Zheng informed him.

'Oh, I know Intendant Hu . . .' said Feng. 'Heard that he lets some pretty rum things go on in his house too. Still, the main thing is that the gal should have turned out all right.'

'I heard from someone at the Grand Secretariat that Yu-cun is to be promoted again,' put in Jia Lian.

'Really? I'm glad to hear that,' said Jia Zheng. 'Has it been made official yet?'

'Most probably,' said Jia Lian.

'Yes, I heard the same myself when I was at the Board of Civil Office earlier today,' said Feng. 'Am I right in thinking that he is a relation of yours, sir?'

'He is,' answered Jia Zheng.

'A close one?'

'It is a long story,' said Jia Zheng. 'He comes originally from Hu-zhou in Chekiang. He left home and was lodging in Soochow, eking out a rather unsatisfactory existence, when he was befriended by a gentleman named Zhen Shi-yin, who provided the means for him to better himself. Yu-cun later went on to become a palace graduate, and passed out with flying colours and an immediate posting as a magistrate in one of the provinces. He took one of this benefactor's maidservants as his concubine; she is now, I believe, his principal wife. Old Zhen himself was reduced to destitution by a strange series of calamities, and finally disappeared without trace.'

'We only came to know Yu-cun,' continued Jia Zheng, 'when my brother-in-law, Lin Ru-hai, who at that time was the Yangchow Salt Commissioner, engaged him as private tutor for his daughter – this was after his dismissal. Then Yu-cun learned of the general reinstatement for dismissed officials and planned to come up to the capital to take advantage of it. My niece – Ru-hai's daughter – was, as it so happened, just about to come and visit us here, so her father persuaded her tutor to travel with her and act as her escort. He also sent me a letter of recommendation, asking me to put in a good word for him where I could. I formed a favourable impression of him, and from then on we saw a good deal of one another. One thing I remember finding most extraordinary about Yu-cun: he seemed to have familiarized himself with every detail of our family history. There was nothing he did not know. Who our ancestors were, how they won their titles, every ramification of the Rong-guo and Ning-guo family trees, exactly how many of us there are, who we all are, where we all live, what we all do – why, he was a mine of information! I liked him for it, I must say.'

Jia Zheng smiled, and went on:

'He's done extremely well for himself in the last few years too. Promoted from Prefect to Censor, then in a few years to Vice-president of the Board of Civil Office, then President of the Board of War. He was demoted three grades for some incident, but now it seems he is to be promoted again.'

'How hard it is to predict the vicissitudes of human life,' commented Feng Zi-ying.

'And yet there is a pattern in all things,' said Jia Zheng. 'Take your pearl for instance. The big one is like a man blessed with fortune; the little ones are his dependants, sheltering in the shade of his influence. If the big one goes, then the little ones are helpless. If the head of a family is in trouble, his wife and children are taken from him, his relations are left destitute, even his friends he may see no more. Prosperity may crumble in the twinkling of an eye, like the passing of a spring cloud or the falling of an autumn leaf. What joy is there in public life? My kinsman Yu-cun has had a comparatively easy time of it. But take a case nearer home, the Zhen family, like our own in so many respects. They too were ennobled for their services to the Throne. Their style of life has always been very like ours. We used to see a great deal of them. I remember not many years ago when they were here in the capital, they sent one of their men round to convey their respects, and all seemed well. Yet not long afterwards their family estate was confiscated, and goodness alone knows what has become of them now. We have had no news of them for so long. My heart goes out to them.'

'What's this about a pearl?' asked Jia She. Jia Zheng and Feng Zi-ying gave him a description of the 'Mother Pearl'.

'We need have no fears,' said Jia She, resuming the previous topic of conversation. 'Nothing can happen to us.'

'Of course not, sir,' said Feng, 'with Her Grace to protect your interests at Court, with such enviable connections and such a host of relations, and with a family that from Lady Jia down to the younger generation has such an impeccable record . . .'

'Granted,' said Jia Zheng somewhat grimly. 'But our respectability is more than balanced by our lack of ability and positive achievement. We are living on borrowed time, and one day it will run out.'

'Do let's put an end to this depressing conversation,' said Jia She, 'and have another drink.'

They did so, and after a few more rounds dinner was served. After dinner, tea was brought in and Feng's page came in and murmured something in his master's ear. Feng took his leave.

'What was that you said?' asked Jia She of the page.

'It's snowing, sir, and they've sounded the first evening watch.'

Jia Zheng sent a servant out who came back to report that the snow was indeed already more than an inch thick on the ground.

'I hope your two curios are well wrapped?' said Jia Zheng.

'They are,' replied Feng. 'Don't forget, if you change your minds, I'm sure we can come to some agreement about the price.'

'I'll bear it in mind,' said Jia Zheng.

'I shall wait to hear from you then. It's cold – please don't bother to see me out. Goodbye.'

Jia She and Jia Zheng instructed Jia Lian to accompany Feng Zi-ying to the gate.

For the sequel, please read the following chapter.

CHAPTER 93

A Zhen retainer seeks shelter
in the Jia household
And shady activities are revealed
behind the Iron Threshold

When Feng Zi-ying had gone, Jia Zheng sent for one of the men on the gate.

'I see there's an invitation here from the Earl of Lin-an,' he said. 'Do you know what sort of an occasion it is?'

'I did inquire, sir,' replied the servant. 'It's only the arrival of a new company of actors at the Prince of Nan-an's. They are said to be first-class, and his lordship wants to celebrate by putting on a dramatic entertainment for a couple of days. Just an informal party for friends, nothing requiring a presentation I should say, sir.'

As the servant was speaking Jia She came over.

'Will you be going tomorrow?' he asked his brother.

'I really ought to,' replied Jia Zheng. 'The Earl has always been most affable.'

Another servant came in from the gate and reported to Jia Zheng:

'There's a clerk from the Ministry, sir; will you please go in to the office tomorrow. The President has some important business for you, so could you be there a little earlier than usual.'

This received a brief acknowledgement from Jia Zheng. Two family servants came in next, whose job it was to collect the land rents from the Rong-guo country estates. They paid their respects, made their kotow and stood humbly to one side.

'Are you from Hao-family village?' asked Jia Zheng.

'Yes, sir.'

Jia Zheng did not inquire any further into their business. He and Jia She talked a little longer and then both left for their apartments, Jia She accompanied by servants bearing lanterns.

When they had gone, Jia Lian asked the rent-collectors for their report.

'We've been as fast as we could with the tenth-month rents, sir,' replied one of them. 'They were due to arrive tomorrow, but we ran into trouble a few miles from town. Our wagons were seized by a patrol and everything was tipped out onto the ground. They didn't let us get a word in. I tried to explain that it was rent-produce for Rong-guo House, not ordinary goods in transit, but they couldn't have cared less. And when I told our wagoner to keep on going, some of the highway-patrol beat him up and impounded two wagons. I've come on ahead to report, sir. The only thing now is for you to send someone to the local yamen and demand our goods back. And you'd be doing everyone a good turn, if you had those hooligans in the highway-patrol brought to order. You may not know it, but the regular goods-wagons have an even worse time with them. They tip out the contents and make off with them, and if the poor old wagoner dares to open his mouth in protest, he has his brains beaten out.'

'What a preposterous state of affairs!' exclaimed Jia Lian. He wrote a note at once and handed it to one of his men.

'Take this to the yamen responsible for impounding the wagons. We want our wagons and all our goods back at once. If we discover the smallest thing missing there'll be trouble.'

He sent for Zhou Rui. Zhou was out, so he sent for Brightie instead, only to be informed that Brightie had gone out at midday and had still not returned.

'The lazy bastards! They're never here when they're wanted! All they do from one year to the next is slack around at our expense!'

Shouting to his pages to find them both at once, Jia Lian retired to his apartment for the night.

*

Next morning brought a reminder from the Earl of Lin-an.

'I shall be busy at the Ministry,' said Jia Zheng to his brother. 'And Lian will have to stay here to sort out this trouble with the rent-wagons. You had better take Bao-yu with you for the day.'

Jia She nodded.

'Very well.'

Jia Zheng sent word to Bao-yu that he was to accompany his uncle to the Earl of Lin-an's theatre party. Bao-yu was thrilled. He changed, and choosing three of his pages, Tealeaf, Sweeper and Ploughboy, to go with him, came out to pay his morning respects to Jia She. They climbed into their carriages and were soon at the Earl's palace. A gateman went in to announce their arrival and returned after a brief interval to escort them in.

Jia She led Bao-yu into the main courtyard, which was packed with a noisy throng. They paid their respects to the Earl and exchanged civilities with the other guests before sitting down and joining in the flow of light-hearted conversation. Before long the manager of the troupe came forward with two playbills, an ordinary one and a fancy one in the form of an ivory tablet, and saluting his patrons by dropping one knee to the ground Manchu-style, announced:

'Will the gentlemen please select their favourite plays?'

Passing along the distinguished company, he came to Jia She, who made his choice. Then catching sight of Bao-yu, he hurried straight towards him, saluted him most elegantly and said:

'Will Master Bao be so good as to choose two from our list?'

Bao-yu studied his face. Those powder-white cheeks,

those lips as red as rouge, that fresh lustre, like a lotus on the water, that lilting gait, like a jade tree swaying in the wind – why, it was his old friend Jiang Yu-han! Bao-yu remembered having heard of his arrival in town with his own troupe. He also remembered wondering why he had still not seen anything of him. Meeting him now in such formal company, he felt unable to rise spontaneously to his feet, and had to content himself with asking:

'When did you arrive?'

Jiang glanced quickly from left to right, then with a confidential smile whispered:

'Surely you knew I was here?'

Bao-yu felt too inhibited to continue the conversation, and made his choice of plays in some confusion.

When Jiang returned backstage, the guests started talking about him.

'He used to play soubrette parts,' volunteered one of them. 'Now that he's older, he's given that up and turned manager. He manages the Prince's resident troupe. Before that he'd already started playing young male leads. He made quite a lot of money, and bought two or three shops. But nothing could keep him from the stage, so he has turned actor-manager.'

Someone asked:

'He must surely be married by now?'

'Not yet,' came the reply. 'He has strong views on the subject. "Marriage," says he, "is a once-and-for-all thing, a lifetime affair, and not to be trifled with." His bride may be rich or poor, of high or low birth, but the one thing she must possess is talent to match his. So, he's remained single to this day.'

'I wonder who the lucky girl will be,' thought Bao-yu secretly to himself, 'to marry such a fine fellow . . .'

By now the plays had started. They performed in a variety of styles; the lyrical *kun-qu*, the noisier *gao-qiang* and *yi-qiang*, and the 'clapper' style from Shensi to the west. It was a splendid show. At midday the tables were set out, and wine and food were served. After an act or two of the afternoon programme, Jia She showed signs of wanting to leave. But the Earl came over and pressed him to stay:

'The day is still young,' he said, 'and I understand that Bijou intends to perform a scene from 'The Queen of the Flowers', their *pièce de résistance*.'

When Bao-yu heard this, he secretly prayed for his uncle to stay. Jia She sat down again.

It was soon time for 'The Queen of the Flowers', with Jiang Yu-han playing Master Qin, the humble oil-vendor. The scene in which he sits up with the drunken flower-girl Jasper Lute had just the right degree of erotic tenderness, while the drinking duet was exactly as it should be, *amoroso delicioso*. Bao-yu hardly noticed Jasper Lute. He only had eyes for Master Qin. That ringing vocal timbre, that crystal diction, that subtle tempo were too much for his sensitive soul. He was enraptured. By the end of the performance he knew beyond any shadow of doubt that Jiang Yu-han was an artist of True Feeling, and not to be compared with the common run of actors. It reminded him of a passage from the chapter 'On Music', in the *Liber Ritualis*:

> 'Feeling stirs within and is embodied in sound. When that sound is fashioned by art, music is born.'

'No wonder true lovers of music make so much of "Knowing the Sound", entering into the essence of the music,' thought Bao-Yu to himself. 'I must get to the heart of it. Poetry conveys feeling, but music strikes to the very core. From now on I must study it in earnest.'

He was awoken from this rapture by Jia She, who had had enough and this time left before his host had another chance to detain him. Bao-yu had no choice but to follow in his uncle's steps.

On their arrival home, Jia She went straight to his own apartment, while Bao-yu went to report to his father, who had just returned from the Board and was discussing with Jia Lian the affair of the impounded rent-wagons.

'I sent a man with a note today,' Jia Lian was saying. 'But the local mandarin was out. The gateman said that his master knew nothing of the affair and had certainly never issued a warrant in connection with it. He said it was a piece of flagrant corruption and extortion on the part of the "scum in the highway-patrol". As this was Jia family property, he said he would have the culprits found and dealt with, and gave his personal guarantee that we would have the vehicles and goods back by tomorrow. If we discover a single thing missing, we are to report to his master and stern measures will be taken. But at present, as his master was away, he asked us as a special favour to be discreet and not bother him with it.'

'How can such a thing be done without any kind of warrant?' said Jia Zheng.

'You don't seem to realize, Uncle,' said Jia Lian, 'that this sort of thing goes on all the time. I think we shall probably have our goods back tomorrow all right.'

Business concluded, Jia Lian left the room. Bao-yu now came forward and reported on his day at the Earl's. His father asked him a few questions, then sent him on to Grandmother Jia's.

Jia Lian had not forgotten yesterday's unaccounted absence on the part of the two menservants, and on leaving Jia Zheng he gave orders for a general assembly of the staff. This time there was a prompt response. After a few preliminary words of reprimand Jia Lian called forward Lai Da, the chief steward.

'Fetch the general register for all household departments and call the roll. Then I want you to write out an announcement. I want everyone to know that if I detect a single case of absence without leave, or failure to come when sent for, or negligence in any other respect whatsoever, I shall have the culprit immediately flogged and dismissed.'

'Yes sir!' replied Lai Da several times. He went out and relayed this to the assembled servants, who all took due note.

*

Not long afterwards there was an unexpected arrival at the main gate. A man in a felt hat, blue cotton gown and sturdy, leather-patched slippers approached and bowed to the janitors on duty. They eyed him up and down and asked him where he hailed from.

'From the Zhen family in the South,' was his reply. 'I have with me a letter from my Master, which I beg you to take in to Sir Zheng.'

When they learned that he was from the Zhen family, the men stood up and made room for the newcomer to sit down.

'You must be tired. Here, sit down. We'll take your letter in for you.'

One of them went in to report his arrival and deliver the letter to Jia Zheng. He opened it, and this is what he read:

'My dear Zheng,

Over many generations our two families have established close ties of friendship and mutual understanding. We have always looked up to your illustrious house with the profoundest respect. Although for my heinous crime a thousand deaths would have been insufficient punishment, thanks to an exceptional act of clemency, I have been favoured with a mild sentence of banishment to the frontier. In the general dispersion of our family establishment, I have a manservant called Bao Yong, who has served me well and though lacking any particular skill, is a thoroughly trustworthy and dependable fellow. If you could see your way to employing him in some humble capacity in your household, my gratitude would be unbounded.

I shall write again when I can. With sincere regards,

Your fellow-graduate and friend,

Zhen Ying-jia.'

Jia Zheng smiled wrily as he reached the end of the letter.

'Here we are overstaffed ourselves,' he mused aloud to himself, 'and the Zhens must send us one of theirs. We shall have to try and find room for him somehow, I suppose.'

He turned to the gateman.

'Send this fellow in to see me, and find somewhere for him to stay. There must be some way in which he can make himself useful.'

The gateman went out, and came back with Bao Yong, who prostrated himself before Jia Zheng and performed a threefold kotow. Rising to his feet, he declared solemnly:

'My Master presents his greetings, sir.'

Then falling on one knee, he continued:

'Bao Yong offers his humble respects, sir.'

Jia Zheng inquired after Zhen Ying-jia, and surveyed Bao Yong. He was something over five feet tall, broad-shouldered and strongly built, with heavy brows and prominent eyes, a protruding forehead, a long beard and a rough, dark complexion. He stood with his arms hanging respectfully at his side.

'Have you been with the Zhens since birth?' asked Jia Zheng. 'Or have you only served them for a number of years?'

Bao Yong: 'Since birth, sir.'

Jia Zheng: 'Why do you wish to leave them now?'

Bao Yong: 'It was not my wish at all, sir. But the Master insisted that I should, and said that I'd find things here very much the same as with them. That is why I have come here.'

Jia Zheng: 'Your master has not deserved the hardship to which he and his family have been reduced.'

Bao Yong: 'It is not my place to say such things but I think the Master is far too good a man, far too honest in his dealings with people. That is what has brought this trouble on him.'

Jia Zheng: 'But honesty is a great virtue.'

Bao Yong: 'Too much of it doesn't always go down well. Some people are irked by it.'

Jia Zheng (with a smile): 'If that is the case, I feel confident that the Supreme Providence will see justice done.'

Bao Yong was about to say something when Jia Zheng went on:

'Am I right in thinking that your master has a son called Bao-yu?'

Bao Yong: 'That is correct, sir.'

Jia Zheng: 'Tell me, does he work hard at his studies?'

Bao Yong: 'That's a very interesting question sir. There's quite a story behind it. In a way our Master Bao-yu is just like his father, very single-minded, very – how shall I say – dedicated. His life has until recently been dedicated to playing with his sisters and lady cousins. The Master and Her Ladyship have given him quite a few thrashings, all to no effect. A year or so ago, however, when Her Ladyship was away on a trip to the capital, our Master Bao fell seriously ill. He had been given up for dead for a long while in fact, and the Master himself was nearly dead with worry. His funeral clothes were even laid out in readiness. In the end he recovered, thank goodness. When he came round, he said that he had been through a great archway, where he met a lady, who showed him a temple full of cabinets. And in these cabinets were a number of registers, which he saw. Then he went into a room full of girls, who turned into ghosts and skeletons. He was scared and cried out, and that was when he woke up.

'After this experience of his, his father had him treated by a doctor and slowly but surely he became well. This time he was indulged and allowed to play with his sisters and cousins to his heart's content. But who would have thought it – he had completely changed his ways! None of his old games appealed to him any more. Now it was all books and studying. And nobody could distract him. He's even learning to help the Master with family business.'

Jia Zheng was silent, lost in thought. Then he said:

'You may go now. When we have need of you we will find you a proper post.'

'Thank you sir,' said Bao Yong, and withdrew from the room. He was shown to his temporary quarters by some of the servants, and there we must leave him.

*

A few days later, Jia Zheng rose early and was passing through the main gate on his way to the Board, when he noticed the porters and servants huddled together in some sort of confabulation. They seemed to be trying to attract his attention, but at the same time were evidently too afraid to speak out, and could only whisper among themselves. He called one of them over and asked:

'What's going on? What's all this muttering in corners about?'

'We daren't tell, sir . . .' replied the servant.

Jia Zheng: 'Daren't tell what?'

Servant: 'Well sir, this morning when I got up to open the gate, I found a sheet of white paper stuck to it with a lot of rude words written on it . . .'

Jia Zheng: 'What's this? What sort of thing do you mean?'

Servant: 'Something about sordid goings-on at the Temple of the Iron Threshold, sir.'

Jia Zheng: 'Show it to me!'

Servant: 'I tried to peel it off in one piece, sir, but it was stuck on so firmly that I couldn't. So I copied the wording down instead and then scrubbed it clean. Li De has just found another one. He showed it to me, and it says much the same. That's the truth, sir.'

He handed Jia Zheng the most recent specimen. Jia Zheng took it and read:

> Jia Qin's a lucky young sod –
> He's in charge of the family nunnery.
> All those girls for just one bod –

Whoring, gambling, loads of funnery!
Now that rakes are running the place,
Rong-guo House is a public disgrace!

Jia Zheng was boiling. His head began to swim, his eyes to swirl. Telling the servants at the gate not to breathe a word of this, he gave secret orders to search every alley-way in the neighbourhood for any further posters, and sent at once for Jia Lian, who came hurrying over.

'Tell me,' asked Jia Zheng, 'have you ever personally checked the arrangements made for the nuns and Taoist novices lodged at the Iron Threshold Temple?'

'Not personally, no,' replied Jia Lian. 'That has always been young Qin's responsibility.'

'And do you know if he is competent or not?' asked Jia Zheng.

'It sounds from what you say as though he must have slipped up over some detail,' said Jia Lian.

'Take a look at this!'

Jia Lian read the poster and exclaimed:

'Why, this is an outrage!'

The words were no sooner out of his mouth than Jia Rong came in with a letter bearing the inscription: 'For the attention of Sir Jia Zheng – *Private and Confidential.*' Jia Zheng opened it and found it to be an anonymous letter couched in the same terms as the posters.

'Tell Lai Da,' he instructed them, 'to take three or four carts at once to the Temple of the Iron Threshold and bring all the novices back here. This must be kept absolutely secret. He is to say that they are wanted at the Palace.'

Lai Da was given his orders and set off.

*

Now when the twenty-four Buddhist and Taoist novices first arrived at the Temple, they had been put under the surveillance of the older Sisters, who gave them their daily lessons and rehearsed them in their liturgies. As the months went by and their services were not once called upon by the Imperial Concubine, the girls became slacker and slacker in their studies. They also began to grow up and show a greater awareness of life. Jia Qin himself was a bit of a young fop, and reckoned that for a pretty young actress such as Parfumée the decision to enter a nunnery must have been a childish whim. She became the first object of his advances, over at Water-moon Priory. To his great surprise he discovered that she was in earnest and not at all willing to comply with his wishes. So he turned his attentions back to the Temple, to two of the young novices, a Buddhist nun called Thurible and a little Taoist nun called Crucible, both extremely attractive and much more cooperative. Many a pleasant hour they spent with him, playing music and singing songs.

In the middle of the tenth month, Jia Qin arrived as usual with the monthly allowance. He had no intention of leaving straight away and announced to them all:

'I have brought you your month's allowance. I'm afraid I shall be too late to catch the city-gates tonight and shall have to find somewhere to stay here. On such a chilly night as this, what could be better than for us to share the wine and the few nuts and things that I happen to have with me and make a little party of it?'

The girls were thrilled and immediately started putting out the tables. They even invited the nuns from Water-moon Priory to join them. Parfumée was the only one to abstain. After a few bowls of wine, Jia Qin suggested a drinking game. Thurible and her friends replied:

'None of us can play those games. Why don't we play guess-fingers instead? Loser to drink a bowl – that would be great fun!'

'It's only just past midday!' objected one of the Sisters. 'It will never do to start rioting about at this hour. I suggest we take a little drink or two now and then those who wish to may leave. Those of you who want to keep Mr

Qin company can drink to your hearts' content this evening. I shall turn a blind eye.'

Just at that moment, however, one of the lay-sisters came bursting into the room.

'Quickly everyone! Break it up! Steward Lai's here, from Rong-guo House!'

The girls rushed around tidying up, and told Jia Qin to hide. He was by now well in his cups, and bragged:

'Why should I hide? I'm here to deliver the month's allowance...'

Lai Da was in at the door before he had finished speaking. Signs of the incipient orgy were all too visible, and Lai Da's loyal breast filled with rage. He was under the Master's instructions to keep the whole operation quiet, however, and inquired with a nonchalant smile:

'Would Mr Qin be here by any chance?'

Qin lurched to his feet.

'Why Mr Lai! What brings you here?'

'Pleased to find you here, sir,' said Lai Da. 'We must get the young ladies ready as quickly as possible, and take them back to town. They're wanted at the Palace.'

Jia Qin and the girls wanted to know more, but Lai Da merely said:

'Come along now. It's getting late. We must hurry or we shall miss the gates.'

So they all bundled into the carts that were waiting for them, and Lai Da mounted his sturdy mule and led the convoy into town.

*

We must return to Jia Zheng. Usually so punctilious in his attendance at the Board, the Master was sitting alone in his study, breathing heavily and brooding over the anonymous posters. Jia Lian hovered within earshot, not daring to leave the house. At last there came the sound of someone at the gate and a messenger came in to report:

'Excellency Zhang is indisposed, and will Sir Zheng please replace him this evening at the Board?'

Jia Zheng had been expecting Lai Da at any moment. It was most annoying to be called away like this. Jia Lian came in.

'Lai Da didn't leave until after lunch, Uncle, and the Temple is over eight miles from town. He won't be back till eleven o'clock at the earliest. As you are 'on call' for this evening I think you should go. When Lai Da gets back, I shall tell him to keep the nuns locked up and not to say anything until you have had an opportunity of settling the affair yourself tomorrow. If Qin comes, I shall say nothing. We shall see how he reacts when you speak to him tomorrow.'

It seemed reasonable enough, and Jia Zheng left with some reluctance for the Board.

As soon as he had gone Jia Lian set off back to his own apartment, brooding as he went on what he was going to say to Xi-feng. He held her to blame for having given Qin this job in the first place. But then he remembered that she was ill and relented. He had better not be too hard on her. He slackened his pace.

*

Meanwhile the news had spread among the servants. It soon reached the ears of Patience, who immediately went to tell her mistress. Xi-feng had had a bad night anyway and was feeling very low. Her feeble state intensified her ever-present anxiety about the various misdeeds that lay on her conscience, in particular her unscrupulous dealings at Water-moon Priory. When she learnt of the anonymous poster, she sat up with a jolt and asked Patience:

'What did it say?'

Patience thoughtlessly replied:

'Oh, nothing much. Something to do with the nuns at Water-moon Priory . . .'

This nearly put paid to Xi-feng. Her guilty conscience spelled out for her the rest of the story. She was undone! A spasm of terror quite deprived her of the power of speech. She felt the heat surging within her, her eyes began to swim. She started coughing and collapsed on her bed, her eyes staring rigidly in front of her.

Patience called out in great agitation:

'I meant the nuns at the Temple of the Iron Threshold! Something to do with the novices. There's no cause for you to take on so, ma'am.'

The words 'Iron Threshold' brought Xi-feng back to her senses.

'Stupid creature! Which is it, for heaven's sake? The nuns at the Temple or the Priory?'

'At first I thought it was the Priory,' replied Patience. 'Then I found out it was the Temple. That's why I got it wrong just now.'

'I thought it must have been the Temple,' said Xi-feng. 'The Priory has nothing to do with me. But I was the one who gave Qin the job of looking after the nuns at the Temple. He's probably been making off with some of the money.'

'No, ma'am,' said Patience, 'I don't think it's anything to do with money. I heard the word 'filth' mentioned several times.'

'Well that's nothing whatever to do with me. Where's Mr Lian got to?'

'He's been in ever since he heard that the Master was in a rage,' replied Patience. 'When I heard what sort of an unpleasant affair it was, I told all the servants to keep quiet about it. I hope their Ladyships haven't heard. The Master has sent Lai Da to bring all the girls back from the Temple. I'll send someone out to see what's happened. Now you settle down, ma'am. You're not well and shouldn't worry your head over such things.'

Just at that moment Jia Lian came in. Xi-feng would have liked to ask him for more details, but thought better of it when she saw the look on his face. He was obviously in a bad mood and she would be best advised to feign ignorance.

Jia Lian had not finished eating his dinner when Brightie came in.

'Lai Da's back, sir.'

'Is Mr Qin with him?'

'Yes, sir.'

'Tell Lai Da the Master has had to go to the Board tonight. He's to put the girls in the Garden for the time being, and tomorrow when the Master gets back we'll see about sending them to the Palace. Tell Mr Qin to wait for me in the inner library.'

Brightie disappeared.

Jia Qin went as instructed to the library. On his way he noticed a lot of pointing and muttering among the servants. He could not make out what it was all about, but it was clearly something to do with him. This was beginning to seem less and less like a summons from the Palace. He would have dearly liked to ask one of them what was going on, but felt too uneasy to do so and could only wait there in ever increasing suspense. When Jia Lian arrived, Jia Qin greeted him and stood nervously with his hands at his side.

'I wonder what Her Grace requires the nuns for at such short notice?' he ventured. 'I had to race all the way here. Luckily I was out there anyway today with the monthly allowance and was able to come back with Lai Da. But I'm sure you know all about that.'

'All about what! You're the one that should know!'

Jia Qin could make neither head nor tail of this, and stood there tongue-tied.

'A fine mess you've made of things!' continued Jia Lian. 'Sir Zheng's in a fuming rage!'

'But I've done nothing!' protested Jia Qin. 'I've delivered the allowance on time every month, the girls know their services by heart . . .'

Jia Lian could see that he knew nothing of what had happened. He and Qin had played together as children, and he sighed.

'You ass! Take a look at this!'

He pulled one of the posters from his boot-flap and threw it in Jia Qin's direction. Jia Qin picked it up and read it. His face grew ashen pale.

'Who could have done this? I've never done anyone any harm. Why should anyone want to blacken my name like this? I only go there once a month with the money – this is all lies! Sir Zheng will be very hard on me, I know he will! I shall die of shame! If my mother finds out, she'll flog me to death!'

He checked that there was no one else in the room and knelt before Jia Lian.

'Uncle! Please help me! Please!'

He went on knocking his head on the ground, tears streaming down his face. Several thoughts were going through Jia Lian's mind.

'Debauchery is Uncle Zheng's pet abomination. If he finds out that there really has been any such thing we'll be in for a major scene. It will only help smear the family name, besides. And give the anonymous author the greatest satisfaction, and then we can expect more of such posters in the future. No, why not take advantage of Uncle Zheng's absence, talk to Lai Da and hush the whole thing up. So far there's no proof that anything ever happened. And no one need be any the wiser.'

Having reached this decision, Jia Lian spoke to Jia Qin again:

'There's no point in trying to fool me. Don't think I don't know about every one of your mucky little pranks. Now listen: if you want to get out of this, you must deny everything, absolutely everything, no matter how hard Sir Zheng presses you. Do you understand? Now get up off the ground, you pathetic creature!'

Jia Lian sent for Lai Da and asked him for his opinion.

'As a matter of fact, sir,' said Lai Da, 'Mr Qin was behaving in a very unbecoming manner. When I arrived at the Temple they were all drinking. I'd say the man who wrote the posters was telling the truth . . .'

'Do you hear that, Qin?' said Jia Lian. 'Is Lai Da maligning you too?'

Jia Qin was by now puce in the face and speechless with embarrassment. Jia Lian took Lai Da by the hand and pleaded with him:

'Spare the lad, Lai. Say you found him at home. When you take him in to see the Master, there's no need to say that I've already seen him. And tomorrow you can ask the Master not to bother with questioning the nuns. Send for a broker and have them all sold off. If Her Grace should really need them again, we can always buy some more.'

Lai Da reflected that there was nothing to be gained by letting the incident blow into a storm. The family's name would only suffer. So he agreed to Jia Lian's proposal.

'You go with Mr Lai now, Qin,' ordered Jia Lian. 'And do whatever he tells you.'

Jia Qin kotowed once more to Jia Lian and followed Lai Da out. When they reached a secluded spot, he also kotowed to Lai Da.

'Excuse me for saying so, Master Qin,' said Lai, 'but it was your fault for behaving in such a manner. I don't know who it is that you offended. Can you think who it could be?'

Jia Qin thought for a while, but could think of no particular enemies. He followed Lai Da listlessly out.

To learn how he extricated himself, you must read the next chapter.

CHAPTER 94

Grandmother Jia gives a crab-blossom party:
a celebration of the ominous
Bao-yu loses his Magic Jade: a strange disappearance
of the numinous

Lai Da led Jia Qin off, to await the Master's return in the morning.

The little novices were thrilled to be back in the Garden and were eager to revisit their favourite haunts, imagining that the next day would be taken up with preparations for their visit to the Palace. Imagine their dismay when they found themselves prisoners: Lai Da's instructions to the old women and pages on duty were to feed them in their rooms and keep them in close confinement. The girls had no idea why they were being treated in this way and spent the night sitting up in suspense. Although the maids in the Garden's various residences knew by now of their arrival, they had only been given the official story and knew nothing of the real facts of the case.

Early next day Jia Zheng, having completed his night duty, was about to leave the Board when another urgent file was passed down to him: the City Wall Repairs Estimates and Accounts for two of the Provincial Capitals, for Immediate Audit. He foresaw a considerable delay, and sent a message home to Jia Lian, authorizing him to go ahead and question Lai Da when he returned from the Temple, and to deal with the case as he saw fit.

Jia Lian received these instructions with relief, mainly on young Qin's behalf, as he would now be spared the Master's wrath. On further reflection, however, it occurred to him that he might attract Jia Zheng's suspicion if he were to brush the entire affair under the carpet. It would be wiser to consult Lady Wang. Then if he incurred the Master's displeasure, at least he would not be solely responsible.

Having decided on this course of action, Jia Lian went to see Lady Wang and told her what had happened, concluding:

'Uncle Zheng was extremely angry about the anonymous poster and gave orders for Lai Da to bring young Qin and all the girls here for questioning. Today Uncle is too busy to deal with this sordid matter himself, and has asked me to consult you about it. What do you think we should do, Aunt?'

'I never heard of such a disgraceful business!' exclaimed Lady Wang in horror. 'If young Qin really has behaved in this degrading fashion, the family should have nothing more to do with him. Mind you, it's a despicable way to carry on, to go putting posters up about people... Do *you* suppose there is any truth in it? Have you asked Qin about it yet? What has he to say for himself?'

'I've questioned him,' replied Lian. 'Only a few moments ago, as a matter of fact. Of course he denied the whole thing. But consider, Aunt; supposing he really had done it, do you think he would admit to it? Personally I don't think he did. He knows that the girls are liable to be called to Court at short notice, and would be too scared of a scandal. We could find out the truth easily enough. But what then? What do you suggest?'

'Where are the girls now?' asked Lady Wang.

'They are locked up in the Garden,' replied Jia Lian.

'Do the others know that they are there?'

'They probably all know by now. But so far as they are concerned the girls are on their way to the Palace. That is what everyone has been told.'

'Good,' said Lady Wang. 'We must get rid of these creatures immediately, once and for all. I never wanted to keep them on in the first place – it was all your idea and Xi-feng's. Didn't I say it would end in trouble? You'd better tell Lai Da to go through them one by one and find out if they've any relatives left at home. Find their contracts and authorize whatever money is necessary to hire a boat for them – twenty or thirty taels should be enough. Put someone dependable in charge and have them all taken home to wherever they came from in the first place. They can take their contracts with them, and that will be the end of that. Even if one or two of them have been up to some mischief, I don't think it would be fair to punish them indiscriminately, by making them all return to lay-life. And if we hand them over to the official broker who usually finds husbands for orphan girls, even though *we* don't want the body price, someone is sure to try and make money out of them, and no one will think of their welfare. Who knows what might happen to them? As for Qin, I want you to tell him in no uncertain manner exactly what we think of him. He is never to come here again except for a clan sacrifice or some other big celebration. He had better keep well out of Sir Zheng's way too, unless he wants a taste of real trouble. And don't forget to tell the accounts people to cancel the relevant entry.

'Send someone to the Temple,' concluded Lady Wang, 'with strict instructions from Sir Zheng that none of the male members of the clan is to be allowed in there, except for the specific purpose of burning paper-money at the grave-site. And if there is any more nonsense, we will have all the Sisters removed too.'

Jia Lian took this all in and went to give Lai Da his orders.

'That is what Her Ladyship says you are to do,' he said. 'Report to me when you've finished, and I shall report back to Her Ladyship. Look smart. When Sir Zheng comes in, all you need do is repeat Her Ladyship's instructions.'

'It's very charitable of Her Ladyship to deal so generously with these worthless people,' commented Lai Da. 'I'll make sure I pick a good 'un to take them all home, carrying on Her Ladyship's good work, so to speak. And I'll bring young Master Qin in here, sir, for you to deal with. As for that anonymous bill-sticker, I'll track him down, and when I lay my hands on him I'll teach him a lesson he won't forget in a hurry.'

Jia Lian nodded.

'Good.'

Jia Qin was summoned and disposed of, and Lai Da dealt with the girls in accordance with Lady Wang's instructions.

When Jia Zheng came home that evening, Jia Lian and Lai Da both went in to report. Jia Zheng was not a man to look for unnecessary trouble, and was content to consider the matter closed. The news that the Jia household had dismissed twenty-four girl novices soon spread, and every young rake in town fancied the idea of getting hold of one of them for himself. What did happen to the girls in the end, and whether or not they ever reached home, our story does not relate, and it would be idle to speculate.

*

Let us return instead to the Naiad's House. With the slight improvement in Dai-yu's health, Nightingale was less busy than usual. Hearing of the arrival of the novices, and curious about the event that called for their presence at Court, she decided to pay a visit to Grandmother Jia's apartment, in the hope of finding out more from one of the maids there. She arrived just as Faithful was coming off duty and the two of them were able to sit down for a chat. Nightingale mentioned the novices. Their presence in the Garden came as a complete surprise to Faithful who exclaimed:

'That's the first I've heard of it! I'll ask Mrs Lian about it later on, she'll be sure to know.'

At that moment two old women from Mr Fu Shi's establishment came to call on Grandmother Jia, and Faithful went to take them through. Grandmother Jia had just retired for her midday nap, however, so the women exchanged a few words with Faithful and went on their way again.

'Where are those two from?' asked Nightingale.

'They're a tiresome pair,' replied Faithful. 'They're always calling on Her Old Ladyship and telling her how wonderful their Miss Fu is – so sweet-natured, beautiful, well-mannered, softly spoken, a perfect needlewoman, deft with her writing-brush, nimble with her abacus, a paragon of daughterly obedience, kind and ladylike towards the servants, and so on and so forth . . . Every time they come they treat Her Old Ladyship to the same recital. I can't bear that sort of thing, but Her Old Ladyship seems to love it. And the strange thing is that Bao-yu, who normally finds old women like that most irritating, makes an exception of these two. A few days ago, when they were here last, they said that Mr Fu wouldn't look at any of his sister's suitors (and there are plenty of them), but had set his heart on her marrying into a family like ours. They sung her praises all over again. Somehow they always seem to say just the thing to please the old lady.'

Nightingale looked thoughtful for a moment. Then she asked with affected nonchalance:

'If Her Old Ladyship is so pleased with what they say, why doesn't she marry Bao-yu to the young lady?'

Faithful was on the very point of explaining to Nightingale the real reason, when she heard a call from inside:

'Her Old Ladyship is awake!'

She hurried in, leaving Nightingale to make her own way home.

As Nightingale reached the Garden and began to walk towards the Naiad's House, she thought to herself:

'Anyone would suppose Bao-yu to be the only boy in the world, from the amount of time we all spend thinking about him! My poor mistress just seems to get more and more besotted with him. Whenever I see her sinking into one of her depressions, I can tell it's because of him.

That's what has been making her fall ill all the time too. What with all the uncertainty about the bond of gold and jade, and now this Miss Fu – I don't know! I always thought Bao-yu loved Miss Lin, but from what Faithful said it seems he just flits from one girl to the next. My poor mistress! All your heartache is wasted on him!'

Nightingale had begun by feeling sad on Dai-yu's account, but the more she thought about it the more wretched and confused she began to feel herself. She would have liked to advise Dai-yu not to wear her heart out in such a futile affair, but was too afraid of incurring her displeasure. And yet how could she just stand by and watch her suffer?

Presently, as she turned the problem over and over in her mind, her compassion gave way to a sudden feeling of annoyance and she chided herself:

'Why should I worry about them anyway? Supposing Miss Lin does marry Bao-yu – she'll still be as difficult to please as ever. And Bao-yu may be friendly enough, but I know how fickle he is too. I tell others not to wear their hearts out in vain, and then do so myself! No, from now on I shall concentrate on doing my duty and not allow myself to get involved.'

In this new spirit of detachment she continued on her way to the Naiad's House, and arrived to find Dai-yu sitting alone on the kang, going over some of her old poems and other writings. As she entered the room Dai-yu looked up and asked:

'Where have you been?'

'Oh, I just went out for a chat with one of the other maids,' replied Nightingale.

'Was it Aroma?'

'What should I want to see her for?'

The off-hand manner of her reply came as a shock to Dai-yu, who felt most put out and said curtly:

'Do as you please, it's all the same to me. Bring me a cup of tea.'

Nightingale smiled inwardly at the outcome of her experiment and went to pour the tea. As she did so she heard a confused hubbub in the Garden, but could not tell what was going on. She began pouring the tea and sent a junior maid out to investigate the disturbance. The maid returned in a short while to report:

'It's the crab-trees at Green Delights. Earlier this year some of them were struck with the blight, and no one bothered to water them. Yesterday Bao-yu went to have a look at them and thought he could see buds on some of the branches. No one believed him or paid any attention to his story at the time. But today there's no doubt about it, they've come out in the most beautiful blossom! It has caused quite a stir and everyone is hurrying over there to have a look. Even Her Old Ladyship and Her Ladyship have been caught up in the excitement and are going along to see the blossom. So Mrs Zhu has given orders for all the paths to be cleared of leaves – that's what all the shouting was about.'

When Dai-yu heard that Grandmother Jia was coming, she got up to change and sent Snowgoose on ahead, telling her to report back the moment Her Old Ladyship arrived. She soon came running back.

'Her Old Ladyship and Her Ladyship and a lot of the other ladies have all arrived! Hurry, Miss!'

Dai-yu took a brief look in the mirror, passed a comb quickly through her hair and set off with Nightingale in the direction of Green Delights. She arrived to find Grandmother Jia installed on Bao-yu's day-couch, and after greeting her and Lady Xing and Lady Wang went on to say hello to Li Wan, Tan-chun, Xi-chun and Xing Xiu-yan. She noticed that several people were absent: Xi-feng was ill in bed, Shi Xiang-yun had gone home to see her uncle who was in the capital on transfer, while Bao-qin had stayed at home with Bao-chai, and the two Li sisters, Wen and Qi, had been taken to live elsewhere by their mother, whom recent events had convinced that Prospect

Garden was a rather unsuitable environment for her daughters.

They were all chatting away, each propounding a different interpretation of the strange phenomenon of the winter-flowering crab-trees.

'They usually flower in the third month, I know,' Grandmother Jia was saying. 'And we are in the eleventh month now. But then the movable terms in the calendar are rather late this year, so we could say this is more like the tenth month, which is after all sometimes called "Little Spring". With the exceptionally warm weather we have been having, a little blossom is only to be expected.'

'You are quite right, Mother,' agreed Lady Wang. 'We need someone of your experience to show us that this is really nothing out of the ordinary.'

Lady Xing however was not so easily convinced.

'I heard that these trees had already been struck by the blight for almost a year... How do you explain the fact that half-dead trees should start flowering now, at such an odd time of the year?'

Li Wan spoke next.

'I think you are both right,' she said with a smile. 'My own humble suggestion is that they have flowered specially to tell us of some happy event that is about to take place in Bao-yu's life.'

Tan-chun, although she remained silent, was secretly thinking to herself:

'This must be an ill-omen. Everything that is in harmony with nature prospers, and things out of season, out of time, fade and die. Plants and trees obey a natural cycle. If a tree flowers out of season, it must be an ill-omen.'

She kept all this to herself, however. It was Dai-yu who spoke next. She had been struck by Li Wan's mention of a happy event, and said with some excitement:

'There was once a family of farmers who had a thorn-bush. There were three sons in the family, and one day these three sons decided to leave home and go their separate ways. No sooner had they gone than the thornbush began to fade away and die. But some time later the brothers began to yearn for each other's company, returned home and were reunited. And at once the thornbush began to flourish again. So you see plants follow closely the fortunes of the people to whom they are attached. Now Cousin Bao is devoting himself seriously to his studies, which pleases Uncle Zheng, which pleases the crab-trees, which is why they are flowering!'

This went down very well with Grandmother Jia and Lady Wang.

'What a well-chosen story! Such an interesting idea!'

Jia She and Jia Zheng now arrived to view the flowers, accompanied by Jia Huan and Jia Lan. Jia She spoke first.

'Cut them down. That's what I say. There's evil work afoot here.'

'On the contrary,' said Jia Zheng. 'Leave them alone. Evil manifestations thrive on such superstition. Ignore them and they disappear.'

'What's all this?' interrupted Grandmother Jia testily. 'We're all gathered here to witness a happy event. Why do you have to start talking about manifestations and what-have-you? When there's good luck then enjoy it while you can. I'll take care of any bad luck. I forbid you to utter another word of such gloomy nonsense.'

This silenced Jia Zheng, and he and Jia She effected an awkward departure. Grandmother Jia was unperturbed and determined to enjoy herself.

'Send someone to the kitchen,' she said. 'We want wine and some nice things to eat. We'll have a little party. I should like you, Bao-yu, Huan and Lan, each to write a poem to celebrate the occasion. Miss Lin has been unwell so she can be excused. If she feels up to it she can help you boys polish yours.'

Turning to Li Wan she continued:

'You and the others come up and have some wine with me.'

'Yes Grannie,' said Li Wan, then turning to Tan-chun she laughed and said:

'This is all your fault, Tan!'

'What do you mean?' protested Tan-chun. 'We've been let off the poetry-writing – my fault for what?'

'Aren't you the founder of the Crab-flower Club?' replied Li Wan. 'I know *that* crab was an Autumn Crab – but can't you see? Now the *real* crab-blossom wants to join in too . . .'

Everyone laughed at the idea.

Food and wine were now served, and they all drank and did their best to humour the old lady with light-hearted conversation. Bao-yu came up to pour himself some wine, and standing there thought up a quatrain which he then wrote out and recited for his grandmother.

> I asked the crab-tree why at blossom-time it failed,
> Yet now profusely bloomed so long before the spring?
> The tree replied: 'Midwinter marks the birth of light.
> Glad tidings to the Mistress of this House I bring.'

It was Huan's turn next. He wrote his out and began to recite:

> Plants should put out buds in spring:
> Our crab tree's timing's topsy-turvy.
> Of all the wonders of the world
> Ours is the only winter-flowering tree.

Then Jia Lan made a careful copy of his poem, in immaculate *kai-shu* calligraphy, and presented it to his great-grandmother, who asked Li Wan to read it out for her.

> Your mist-congealed beauty blighted in the spring,
> Your frosted petals blush now in the snow.
> Hail Tree of Wisdom! Whose Rebirth
> Adds lustre to our Family Hearth.

When she reached the end, Grandmother Jia commented:

'I don't know much about poetry, but I should judge

Lan's good, while I should say that Huan's was poor. Come on now, everybody come and have something to eat.'

Bao-yu was affected by her jolly mood. But then he thought to himself:

'Last year when the crab-trees died was the year Skybright died. Now the crab-trees have come back to life. That's all very well for us; but Skybright can never live again . . .'

This thought threw him into a sudden depression; then he remembered what Qiao-jie had recently said, that Xi-feng might be sending him pretty Fivey. Perhaps it was her imminent arrival that the strange blossoming portended? This prospect dispelled his gloom and he became his smiling self once more.

Grandmother Jia stayed a while longer, then returned to her apartment, leaning on Pearl and escorted by Lady Wang and the others. As she was leaving, Patience came hurrying up, her face wreathed in smiles:

'Mrs Lian heard that you were here viewing the flowers,' she said, 'and though she couldn't come herself, she asked me to come and attend to Your Ladyships and to bring this parcel. It contains two rolls of red silk for Master Bao to decorate the trees with, and comes with Mrs Lian's congratulations on the happy event.'

Aroma came forward to receive the parcel and presented it to Grandmother Jia, who beamed with delight.

'Trust Fengie to think of the right thing! What a nice idea! So distinguished!'

Aroma gave Patience a smile.

'Please thank Mrs Lian for Master Bao when you go back, will you?' she said. 'The happy event she is referring to is one that will make all of us happy, I'm sure . . .'

When Aroma said this, it dawned on Grandmother Jia that Xi-feng was thinking of Bao-yu's marriage, and her face lit up.

'Aiyo!' she exclaimed. 'Of course! It never occurred to

me! Fengie may be laid up in bed, but she's still the cleverest of us all. What a perfect thing to send!'

As she said this, she was already walking away from Green Delights, followed by her entourage. Patience whispered to Aroma:

'Actually Mrs Lian says this flowering is an ill-omen, and you're to cut strips of this red silk and hang them on the trees; that will help turn the bad luck into good. And in future you're to avoid any superstitious chat about it.'

Aroma nodded and saw Patience out.

*

Earlier that day, Bao-yu had been lounging around indoors, casually dressed in a fur-lined gown with slits at the sides. When he caught sight of the flowering crab-trees through the window, he went out to look at them. The more he gazed at the blossom the more lovely and poignant it seemed, the more strangely it seemed to reflect the mysterious vagaries of destiny, the joy and pathos of life. It was the embodiment of his own thoughts and feelings. Then, when he heard that Grandmother Jia was coming over, he hurried in to change into more formal attire, choosing a pale fox-lined robe with cut-away archer's sleeves and a darker jacket, also fox-lined, to go with it. He emerged again properly dressed to receive his grandmother, and in his hurry quite forgot to put on his Magic Jade.

When Grandmother Jia left he went in again to change back into his comfortable clothes, and it was then that Aroma detected the absence of the jade and asked him where it was.

'I was in such a rush when I came in to change,' he replied. 'I took it off and left it on the kang-table. Then I forgot to put it on again.'

Aroma looked but it was not on the table. She searched everywhere but could see no sign of it. She began to feel frightened, and broke into a cold sweat.

'Please don't worry,' Bao-yu begged her. 'It must be somewhere in the room. It's bound to turn up. Ask the others – they might know.'

It occurred to Aroma that Musk or one of the other maids might have hidden it somewhere as a practical joke and she bore down on them with an expression of playful accusation:

'You mean lot! Can't you think of a better way of amusing yourselves? Come on, where have you hidden it? Don't take this too far! If it really did get lost we'd be in real trouble, all of us!'

But Musk replied with a straight face:

'What on earth do you mean? We'd know better than to play a trick like that. We're not that silly. You're the one who should stop and think a minute. Try to remember where you put it, instead of laying the blame on us!'

Aroma could tell that Musk was in earnest and cried out in alarm:

'Heaven save us then! Oh little ancestor, where *can* you have put it? You must try to remember!'

'I do,' replied Bao-yu, 'I remember quite clearly putting it on the kang-table. Have another look for it.'

The maids were too scared to tell anyone else, and joined together in a furtive search. This went on for most of the day but there was still no sign of the jade. They emptied every box, and rummaged in every trunk, until there simply was nowhere left to look and they began to wonder if perhaps one of the visitors might have picked it up earlier in the day.

'How would anyone dare do such a thing?' said Aroma. 'Everyone knows how important it is, and that Master Bao's very life hinges on it. Ask about it, but be very discreet. If you find out that one of the maids has taken it and is playing a trick on us, kotow to her and beg for it back. If it's a junior maid who's stolen it, don't tell a soul, just do whatever is necessary to get it back. Give her whatever you like in exchange. This is very serious. It would be terrible if we lost the jade, worse even than losing Master Bao himself!'

Musk and Ripple set off on this mission. Aroma hurried out after them with a few final words of instruction:

'On second thoughts, leave the people who were here at lunch-time till last. If it turns out to be someone else, we don't want to offend them and cause a lot of ill-feeling to no purpose.'

The two maids split up to make their inquiries, but everywhere they went it was the same story. Nobody knew anything about it. Everybody was equally taken aback by the news. They hurried back to report their lack of success, and stared at one another in despondent silence. Bao-yu himself was now beginning to look rather stunned, and Aroma was so desperate that she could only weep helplessly. What could they do? There was nowhere left to look. They were too scared to tell any of the elder members of the family. The entire establishment at Green Delights was immobilized with fear and resembled a group of wooden statues or clay dolls.

One by one the others who had heard the news began to arrive, among them Tan-chun, who immediately gave orders for the Garden gate to be shut and sent an old serving-woman and two maids on another comprehensive search, announcing to everyone present that there would be a substantial reward for the recovery of the jade. They were all keen to establish their own innocence, and this, with the added incentive of winning the reward, now led to a flurry of indiscriminate searching. Every nook and cranny of the Garden was explored, not excluding the lavatories, but to no avail. It was as hopeless as hunting for an embroidery needle, and as evening drew on there was still no trace of the missing jade. Li Wan now sensed the urgency of the situation and said:

'I have a suggestion to make. It's not the sort of thing I would usually like to suggest but in the present circumstances I feel I must...'

They all gave her their attention.

'Things are so desperate that I think we have to try anything. Now apart from Bao-yu, all the residents of the Garden are girls. I should like you all to ask your maids to remove their dresses, so that we can search everyone properly. If that produces no results, then we should send them to search the older serving-women and cleaners. Do you all agree?'

The consensus of opinion was that she was right. With so many people involved, and such confusion, this seemed the only way of establishing anyone's innocence. Tan-chun was the only one to abstain from making any comment.

The maids were eager to clear themselves, and Patience was the first to volunteer. One by one they all undid their dresses and filed past, while Li Wan supervised the examination. Tan-chun could contain herself no longer.

'My dear Wan, can't you see what a futile waste of time this all is? Supposing someone has stolen it; do you really think he or she would be foolish enough to carry it around? Anyway, why should anyone want to steal it? It means a lot to us, but outside this household it's quite valueless. If you ask me, someone's doing this out of spite.'

They all knew immediately whom she was referring to. Jia Huan had been in and out of Green Delights many times that day. No one was prepared to mention his name, however, and she was obliged to be more specific herself:

'It must be Huan. Who else would play such a nasty trick? Send someone secretly over to his room and bring him here. Get him on his own and talk him into producing the jade, then threaten to expose him unless he keeps his mouth shut, and there's our mystery solved.'

Amid much nodding of heads, Li Wan turned to Patience and said:

'You'd better go. This will require all your tact.'

'Yes ma'am,' replied Patience, and hurried off.

A few minutes later, when she returned with Jia Huan, the others pretended hardly to notice his arrival. One of them made him a pot of tea and placed it on a table in the inner room. Then they all shuffled out and left the scene clear for Patience. She gave him an ingenuous smile.

'Master Bao's jade has gone missing... I don't suppose you've seen it anywhere have you?'

Jia Huan's face instantly flushed to an ugly shade of purple. He glowered at her.

'Just because somebody's lost something, does that mean that I automatically become the suspect and get called in for interrogation? Have I got a criminal record or something?'

Patience decided to change tack, and said with a smile:

'Of course no one would dream of suggesting you stole it! They just thought that perhaps you might have hidden it somewhere as a practical joke, and that by asking you if you'd seen it I might be able to get a few clues as to where they should look for it.'

'It's *his* jade, isn't it?' replied Jia Huan indignantly. 'He's the one that wears the thing – ask him, not me! You're all so keen to please him, that's your trouble! If something's found I never get to hear of it! But the moment anything's lost, it's me that gets the blame!'

He got up and stomped out of the room. The maids stepped back to let him through.

All this only served to exasperate Bao-yu.

'The amount of trouble that wretched thing has caused!' he said. 'I've no desire for it and I wish you would all forget about it. Now look what we've done. Huan will go and tell everybody and we'll never hear the end of it.'

'Little ancestor, *please*...' came tearfully from where Aroma stood in the throng of distraught maids. 'It's all very well for you to say "forget about it"! But what *you* seem to have forgotten is that if their Ladyships get to hear, the likes of us will be torn to shreds and ground to powder!'

This was followed by prolonged wailing. It soon

became clear to them all that things could not be hushed up for much longer. They would have to agree on a story to tell Grandmother Jia and the other ladies.

'That's easy,' said Bao-yu. 'Just tell them I smashed it myself.'

'No no! That's no good!' said Patience. 'Can't you see? They'll want to know why you smashed it, and then things will look just as black for Aroma and the others. And besides, what if they want to see the pieces?'

'Well then, say I lost it on a trip to town.'

There was a moment's silence as they all pondered this suggestion.

'We might possibly have got away with that,' said someone at last. 'But during the past few days you haven't been to school, and you haven't been out anywhere either.'

'Yes I have,' Bao-yu corrected them. 'A few days ago I went to the Earl of Lin-an's to watch the plays. You can say I lost it then.'

'No, that won't do,' said Tan-chun. 'If you lost it as long ago as that, they'll want to know why it hasn't been reported till now.'

They were still busy discussing the relative merits of these various fictions when suddenly they heard the voice of Aunt Zhao, cursing and wailing her way towards them.

'If you lose something, why can't you look for it yourselves, instead of sneaking up and blaming my boy? Well, here he is! Take him! Sacrifice him if you think it will do you any good! Kill him! Hack him to pieces! Do what you like with him!'

She propelled Jia Huan into the room, crying:

'Thief! Hurry up and confess your crime!'

This brought loud and angry protestations from Huan. Li Wan was just bracing herself to intervene and make the peace when a maid came rushing in and announced:

'Her Ladyship is here!'

Aroma and the maids could see that a confrontation was

now inevitable. Bao-yu and the girls went out at once to receive Lady Wang. Aunt Zhao's wrath subsided for a moment and she followed them out. From the startled look on their faces Lady Wang could see that what she had heard must be true.

'Is it really lost?' she cried.

No one dared reply. Lady Wang walked in, sat down and called Aroma forward. Aroma fell trembling to her knees. In a choked voice she murmured 'Yes.'

'Well, get up!' said Lady Wang. 'We must have a thorough search made. Come on, this helpless attitude will never do.'

Aroma was sobbing and could not say a word. Bao-yu finally spoke up, fearful that she might blurt out the truth.

'Mother, this has nothing to do with Aroma. I lost it the other day on my way back from seeing the plays at the Earl of Lin-an's.'

'Then why didn't you look for it at the time?'

'I didn't want anyone to know. I just told Tealeaf to look for it everywhere along the street.'

'Nonsense! You know perfectly well that Aroma or one of your other maids would have noticed. That's their job. They are always with you when you change. Whenever you come in from a party or any kind of excursion, if one of your handkerchiefs is missing, or a little purse, they're bound to ask you where it's gone – do you really think that they would allow something as irreplaceable as your jade to disappear, and not say a word?'

Bao-yu was stumped for an answer. Aunt Zhao, who was gloating over his discomfiture, hastened to put in:

'If you're so sure you lost it outside, why try to pin the blame on Huan?'

'That's enough from you!' said Lady Wang sharply. 'You keep out of this!'

Aunt Zhao was reduced to silence. It was left to Li Wan and Tan-chun to give the true story, which brought tears to Lady Wang's eyes. In her agitation she was for telling

Grandmother Jia and going over to Lady Xing's apartment to question the members of her household who had been to Green Delights earlier in the day.

The news had meanwhile reached Xi-feng on her sickbed. When she heard that Lady Wang had arrived at Green Delights she felt obliged to put in an appearance and, leaning on Felicity's arm, made her way towards the Garden. She arrived just as Lady Wang was about to leave.

'Good evening, Aunt.'

Xi-feng's voice trembled slightly as she spoke. Bao-yu and the others came up to greet her.

'So you've heard the news too!' said Lady Wang to Xi-feng. 'Most extraordinary! It vanished just like that, and can't be found anywhere. Think for a moment: of all the maids, including all of Lady Jia's and even your own Patience, which would you say showed thieving tendencies, or had a malicious disposition? I intend to tell Lady Jia, and to order a thorough search. Until we find it, Bao-yu's life hangs in the balance!'

'Ours is such a large household,' said Xi-feng, 'and, as the saying goes, you can know a man's face, but never his heart. With all the commotion of a search, everyone is bound to hear, and the thief will be so scared of the consequences that rather than be caught, he could well panic and destroy the evidence – the jade itself – and *then* where would we be? No, my advice, for what it is worth, is that we should let it be known that Bao-yu threw it away in disgust and that it really doesn't matter. Everyone must be very discreet so as to keep Her Old Ladyship and Sir Zheng from knowing. Meanwhile we can search everywhere in secret, and if we're clever we should end up with both the jade and the thief. Does that make sense to you, Aunt?'

After a long pause Lady Wang replied:

'It's all very well, but will we ever succeed in keeping this from Sir Zheng?'

She called Jia Huan to her.

'It was very silly of you to go shouting your head off about Bao-yu's jade, just because they asked you about it. If the thief has heard and destroys the jade, you will pay for it with your life!'

'I promise never to mention it again!' wailed Jia Huan in terror. This time Aunt Zhao held her tongue.

'There must be some places left where you haven't looked,' Lady Wang continued, addressing the assembled maids. 'It must be somewhere here. It's hardly going to fly away, is it? But when you look, be as quiet as possible. Aroma, I give you three days to find it. If we still haven't found it by then, we shan't be able to keep it from Her Old Ladyship and Sir Zheng any longer. And everyone knows what that will mean!'

Bidding Xi-feng accompany her, Lady Wang set off for Lady Xing's apartment, for further consultations on how to apprehend the thief.

Li Wan and the others continued to debate what to do. They sent for the various domestics in charge of the Garden and gave orders for the gates to be securely locked. Steward Lin's wife was also summoned and given confidential instructions.

'Tell the servants on both gates that absolutely no one is to be allowed *out* of the Garden for the next three days. We can allow freedom of movement *within* the Garden, but no one must leave. Say that something has been lost and that no one can go out until it's found.'

'Yes, Mrs Zhu,' said Lin's wife. 'Excuse me, ma'am,' she went on, 'but we lost something at home the other day – nothing of any value of course, but my husband was determined to find it, and he went and consulted one of those word-diviners that set themselves up at street corners. Iron Mouth Liu I think this one's name was. His reading was very clear. My husband followed his instructions, and found the missing item straight away.'

When Aroma heard this she begged her to help them.

'Oh, Mrs Lin! Please go and ask your husband to consult this man for us!'

'Indeed I will. Straight away.'

Lin's wife bustled off. Xing Xiu-yan now had a suggestion to make.

'If you ask me, those word-diviners and fortune-tellers you find on street corners are all charlatans. But when I knew Adamantina, in the South, before she came to live here, I heard of her gift for the planchette. Why don't we ask her to hold a séance for us? Didn't Bao-yu's jade have a mysterious origin anyway? It would surely lend itself to that sort of approach.'

The others seemed greatly surprised to hear this, and reflected that in all the time they had known her, Adamantina had never once mentioned such a gift. Musk earnestly beseeched Xiu-yan:

'Oh, Miss! I don't think she would agree to do it for anyone but you! Please, *please*, will you ask her for us? I'll kotow to you – if she finds the answer, I'll be indebted to you for a lifetime!'

She was about to perform a kotow, but Xiu-yan raised her from the ground. Dai-yu and the others added their entreaties to Musk's, and Xiu-yan left with all speed for Green Bower Hermitage.

No sooner had she gone, than Steward Lin's wife returned from her mission.

'Ladies!' she announced with great jubilation. 'I bring good news! My husband has been to see the man, and he says the jade is sure to turn up. Someone will definitely bring it back.'

She had yet to convince her audience however – except for Aroma and Musk, who were ready to grasp at the slightest hope. Tan-chun asked:

'What word came up, and what was the reading?'

'He said a lot,' replied Lin's wife, 'and some of it I couldn't understand. But I know the word was *shang* (1) meaning "to reward". Iron Mouth Liu took one look at it and said, "You've lost something, haven't you?"!'

'Goodness! He sounds pretty good!' exclaimed Li Wan.

Lin's wife continued:

'Then he went on to say that as *shang* was made up of *xiao* (2) meaning "small" on top, with *kou* (3) meaning "mouth" in the middle, the lost object was small enough to fit inside the mouth. It must be some jewel or precious stone.'

Amid cries of 'Miraculous!' and 'Go on!', Lin's wife continued:

'Then he said that we should be careful to notice that the radical element was *bei* (4) meaning "a cowry shell" and *not* the similar radical *jian* (5) meaning "to appear", hence the object's *dis*appearance... And the top element of the word taken as a whole was very like *dang* (6) meaning "to pawn", so we should go straight to the pawnshop. Then he pointed out that by adding a *ren* (7) "man" to the

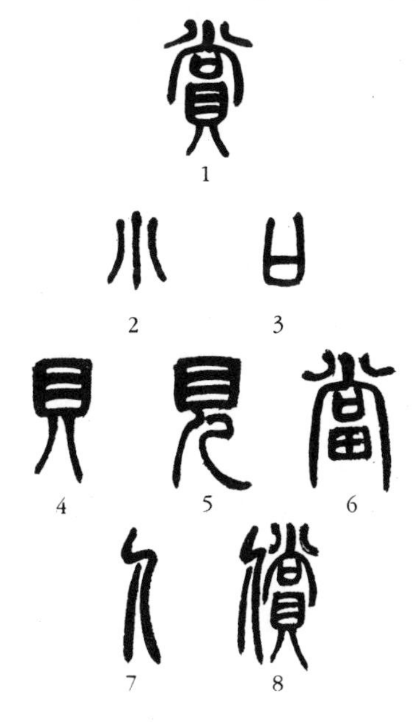

left-hand side, the compound *chang* (8) meaning "to redeem" was formed. Find the man in the pawnshop, pay the price, and the lost object will be redeemed . . .'

'What are we waiting for?' cried the girls. 'Search the neighbourhood! If we work our way through the pawnshops, we're sure to find the right one sooner or later. And once we've found the jade, it will be easy enough to find the thief.'

'Find the jade and we needn't even bother who the thief is,' said Li Wan. Turning to Steward Lin's wife she continued: 'Go and tell Mrs Lian what you have just told us. Then she can tell Her Ladyship and set her mind at rest. And ask Mrs Lian to send someone out to search the pawnshops.'

Lin's wife set off at once.

Things seemed more hopeful now, and relative calm was restored. They were waiting in a somewhat bemused state for Xiu-yan to return when they saw Tealeaf beckoning from the gateway to one of the junior maids. She ran out and he said:

'Quick! Go in and tell Master Bao and their Ladyships and the ladies and young misses that I've got the most wonderful piece of news!'

'Well come on!' burst out the maid. 'What is it? Out with it!'

Tealeaf started laughing and clapping his hands.

'All right, I'll tell you. And then you can go in and tell them, and we can split the reward between us. Guess what? The most reliable information has reached me as to the whereabouts of the Missing Jade!'

The outcome of all this excitement will be related in the next chapter.

CHAPTER 95

A rumour comes true and the Imperial Consort passes away
A counterfeit is deceptively like the real thing, and Bao-yu loses his wits

There was Tealeaf at the entrance to Green Delights, proclaiming his discovery of the missing jade. A junior maid hurried in to tell Bao-yu. The others, when they heard, propelled Bao-yu towards the entrance to question Tealeaf, while they stood listening in the covered gallery. Bao-yu, greatly relieved at the news, walked out and asked Tealeaf:

'Where did you find it? Come on, give it to me.'

Tealeaf replied:

'I'm afraid I couldn't bring it with me. I need a guarantor.'

'But how did you find it? Tell me, and I'll send someone to fetch it.'

'I heard that Steward Lin was going to consult the word-diviner,' said Tealeaf, 'so I went along with him. When I heard the word 'pawnshop', I didn't wait to hear the rest, but went racing round the pawnshops. I described the jade to them, and eventually one of them said, "We've got it." I asked him to hand it over, but he insisted on having the pawn-ticket. When I asked him how much it had been pawned for, he said he had one for three hundred taels and another for five hundred. The one for three hundred was brought in the day before yesterday, the one for five hundred came in today.'

'Quick,' interrupted Bao-yu. 'Take three hundred taels *and* five hundred. Get them both, and we can see which is the right one.'

But Aroma called out jeeringly from within:

'You're not going to take any notice of him, are you? I remember my elder brother telling me when I was a little girl, that the people who deal in that kind of jade pawn one or two from their stock when they are short of cash. Every pawnshop must have at least one of them.'

At first everyone had been carried away by Tealeaf's story. But now, after reflecting on what Aroma had just said, they all began to laugh.

'Come inside, Master Bao. Don't listen to that fool. Whatever it is he's talking about, it obviously isn't the real thing.'

Bao-yu laughed too. At that moment, Xiu-yan returned from her mission.

On her arrival at Green Bower Hermitage, she had come straight to the point. Would Adamantina consult the planchette for them? Her request met with a scornful laugh.

'I thought you were above such worldly things, Xiu-yan. I am sure we should never have been such friends if I had known you would ever let idle talk induce you to come bothering me. Anyway, I'm afraid this planchette you mention is something I am not familiar with.'

With this, she clearly intended to dismiss the subject, and Xiu-yan regretted ever having come. She knew what a difficult disposition Adamantina had. But now that she had broached the subject, it seemed such a pity to return empty-handed. She made no attempt to insist on her friend's psychic powers, but instead tried to win Adamantina around by speaking of the urgent light in which Aroma and the others viewed the loss. At this, Adamantina showed signs of relenting, and Xiu-yan rose to her feet and bowed humbly before her several times. Adamantina sighed.

'Are we to be at everyone's beck and call? Since I have been here, I have kept this a secret. Now, if I make an exception for you, I shall never be left in peace.'

'I felt I had to come, their need seemed so great,' replied Xiu-yan. 'I knew that you would feel sorry for them. If anyone else should ask, you will be quite free to say no. No one would ever press you into it.'

Adamantina laughed. She told one of the lay-sisters to light some incense, and went herself to fetch the tray of sand and the planchette-wand from a chest. After writing out the requisite incantation, she told Xiu-yan to kneel and pray. When this was done, they both stood and held the wand by its double handle. Before long it began to move across the tray. The characters it traced with a rapid motion in the sand read as follows:

> ALAS!
> IT LEFT NOR TRACE
> NOR SIGN.
> GONE TO GREEN-SICKNESS PEAK, TO LIE
> AT THE FOOT OF AN AGE-OLD PINE.
> WHY TRAVERSE COUNTLESS MOUNTAINS,
> SEARCHING FOR YOUR FRIEND?
> FOLLOW ME AND LAUGH TO SEE
> YOUR JOURNEY AT AN END!

The writing ceased, and the wand came to rest.

'Which spirit did you invoke?' asked Xiu-yan.

'Iron Crutch Li,' replied Adamantina.

Xiu-yan copied down the writing, and asked Adamantina to give an explanation of the lines.

'How could I?' she replied. 'I don't understand them myself. Take it back to the others. Many of them are far cleverer than I am, I'm sure.'

Xiu-yan did not press her, but returned to Green Delights. On her arrival, she was besieged with questions.

'Tell us what happened!' they all cried.

Instead of giving them a lengthy description of the séance, Xiu-yan handed her transcript straight to Li Wan. The girls and Bao-yu crowded round to read it. Between them they came to the following interpretation of the lines: the jade would not be found by looking for it, and yet it was not irretrievably lost. At some unforeseeable time, when no one was looking for it, it would just turn up. But as for Green-sickness Peak, no one had any idea where that could be.

'It may be some sort of hidden clue,' suggested Li Wan. 'We've certainly never had such a mountain in our garden, and one is not going to spring suddenly from nowhere. The only explanation I can think of is that whoever stole the jade lost his nerve and threw it away, and now it's lying beneath some miniature mountain in a rockery somewhere near a pine-tree. But what's all this about 'follow me' at the end?'

'Who was the spirit invoked?' asked Dai-yu.

'Iron Crutch Li,' Xiu-yan informed her.

'He'd be a hard one to follow!' protested Tan-chun.

Aroma, meanwhile, in her desperation, took the words quite literally and set to in earnest, searching blindly everywhere. She left no stone in the garden unturned, but all to no avail. When she returned, Bao-yu did not even ask her if she had had any success, but just gave her a silly grin.

'Little ancestor!' cried Musk. 'For pity's sake tell us where you lost it! At least then if we have to suffer for it, we will know why!'

'You wouldn't listen to me when I said I'd lost it outside,' protested Bao-yu. 'How am I supposed to know any better now?'

Li Wan and Tan-chun suggested that they had all had a long and tiring day. It was now eleven o'clock. Dai-yu, they observed, had been too weary to stay up any longer, and had gone home on her own.

'We should all go to bed now,' they proposed. 'Tomorrow we can start afresh.'

The gathering dispersed. Bao-yu went straight to sleep. Aroma and the other maids, however, were quite unable to get to sleep, and sat up all night long, weeping and brooding by turns.

*

But we must leave them for a while, and turn our attention to Dai-yu. When she reached home, her thoughts turned once more to the subject that had always preoccupied her, the bond of gold and jade between Bao-yu and Bao-chai. On this occasion, her conclusions were more gratifying than usual.

'How can there have been any truth in the prophecy made by the Monk and the Taoist?' she argued with herself. 'If there really were a bond of gold and jade, how could Bao-yu lose his jade like this? Perhaps I am an unforeseen circumstance that has broken the bond...'

More reflections of this kind brought her an unwonted peace of mind. Her weariness after the day's exertions seemed to fall from her, and she began reading again. Nightingale, however, was worn out, and urged her mistress repeatedly to go to sleep. Dai-yu lay down, but continued to think. This time it was the crab-trees that occupied her thoughts.

'Bao-yu's jade is no ordinary stone. He was born with it, and whatever happens to it is highly significant. If the crab-blossom were a good omen, then why should he lose his jade at the same time? It must be inauspicious. I'm afraid something unlucky will happen to him.'

Down went her spirits again. And then she saw it in yet another light, and became optimistic once more. Perhaps both the blossoming *and* the loss of the jade were meant to happen, were both in some way timely and auspicious. She lay awake in the throes of these conflicting emotions, and only fell asleep in the early hours.

Early the next morning, Lady Wang sent servants to make inquiries in the pawnshops, while Xi-feng set in motion her own secret investigations. Several days went by, but despite their combined efforts, there was still no sign of the missing jade. Luckily word of the disaster had as yet reached neither Grandmother Jia nor Jia Zheng. But Aroma and the other maids lived from day to day in unbearable suspense, while Bao-yu, who had now been absent from school for several days, was becoming progressively more morose, listless and silent. Lady Wang was not too worried by this, judging it to be a temporary affliction brought on by the loss of his jade.

She was sitting one day lost in thought, when Jia Lian came into her room, and having paid his respects, announced with a complacent smile:

'Uncle Zheng has today had word from Yu-cun that Uncle Wang Zi-teng has been promoted to a position in the Grand Secretariat. He has received an Imperial Decree to proceed to the capital. His official instatement is to be on the twentieth of the First month of next year, and an urgent dispatch has been sent to summon him from the frontier. He will be travelling day and night, and should be here in half a month or so. I have come especially to bring you this news, Aunt.'

Lady Wang was absolutely delighted. She had only just been thinking how few of her own family she had around her, a deficiency that had been highlighted during her sister's latest troubles. Her brother Zi-teng had been too far away to be able to wield any influence on their behalf. But now, with his new appointment and return to the capital, she could expect a revival of Wang family prestige from which Bao-yu too would be able to benefit. For the time being she felt able to dismiss her anxiety over the missing jade, and looked forward more and more to her brother's return.

A day or two later, Jia Zheng came in unexpectedly, and with tear-stained face and voice choking with emotion, told her:

'You must inform Mother immediately that her presence is required at once at the Palace. There is no need for a large party to go. It will be sufficient if you escort Mother. Her Grace has suddenly been taken ill, and has fallen into a coma. There is a court eunuch waiting outside. He says the official diagnosis by the College of Physicians is an incurable stroke.'

Lady Wang burst into tears.

'This is no time for crying,' said Jia Zheng. 'You must go and tell Mother at once. Break it to her gently. We must not cause the old lady too much of a shock.'

So saying, Jia Zheng went out to give the staff their instructions. Lady Wang dried her eyes and went in to Grandmother Jia's apartment. She said simply that Yuan-chun was ill, and that they must go to the Palace to present their respects.

'Merciful Buddha!' exclaimed Grandmother Jia. 'How can she have fallen ill again? Last time if you remember I had such a fright, and then we found out that I had been imagining it all. If only I were imagining it now!'

Lady Wang talked to the old lady, and at the same time urged Faithful and the other maids to look out her court robes and begin attiring her. She then went in haste to her own apartment, dressed and returned to wait on Grandmother Jia. In a short while they were ready, and walked out from the main hall to the sedan-chairs that were waiting to carry them to the palace.

Yuan-chun, since her elevation to the Imperial Bedchamber, had been the cherished object of the emperor's favours, and had become as a result somewhat plump. From the constant pressure and daily exhaustion of life at court, she had also developed a chronic bronchial condition. A few days previously, when returning late from attendance at a banquet, she had caught a chill, which soon brought on her old complaint. This time, however, it was a severe attack. Phlegm completely obstructed her passages, causing a coldness and faintness in her limbs. The emperor was informed, and a court physician summoned at once. But she could swallow none of the medicines that he prescribed, and even the decongestant salts they tried to administer had no beneficial effect. Concerned at her critical condition, her attendant eunuchs reported again to His Majesty, requesting that the necessary precautions be taken. And so her immediate family were summoned to the Palace.

Grandmother Jia and Lady Wang presented themselves at the palace, and entered the Imperial Concubine's Bed-chamber, to find her choked with phlegm, with saliva dribbling from her mouth, no longer capable of speech. When she saw her grandmother coming towards her, her face took on the most pitiful expression, as if she wanted to weep but no longer had the strength to do so. Grand-mother Jia came forward to do homage, and offered a few words of comfort. A little later, the official cards of Jia Zheng and company were brought in, and a lady-in-waiting presented them for Her Grace's inspection. She no longer had the strength to look at them, however, and her face was growing paler minute by minute.

The eunuchs were about to report to the emperor again, and foreseeing that the other concubines would soon arrive to pay their last respects, asked the Jia relatives if they would kindly step outside and wait in one of the ante-chambers of the Palace. Grandmother Jia and Lady Wang had no choice but to conform to court regulations, and wrench themselves away. Holding back their tears, they left the chamber with sorrowful hearts.

They could see messages being passed within the Palace, and shortly afterwards a eunuch came out and sent for an official from the Imperial Board of Astronomy. Grand-mother Jia knew only too well what this meant. He was requesting an auspicious date for the funeral. It was all over. But still she dared not make a move. It was not long before a junior eunuch came out to make the official announcement:

'Her Grace the Jia Concubine has passed away.'

It was the nineteenth of the twelfth month. Spring Commencement fell on the eighteenth of the twelfth month of that year, being the year *Jia Yin*; the nineteenth of the month was therefore also, astrologically speaking, within the month *Yin* of the following *Mao* year. Her Grace was forty-three years old.

Grandmother Jia rose, and doing her best to remain composed, left the Palace, climbed into her sedan and was carried home. Jia Zheng and company had also been informed, and they too made the sad journey home. Lady Xing, Li Wan, Xi-feng, Bao-yu and other members of the family were lined up on both sides of the courtyard before the main hall of Rong-guo House to greet first Grandmother Jia, then Jia Zheng and Lady Wang as they returned. Our narrative passes over the tearful family scene.

Early next day, all members of the family with official rank went to the Palace to pay their last respects, and to mourn as the rites prescribed. The details of Yuan-chun's tomb were the responsibility of the Minister of Works, and Jia Zheng found himself being frequently entertained by his President, and consulted by his colleagues. It was a very busy time – not at all like the period of the previous court funerals for the Dowager Empress and the Zhou Concubine. Because Yuan-chun had died without issue, she was given the posthumous title: 'Illustrious and Chaste Imperial Concubine'. This was in conformity with state precedent. But of this no more.

Everyone in the Jia family was kept extremely busy, travelling to and from the Palace daily for the duration of the funeral. Luckily Xi-feng's health had improved a little of late, and she was able to get up and manage the household. She was also preparing to celebrate the return of Wang Zi-teng. Her own elder brother, Wang Ren, now that his uncle was to be a Privy Councillor and in a position of such influence, was also on his way to the capital with his family. Xi-feng was glad of this. The knowledge that she would have these extra Wangs around her also gave her renewed confidence, and had a beneficial effect on her health. Lady Wang, now that Xi-feng was up and about again, unloaded half of her responsibilities onto her, and with the reassuring prospect of having her elder brother back in the capital soon, felt more at peace.

Bao-yu was not entitled to attend any of his eldest sister's funeral ceremonies, as he held no official rank. He did no work either, and was left undisturbed in his idleness; the Preceptor attributed his state to the recent family events, while Jia Zheng was far too busy to keep a check on his son's studies. Our hero might have been expected to seize this as an ideal opportunity to amuse himself in the delightful company of his sister and cousins. But from the day he lost his jade, he just sat around all the time doing nothing, and if he spoke, did so in an incoherent mumble. When Grandmother Jia and the others returned from the Palace, he went over to pay his respects if told to do so; if not, he stayed where he was. All this time Aroma and his other maids grew more and more guilty and apprehensive. They dared not take him to task, for fear that he might have a tantrum. Each day he drank his tea and ate his meals, when they were placed before him. But he would as soon have gone without.

It eventually dawned on Aroma that this was not just a mood of his, but a genuine illness. When she had a free moment, she slipped over to the Naiad's House, and had a word with Nightingale.

'If only your Mistress would talk to him, and try to cheer him up,' she said.

Nightingale passed this message on to Dai-yu straight away. But Dai-yu now saw herself as Bao-yu's future bride, and felt a need to behave towards him with scrupulous modesty.

'If he should come to see me,' she argued with herself, 'I should have to receive him politely, for the sake of our childhood friendship. But as for going over to see him myself, that is quite out of the question.'

So she turned a deaf ear to Aroma's entreaties. Aroma next went secretly to tell Tan-chun. But Tan-chun was herself plunged in gloom. To her mind, the strange flowering of the crab-trees had been the first of a series of ill omens, followed by the still stranger loss of the Precious Jade, and now by her sister's death. With the family fortunes so evidently on the decline, how could she find it in herself to rally Bao-yu's spirits? Besides, as brother and sister, they were obliged to maintain a certain distance. She did visit him once or twice, but he seemed indifferent to her presence and she made no further efforts.

Bao-chai also knew of the missing jade. Her mother had already told her of her proposed betrothal to Bao-yu, the day she discussed it with Lady Wang and all but consented.

'Although it is your Aunt Wang's proposal,' she had said to Bao-chai, 'I have still not given my final consent. I said we should have to wait until Pan comes home. What do you say to the idea? Are you willing?'

'Mother,' replied Bao-chai, in a most serious tone, 'you don't need to ask me. A daughter's future lies in her parents' hands. Since Father is dead, the decision is entirely yours. Consult Pan, if you wish, but why me?'

Aunt Xue was most touched by this display of modesty in her daughter, proof that her basically sound character had not been in any way spoiled by her luxurious upbringing. She would not mention Bao-yu's name to her again. Bao-chai for her part maintained a strict taboo from that day forth on those two syllables. So when she came to hear of the missing jade, despite the concern she felt, she refrained from inquiring any further and contented herself with what she gleaned from those around her, while maintaining a show of complete indifference.

Aunt Xue, on the other hand, sent a maid over several times to inquire after Bao-yu. She was also greatly concerned about her own son, and awaited her elder brother's arrival with impatience. His influence would surely secure Pan's release. With the death of the Imperial Concubine, she could see how busy the Jias were. But as Xi-feng was well enough to take charge of the household management, she did not feel it necessary to visit them often.

The one to suffer most during all this was Aroma, although she tried to remain quiet and calm, and to comfort Bao-yu and minister to his needs. He seemed to understand nothing, and she could only watch over him in secret anguish.

After a few days, Yuan-chun's coffin was laid out in the Imperial Chapel of Rest, and Grandmother Jia and the other senior members of the family attended funeral services there for several days. Bao-yu was becoming daily more and more of an imbecile. He had no fever and was not in any physical pain, but he was eating little and sleeping less and becoming quite incoherent in his speech. Aroma, Musk and the other maids were at their wits' end, and several times went to report to Xi-feng, who came over constantly to see how he was. At first she had thought that he was simply upset that his jade had not been found. But now, seeing the deranged state into which he was sinking, she sent for the doctor. The doctor paid daily visits, and more than one kind of medicine was prescribed, but all seemed to do more harm than good. To all inquiries as to where he felt pain, he was quite unable to reply.

When Yuan-chun's funeral ceremonies were over, Grandmother Jia's thoughts turned again to Bao-yu, and she came to the Garden to visit him, accompanied by Lady Wang. Aroma told Bao-yu to go out and greet her properly. Bao-yu was still able to get about, and managed to greet his grandmother presentably, with Aroma at his side prompting him at every turn.

'My dear boy!' exclaimed Grandmother Jia. 'I am so relieved! I was led to believe that you were seriously ill. But now I see that you are quite your normal self.'

Lady Wang too seemed pleasantly surprised. Bao-yu said nothing and gave an inane grin. They went in and sat down. When Grandmother Jia asked him a question, he could only repeat whatever Aroma said. It soon became clear to them all that so far from being his normal self, he was now little more than a halfwit. The more Grandmother Jia saw, the more it puzzled and distressed her.

'When I came in,' she said, 'he seemed quite well. But I can see now that he really is seriously ill. He seems to have quite lost his wits. Will someone please tell me what has happened?'

Lady Wang realized that they could not keep it from her any longer. For Aroma's sake, who stood there in mortal terror, she stuck to Bao-yu's story and told Grandmother Jia that he had lost his jade at the Earl of Lin-an's party, whispering it all in the old lady's ear, afraid it might come as too great a shock to her.

'The servants have been told to look everywhere,' she added. 'We have asked several fortune-tellers, and they all say that it's in a pawnshop, so it can only be a matter of time before we find it.'

Grandmother Jia rose to her feet in great agitation, tears streaming down her cheeks.

'How could he lose such a precious thing? You are not fit to look after him! What about his father? Surely he has not washed his hands of it too?'

Lady Wang could see that Grandmother Jia was in a rage. She told Aroma and the others to kneel, and herself replied, with contrite face and lowered head:

'I was afraid you would be upset, Mother, and that his father would be angry, so I still have not told him.'

'But can't you see?' cried Grandmother Jia. 'The jade is Bao-yu's very life. Losing it is what has made him lose his wits. What *are* we going to do? People all over town have heard of the jade. If someone picks it up, he's hardly going to hand it in. Send someone at once to his father and ask him to come here. I must speak to him about this.'

Lady Wang, Aroma and all the others present were

terrified of the possible consequences and entreated Grandmother Jia to relent.

'Imagine how angry Sir Zheng will be, Mother! Think of poor Bao-yu! For his sake, give us one last chance. We will search for all we are worth.'

'Why should you fear his father's wrath? I shall be here,' said the old lady firmly.

She told Musk to send someone for Jia Zheng. Minutes later, the message returned that he was out visiting a friend.

'Well, we'll go ahead without him,' said Grandmother Jia. 'For the present, none of the servants is to be punished. Those are my instructions, and I shall take full responsibility. Send for Lian and tell him to write out a Notice of Reward, and post copies of it wherever Bao-yu went on the day he lost his jade. It is to say: "Reward for return of jade, ten thousand taels of silver. Reward for information leading to its recovery, five thousand taels." And there is to be no question of not paying up in full if someone does come forward. This is the only way we shall ever find it. If we rely on our own people, we could go on searching for the rest of our lives.'

Lady Wang did not dare voice her reservations about this plan of action. Jia Lian was sent for, and told to have the posters made up with all speed.

'Move Bao-yu's things to my apartment,' Grandmother Jia ordered one of the servants. 'I shall only need Aroma and Ripple to wait on him. The rest can stay here and look after his apartment.'

Bao-yu remained silent throughout all of this, grinning inanely. Grandmother Jia took him by the hand and led him out, Aroma and the others clustering round to support him as far as the garden gate. When they reached her apartment, Grandmother Jia told Lady Wang to sit down, and herself supervised the putting in order of the inner room. When this was done, she spoke to Lady Wang:

'You know why I have brought him over here, don't

you? In the first place, there are so few people living in the garden now, and I can't help feeling there's something odd about the way those crab-trees in his courtyard died so suddenly, and then so suddenly flowered. Before now he could always rely on his jade to keep any evil influences at bay. But now that it is lost, I am afraid the evil can get in more easily. So I thought it best for him to stay here with me. He had better not go out for a few days. When the doctor comes, he can see him here.'

'Of course you are right,' said Lady Wang promptly. 'Your good luck will shelter him from any such influences, now that he is here.'

'My luck! Nothing of the sort! It is quieter here, that is all, and there are plently of sutras for him to read, to help settle his mind. Ask him if he agrees.'

When his mother put the question to him, Bao-yu merely smiled. Finally, prompted by Aroma, he answered, 'Yes Mother.' Lady Wang was moved to tears by the pitiful spectacle her son presented, but contained herself in Grandmother Jia's presence. Grandmother Jia could see that she was somewhat overwrought, and told her to go back to her own apartment.

'Leave him to me. I shall look after him. When his father gets home this evening, tell him there is no need for him to come and see me today. I do not want him to know yet.'

When Lady Wang had left, Grandmother Jia told Faithful to bring her one of her sedative remedies. Bao-yu took it; and there we must leave them for the present.

Jia Zheng, on his way home that evening, heard from within his carriage the following conversation in the street:

'If you want to get rich, I know of an easy way . . .'

'Oh? What's that?'

'I heard today that at Rong-guo House one of the young nobs has lost a jade, and they've posted a notice of reward, with all the details – shape, size, colour, etc. Ten thousand they're offering to anyone who hands it in, and five thousand for information!'

Jia Zheng did not catch every word. But he heard enough to be considerably alarmed. He hurried home, and on arrival summoned one of the janitors and questioned him about the whole affair.

'I knew nothing of all this until today, sir,' replied the janitor. 'The first I heard of it was this afternoon, when Mr Lian gave us Her Old Ladyship's orders to put the posters up.'

'We are doomed!' said Jia Zheng to himself with a bitter sigh. 'This son of mine is the bane of our lives! When he was a child he was the talk of the neighbourhood. It has taken us these last ten years or more to stop their tongues, and now we have to go putting up a poster like this, announcing our troubles to the world!'

He went in without further delay and questioned Lady Wang, who told him the whole story. When he learnt that the reward was the old lady's idea, Jia Zheng knew that he could not very well openly oppose it. He criticized Lady Wang instead for her part in it, and going out once more, gave orders for the posters to be taken down without Grandmother Jia's knowledge. As it turned out, some local loafers had already pulled them down.

Despite this, a day or two later, a man did arrive at the main gate of Rong-guo House, claiming to have brought the jade. The servants were ecstatic. 'Give it here!' they cried. 'We'll take it in for you.'

'Not so fast!' The man fumbled inside his gown, and brought out the reward poster. 'Look here,' he said, pointing to the wording on the poster. 'This is what your masters put up, isn't it? "Ten thousand taels for return of jade" – plain as daylight. I may be a pauper today, my man, but wait till I come into my ten thousand. You'll sing a different tune then.'

The gateman could see he was a difficult customer.

'Well at least give us a look, so we can go in and report.'

At first the man refused. But eventually he allowed himself to be persuaded, and producing it from within his gown, he exhibited the jade to them fleetingly on the palm of his hand, saying:

'Isn't this what you are looking for?'

Now these servants were all employed on external duties, and though they had heard tell of Bao-yu's jade, had hardly ever set eyes on it. This was in fact their first opportunity of inspecting the thing at close quarters. This did not deter them from running into the house in a great state of excitement, racing to be the first with the news.

They found that both Jia Zheng and Jia She were out. It was Jia Lian who received their report.

'Is it genuine or a fake?' he asked them sceptically.

'I saw it with my own eyes!' replied one of them. 'He wouldn't hand it over to us though, but insisted on seeing one of the masters, so that he could exchange it directly for the money.'

Jia Lian could not help being infected by their enthusiasm, and went in straight away to tell Lady Wang and Grandmother Jia. Aroma, when she heard, was overjoyed, and brought her hands piously together in a prayer of thanks to Lord Buddha. Grandmother Jia stood firmly by her word.

'Tell Lian to invite him into the study at once,' she said to Lady Wang in a flurry of excitement. 'Once we have had a look at it, he will get his money straight away.'

Jia Lian did as instructed and invited the stranger in, treating him most politely and expressing profuse thanks.

'I should just like to let the owner have a look at it, if I may,' he said. 'Then you shall have your money, every penny of it, I assure you.'

Reluctantly, the man handed him a little parcel wrapped in red silk. Jia Lian opened it. There lay a lustrous jade. Surely this was it! Jia Lian, to tell the truth, had never taken much notice of it while it hung round Bao-yu's neck. Now he looked closely at it for some time. The inscription was certainly familiar. He remembered some of the words, such as "dispels the harms of witchcraft". With a jubilant air, he strode in to show it to the ladies, leaving a servant to wait on the stranger.

By now the whole family had heard the news, and were gathered in Grandmother Jia's apartment, waiting eagerly, each one anxious to be the first to see. Xi-feng saw Jia Lian come in, and thrusting forward her hand, snatched the parcel from him and without looking at it herself, placed it in Grandmother Jia's hand.

'Can't you even let me take the credit for a small thing like this?' said Jia Lian with a sneer.

Grandmother Jia opened the silk bundle and examined the stone. It seemed a great deal duller than she remembered. She rubbed it between her fingers. Faithful brought her spectacles, and put them on for her. She examined it again.

'How peculiar! This must surely be it; and yet it seems to have lost its original lustre entirely.'

Lady Wang now inspected it. She too felt unable to identify it with any certainty, and told Xi-feng to come over and take a look.

'There is a certain similarity,' said Xi-feng after her inspection. 'But the colour is not quite right. We should show it to Bao-yu himself. He will be able to tell.'

Aroma was standing at her side, and had managed to have a look at the stone. Her eyes told her that it was not the one, but her heart was too full of hope to allow her to voice her misgivings. Xi-feng took the stone from Grandmother Jia's hands and went with Aroma to show it to Bao-yu, who had just awoken.

'Your stone has been found!' announced Aroma.

Bao-yu's eyes were still heavy with sleep. He took the stone in his hand, and without so much as a glance, let it drop to the ground.

'Why try to fool me!' he said, smiling strangely.

Xi-feng picked it up promptly.

'That's odd,' she said. 'How can you tell without even looking at it?'

Bao-yu only smiled again. Lady Wang had come in meanwhile, and observed what happened.

'It is perfectly natural,' she commented. 'That strange jade came into the world with him, it is his very own. He would be bound to know whether this was genuine or not. Someone must have read the reward-notice and faked it.'

The truth dawned on them all. Jia Lian, who heard it all from the outer room, said at once:

'If it is a fake, give it to me! I'll have it out with this impostor! How dare he play a trick on us, in such a serious matter!'

'No, Lian!' ordered Grandmother Jia. 'Give it back to him, and tell him to leave. No doubt he was desperately poor, and when he read the notice, saw a way of making a few pennies. It's understandable. Now he has been found out, and whatever it cost him to make the thing has been wasted too. Don't be too hard on him. Give him back the jade, and just say that it's not ours, and there's been a mistake. Give him a few taels of silver. If people hear that he's been well treated, it will encourage someone with genuine information to come forward. If we treat this one harshly, no one will bring it in even if they do find it.'

Jia Lian went as bidden. The impostor had been waiting in the study, and as time went by and no one returned, had already begun to lose his nerve. Now he saw the irate figure of Jia Lian advancing into the room. For the outcome of their subsequent interview, please read the next chapter.

CHAPTER 96

Xi-feng conceives an ingenious plan of deception
And Frowner is deranged by an inadvertent disclosure

When he saw the scowl on Jia Lian's face, the impostor's heart sank. He rose nervously to greet him, but before he could say a word, Jia Lian gave a chilling laugh and silenced him with:

'Impudent fool! I should like to wring your miserable little... Do you realize who you are dealing with? How dare you play such tricks on us?'

Turning, he called for his pages. The order was echoed outside like a clap of thunder, and several pages responded in unison and presented themselves.

'Fetch a rope and bind this fellow!' order Jia Lian. 'When the Master returns, I shall report the matter and pack him off to the yamen.'

'Ready, sir!' cried the chorus of pages. But not one of them moved a muscle.

The impostor was at first immobilized with terror. But Jia Lian's hectoring, and the prospect of being taken to court, finally stirred him to action. He fell on his knees and kotowed frantically in Jia Lian's direction, jabbering:

'Your Honour! Spare me! It was poverty forced me to it! I know it was a shameful thing to do. I had to borrow money to have it made, but please keep it and give it to the young master of the house with my humble compliments, to play with!'

Repeated head-knocking followed. Jia Lian spat contemptuously.

'Idiot! We certainly don't want any of your trash here!'

At this point, Lai Da came into the room.

'Do not waste your anger on this creature, sir,' he interceded, with a placatory smile. 'Spare him this once, and throw him out.'

'Why should I? The worm . . .'

While Jia Lian and Lai Da continued to haggle over the poor man's fate, the servants standing in the doorway offered him their advice:

'Come on, you great ninny! Kotow to Mr Lian and Mr Lai, and clear off! What are you waiting for? A kick in the stomach?'

The man was down in a flash, kotowed to Jia Lian and Lai Da, wrapped his hands round the back of his head and fled like a rat.

This episode became known in the locality as 'the case of Master Jia Bao-yu and the Counterfeit (Jia) Precious Jade (Bao-yu).

*

When Jia Zheng returned home that same day from a visit, no one told him what had happened in his absence. They thought that with the Lantern Festival coming up, it would be a mistake to make him angry about something that was, after all, over and done with. What with Yuan-chun's death, and their concern at Bao-yu's illness, the family was far too gloomy and preoccupied to celebrate New Year in anything but a perfunctory fashion, and it passed by without any event worthy of notice in this chronicle.

By the seventeenth of the first month, when Lady Wang was expecting her brother to arrive in the capital any day, she had an unannounced visit from Xi-feng:

'Lian has just come home with a piece of bad news, Aunt. It is about Uncle Zi-teng. He was travelling post-haste on his way to the capital, and was only seventy miles from here, when he died. Had you heard?'

'No!' exclaimed Lady Wang, aghast. 'Sir Zheng didn't mention anything of the sort yesterday evening. Where did Lian hear this?'

'At the home of Excellency Zhang from the Privy Council.'

Lady Wang stared in silence. Tears started from her eyes. Wiping them away, she finally said:

'Go and tell Lian to get confirmation of the news, and to see me as soon as he has.'

Xi-feng departed as bidden. Left on her own, Lady Wang gave way to her tears. A brother and daughter dead, a son deranged – she could contain her burden of grief and anxiety no longer. She began to feel a pain in her chest. And here was Jia Lian to confirm the story:

'Uncle was exhausted by the strain of the journey, and caught a chill. They were at Ten Mile Village when this happened. A doctor was called, but the only one available in such a remote spot turned out to be incompetent. He prescribed the wrong drugs, and the first dose proved fatal. Uncle's own family have set out for the place already, but I do not know if they have arrived yet.'

These details touched Lady Wang to the quick, and the pain in her chest became so severe that she could no longer sit upright. She told Suncloud to help her onto the kang, and struggling to keep a grip on herself, told Jia Lian to report at once to Jia Zheng.

'Pack your things as quickly as you can, and go straight there to join the family and help them with the funeral arrangements. Come back as soon as possible and let us know how things stand. I know Xi-feng will not set her mind at rest until you are back.'

Jia Lian could see that it would be inappropriate to raise any objections. He took his leave of Jia Zheng, and set out for Ten Mile Village.

Jia Zheng had learned the news of Wang Zi-teng's death independently. Depressed already by the moronic decline into which his son had fallen since the loss of his jade, a condition no doctor seemed able to cure, he responded with extreme gloom to this latest blow and to Lady Wang's attack following upon it. The time had come round for the triennial review of civil servants stationed in the capital. Jia Zheng's Board gave him a high commendation, and in the second month the Board of Civil Office presented him for an audience with the Emperor. His Majesty, in view of Jia Zheng's record as a 'diligent, frugal, conscientious and prudent servant of the Throne', appointed him immediately to the post of Grain Intendant for the province of Kiangsi. The same day, Jia Zheng offered his humble acceptance and gratitude for the honour, and suggested a day for his departure. Friends and relatives were all eager to celebrate, but he was not in festive mood. He was loth to leave the capital at a time when things were so unsettled at home, although at the same time he knew that he could not delay his departure.

He was pondering this dilemma, when a message came to summon him to Grandmother Jia's presence. He made his way promptly to her apartment, where he found Lady Wang also present, despite her illness. He paid his respects to Grandmother Jia, who told him to be seated and then began:

'In a few days, you will be leaving us to take up your post. There is something I should like to discuss with you, if you are willing.'

The old lady's eyes were wet with tears. Jia Zheng rose swiftly to his feet, and said:

'Whatever you have to say, Mother, please speak: your word is my command.'

'I shall be eighty-one this year,' said Grandmother Jia, sobbing as she spoke. 'You are going away to a post in the provinces, and with your elder brother still at home, you will not be able to apply for early retirement to come and look after me. When you are gone, of the ones closest to my heart I shall only have Bao-yu left to me. And he, poor darling, is in such a wretched state, I don't know what we can do for him! The other day I sent out Lai Sheng's wife to have the boy's fortune told. The man's reading was uncanny. What he said was: "This person must marry a lady with a destiny of gold, to help him and support him. He must be given a marriage as soon as possible to turn his luck. If not, he may not live." Now I know you don't believe in such things, which is why I sent for you, to talk it over with you. You and his mother must discuss it among yourselves. Are we to save him, or are we to do nothing and watch him fade away?'

Jia Zheng smiled anxiously.

'Could I, who as a child received such tender love and care from you, Mother, not have fatherly feelings myself? It is just that I have been exasperated by his repeated failure to make progress in his studies, and have perhaps been too ambitious for him. You are perfectly right in wanting to see him married. How could I possibly wish to oppose you? I am concerned for the boy, and his recent illness has caused me great anxiety. But as you have kept him from me, I have not ventured to say anything. I should like to see him now for myself, and form my own impression of his condition.'

Lady Wang saw that his eyes were moist, and knew that he was genuinely concerned. She told Aroma to fetch Bao-yu and help him into the room. He walked in, and when Aroma told him to pay his respects to his father, did exactly as she said. Jia Zheng saw how emaciated his face had grown, how lifeless his eyes were. His son was like some pathetic simpleton. He told them to take him back to his room.

'I shall soon be sixty myself,' he mused. 'With this provincial posting, it is difficult to tell how many years it will be before I return. If anything were to happen to Bao-yu, I should be left without an heir in my old age. I have a grandson, but that is not the same. And then Bao-yu is the old lady's favourite. If anything untoward occurred, I should be still more deeply at fault.'

He glanced at Lady Wang. Her face was wet with tears. He thought of the sorrow it would cause her too, and stood up again to speak.

'If, from your wealth of experience, you have thought of a way to help him, Mother, then how could I possibly raise any objection? We should do whatever you think is best. But has Mrs Xue been informed?'

'My sister has already expressed her agreement,' replied Lady Wang. 'We have only been biding our time because Pan's court-case has still not been settled.'

'Yes, that is certainly the first obstacle,' commented Jia Zheng. 'How can a girl be given in marriage while her elder brother is in jail? And besides there is Her Grace's death. Although that does not strictly entail any such prohibition, Bao-yu should at least abide by the set term of mourning for a deceased elder sister, which would mean a period of nine months during which marriage would be highly irregular. And then, my own date of departure has already been reported to the throne, and I cannot postpone it now. That only leaves us a few days. There is not enough time.'

Grandmother Jia pondered her son's words. 'What he says is true,' she thought to herself. 'If we wait for all of these conditions to be fulfilled, his father will have left, and who knows to what state the boy's health may deteriorate. And then it may be too late. We shall have to put aside the rules for once. There is no other way.'

Having reached this conclusion in her own mind, she spoke to Jia Zheng again.

'If you will agree to this for him, I shall take care of any problems that may arise. There is nothing that cannot be ironed out, of that I am confident. His mother and I shall go over and put the matter personally to Mrs Xue. As for Pan, I shall ask young Ke to go to him and explain that we are doing this to save Bao-yu's life. When he knows the reason, I am sure he will agree. As for marrying during a period of mourning, strictly speaking one shouldn't, I know. And besides, it is not right for him to marry while he is so ill. But it's a question of turning his luck. Both families are willing, and as the children have the bond of gold and jade to justify their union, we can dispense with the usual reading of horoscopes. We just need to choose an auspicious day to exchange presents in proper style, and then set a date for the wedding itself, possible afterwards. No music during the wedding itself, but otherwise we can follow court practice: twelve pairs of long-handled lanterns and an eight-man palanquin for the bride. We shall have the ceremony in our southern form, and keep our old customs of throwing dried fruit onto the bridal bed and so forth. That will be enough to make it quite a proper wedding. Bao-chai is a sensible girl. We need not worry on her account. And Aroma is a very reliable person. We can count on her to have a calming influence on Bao-yu. She gets on well with Bao-chai too.

'One other thing: Mrs Xue once told us that a monk said Bao-chai should only marry someone with a jade to match her golden locket. Perhaps when she comes to live as Bao-yu's wife, her locket will draw the jade back. Once they are married, things will look up and the whole family will benefit. So, we must prepare a courtyard and decorate it nicely – I should like you to choose it. We shan't be inviting any friends or relations to the wedding, and we can have the party later, when Bao-yu is better and the mourning period is over. This way, everything will be done in time, and you will be able to see the young people married and set off with an easy mind.'

Jia Zheng had grave doubts about the proposal. But as it was Grandmother Jia's, he knew he could not go against it. He smiled dutifully, and hastened to reply:

'You have thought it all out very well, Mother, and have taken everything into account. We must tell the servants not to go talking about this to everyone they meet. It would hardly redound to our credit if people knew. And personally I doubt if Mrs Xue will agree to the idea. But if she does, then I suppose we should do as you suggest.'

'You need not worry about Mrs Xue,' said the old lady. 'I can explain things to her. Off you go then.'

Jia Zheng took his leave. He felt extremely uneasy about the whole idea. Official business soon engulfed him, however – acceptance of his new papers of appointment, recommendations of staff from friends and relatives, an endless round of social gatherings of one sort or another – and he delegated all responsibility for the marriage plans to Grandmother Jia, who in turn left the arrangements to Lady Wang and Xi-feng. Jia Zheng's only contribution was to designate a twenty-frame building in a courtyard behind the Hall of Exalted Felicity, to the side of Lady Wang's private apartment, as Bao-yu's new home. Grandmother Jia's mind was now quite made up, and when she sent someone to communicate this to Jia Zheng he just replied: 'Very well.' But of this, more later.

*

Bao-yu, after his brief interview with his father, was escorted back by Aroma to his kang in the inner room. Intimidated by the Master's presence in the next room, none of the maids dared speak to him and he soon fell into a deep sleep. As a consequence he did not hear a word of the conversation between his father and Grandmother Jia. Aroma and the others did, however, and stood in complete silence taking it all in. Aroma had heard rumours of this marriage-plan, rumours whose likelihood, it is true, had been strengthened by Bao-chai's repeated absence from family gatherings. Now that she knew it for a fact, all became crystal clear. She was glad.

'They've shown some sense at last!' she thought to herself. 'Those two will make by far the better match. And I shall be better off too. With Miss Chai here I'll be able to unload a lot of my responsibilities. The only trouble is, Master Bao still thinks of no one but Miss Lin... It's a good thing he didn't hear just now. If he knew what they are planning, I dread to think what trouble we'd have.'

This cast a shadow over her previous optimism. 'What's to be done?' she continued to brood to herself. 'Her Old

Ladyship and Her Ladyship obviously don't know about the secret feelings Master Bao and Miss Lin have for each other, and in their enthusiasm they could tell him their plan, to try and cure him. But if he still feels as he did – when he first saw Miss Lin, for instance, and hurled his jade to the ground and wanted to smash it to pieces; or last summer in the Garden, when he mistook me for her and poured his heart out to me; or when Nightingale teased him by saying that Miss Lin was going away, and had him in such floods of tears – and if they go and tell him now that he's betrothed to Miss Chai and will have to give Miss Lin up for ever, so far from turning his luck they'll probably kill him! (Unless of course he's going through one of his deaf-and-dumb spells, in which case he probably won't even notice.) I'd better tell them what I know, or three people may suffer!'

Aroma's mind was made up. As soon as Jia Zheng had taken his leave of the ladies, she left Ripple to look after Bao-yu, and went into the outer room. She walked over to Lady Wang and whispered that she would like a word with her privately in the room to the rear of Grandmother Jia's apartment. Grandmother Jia imagined it to be some message from Bao-yu and did not pay much attention, but continued to engross herself in the wedding arrangements. Lady Wang rose to leave, and Aroma followed her into the rear chamber, where she at once fell on her knees and began crying. Lady Wang had no idea what it was all about, and taking her by the hand, said:

'Come now! What is all this? Has someone done you wrong? If so, stand up, and tell me.'

'It is something I shouldn't really say, but in the circumstances I feel I must.'

'Well, tell me then. And take your time.'

'You and Her Old Ladyship have made an excellent decision, in choosing Miss Bao-chai as Bao-yu's future bride . . .' began Aroma. 'But, I wonder, ma'am, if you have noticed which of the two young ladies Bao-yu is more closely attached to, Miss Chai, or Miss Lin?'

'As they have lived together since they were children,' replied Lady Wang, 'I suppose he would be a little closer to Miss Lin.'

'More than a little!' protested Aroma, and went on to give Lady Wang a detailed history of how things had always stood between Bao-yu and Dai-yu, and of the various incidents that had occurred between them.

'These are all things that you would have seen for yourself, ma'am,' she added, 'with the exception of his outburst during the summer, which I have not mentioned to a soul until now.'

Lady Wang drew Aroma towards her.

'Yes, most of what you have told me I have been able to deduce for myself. What you have said simply bears out my own observations. But you must all have heard the Master's words. Tell me, how did Bao-yu react?'

'As things are at present, ma'am, Bao-yu smiles if someone talks to him, but otherwise he just sleeps. He heard nothing.'

'In that case, what are we to do?'

'It is not my place to say,' replied Aroma. 'Your Ladyship should inform Her Old Ladyship of what I have said, and think of a suitable way of solving the problem.'

'Then you had better go,' said Lady Wang, 'and leave it to me. Now would not be a good moment to bring it up; there are too many people in the room. I shall wait for an opportunity to tell Her Old Ladyship, and we will discuss what to do.'

Lady Wang returned to Grandmother Jia's apartment. The old lady was talking to Xi-feng, and when she saw Lady Wang come in, asked:

'What did Aroma want? What was all that mysterious whispering about?'

Lady Wang answered her directly, and told the

whole story of Bao-yu's love for Dai-yu, as Aroma had told it her. When she had finished, Grandmother Jia was silent for a long while. Neither Lady Wang nor Xi-feng dared say a word. At last, Grandmother Jia sighed and said:

'Everything else seemed somehow soluble. It does not matter so much about Dai-yu. But if Bao-yu really feels this way about her, it seems we have run into an insoluble problem.'

Xi-feng looked very thoughtful for a minute, then said:

'Not insoluble. I think I can see a solution. But I am not sure if you would agree to it or not, Aunt.'

'Whatever your idea is,' said Lady Wang, 'speak up and let Mother know. Then we can all discuss it together.'

'There is only one solution that I can think of,' said Xi-feng. 'It involves two things: a white lie, and a piece of discreet substitution.'

'Substitution? What do you mean?' asked Grandmother Jia.

'First of all,' replied Xi-feng, 'whether Bao-yu knows anything yet or not, we let it be known that Sir Zheng proposes to betroth him to Miss Lin. We must watch for his reaction. If he is quite unaffected, then there is no need to bother with my plan. But if he does seem at all pleased at the news, it will make things rather more complicated.'

'Supposing he is pleased?' asked Lady Wang. 'What then?'

Xi-feng went over and whispered at some length in Lady Wang's ear. Lady Wang nodded, smiled and said:

'Well, well . . . An ingenious idea, I must say!'

'Come on, you two!' exclaimed Grandmother Jia. 'Let me in on the secret: what are you whispering about?'

Xi-feng was afraid that Grandmother Jia might not grasp her idea at once, and might inadvertently give the game away. She leant across and whispered in the old lady's ear. Grandmother Jia did seem rather puzzled at first. Xi-feng smiled, and added a few more words of explanation. Grandmother Jia finally said with a smile:

'Why not? But isn't it rather hard on Bao-chai? And what about Miss Lin? What if she gets to hear of it?'

'We shall only tell Bao-yu' replied Xi-feng. 'No one else will be allowed to mention it. That way no one need know.'

A maid came in and informed them that Mr Lian had returned. Lady Wang was worried that Grandmother Jia might inquire into the distressing news that had occasioned his journey, and cast a meaningful glance in Xi-feng's direction. Xi-feng went out to intercept him, and signalled to him with her lips to accompany her to Lady Wang's apartment and wait there. It was not long before Lady Wang came in, to find Xi-feng red-eyed from weeping. Jia Lian paid his respects to Lady Wang, and gave her an account of the funeral arrangements for Wang Zi-teng at Ten Mile Village.

'He has been posthumously awarded the rank of Grand Secretary, by Imperial Decree,' Jia Lian went on, 'and the title Lord Wen-qin. The Court has given instructions for the family to accompany the coffin *en cortège* to Nanking, and all local mandarins have been instructed to look after them en route. The whole family left yesterday for the South. Uncle's widow asked me to convey her respects. She said that there was so much she wanted to talk to you about, but that she would not be able to come to the capital at present. My brother-in-law Wang Ren is coming here, so I heard, and if they meet him on the way, they will tell him to come and give us the latest news.'

Lady Wang responded to all of this with a grief that the reader can surely imagine.

'Why don't you lie down for a while, Aunt?' said Xi-feng. 'In the evening, we can talk further about Bao-yu's affairs.'

Having uttered these comforting words, Xi-feng returned with Jia Lian to her own apartment, where she informed him of all that had been decided and told him to give instructions for the cleaning and refurbishing of the courtyard that was to be the couple's new home. But of this no more for the present.

*

A day or two after these events, Dai-yu, having eaten her breakfast, decided to take Nightingale with her to visit Grandmother Jia. She wanted to pay her respects, and also thought the visit might provide some sort of distraction for herself. She had hardly left the Naiad's House, when she remembered that she had left her handkerchief at home, and sent Nightingale back to fetch it, saying that she would walk ahead slowly and wait for her to catch up. She had just reached the corner behind the rockery at Drenched Blossoms Bridge – the very spot where she had once buried the flowers with Bao-yu – when all of a sudden she heard the sound of sobbing. She stopped at once and listened. She could not tell whose voice it was, nor could she distinguish what it was that the voice was complaining of, so tearfully and at such length. It really was most puzzling. She moved forward again cautiously and as she turned the corner, saw before her the source of the sobbing, a maid with large eyes and thick-set eyebrows.

Before setting eyes on this girl, Dai-yu had guessed that one of the many maids in the Jia household must have had an unhappy love-affair, and had come here to cry her heart out in secret. But now she laughed at the very idea. 'How could such an ungainly creature as this know the meaning of love?' she thought to herself. 'This must be one of the odd-job girls, who has probably been scolded by one of the senior maids.' She looked more closely, but still could not place the girl. Seeing Dai-yu, the maid ceased her weeping, wiped her cheeks, and rose to her feet.

'Come now, what are you so upset about?' inquired Dai-yu.

'Oh Miss Lin!' replied the maid, amid fresh tears. 'Tell

me if you think it fair. *They* were talking about it, and how was I to know better? Just because I say one thing wrong, is that a reason for sister to start hitting me?'

Dai-yu did not know what she was talking about. She smiled, and asked again:

'Who is your sister?'

'Pearl,' answered the maid.

From this, Dai-yu concluded that she must work in Grandmother Jia's apartment.

'And what is your name?'

'Simple.'

Dai-yu laughed. Then:

'Why did she hit you? What did you say that was so wrong?'

'That's what I'd like to know! It was only to do with Master Bao marrying Miss Chai!'

The words struck Dai-yu's ears like a clap of thunder. Her heart started thumping fiercely. She tried to calm herself for a moment, and told the maid to come with her. The maid followed her to the secluded corner of the garden, where the Flower Burial Mound was situated. Here Dai-yu asked her:

'Why should she hit you for mentioning Master Bao's marriage to Miss Chai?'

'Her Old Ladyship, Her Ladyship and Mrs Lian,' replied Simple, 'have decided that as the Master is leaving soon, they are going to arrange with Mrs Xue to marry Master Bao and Miss Chai as quickly as possible. They want the wedding to turn his luck, and then . . .'

Her voice tailed off. She stared at Dai-yu, laughed and continued:

'Then, as soon as those two are married, they are going to find a husband for you, Miss Lin.'

Dai-yu was speechless with horror. The maid went on regardless:

'But how was I to know that they'd decided to keep it quiet, for fear of embarrassing Miss Chai? All I did was say to Aroma, that serves in Master Bao's room: "Won't it be a fine to-do here soon, when Miss Chai comes over, or Mrs Bao . . . what *will* we have to call her?" That's all I said. What was there in that to hurt sister Pearl? Can *you* see, Miss Lin? She came across and hit me straight in the face and said I was talking rubbish and disobeying orders, and would be dismissed from service! How was I to know their Ladyships didn't want us to mention it? Nobody told me, and she just hit me!'

She started sobbing again. Dai-yu's heart felt as though oil, soy-sauce, sugar and vinegar had all been poured into it at once. She could not tell which flavour predominated, the sweet, the sour, the bitter or the salty. After a few moments' silence, she said in a trembling voice:

'Don't talk such rubbish. Any more of that, and you'll be beaten again. Off you go!'

She herself turned back in the direction of the Naiad's House. Her body felt as though it weighed a hundred tons, her feet were as wobbly as if she were walking on cotton-floss. She could only manage one step at a time. After an age, she still had not reached the bank by Drenched Blossoms Bridge. She was going so slowly, with her feet about to collapse beneath her, and in her giddiness and confusion had wandered off course and increased the distance by about a hundred yards. She reached Drenched Blossoms Bridge only to start drifting back again along the bank in the direction she had just come from, quite unaware of what she was doing.

Nightingale had by now returned with the handkerchief, but could not find Dai-yu anywhere. She finally saw her, pale as snow, tottering along, her eyes staring straight in front of her, meandering in circles. Nightingale also caught sight of a maid disappearing in the distance beyond Dai-yu, but could not make out who it was. She was most bewildered, and quickened her step.

'Why are you turning back again, Miss?' she asked softly. 'Where are you heading for?'

Dai-yu only heard the blurred outline of this question. She replied:

'I want to ask Bao-yu something.'

Nightingale could not fathom what was going on, and could only try to guide her on her way to Grandmother Jia's apartment. When they came to the entrance, Dai-yu seemed to feel clearer in mind. She turned, saw Nightingale supporting her, stopped for a moment, and asked:

'What are you doing here?'

'I went to fetch your handkerchief,' replied Nightingale, smiling anxiously. 'I saw you over by the bridge and hurried across. I asked you where you were going, but you took no notice.'

'Oh!' said Dai-yu with a smile. 'I thought you had come to see Bao-yu. What else did we come here for?'

Nightingale could see that her mind was utterly confused. She guessed that it was something that the maid had said in the garden, and only nodded with a faint smile in reply to Dai-yu's question. But to herself she was trying to imagine what sort of an encounter this was going to be, between the young master who had already lost his wits, and her young mistress who was now herself a little touched. Despite her apprehensions, she dared not prevent the meeting, and helped Dai-yu into the room. The funny thing was that Dai-yu now seemed to have recovered her strength. She did not wait for Nightingale but raised the portière herself, and walked into the room. It was very quiet inside. Grandmother Jia had retired for her afternoon nap. Some of the maids had sneaked off to play, some were having forty winks themselves and others had gone to wait on Grandmother Jia in her bedroom. It was Aroma who came out to see who was there, when she heard the swish of the portière. Seeing that it was Dai-yu, she greeted her politely:

'Please come in and sit down, Miss.'

'Is Master Bao at home?' asked Dai-yu with a smile.

Aroma did not know that anything was amiss, and was

about to answer, when she saw Nightingale make an urgent movement with her lips from behind Dai-yu's back, pointing to her mistress and making a warning gesture with her hand. Aroma had no idea what she meant and dared not ask. Undeterred, Dai-yu walked on into Bao-yu's room. He was sitting up in bed, and when she came in made no move to get up or welcome her, but remained where he was, staring at her and giving a series of silly laughs. Dai-yu sat down uninvited, and she too began to smile and stare back at Bao-yu. There were no greetings exchanged, no courtesies, in fact no words of any kind. They just sat there staring into each other's faces and smiling like a pair of half-wits. Aroma stood watching, completely at a loss.

Suddenly Dai-yu said:

'Bao-yu, why are you sick?'

Bao-yu laughed.

'I'm sick because of Miss Lin.'

Aroma and Nightingale grew pale with fright. They tried to change the subject, but their efforts only met with silence and more senseless smiles. By now it was clear to Aroma that Dai-yu's mind was as disturbed as Bao-yu's.

'Miss Lin has only just recovered from her illness,' she whispered to Nightingale. 'I'll ask Ripple to help you take her back. She should go home and lie down.' Turning to Ripple, she said: 'Go with Nightingale and accompany Miss Lin home. And no stupid chattering on the way, mind.'

Ripple smiled, and without a word came over to help Nightingale. The two of them began to help Dai-yu to her feet. Dai-yu stood up at once, unassisted, still staring fixedly at Bao-yu, smiling and nodding her head.

'Come on, Miss!' urged Nightingale. 'It's time to go home and rest.'

'Of course!' exclaimed Dai-yu. 'It's time!'

She turned to go. Still smiling and refusing any assistance from the maids, she strode out at twice her normal speed. Ripple and Nightingale hurried after her. On leaving Grandmother Jia's apartment, Dai-yu kept on walking, in quite the wrong direction. Nightingale hurried up to her and took her by the hand.

'This is the way, Miss.'

Still smiling, Dai-yu allowed herself to be led, and followed Nightingale towards the Naiad's House. When they were nearly there, Nightingale exclaimed:

'Lord Buddha be praised! Home at last!'

She had no sooner uttered these words when she saw Dai-yu stumble forwards onto the ground, and give a loud cry. A stream of blood came gushing from her mouth.

To learn if she survived this crisis, please read the next chapter.

CHAPTER 97

Lin Dai-yu burns her poems
to signal the end of her heart's folly
And Xue Bao-chai leaves home
to take part in a solemn rite

We have seen how Dai-yu, on reaching the entrance of the Naiad's House, and on hearing Nightingale's cry of relief, slumped forward, vomited blood and almost fainted. Luckily Nightingale and Ripple were both at hand to assist her into the house. When Ripple left, Nightingale and Snowgoose stood by Dai-yu's bedside and watched her gradually come round.

'Why are you two standing round me crying?' asked Dai-yu, and Nightingale, greatly reassured to hear her talking sense again, replied:

'On your way back from Her Old Ladyship's, Miss, you had quite a nasty turn. We were scared and did not know what to do. That's why we were crying.'

'I am not going to die yet!' said Dai-yu, with a bitter smile. But before she could even finish this sentence, she was doubled up and gasping for breath once more.

When she had learned earlier that day that Bao-yu and Bao-chai were to be married, the shock of knowing that what she had feared for so long was now about to come true, had thrown her into such a turmoil that at first she had quite taken leave of her senses. Now that she had brought up the blood, her mind gradually became clearer. Though at first she could remember nothing, when she saw Nightingale crying, Simple's words slowly came back to her. This time she did not succumb to her emotions, but set her heart instead on a speedy death and final settlement of her debt with fate.

Nightingale and Snowgoose could only stand by helplessly. They would have gone to inform the ladies, but were afraid of a repetition of the last occasion, when Xi-feng had rebuked them for creating a false alarm. Ripple had already given all away, however, by the look of horror on her face when she returned to Grandmother Jia's apartment. The old lady, who had just risen from her midday nap, asked her what the matter was, and in her shocked state Ripple told her all that she had just witnessed.

'What a terrible thing!' exclaimed Grandmother Jia, aghast. She sent for Lady Wang and Xi-feng at once, and told them both the news.

'But I gave instructions to everyone to observe strict secrecy,' said Xi-feng. 'Who can have betrayed us? Now we have another problem on our hands.'

'Never mind that for the moment,' said Grandmother Jia. 'We must first find out how she is.'

She took Lady Wang and Xi-feng with her to visit Dai-yu, and they arrived to find her barely conscious, breathing in faint little gasps, her face bloodless and white as snow. After a while she coughed again. A maid brought the spittoon and they watched with horror as she spat out a mouthful of blood and phlegm. Dai-yu faintly opened her eyes, and seeing Grandmother Jia standing at her bedside, struggled to find breath to speak.

'Grandmother! Your love for me has been in vain.'

Grandmother Jia was most distraught.

'There now, my dear, you must rest. There is nothing to fear.'

Dai-yu smiled faintly and closed her eyes again. A maid came in to tell Xi-feng that the doctor had arrived. The ladies withdrew, and doctor Wang came in with Jia Lian. He took Dai-yu's pulses, and said:

'As yet, there is no cause for alarm. An obstruction of

morbid humours has affected the liver, which is unable to store the blood, and as a consequence her spirit has been disturbed. I shall prescribe a medicine to check the Yin, and to halt the flow of blood. I think all will be well.'

Doctor Wang left the room, accompanied by Jia Lian, to write out his prescription.

Grandmother Jia could tell that this time Dai-yu was seriously ill, and as they left the room, she said to Lady Wang and Xi-feng:

'I do not wish to sound gloomy or bring her bad luck, but I fear she has small hope of recovery, poor child. You must make ready her grave-clothes and coffin. Who knows, such preparations may even turn her luck. She may recover, which will be a mercy for us all. But it would be sensible anyway to be prepared for the worst, and not be taken unawares. We shall be so busy over the next few days.'

Xi-feng said she would make the necessary arrangements. Grandmother Jia then questioned Nightingale, but she had no idea who it was that had upset Dai-yu. The more she thought about it, the more it puzzled Grandmother Jia, and she said to Xi-feng and Lady Wang:

'I can understand that the two of them should have grown rather fond of one another, after growing up together and playing together as children. But now that they are older and more mature, the time has come for them to observe a certain distance. She must behave properly, if she is to earn my love. It's quite wrong of her to think she can disregard such things. Then all my love *will* have been in vain! What you have told me troubles me.'

She returned to her apartment and sent for Aroma again. Aroma repeated to her all that she had told Lady Wang on the previous occasion, and in addition described the scene earlier that day between Dai-yu and Bao-yu.

'And yet, when I saw her just now,' said Grandmother Jia, 'she still seemed able to talk sense. I simply cannot understand it. Ours is a decent family. We do not tolerate unseemly goings-on. And that applies to foolish romantic attachments. If her illness is of a respectable nature, I do not mind how much we have to spend to get her better. But if she is suffering from some form of lovesickness, no amount of medicine will cure it and she can expect no further sympathy from me either.'

'You really shouldn't worry about Cousin Lin, Grandmother,' said Xi-feng. 'Lian will be visiting her regularly with the doctor. We must concentrate on the wedding arrangements. Early this morning I heard that the finishing touches were being put to the bridal courtyard. You and Aunt Wang and I should go over to Aunt Xue's for a final consultation. There is one thing that occurs to me, however: with Bao-chai there, it will be rather awkward for us to discuss the wedding. Maybe we should ask Aunt Xue to come over here tomorrow evening, and then we can settle everything at once.'

Grandmother Jia and Lady Wang agreed that her proposal was a good one, and said:

'It is too late today. Tomorrow after lunch, let us all go over together.'

Grandmother Jia's dinner was now served, and Xi-feng and Lady Wang returned to their apartments.

Next day, Xi-feng came over after breakfast. Wishing to sound out Bao-yu according to her plan, she advanced into his room and said:

'Congratulations, Cousin Bao! Uncle Zheng has already chosen a lucky day for your wedding! Isn't that good news?'

Bao-yu stared at her with a blank smile, and nodded his head faintly.

'He is marrying you,' went on Xi-feng, with a studied smile, 'to your cousin Lin. Are you happy?'

Bao-yu burst out laughing. Xi-feng watched him carely, but could not make out whether he had understood her, or was simply raving. She went on:

'Uncle Zheng says, you are to marry Miss Lin, *if* you get better. But not if you carry on behaving like a half-wit.'

Bao-yu's expression suddenly changed to one of utter seriousness, as he said:

'I'm not a half-wit. You're the half-wit.'

He stood up.

'I am going to see Cousin Lin, to set her mind at rest.'

Xi-feng quickly put out a hand to stop him.

'She knows already. And, as your bride-to-be, she would be much too embarrassed to receive you now.'

'What about when we're married? Will she see me then?'

Xi-feng found this both comic and somewhat disturbing.

'Aroma was right,' she thought to herself. 'Mention Dai-yu, and while he still talks like an idiot, he at least seems to understand what's going on. I can see we shall be in real trouble, if he sees through our scheme and finds out that his bride is not to be Dai-yu after all.'

In reply to his question, she said, suppressing a smile:

'If you behave, she will see you. But not if you continue to act like an imbecile.'

To which Bao-yu replied:

'I have given my heart to Cousin Lin. If she marries me, she will bring it with her and put it back in its proper place.'

Now this was madman's talk if ever, thought Xi-feng. She left him, and walked back into the outer room, glancing with a smile in Grandmother Jia's direction. The old lady too found Bao-yu's words both funny and distressing.

'I heard you both myself,' she said to Xi-feng. 'For the present, we must ignore it. Tell Aroma to do her best to calm him down. Come, let us go.'

Lady Wang joined them, and the three ladies went across to Aunt Xue's. On arrival there, they pretended to be concerned about the course of Xue Pan's affair. Aunt Xue expressed her profound gratitude for this concern, and gave them the latest news. After they had all taken tea, Aunt Xue was about to send for Bao-chai, when Xi-feng stopped her, saying:

'There is no need to tell Cousin Chai that we are here, Auntie.'

With a diplomatic smile, she continued:

'Grandmother's visit today is not purely a social one. She has something of importance to say, and would like you to come over later so that we can all discuss it together.'

Aunt Xue nodded.

'Of course.'

After a little more chat, the three ladies returned.

That evening Aunt Xue came over as arranged, and after paying her respects to Grandmother Jia, went to her sister's apartment. First there was the inevitable scene of sisterly commiseration over Wang Zi-teng's death. Then Aunt Xue said:

'Just now when I was at Lady Jia's, young Bao came out to greet me and seemed quite well. A little thin perhaps, but certainly not as ill as I had been led to expect from your description and Xi-feng's.'

'No, it is really not that serious,' said Xi-feng. 'It's only Grandmother who will worry so. Her idea is that it would be reassuring for Sir Zheng to see Bao-yu married before he leaves, as who knows when he will be able to come home from his new posting. And then from Bao-yu's own point of view, it might be just the thing to turn his luck. With Cousin Chai's golden locket to counteract the evil influence, he should make a good recovery.'

Aunt Xue was willing enough to go along with the idea, but was concerned that Bao-chai might feel rather hard done by.

'I see nothing against it,' she said. 'But I think we should all take time to think it over properly.'

In accordance with Xi-feng's plan, Lady Wang went on:

'As you have no head of family present, we should like you to dispense with the usual trousseau. Tomorrow you should send Ke to let Pan know that while we proceed with the wedding, we shall continue to do our utmost to settle his court-case.'

She made no mention of Bao-yu's feelings for Dai-yu, but continued:

'Since you have given your consent, the sooner they are married, the sooner things will look up for everyone.'

At this point, Faithful came in to take back a report to Grandmother Jia. Though Aunt Xue was still concerned about Bao-chai's feelings, she saw that in the circumstances she had no choice, and agreed to everything they had suggested. Faithful reported this to Grandmother Jia, who was delighted and sent her back again to ask Mrs Xue to explain to Bao-chai why it was that things were being done in this way, so that she would not feel unfairly treated. Aunt Xue agreed to do this, and it was settled that Xi-feng and Jia Lian would act as official go-betweens. Xi-feng retired to her apartment, while Aunt Xue and Lady Wang stayed up talking together well into the night.

Next day, Aunt Xue returned to her apartment and told Bao-chai the details of the proposal, adding:

'I have already given my consent.'

At first Bao-chai hung her head in silence. Then she began to cry. Aunt Xue said all that she could to comfort her, and went to great lengths to explain the reasoning behind the decision. Bao-chai retired to her room, and Bao-qin went in to keep her company and cheer her up. Aunt Xue also spoke to Ke, instructing him as follows:

'You must leave tomorrow. Find out the latest news of Pan's judgement, and then convey this message to him. Return as soon as you possibly can.'

Xue Ke was away for four days, at the end of which time he returned to report to Aunt Xue.

'The Circuit Judge has ratified the verdict of manslaughter, and after the next hearing his final memorial will be presented to the Provincial Supreme Court for confirmation. We should have the commutation money ready. As for Cousin Chai's affair, Cousin Pan approves entirely of your decision, Aunt. And he says that curtailing the formalities will save us a lot of money too. You are not to wait for him, but should do whatever you think best.'

Aunt Xue's mind was greatly eased by the knowledge that Xue Pan would soon be free to come home, and that there were now no further obstacles to the marriage. She could see that Bao-chai was unwilling to be married in this way, but reasoned with herself: 'Even if this is not what she ideally wants, she is my daughter and has always been obedient and well-bred. She knows I have agreed to it, and will not go against my wishes.'

She instructed Xue Ke:

'We must prepare the betrothal-card. Take some fine gold-splash paper and write on it the Stems and Branches of Bao-chai's birth. Then take it to Cousin Lian. Find out which day has been fixed for the exchange of presents, and make all the necessary preparations for sending ours. We shall not be inviting any friends or relatives to the wedding. Pan's friends are a worthless lot, as you yourself said, while our relations consist mainly of the Jias and the Wangs. The Jias are groom's family, and there are no Wangs in the capital at present. When Xiang-yun was engaged, the Shis did not invite us, so we need not get in touch with them. The only person I think we should invite is our business manager, Zhang De-hui. He is an older man and experienced in such things, and will be a help to us.'

Xue Ke carried out these instructions, and sent a servant

over with the betrothal-card. Next day, Jia Lian came to visit Aunt Xue. After paying his respects, he said:

'I have consulted the almanac, and tomorrow is a most propitious day. I have come here today to propose that our two families exchange presents tomorrow. And please, Aunt Xue, do not be too critical about the arrangements.'

He presented the groom's notice, which bore the date of the wedding. Aunt Xue said a few polite words of acceptance and nodded her assent. Jia Lian returned at once and reported to Jia Zheng.

'Report to your Grandmother,' said Jia Zheng, 'and say that as we are not inviting anybody, the wedding should be kept very simple. She can exercise her discretion over the presents. There is no need to consult me any further.'

Jia Lian bowed, and went in to convey this message to Grandmother Jia. Meanwhile Lady Wang had told Xifeng to bring in the presents that were being given on Bao-yu's behalf, for Grandmother Jia's inspection. She also told Aroma to bring Bao-yu in to see them. He seemed highly amused by the whole business, and said:

'It seems such a waste of everyone's time, to send all these things from here to the Garden, and then have them brought all the way back, when it's all in the family anyway!'

This seemed to Lady Wang and Grandmother Jia sufficient proof that, whatever anyone might have said to the contrary, Bao-yu still had his wits about him, and they said as much to each other in tones of some satisfaction. Faithful and the other maids could not help but smile too. They brought the presents in and displayed them one by one, describing them as they went along:

'A gold necklace and other jewellery in gold and precious stones – altogether eighty pieces; forty bolts of dragon-brocade for formal wear and one hundred and twenty bolts of silks and satins in various colours; one hundred and twenty costumes for the four seasons of the year. They have not had time in the kitchen to prepare the sheep and wine, so this is money in lieu.'

Grandmother Jia expressed her approval, and said softly to Xi-feng:

'You must tell Mrs Xue not to think of this as an empty formality. In due course, when Pan is back and she has that weight off her mind, she can have these made up into dresses for Chai. In the meantime, we shall take care of all the bedcovers for the wedding-day.'

'Yes Grandmother,' replied Xi-feng, and returned to her apartment. She sent Jia Lian over first to Aunt Xue's, then summoned Zhou Rui and Brightie to receive their instructions.

'When delivering the presents,' she said, 'you are not to use the main gate. Use the little side-gate in the garden, that used to be kept open. I shall be going over myself shortly. The side-gate has the advantage of being a long way from the Naiad's House. If anyone from any other apartment notices you, you are to tell them on no account to mention it at the Naiad's House.'

'Yes ma'am.'

The two men departed for Aunt Xue's apartment at the head of a contingent of servants bearing the presents.

Bao-yu was quite taken in by all this. His new feeling of happy anticipation had caused a general improvement in his health, though his manner of speech remained rather eccentric at times. When the present-bearers returned, the whole thing was accomplished without a single name being mentioned. The family and all the staff knew, but were under orders from Xi-feng to maintain absolute secrecy, and no one dared disobey.

*

Dai-yu meanwhile, for all the medicine she took, continued to grow iller with every day that passed. Nightingale did her utmost to raise her spirits. Our story finds her standing once more by Dai-yu's bedside, earnestly beseeching her:

'Miss, now that things have come to this pass, I simply must speak my mind. We know what it is that's eating your heart out. But can't you see that your fears are groundless? Why, look at the state Bao-yu is in! How can he possibly get married, when he's so ill? You must ignore these silly rumours, stop fretting and let yourself get better.'

Dai-yu gave a wraithlike smile, but said nothing. She started coughing again and brought up a lot more blood. Nightingale and Snowgoose came closer and watched her feebly struggling for breath. They knew that any further attempt to rally her would be to no avail, and could do nothing but stand there watching and weeping. Each day Nightingale went over three or four times to tell Grandmother Jia, but Faithful, judging the old lady's attitude towards Dai-yu to have hardened of late, intercepted her reports and hardly mentioned Dai-yu to her mistress. Grandmother Jia was preoccupied with the wedding arrangements, and in the absence of any particular news of Dai-yu, did not show a great deal of interest in the girl's fate, considering it sufficient that she should be receiving medical attention.

Previously, when she had been ill, Dai-yu had always received frequent visits from everyone in the household, from Grandmother Jia down to the humblest maidservant. But now not a single person came to see her. The only face she saw looking down at her was that of Nightingale. She began to feel her end drawing near, and struggled to say a few words to her:

'Dear Nightingale! Dear sister! Closest friend! Though you were Grandmother's maid before you came to serve me, over the years you have become as a sister to me...'

She had to stop for breath. Nightingale felt a pang of pity, was reduced to tears and could say nothing. After a long silence, Dai-yu began to speak again, searching for breath between words:

'Dear sister! I am so uncomfortable lying down like this. Please help me up and sit next to me.'

'I don't think you should sit up, Miss, in your condition. You might get cold in the draught.'

Dai-yu closed her eyes in silence. A little later she asked to sit up again. Nightingale and Snowgoose felt they could no longer deny her request. They propped her up on both sides with soft pillows, while Nightingale sat by her on the bed to give further support. Dai-yu was not equal to the effort. The bed where she sat on it seemed to dig into her, and she struggled with all her remaining strength to lift herself up and ease the pain. She told Snowgoose to come closer.

'My poems . . .'

Her voice failed, and she fought for breath again. Snowgoose guessed that she meant the manuscripts she had been revising a few days previously, went to fetch them and laid them on Dai-yu's lap. Dai-yu nodded, then raised her eyes and gazed in the direction of a chest that stood on a stand close by. Snowgoose did not know how to interpret this and stood there at a loss. Dai-yu stared at her now with feverish impatience. She began to cough again and brought up another mouthful of blood. Snowgoose went to fetch some water, and Dai-yu rinsed her mouth and spat into the spittoon. Nightingale wiped her lips with a handkerchief. Dai-yu took the handkerchief from her and pointed to the chest. She tried to speak, but was again seized with an attack of breathlessness and closed her eyes.

'Lie down, Miss,' said Nightingale. Dai-yu shook her head. Nightingale thought she must want one of her handkerchiefs, and told Snowgoose to open the chest and bring her a plain white silk one. Dai-yu looked at it, and dropped it on the bed. Making a supreme effort, she gasped out:

'The ones with the writing on . . .'

Nightingale finally realized that she meant the handkerchiefs Bao-yu had sent her, the ones she had inscribed with her own poems. She told Snowgoose to fetch them, and herself handed them to Dai-yu, with these words of advice:

'You must lie down and rest, Miss. Don't start wearing yourself out. You can look at these another time, when you are feeling better.'

Dai-yu took the handkerchiefs in one hand and without even looking at them, brought round her other hand (which cost her a great effort) and tried with all her might to tear them in two. But she was so weak that all she could achieve was a pathetic trembling motion. Nightingale knew that Bao-yu was the object of all this bitterness but dared not mention his name, saying instead:

'Miss, there is no sense in working yourself up again.'

Dai-yu nodded faintly, and slipped the handkerchiefs into her sleeve.

'Light the lamp,' she ordered.

Snowgoose promptly obeyed. Dai-yu looked into the lamp, then closed her eyes and sat in silence. Another fit of breathlessness. Then:

'Make up the fire in the brazier.'

Thinking she wanted it for the extra warmth, Nightingale protested:

'You should lie down, Miss, and have another cover on. And the fumes from the brazier might be bad for you.'

Dai-yu shook her head, and Snowgoose reluctantly made up the brazier, placing it on its stand on the floor. Dai-yu made a motion with her hand, indicating that she wanted it moved up onto the kang. Snowgoose lifted it and placed it there, temporarily using the floor-stand, while she went out to fetch the special stand they used on the kang. Dai-yu, far from resting back in the warmth, now inclined her body slightly forward – Nightingale had to support her with both hands as she did so. Dai-yu took the handkerchiefs in one hand. Staring into the flames and nodding thoughtfully to herself, she dropped them into the brazier. Nightingale was horrified, but much as she would have liked to snatch them from the flames, she did not dare move her hands and leave Dai-yu unsupported. Snowgoose was out of the room, fetching the brazier-stand, and by now the handkerchiefs were all ablaze.

'Miss!' cried Nightingale. 'What are you doing?'

As if she had not heard, Dai-yu reached over for her manuscripts, glanced at them and let them fall again onto the kang. Nightingale, anxious lest she burn these too, leaned up against Dai-yu and freeing one hand, reached out with it to take hold of them. But before she could do so, Dai-yu had picked them up again and dropped them in the flames. The brazier was out of Nightingale's reach, and there was nothing she could do but look on helplessly.

Just at that moment Snowgoose came in with the stand. She saw Dai-yu drop something into the fire, and without knowing what it was, rushed forward to try and save it. The manuscripts had caught at once and were already ablaze. Heedless of the danger to her hands, Snowgoose reached into the flames and pulled out what she could, throwing the paper on the floor and stamping frantically on it. But the fire had done its work, and only a few charred fragments remained.

Dai-yu closed her eyes and slumped back, almost causing Nightingale to topple over with her. Nightingale, her heart thumping in great agitation, called Snowgoose over to help her settle Dai-yu down again. It was too late now to send for anyone. And yet, what if Dai-yu should die during the night, and the only people there were Snowgoose, herself and the one or two other junior maids in the Naiad's House? They passed a restless night. Morning came at last, and Dai-yu seemed a little more comfortable. But after breakfast she suddenly began coughing and vomiting, and became tense and feverish again. Nightingale could see that she had reached a crisis. She called Snowgoose and the other juniors in and told them to mount watch, while she went to report to Grandmother Jia. But when she reached Grandmother Jia's apartment, she found it almost deserted. Only a few old nannies and charladies were there, keeping an eye.

'Where is Her Old Ladyship?' asked Nightingale.

'We don't know,' came the reply in chorus.

That was very odd, thought Nightingale. She went into Bao-yu's room and found that too quite empty, save for a single maid who answered with the same 'Don't know'. By now Nightingale had more or less guessed the truth. How could they be so heartless and so cruel? And to think that not a soul had come to visit Dai-yu during the past few days! As the bitterness of it struck her with full force, she felt a great wave of resentment break out within her, and turned abruptly to go.

'I shall go and find Bao-yu, and see how *he* is faring! I wonder how he will manage to brazen it out in front of me! I remember last year, when I made up that story about Miss Lin going back to the South, he fell sick with despair. To think that now he should be openly doing a thing like this! Men must have hearts as cold as ice or snow. What hateful creatures they are!'

She was already at Green Delights, and found the courtyard gate ajar. All was quiet within. Suddenly she realized:

'Of course! If he is getting married, he will have a new apartment. But where?'

She was looking around her in uncertainty, when she saw Bao-yu's page boy Inky rush past, and called to him to stop. He came over, and with a broad smile asked:

'What are you doing here, Miss Nightingale?'

'I heard that Master Bao was getting married,' replied Nightingale, 'and I wanted to watch some of the fun. But I can seen I've come to the wrong place. And I don't know when the wedding is taking place, either.'

'If I tell you,' said Inky in a confidential tone, 'you must promise not to tell Snowgoose. We've been given orders not to let any of you know. The wedding's to be tonight. Of course it's not being held here. The Master told Mr Lian to set aside another apartment.'

'What's the matter?' continued Inky, after a pause.

'Nothing,' replied Nightingale. 'You can go now.'

Inky rushed off again. Nightingale stood there for a while, lost in thought. Suddenly she remembered Dai-yu. She might already be dead! Her eyes filled with tears, and clenching her teeth, she said fiercely:

'Bao-yu! If she dies, you may think you can wash your hands of her in this callous way: but when you are happily married, and have your heart's desire, you needn't think you can look *me* in the face again!'

As she walked, she began to weep. She made her way, sobbing pitifully, across the Garden. She was not far from the Naiad's House, when she saw two junior maids standing at the gate, peeping out nervously. They saw her coming, and one of them cried out:

'There's Miss Nightingale! At last!'

Nightingale could see that all was not well. Gesturing to them anxiously to be silent, she hurried in, to find Dai-yu red in the face, the fire from her liver having risen upwards and inflamed her cheeks. This was a dangerous sign, and Nightingale called Dai-yu's old wet-nurse, Nannie Wang, to come and take a look. One glance was enough to reduce this old woman to tears. Nightingale had turned to Nannie Wang as an older person, who could be expected to lend them some courage in this extremity. But she turned out to be quite helpless, and only made Nightingale more distraught than before. Suddenly she thought of someone else she could turn to, and sent one of the younger maids to fetch her with all speed. Her choice might seem a strange one; but Nightingale reasoned that as a widow, Li Wan would certainly be excluded from Bao-yu's wedding festivities. Besides she was in general charge of affairs in the Garden, and it would be in order to ask her to come.

Li Wan was at home correcting some of Jia Lan's poems, when the maid came rushing frantically in and cried:

'Mrs Zhu! Miss Lin's dying! Everyone over there is in tears!'

Li Wan rose startled to her feet and without a word set off at once for the Naiad's House, followed by her maids Candida and Casta. As she walked, she wept and lamented to herself:

'When I think of all the times we have spent together – oh my poor cousin! So lovely, so gifted! There is hardly another like her. Only Frost Maiden and the Goddess of the Moon could rival her. How can she be leaving us at such a tender age, for that distant land from whence no travellers return . . . And to think that because of Xi-feng's deceitful scheme, I have not been able to show myself at the Naiad's House and have done nothing to show my sisterly affection! Oh the poor, dear girl!'

She was already at the gate of the Naiad's House. There was no sound from within. She began to fret.

'I must be too late! She must have died already and they are resting between their lamentations. I wonder if her grave-clothes and coverlet are ready?'

She quickened her step and hurried on into the room. A young maid standing at the inner doorway had already seen her, and called out:

'Mrs Zhu is here!'

Nightingale hurried out to meet her.

'How is she?' asked Li Wan.

Nightingale tried to answer but all she could muster was a choked sob. Tears poured down her cheeks like pearls from a broken necklace, as she pointed silently to where Dai-yu lay. Realizing with a pang what Nightingale's pitiable condition must portend, Li Wan asked no more, but went over at once to see for herself. Dai-yu no longer had the strength to speak. When Li Wan said her name a few times, her eyes opened a slit as if in recognition of the voice. But her eyelids and lips could only make a trembling suggestion of a movement. Although she still breathed, it was now more than she could manage to utter a single word, or shed a single tear.

Li Wan turned around and saw that Nightingale was no longer in the room. She asked Snowgoose where she was, and Snowgoose replied:

'In the outer room.'

Li Wan hurried out, to find Nightingale lying on the empty bed, her face a ghastly green, her eyes closed, tears streaming down her cheeks. Where her head lay on the embroidered pillow, with its border of fine brocade, was a patch the size of a small plate, wet with her tears and the copious effusions of her nose. When Li Wan called to her, she opened her eyes slowly, and raised herself slightly on the bed.

'Silly girl!' Li Wan upbraided her. 'Is this a time for tears? Fetch Miss Lin's grave-clothes and dress her in them. Are you going to leave it till it is too late? Would you have her go naked from the world? Would you ruin her honour?'

This released a fresh flood of tears on Nightingale's part. Li Wan wept herself, fretfully wiping her eyes and patting Nightingale on the shoulder.

'Dear girl! Look how you are upsetting me now, and making me cry. Hurry and get her things ready. If we delay much longer, it will all be over.'

They were in this state of trepidation, when they heard footsteps outside, and someone came running into the room in a great flurry, causing Li Wan to start back in alarm. It was Patience. When she saw their tear-stained faces, she stopped abruptly and stared at them aghast for a while.

'Why aren't you over there?' asked Li Wan. 'What do you want here?'

As she spoke, Steward Lin's wife also came into the room. Patience answered:

'Mrs Lian was worried, and sent me to see how things were. As you are here, Mrs Zhu, I can tell her to set her mind at rest.'

Li Wan nodded. Patience went on:

'I should like to see Miss Lin myself.' So saying, she walked into Dai-yu's bed-chamber, with tears on her cheeks. Li Wan turned to Steward Lin's wife and said:

'You have come just in time. Go and find your husband, and tell him to prepare Miss Lin's coffin and whatever else is necessary. When everything has been satisfactorily arranged, he is to let me know. There is no need to go over to the house.'

'Yes, ma'am,' replied Lin's wife, but made no move to go.

'Well? Is there something else?' asked Li Wan.

'Mrs Lian and Her Old Ladyship,' replied the steward's wife, 'have decided that they need Miss Nightingale in attendance over there.'

Before Li Wan could say anything, Nightingale spoke up for herself:

'Mrs Lin, will you be so kind as to leave now? Can't you even wait until she is dead? We will leave her then, you need not fear. How can you be so . . .'

She stopped short, thinking it inadvisable to be so rude, and changing her tone somewhat, said:

'Besides, after waiting on a sick person, I fear we would not be fit for such an occasion. And while Miss Lin is still alive, she may ask for me at any time.'

Li Wan tried to make the peace between them.

'The truth is,' she said, 'that this maid and Miss Lin have an affinity from a past life. Snowgoose, I know, was Miss Lin's original maid from home, but even she is not so indispensable as Nightingale. We really cannot separate them just now.'

Lin's wife, who had been considerably put out by

Nightingale's outspoken response, was obliged to contain herself when Li Wan came to the maid's defence. Seeing Nightingale reduced to floods of tears, she eyed her with a hostile smile and said:

'I shall ignore Miss Nightingale's rudeness. But am I to report what you have just said to Her Old Ladyship? And am I to tell Mrs Lian?'

As she was speaking, Patience came out of Dai-yu's bedchamber, wiping her eyes.

'Tell Mrs Lian what?' she asked.

Lin's wife told her the substance of their conversation. Patience lowered her head in thought. After a moment, she said:

'Why can't you take Snowgoose?'

'Would she do?' asked Li Wan. Patience went up to her and whispered a few words in her ear. Li Wan nodded, and said:

'Well in that case, it will be just as good if we send Snowgoose.'

'Will Miss Snowgoose do?' Lin's wife asked Patience.

'Yes,' replied Patience. 'She will do just as well.'

'Then will you please tell her to come with me straight away,' said Lin's wife. 'I shall report to Her Old Ladyship and Mrs Lian. I shall say that you are both responsible for the arrangement, mind. And later you can tell Mrs Lian yourself, Miss Patience.'

'Of course,' replied Li Wan curtly. 'Do you mean to say that someone as old and experienced as you cannot even take the responsibility for a small thing like this?'

Lin's wife smiled.

'It is not that I can't take the responsibility. It is just that Her Old Ladyship and Mrs Lian have arranged everything and the likes of us don't really know what's going on. In the circumstances, it seems only right to mention you and Miss Patience.'

Patience had already told Snowgoose to come out. Over the past few days Snowgoose had fallen rather into disfavour with Dai-yu, who had called her a 'silly, ignorant child', and her feelings of loyalty towards her mistress had as a consequence been rather blunted. Besides there was no question of her disobeying an order from Her Old Ladyship and Mrs Lian. She therefore tidied her hair quickly and made ready to go. Patience told her to change into her smartest clothes and to go with Mrs Lin. Patience herself stayed on and spoke for a short while with Li Wan. Before she left, Li Wan instructed her to call in on Lin's wife on her way and tell her that her husband should make the necessary preparations for Dai-yu with all possible speed. This Patience agreed to do and went on her way. As she turned a corner in the Garden, she caught sight of Lin's wife walking ahead of her with Snowgoose and called to her to wait.

'I will take Snowgoose with me. You go and tell your husband to prepare Miss Lin's things. I will report to Mrs Lian for you.'

'Yes, Miss Patience,' said Lin's wife, and went on her errand.

Patience then took Snowgoose to the bridal apartment, and reported there herself before going to see to her own affairs.

*

When Snowgoose saw the wedding preparations in full swing and thought of Dai-yu lying at death's door, she felt a pang of grief. But she dared not show her feelings in the presence of Grandmother Jia and Xi-feng. 'What can they want me for?' she wondered. 'I must see what is going on. I know Bao-yu used to be head over heels in love with Miss Lin. And yet now he seems to have deserted her. I begin to wonder if this illness of his is genuine or just a pretence. He may have made the whole thing up so as to avoid upsetting Miss Lin. By pretending to lose his jade and acting like an idiot, perhaps he thinks he can put her off, and marry Miss Chai with a clear conscience? I must watch him closely, and see if he acts the fool when he sees me. Surely he won't keep up the pretence on his wedding-day?' She slipped in and stood spying at the inner doorway.

Now, though Bao-yu's mind was still clouded from the loss of his jade, his sense of joy at the prospect of marrying Dai-yu – in his eyes the most blessed, the most wonderful thing that had happened in heaven or earth since time began – had caused a temporary resurgence of physical well-being, if not a full restoration of his mental faculties. Xi-feng's ingenious plan had had exactly the intended effect, and he was now counting the minutes till he should see Dai-yu. Today was the day when all his dreams were to come true, and he was filled with a feeling of ecstasy. He still occasionally let slip some tell-tale imbecile remark, but in other respects gave the appearance of having completely recovered. All this Snowgoose observed, and was filled with hatred for him and grief for her mistress. She knew nothing of the true cause of his joy.

While Snowgoose slipped away unobserved, Bao-yu told Aroma to hurry and dress him in his bridegroom's finery. He sat in Lady Wang's chamber, watching Xi-feng and You-shi bustling about their preparations, himself bursting with impatience for the great moment.

'If Cousin Lin is coming from the Garden,' he asked Aroma, 'why all this fuss? Why isn't she here yet?'

Suppressing a smile, Aroma replied:

'She has to wait for the propitious moment.'

Xi-feng turned to Lady Wang and said:

'Because we are in mourning, we cannot have music in the street. But the traditional ceremony would seem so drab without any music at all, so I have told some of the women-servants with a bit of musical knowledge, the ones who used to look after the actresses, to come and play a little, to add a bit of a festive touch.'

Lady Wang nodded, and said she thought this a good

idea. Presently the great bridal palanquin was born in through the main gate. The little ensemble of women-servants played, as it entered down an avenue of twelve pairs of palace-lanterns, creating a passably stylish impression. The Master of Ceremonies requested the bride to step out of her palanquin, and Bao-yu saw the Matron of Honour, all in red, lead out his bride, her face concealed by the bridal veil. There was a maid in attendance, and Bao-yu saw to his surprise that it was Snowgoose. This puzzled him for a moment.

'Why Snowgoose, and not Nightingale?' he asked himself. Then: 'Of course. Snowgoose is Dai-yu's original maid from the South, whereas Nightingale was one of our maids, which would never do.'

And so, when he saw Snowgoose, it was as if he had seen the face of Dai-yu herself beneath the veil.

The Master of Ceremonies chanted the liturgy, and the bride and groom knelt before Heaven and Earth. Grandmother Jia was called forth to receive their obeisances, as were Sir Zheng, Lady Wang and other elders of the family, after which they escorted the couple into the hall and thence to the bridal chamber. Here they were made to sit on the bridal bed, were showered with dried fruit and subjected to the various other practices customary in old Nanking families such as the Jias, which we need not describe in detail here.

Jia Zheng, it will be remembered, had gone along with the plan grudgingly, in deference to Grandmother Jia's wishes, retaining grave though unspoken doubts himself as to her theory of 'turning Bao-yu's luck'. But today, seeing Bao-yu bear himself with a semblance of dignity, he could not help but be pleased.

The bride was now sitting alone on the bridal bed, and the moment had come for the groom to remove her veil. Xi-feng had made her preparations for this event, and now asked Grandmother Jia, Lady Wang and others of the ladies present to step forward into the bridal chamber to assist her. The sense of climax seemed to cause Bao-yu to revert somewhat to his imbecile ways, for as he approached his bride he said:

'Are you better now, coz? It's such a long time since we last saw each other. What do you want to go wrapping yourself up in that silly thing for?'

He was about to raise the veil. Grandmother Jia broke into a cold sweat. But he hesitated, thinking to himself:

'I know how sensitive Cousin Lin is. I must be very careful not to offend her.'

He waited a little longer. But soon the suspense became unbearable, and he walked up to her and lifted the veil. The Matron of Honour took it from him, while Snowgoose melted into the background and Oriole came forward to take her place. Bao-yu stared at his bride. Surely this was Bao-chai? Incredulous, with one hand holding the lantern, he rubbed his eyes with the other and looked again. It *was* Bao-chai. How pretty she looked, in her wedding-gown! He gazed at her soft skin, the full curve of her shoulders, and her hair done up in tresses that hung from her temples! Her eyes were moist, her lips quivered slightly. Her whole appearance had the simple elegance of a white lily, wet with pendant dew; the maidenly blush on her cheeks resembled apricot-blossom wreathed in mist. For a moment he stared at her in utter astonishment. Then he noticed that Oriole was standing at her side, while Snowgoose had quite vanished. A feeling of helpless bewilderment seized him, and thinking he must be dreaming, he stood there in a motionless daze. The maids took the lamp from him and helped him to a chair, where he sat with his eyes fixed in front of him, still without uttering a single word. Grandmother Jia was anxious lest this might signal the approach of another of his fits, and herself came over to rally him, while Xi-feng and You-shi escorted Bao-chai to a chair in the inner part of the room. Bao-chai held her head bowed and said nothing.

After a while, Bao-yu had composed himself sufficiently to think. He saw Grandmother Jia and Lady Wang sitting opposite him, and asked Aroma in a whisper:

'Where am I? This must all be a dream.'

'A dream? Why, it's the happiest day of your life!' said Aroma. 'How can you be so silly? Take care: Sir Zeng is outside.'

Pointing now to where Bao-chai sat, and still whispering, Bao-yu asked again:

'Who is that beautiful lady sitting over there?'

Aroma found this so comical that for a while she could say nothing, but held her hand to her face to conceal her mirth. Finally she replied:

'That is your bride, the new Mrs Bao-yu.'

The other maids also turned away, unable to contain their laughter.

Bao-yu: 'Don't be so silly! What do you mean, "Mrs Bao-yu"? Who *is* Mrs Bao-yu?'

Aroma: 'Miss Chai.'

Bao-yu: 'But what about Miss Lin?'

Aroma: 'The Master decided you should marry Miss Chai. What's Miss Lin got to do with it?'

Bao-yu: 'But I saw her just a moment ago, and Snowgoose too. They couldn't have just vanished! What sort of trick is this that you're all playing on me?'

Xi-feng came up and whispered in his ear:

'Miss Chai is sitting over there, so please stop talking like this. If you offend her, Grannie will be very cross with you.'

Bao-yu was now more hopelessly confused than ever. The mysterious goings-on of that night, coming on top of his already precarious mental state, had wrought him up to such a pitch of despair that all he could do was cry – 'I must find Cousin Lin!' – again and again. Grandmother Jia and the other ladies tried to comfort him but he was impervious to their efforts. Furthermore, with Bao-chai in the room, they had to be careful what they said. Bao-yu was clearly suffering from a severe relapse, and they now abandoned their attempts to rally him and instead helped him to bed, while ordering several sticks of gum benzoin incense to be lit, the heavy, sedative fumes of which soon filled the room. They all stood in awesome hush. After a short while, the incense began to take effect and Bao-yu sank into a heavy slumber, much to the relief of the ladies, who sat down again to await the dawn. Grandmother Jia told Xi-feng to ask Bao-chai to lie down and rest, which she did, fully dressed as she was, behaving as though she had heard nothing.

Jia Zheng had remained in an outer room during all of this, and so had seen nothing to disillusion him of the reassuring impression he had received earlier on. The following day, as it happened, was the day selected according to the almanac for his departure to his new post. After a short rest, he took formal leave of the festivities and returned to his apartment. Grandmother Jia, too, left Bao-yu sound asleep and returned to her apartment for a brief rest.

The next morning, Jia Zheng took leave of the ancestors in the family shrine and came to bid his mother farewell. He bowed before her and said:

'I, your unworthy son, am about to depart for afar. My only wish is that you should keep warm in the cold weather and take good care of yourself. As soon as I arrive at my post, I shall write to ask how you are. You are not to worry on my account. Bao-yu's marriage has now been celebrated in accordance with your wishes, and it only remains for me to beg you to instruct him, and impart to him the wisdom of your years.'

Grandmother Jia, for fear that Jia Zheng would worry on his journey, made no mention of Bao-yu's relapse but merely said:

'There is one thing I should tell you. Although the rites were performed last night, Bao-yu's marriage was not properly consummated. His health would not allow it. Custom, I know, decrees that he should see you off today. But in view of all the circumstances, his earlier illness, the luck turning, his still fragile state of convalescence and yesterday's exertions, I am worried that by going out he might catch a chill. So I put it to you: if you wish him to fulfil his filial obligations by seeing you off, then send for him at once and instruct him accordingly; but if you love him, then spare him and let him say goodbye and make his kotow to you here.'

'Why should I want him to see me off?' returned Jia Zheng. 'All I want is that from now on he should study in earnest. That would bring me greater pleasure by far.'

Grandmother Jia was most relieved to hear this. She told Jia Zheng to be seated and sent Faithful, after imparting to her various secret instructions, to fetch Bao-yu and to bring Aroma with him. Faithful had not been away many minutes, when Bao-yu came in and with the usual promptings, performed his duty to his father. Luckily the sight of his father brought him, for a few moments, sufficient clarity to get through the formalities without any gross lapses. Jia Zheng delivered himself of a few exhortatory words, to all of which his son gave the correct replies. Then Jia Zheng told Aroma to escort him back to his room, while he himself went to Lady Wang's apartment. There he earnestly enjoined Lady Wang to take charge of Bao-yu's moral welfare during his absence.

'There must be none of his previous unruliness,' he added. 'He must now prepare himself to enter for next year's provincial examination.'

Lady Wang assured him that she would do her utmost, and without mentioning anything else, at once sent a maid to escort Bao-chai into the room. Bao-chai performed the rite proper to a newly-married bride seeing off her father-in-law, and then remained in the room when Jia Zheng left. The other women-folk accompanied him as far as the inner gate before turning back. Cousin Zhen and the other young male Jias received a few words of exhortation, drank a farewell toast, and, together with a crowd of other friends and relatives, accompanied him as far as the

Hostelry of the Tearful Parting, some three or four miles beyond the city walls, where they bid their final farewell.

But of Jia Zheng's departure no more. Let us return to Bao-yu, who on leaving his father, had suffered an immediate relapse. His mind became more and more clouded, and he could swallow neither food nor drink. Whether or not he was to emerge from this crisis alive will be revealed in the next chapter.

CHAPTER 98

Crimson Pearl's suffering spirit returns
to the Realm of Separation
And the convalescent Stone-in-waiting weeps
at the scene of past affection

On his return from seeing his father, Bao-yu, as we have seen, regressed into a worse state of stupor and depression than ever. He was too lacking in energy to move, and could eat nothing, but fell straight into a heavy slumber. Once more the doctor was called, once more he took Bao-yu's pulses and made out a prescription, which was administered to no effect. He could not even recognize the people around him. And yet, if helped into a sitting position, he could still pass for someone in normal health. Provided he was not called upon to do anything, there were no external symptoms to indicate how seriously ill he was. He continued like this for several days, to the increasing anxiety of the family, until the Ninth Day after the wedding, when according to tradition the newly-married couple should visit the bride's family. If they did not go, Aunt Xue would be most offended. But if they went with Bao-yu in his present state, whatever were they to say? Knowing that his illness was caused by his attachment to Dai-yu, Grandmother Jia would have liked to make a clean breast of it and tell Aunt Xue. But she feared that this too might cause offence and ill-feeling. It was also difficult for her to be of any comfort to Bao-chai, who was in a delicate position as a new member of the Jia family. Such comfort could only be rendered by a visit from the girl's mother, which would be difficult if they had already offended her by not celebrating the Ninth Day. It must be gone through with. Grandmother Jia imparted her views on the matter to Lady Wang and Xi-feng:

'It is only Bao-yu's mind that has been temporarily affected. I don't think a little excursion would do him any harm. We must prepare two small sedan-chairs, and send a maid to support him. They can go through the Garden. Once the Ninth Day has been properly celebrated, we can ask Mrs Xue to come over and comfort Bao-chai, while we do our utmost to restore Bao-yu to health. They will both benefit.'

Lady Wang agreed and immediately began making the necessary preparations. Bao-chai acquiesced in the charade out of a sense of conjugal duty, while Bao-yu in his moronic state was easily manipulated. Bao-chai now knew the full truth, and in her own mind blamed her mother for making a foolish decision. But now that things had gone this far she said nothing. Aunt Xue herself, when she witnessed Bao-yu's pitiful condition, began to regret having ever given her consent, and could only bring herself to play a perfunctory part in the proceedings.

When they returned home, Bao-yu's condition seemed to grow worse. By the next day he could not even sit up in bed. This deterioration continued daily, until he could no longer swallow medicine or water. Aunt Xue was there, and she and the other ladies in their frantic despair scoured the city for eminent physicians, without finding one that could diagnose the illness. Finally they discovered, lodging in a broken-down temple outside the city, a down-and-out practitioner by the name of Bi Zhi-an, who diagnosed it as a case of severe emotional shock, aggravated by a failure to dress in accordance with the seasons and by irregular eating habits, with consequent accumulation of choler and obstruction of the humours. In short, an internal disorder made worse by external factors. He made out a prescription in accordance with this diagnosis, which was administered that evening. At about ten o'clock it began to take effect. Bao-yu began to show signs of consciousness and asked for water to drink. Grandmother Jia, Lady Wang and all the other ladies congregated round the sick-bed felt that they could at last have a brief respite from their vigil, and Aunt Xue was invited to bring Bao-chai with her to Grandmother Jia's apartment to rest for a while.

His brief access of clarity enabled Bao-yu to understand the gravity of his illness. When the others had gone and he was left alone with Aroma, he called her over to his side and taking her by the hand said tearfully:

'Please tell me how Cousin Chai came to be here? I remember Father marrying me to Cousin Lin. Why has *she* been made to go? Why has Cousin Chai taken her place? She has no right to be here! I'd like to tell her so, but I don't want to offend her. How has Cousin Lin taken it? Is she very upset?'

Aroma did not dare tell him the truth, but merely said:

'Miss Lin is ill.'

'I must go and see her,' insisted Bao-yu. He wanted to get up, but days of going without food and drink had so sapped his strength that he could no longer move, but could only weep bitterly and say:

'I know I am going to die! There's something on my mind, something very important, that I want you to tell Grannie for me. Cousin Lin and I are both ill. We are both dying. It will be too late to help us when we are dead; but if they prepare a room for us now and if we are taken there before it is too late, we can at least be cared for together while we are still alive, and be laid out together when we die. Do this for me, for friendship's sake!'

Aroma found this plea at once disturbing, comical and moving. Bao-chai, who happened to be passing with Oriole, heard every word and took him to task straight away.

'Instead of resting and trying to get well, you make

yourself iller with all this gloomy talk! Grandmother has scarcely stopped worrying about you for a moment, and here you are causing more trouble for her. She is over eighty now and may not live to acquire a title because of your achievements; but at least, by leading a good life, you can repay her a little for all that she has suffered for your sake. And I hardly need mention the agonies Mother has endured in bringing you up. You are the only son she has left. If you were to die, think how she would suffer! As for me, I am wretched enough as it is; you don't need to make a widow of me. Three good reasons why even if you want to die, the powers above will not let you and you will not be able to. After four or five days of proper rest and care, your illness will pass, your strength will be restored and you will be yourself again.'

For a while Bao-yu could think of no reply to this homily. Finally he gave a silly laugh and said:

'After not speaking to me for so long, here you are lecturing me. You are wasting your breath.'

Encouraged by this response to go a step further, Bao-chai said:

'Let me tell you the plain truth, then. Some days ago, while you were unconscious, Cousin Lin passed away.'

With a sudden movement, Bao-yu sat up and cried out in horror:

'It can't be true!'

'It is. Would I lie about such a thing? Grandmother and Mother knew how fond you were of each other, and wouldn't tell you because they were afraid that if they did, you would die too.'

Bao-yu began howling unrestrainedly and slumped back in his bed. Suddenly all was pitch black before his eyes. He could not tell where he was and was beginning to feel very lost, when he thought he saw a man walking towards him and asked in a bewildered tone of voice:

'Would you be so kind as to tell me where I am?'

'This,' replied the stranger, 'is the road to the Springs of the Nether World. Your time is not yet come. What brings you here?'

'I have just learned of the death of a friend and have come to find her. But I seem to have lost my way.'

'Who is this friend of yours?'

'Lin Dai-yu of Soochow.'

The man gave a chilling smile:

'In life Lin Dai-yu was no ordinary mortal, and in death she has become no ordinary shade. An ordinary mortal has two souls which coalesce at birth to vitalize the physical frame, and disperse at death to rejoin the cosmic flux. If you consider the impossibility of tracing even such ordinary human entities in the Nether World, you will realize what a futile task it is to look for Lin Dai-yu. You had better return at once.'

After standing for a moment lost in thought, Bao-yu asked again:

'But if as you say, death is a dispersion, how can there be such a place as the Nether World?'

'There is,' replied the man with a superior smile, 'and yet there is not, such a place. It is a teaching, devised to warn mankind in its blind attachment to the idea of life and death. The Supreme Wrath is aroused by human folly in all forms – whether it be excessive ambition, premature death self-sought, or futile self-destruction through debauchery and a life of overweening violence. Hell is the place where souls such as these are imprisoned and made to suffer countless torments in expiation of their sins. This search of yours for Lin Dai-yu is a case of futile self-delusion. Dai-yu has already returned to the Land of Illusion and if you really want to find her you must cultivate your mind and strengthen your spiritual nature. Then one day you will see her again. But if you throw your life away, you will be guilty of premature death self-sought and will be confined to Hell. And then, although you may be allowed to see your parents, you will certainly never see Dai-yu again.'

When he had finished speaking, the man took a stone from within his sleeve and threw it at Bao-yu's chest. The words he had spoken and the impact of the stone as it landed on his chest combined to give Bao-yu such a fright that he would have returned home at once, if he had only know which way to turn. In his confusion he suddenly heard a voice, and turning, saw the figures of Grandmother Jia, Lady Wang, Bao-chai, Aroma and his other maids standing in a circle around him, weeping and calling his name. He was lying on his own bed. The red lamp was on the table. The moon was shining brilliantly through the window. He was back among the elegant comforts of his own home. A moment's reflection told him that what he had just experienced had been a dream. He was in a cold sweat. Though his mind felt strangely lucid, thinking only intensified his feeling of helpless desolation, and he uttered several profound sighs.

Bao-chai had known of Dai-yu's death for several days. While Grandmother Jia had forbidden the maids to tell him for fear of further complicating his illness, she felt she knew better. Aware that it was Dai-yu who lay at the root of his illness and that the loss of his jade was only a secondary factor, she took the opportunity of breaking the news of her death to him in this abrupt manner, hoping that by severing his attachment once and for all she would enable his sanity and health to be restored. Grandmother Jia, Lady Wang and company were not aware of her intentions and at first reproached her for her lack of caution. But when they saw Bao-yu regain consciousness, they were all greatly relieved and went at once to the library to ask doctor Bi to come in and examine his patient again. The doctor carefully took his pulses.

'How odd!' he exclaimed. 'His pulses are deep and still, his spirit calm, the oppression quite dispersed. Tomorrow he must take a regulative draught, which I shall prescribe, and he should make a prompt and complete recovery.'

The doctor left and the ladies all returned to their apartments in much improved spirits.

Although at first Aroma greatly resented the way in which Bao-chai had broken the news, she did not dare say so. Oriole, on the other hand, reproved her mistress in private for having been, as she put it, too hasty.

'What do you know about such things?' retorted Bao-chai. 'Leave this to me. I take full responsibility.'

Bao-chai ignored the opinions and criticisms of those around her and continued to keep a close watch on Bao-yu's progress, probing him judiciously, like an acupunturist with a needle.

A day or two later, he began to feel a slight improvement in himself, though his mental equilibrium was still easily disturbed by the least thought of Dai-yu. Aroma was constantly at his side, with such words of consolation as:

'The Master chose Miss Chai as your bride for her more dependable nature. He thought Miss Lin too difficult and temperamental for you, and besides there was always the fear that she would not live long. Then later Her Old Ladyship thought you were not in a fit state to know what was best for you and would only be upset and make yourself iller if you knew the truth, so she made Snowgoose come over, to try and make things easier for you.'

This did nothing to lessen his grief, and he often wept inconsolably. But each time he thought of putting an end to his life, he remembered the words of the stranger in his dream; and then he thought of the distress his death would cause his mother and grandmother and knew that he could not tear himself away from them. He also reflected that Dai-yu was dead, and that Bao-chai was a fine lady in her own right; there must after all have been some truth in the bond of gold and jade. This thought eased his mind a little. Bao-chai could see that things were improving, and herself felt calmer as a result. Every day she scrupulously performed her duties towards Grandmother Jia and Lady Wang, and when these were completed, did all she could to cure Bao-yu of his grief. He was still not able to sit up for long periods, but often when he saw her sitting by his bedside he would succumb to his old weakness for the fairer sex. She tried to rally him in an earnest manner, saying:

'The important thing is to take care of your health. Now that we are married, we have a whole lifetime ahead of us.'

He was reluctant to listen to her advice. But since his grandmother, his mother, Aunt Xue and all the others took it in turns to watch over him during the day, and since Bao-chai slept on her own in an adjoining room, and he was waited on at night by one or two maids of Grandmother Jia's, he found himself left with little choice but to rest and get well again. And as time went by and Bao-chai proved herself a gentle and devoted companion, he found that a small part of his love for Dai-yu began to transfer itself to her. But this belongs to a later part of our story.

*

Let us return to the wedding-day. Dai-yu, it will be remembered, had lost consciousness while it was still light, and was holding onto life by the slenderest thread. Her weak breathing and precarious heart-beat caused Li Wan and Nightingale to weep in despair. By evening however, she seemed easier again. She feebly opened her eyes, and seemed to be asking for water or medicine. Snowgoose had already left, and only Li Wan and Nightingale were at her bedside. Nightingale brought her a little cup of pear-juice blended with a decoction of longans, and with a small silver spoon fed her two or three spoonfuls of it. Dai-yu closed her eyes and rested for a while. Consciousness would flicker momentarily within her, then fade away again. Li Wan recognized this peaceful state as the last transient revival of the dying, but thinking that the end would not come for a few hours, she returned briefly to Sweet-rice Village to see to her own affairs.

Dai-yu opened her eyes again. Seeing no one in the room but Nightingale and her old wet-nurse and a few other junior maids, she clutched Nightingale's hand and said with a great effort:

'I am finished! After the years you have spent seeing to my every need, I had hoped the two of us could always be together. But now . . .'

She broke off, panting for breath, closed her eyes and lay still, gripping Nightingale's hand tightly. Nightingale did not dare to move. She had thought that Dai-yu seemed so much better, had even hoped she might pull through after all; but these words sent a chill down her spine. After a long pause, Dai-yu spoke again:

'Sister Nightingale! I have no family of my own here. My body is pure: promise me you'll ask them to bury me at home!'

She closed her eyes again and was silent. Her grip tightened still further around Nightingale's hand, and she was seized with another paroxysm of breathlessness. When she could breathe again, her outward breaths became longer, her inward breaths shorter and more feeble. They quickened at a rate that caused Nightingale great alarm, and she sent at once for Li Wan. Tan-chun happened to arrive at that very moment. Nightingale said to her in an urgent whisper:

'Miss! Come and look at Miss Lin!' As she spoke, her tears fell like drops of rain. Tan-chun came over and felt Dai-yu's hand. It was already cold, and her eyes were glazed and lifeless. Tan-chun and Nightingale wept as they gave orders for water to be brought and for Dai-yu to be washed. Now Li Wan came hurrying in. She, Tan-chun and Nightingale looked at each other, but were too shocked to say a word. They began wiping Dai-yu's face with a flannel, when suddenly she cried out in a loud voice:

'Bao-yu! Bao-yu! How could you . . .'

Her whole body broke into a cold sweat and she could say no more. They tried to calm her down and support her. She sweated more and more profusely and her body became colder by degrees. Tan-chun and Li Wan told the maids to put up her hair and dress her in her grave-clothes, and to be quick about it. Her eyes rolled upwards. Alas!

> Her fragrant soul disperses, wafted on the breeze;
> Her sorrows now a dream, drifting into the night.

The moment Dai-yu breathed her last was the very moment that Bao-yu took Bao-chai to be his wife. Nightingale and Dai-yu's other maids began to wail and lament. Li Wan and Tan-chun recalled all their past affection for her, a memory made the more poignant by the lonely circumstances of her death, and they too shed many bitter and heartfelt tears. The wedding chamber was a long way off, and the guests heard nothing of the weeping, but from the Naiad's House, in a brief interval of silence between their lamentations, they heard a faint snatch of music in the distance. They strained their ears to catch it, but it was gone. Tan-chun and Li Wan went out into the garden to listen again, but all they could hear was the rustling of the bamboos in the wind. The moonlight cast a wavering shadow on the wall. It was an eerie, desolate night.

Presently they sent for Steward Lin's wife and had Dai-yu properly laid out. Maids were set to watch the body. Early next morning they reported her death to Xi-feng, who was now placed in an acute dilemma: Grandmother Jia and Lady Wang were both extremely busy and distraught, Jia Zheng was about to leave, Bao-yu in a worse stupor than ever; if she broke the bad news to them now, she was afraid for Grandmother Jia's and Lady Wang's health. They were already burdened with so many worries, and might not be equal to the shock. She decided to go to the Garden herself. When she arrived at the Naiad's

House and went inside, she could not help but weep. She spoke to Li Wan and Tan-chun, and learned that all the correct preparations had been made for the laying out.

'Good,' she said, resuming her brisk tone of voice. 'But I wish you had told me earlier. I have been so worried.'

'How could we?' they replied. 'Sir Zheng was just leaving.'

'Perhaps it was considerate of you,' said Xi-feng, on reflection. 'Well, I must go back and see to the other half of this lovesick pair. I really do not know what to do for the best. I ought to tell them today. But if I do, I am afraid it may be too much for Grandmother.'

'You do what you think best,' said Li Wan.

Xi-feng nodded and hurried back. She arrived to find the doctor with Bao-yu. Hearing him say that Bao-yu's condition was nothing to worry about, and seeing that Grandmother Jia and Lady Wang were calmer as a consequence, she decided to tell them without further delay. She broke it to them as gently as possible, in a place where there was no chance of Bao-yu overhearing. The news had a shattering effect, and Grandmother Jia broke down in tears.

'I am to blame! I have brought this on her! But why did she have to be so obstinate and foolish?'

She wanted to go to the Garden to mourn, but was torn between that and her concern for Bao-yu. Lady Wang and the others all tried to dissuade her, containing their own grief as best they could, and saying:

'You shouldn't go, Mother. You must take care of yourself.'

Grandmother Jia submitted to their counsel, and had to content herself with sending Lady Wang in her place.

'Give her spirit this message from me. Tell her: "It is not because I am hard-hearted that I have not come to bid you farewell, but because my grandson needs me here. You are my daughter's child, I know. But Bao-yu is a Jia, and I cannot leave him now. If I did and he were to die, how would I ever be able to look his father in the face again?"'

The old lady broke down again. Lady Wang tried to console her.

'We all know how much you loved Miss Lin, Mother. But the fates have decreed her an early death. She is dead now and there is nothing more we can do for her, except give her the best possible funeral. That at least will be some expression of our love for her, and will bring some peace to her departed spirit, and that of her dear mother.'

These words brought a fresh and still more heartbroken outburst of tears from Grandmother Jia. Xi-feng was worried that she might damage her health through excess of grief and decided to take advantage of Bao-yu's clouded state of mind to create a distraction. She gave secret instructions to one of the maids, who left the room. Shortly afterwards another maid came in with the timely news that Bao-yu was demanding to see his grandmother. Grandmother Jia stopped crying at once, and asked:

'Gracious! Is anything the matter?'

Xi-feng smiled coaxingly.

'Of course not, Grannie. He is probably just missing you.'

Grandmother Jia immediately put a hand on Pearl's shoulder and set off, accompanied by Xi-feng. They were half-way to Bao-yu's apartment, when they met Lady Wang returning from the Naiad's House. She gave a minute account of her mission, which Grandmother Jia found most moving. But she was intent upon visiting Bao-yu, and had to check her tears and contain her grief.

'Since you have been there and all is in order, I shall not go myself but leave it all to you. It would grieve me too much to see her. I shall rely on you to do things properly.'

Lady Wang and Xi-feng replied that she was quite right to do so, and left her to continue on her way to Bao-yu. When she saw him, she asked:

'What did you want me for?'

He smiled wanly, and said:

'Yesterday evening I saw Cousin Lin, and she told me she was going back to the South. I have been thinking that there is no one here to persuade her to stay, except you, Grannie. Will you, for my sake?'

'Of course I will,' replied Grandmother Jia. 'Don't worry.'

Aroma helped Bao-yu to lie down again, and Grandmother Jia went into Bao-chai's room. This was before Bao-chai had celebrated her Ninth Day, and she still felt rather shy in her new surroundings. When Grandmother Jia came in, she saw that the old lady's face was wet with tears. She served her with a cup of tea, after which Grandmother Jia asked her to be seated, which she did with great diffidence, sitting by her side on the edge of the couch and saying:

'I hear that Cousin Lin has been ill. I hope she is getting better now.'

Tears began to stream from Grandmother Jia's eyes.

'My child! If I tell you, you must promise not to tell Bao-yu. It is all because of your Cousin Lin that you have been made to suffer so. But now that you are Bao-yu's wife, I must tell you the truth. Your Cousin Lin has been dead now for some time. She died just at the time you were married. This present illness of Bao-yu's is all because of her. The three of you were neighbours at one time in the Garden, so I am sure you know what I mean.'

The colour rose in Bao-chai's cheeks. She began to weep too, as she thought of her departed friend. Grandmother Jia talked with her a little longer, and then left.

It was from this moment that Bao-chai began to rack her brains for a cure for Bao-yu. She still felt the need to be cautious, and it was only after the Ninth Day that she acquired the confidence to begin the course of treatment which was to prove so efficacious. With Bao-yu's recovery, it became possible for everyone to talk to him more openly again. But although his health showed a marked daily improvement, nothing could abate his obsessive love for Dai-yu, and he began to insist on going over himself to weep by her corpse. Grandmother Jia forbade it, on the grounds that he was not yet fully cured and any such excursion might upset him. But cooped up as he was in his room, his depression grew almost intolerable and he began to suffer from his old fits again. It was finally the doctor who, in view of the psychological nature of the illness, positively recommended the excursion, to enhance the efficacy of his medicines and speed up the cure. Bao-yu, when he heard this, wanted to go to the Naiad's House at once. This time Grandmother Jia reluctantly gave her permission, and told them to bring a bamboo carrying-chair and help him into it. She and Lady Wang led the way. When they arrived and saw Dai-yu's coffin, Grandmother Jia nearly wept herself into a fit, and was only kept from doing so by the repeated intervention of Xi-feng and the others present. Lady Wang wept too. Li Wan then asked Grandmother Jia and Lady Wang to retire to the inner room, which they did, still weeping. As Bao-yu arrived, his thoughts went back to the days before Dai-yu had fallen ill, before things had taken this turn. The sight of the familiar room was too much for him, and he started howling wildly. How close they had once been! What a gulf death had put between them! His passionate display of grief began to concern them all. They were afraid it might be dangerous, coming so soon after his illness, and all tried to console him. He was already beside himself with weeping, however, and the most they could do was help him to lie down and rest. The others who had accompanied him, including Bao-chai, all wept most bitterly.

Bao-yu, once he had sufficiently recovered, insisted on seeing Nightingale and asking her what Dai-yu's last words had been. Nightingale had formed a most damning opinion of him; but seeing him now so overwhelmed with grief, she softened a little towards him. Besides, Grandmother Jia and Lady Wang were there and she did not dare to be disrespectful towards him in their presence. So she gave him a full account of how her mistress had been taken ill again so suddenly, of how she had destroyed the handkerchiefs and poems, and of the few words she had uttered before her death. Bao-yu cried himself hoarse. Tan-chun now took the opportunity to mention that just before she died Dai-yu had asked for her coffin to be taken to the South. This set Grandmother Jia and Lady Wang weeping again. Luckily Xi-feng was at hand with more words of consolation, and she prevailed upon them to contain their grief. She then politely suggested that they should return to their apartments. Bao-yu could not bring himself to leave. It was only when Grandmother Jia insisted, that he tore himself away and returned to his apartment.

Grandmother Jia, because of her age, and the state of permanent unrest that had prevailed in the household ever since the onset of Bao-yu's illness, was beginning to show signs of strain. This latest scene of grief and lamentation affected her so deeply that she felt a feverishness and faintness coming on, and for all her concern for Bao-yu she no longer felt equal to the situation, but was forced to retire to her room and sleep. Lady Wang was if anything even more inconsolably affected, and retired likewise, giving Suncloud instructions to help Aroma in looking after Bao-yu, and adding:

'If he seems to be taking it badly again, come and tell me at once.'

Bao-chai knew how strong the attachment was that bound Bao-yu to Dai-yu, but rather than try to console him, she continued to take him to task in the same pointed manner as before. He, anxious not to cause her any offence, soon put an end to his weeping and tried to moderate his grief. He went to sleep, and the night passed uneventfully. Early next morning when they came to see how he was, he was still weak and lacking in energy, but seemed to be over the worst. They tended him with renewed care, and gradually he began to recover his strength. Fortunately, Grandmother Jia did not fall sick. It was Lady Wang on whom the shock seemed to leave the most permanent mark.

When Aunt Xue came over to visit the convalescent, she was pleasantly surprised to find him in much better spirits. She stayed for a few days. On one of these days, Grandmother Jia made a point of inviting her over for a talk.

'We owe Bao-yu's life to you,' she began. 'He is out of danger now, I think. I only feel sorry for Bao-chai, after the way things have happened. Bao-yu has been convalescing for a hundred days, and is really quite fit again; and now that the mourning period for Her Grace is over, we can think of celebrating the Consummation. I should like you to choose a lucky day in the calendar for the occasion.'

'Your idea is an excellent one,' returned Aunt Xue. 'But why should you ask me? Bao-chai may not be a very clever girl, but she has a sensible nature, and understands these things. I think you must be familiar with her disposition. If the two of them can live in harmony together, it will be such a relief for you, such a comfort to my sister, and it will set my mind at ease too. You must choose the day. Will we be inviting relatives and friends to the celebrations?'

'I think we should,' replied Grandmother Jia. 'After all, it is the most important event in their lives. There have been so many problems and complications, but now at last they all seem to have been resolved. I think we should send out invitations and make a proper party of it. We will invite all our friends and relations. It will be a way of giving thanks, and besides, I feel that I deserve a bit of fun too, as a little reward for all the heartache this has caused me.'

Aunt Xue was very pleased. She went on to talk of her

plans for preparing Bao-chai's trousseau. Grandmother Jia protested:

'As this is all within the family, there is no need for you to go to such trouble. They already have all the furniture they need. By all means bring some of Bao-chai's favourite things. But please don't bother with anything else. Yes, Bao-chai is such a calm, understanding girl, not at all like my poor granddaughter, whose over-sensitive nature was the cause of her death at such a tender age.'

Aunt Xue now began to cry too. Luckily Xi-feng came in at this moment, and inquired with a smile:

'Grandmother, Auntie, what is troubling you?'

'We were talking about Miss Lin,' answered Aunt Xue. 'It is so sad.'

Xi-feng smiled again.

'You must not allow it to upset you. Listen to this – it's a joke I have just heard.'

Grandmother Jia wiped away her tears, and managed a feeble smile.

'Who are you going to make fun of now? Come on, we are listening. If you don't make us laugh, we will not let you off lightly.'

Xi-feng began gesturing with her hands, but was doubled up with laughter before she could get a word out. To learn what it was she had in mind to tell them, you must turn to the next volume.

EXPLICIT QUARTA PARS LAPIDIS HISTORIAE

APPENDIX I

Prefaces to the first Cheng-Gao edition

a. *Preface by Cheng Weiyuan*

The novel *Hong-lou meng* (*A Dream of Red Mansions*) was originally entitled *Shi-tou ji* (*The Story of the Stone*). There are several conflicting traditions of authorship, and we no longer know who wrote it. We only have the statement in the novel itself, that Mr Cao Xueqin worked on it and rewrote it several times.

Curious readers used to make their own transcriptions of the book, and to buy one of these at the periodic Temple Markets could cost a small fortune. It was a true case of circulation by 'legless locomotion'. But the copies going round are incomplete, as they all consist of eighty chapters, whereas the original table of contents gives a hundred and twenty. Even if some of them claim to be complete, on examination they turn out to have only eighty chapters – altogether a most frustrating experience for the reader!

Surely, I thought to myself, if the table of contents lists one hundred and twenty chapters, a complete version must exist somewhere. I searched everywhere, from antiquarian book-collectors to piles of old discarded papers, leaving no stone unturned, and over a number of years I managed with difficulty to assemble twenty-odd chapters. Then one day, by a stroke of luck, I acquired ten or so more chapters from a peddler. He only agreed to sell them to me for a high price. On perusing these chapters, I discovered to my great delight that the episodes in them could more or less be dovetailed into those in the other chapters that I had previously collected. But the manuscripts were in a hopeless muddle. With the help of a friend, I carefully edited the material, removing what seemed superfluous and making good any gaps, and then transcribed the whole for publication.

So this is the first time that *Hong-lou meng* has been published in its complete form. Now that it is ready, I have appended this account to inform our readers of the circumstances in which this good fortune came about. All who share my love for the book will I am sure be eager to read it without any further delay!

Cheng Weiyuan (Little Spring)

b. *Preface by Gao E*

It is over twenty years since I first heard of *Hong-lou meng* and the great fascination it holds for its readers (despite the fact that there has never been a complete or definitive text). I was once lucky enough to borrow a copy from a friend. Reading it (in this incomplete state) was indeed a tantalizing experience.

In the spring of this year, my friend Cheng Weiyuan came to see me and showed me the complete text that he had purchased. 'This,' he said, 'is the fruit of my labours over several years. Bit by bit I have pieced it together, with a view to publishing it for fellow-lovers of the novel. As you are at a bit of a loose end, and in need of a restorative, will you share the labour [of preparing the manuscript for the press] with me?'

Although it was only a novel, the book contained nothing contrary to the tenets of Confucian teaching, and so I gladly accepted, and fell upon the task with the eagerness of the Persian slave when he saw his pearl! Now that the work is done, I have described these circumstances for the reader's information.

Written in my hand this year *xinhai* of the reign-period Qianlong, the fifth day after the Winter Solstice (27 December 1791).

Gao E of Tieling

Joint Foreword to the subsequent Cheng-Gao edition

1. Collectors have been making their own hand-written copies of the first eighty chapters of this book for nearly thirty years. We have now acquired the last forty chapters and are able to put the

two together to form a complete whole. What with friends borrowing the text to make their own transcriptions, and many others eagerly competing to look at it, it was hard to find time to prepare it properly for the printer (for the first printing). In view of the great length of time needed for woodblock engraving, we decided to bring out a movable-type edition in the first instance. In our eagerness to present the book to fellow readers, we failed to be sufficiently meticulous in collating and proof-reading the first edition, and there were some serious errors contained in it. We have now reassembled the various original texts and made a detailed second recension, which has resulted in an improved text and the removal of many errors. We hope [our previous negligence] will be viewed with indulgence by our readers.

II. Transcriptions of the first eighty chapters varied from copy to copy. We have brought together and collated a large number of these transcriptions, and have exercised our judgement and used our common sense in filling any gaps and rectifying any textual errors. Where any words have been added or subtracted, it has been done to make fluent reading, not out of any presumptuous desire to outdo the original with improvements of our own.

III. Because the novel has been 'unofficially' transmitted over so many years, the copies that come onto the market and those in the possession of private collectors contain many discrepancies. For example, chapter 67 is present in some versions but missing in others. And even if its chapter-heading may be the same, its content varies. In such cases, it is impossible to set up any absolute standard of authenticity. In establishing our text, we have merely followed whatever reading seemed to make the best sense.

IV. The last forty chapters have been acquired over a number of years, and pieced together like a fox-fur patchwork. There have been no other texts to refer to. Our sole object in making the slight modifications we have made has been to integrate earlier and later stages of the plot, and to achieve a degree of continuity and inner consistency. We have not ventured to make any arbitrary alterations, as there is still the hope that we may find a better text and be able to bring out an improved edition. We did not want to swamp the original with matter of our own.

V. The subtlety and originality of this book have long been treasured and commented on by distinguished littérateurs. In preparing it for publication, the sheer bulk of the text itself, and the daunting volume of work involved, led us to exclude the critical comments previously transcribed with it. The reader can, after all, appreciate for himself the brilliant ironic counterpoint of the writing, the interplay between the openly stated and the hidden or implied.

VI. In the past, when men wrote prefaces or signed their names to romances and novels, they were mostly famous writers. These few introductory words of ours, which do not constitute a formal preface, have been written because this book, after having been incomplete for so many years, has suddenly become a whole. This will be a source of great joy to others, and we are glad to let our names be known [in connection with it] and [to celebrate our] good fortune [in having helped to make] this book complete.

VII. Our original motive for printing the book was to give fellow-enthusiasts the opportunity to share its delights. There has subsequently been such a great demand for it from the bookshops that we have arrived at a fixed price to cover publication costs [?for a bigger 'run' of copies]. We do not wish to hoard this treasure!

Little Stream (Cheng Weiyuan)
Orchid Lodge (Gao E)
The day after Flower Morning, the year *renzi*
(4 March 1792)

APPENDIX II

The Octopartite Composition or 'bagu wenzhang.'

The Octopartite Composition, or Eight-legged Essay, was the core of the Chinese educational curriculum and the most important subject in the official examination for nearly five hundred years. Until it was abolished in 1898, every student had to devote a disproportionate amount of energy to mastering its structure and stylistic intricacies. He would be given a *Thema* from either the Four Books or the Five Classics, and had to proceed from one 'leg' to the next of his treatment according to a definite sequence, using the appropriate formulae and rhetorical devices. There was very little room for originality of thought, and a great deal of room for the regurgitation of model essays learnt by heart from the many collections in circulation. Even today in the People's Republic of China, the expression 'Octopartite' is used to refer to cliché-ridden writing, e.g. *dang-bagu* (Communist Party Octopartite, writing full of political jargon).

As early as the seventeenth century, the great scholar Gu Yanwu claimed that the use of the Octopartite in the public exams had done more harm to Chinese culture than the Burning of the Books. But there have also been those who, like Lin Dai-yu, felt that the Octopartite was not *all* bad. A modern scholar, for example, writing of its influence on the famous seventeenth-century critic and poet Jin Shengtan has said:

> In spite of its stifling effects on the intellectual life of China, when viewed simply as a piece of literary composition, the Octopartite has at least the two following merits to recommend it. First, it teaches the writer how to write tightly woven compositions, in which each segment contributes substantially to the whole. Second, it forces the writer to write economically by presenting his main point without bringing in any unnecessary words.[1]

1. John C. Y. Wang, *Chin Sheng-t'an*, New York, 1972, p. 26.

Wang Tao, one of the pioneers of Chinese journalism, writing in the mid-nineteenth century, went even further in its defence:

It is very common nowadays to show how cultivated you are by attacking the style of writing demanded in the official exams, and by sneering at those who cultivate it as a lot of pedants. Actually, the exam style is a definite kind of prose style, and cannot be dismissed lightly. Among the works of the best writers of it you will find pieces equal to anything in classical literature, and worthy to be mentioned in their own way side by side with Tang poetry and Yuan drama.[2]

I doubt if many people today would go quite so far! But it is true that with the abolition of the Octopartite, the aspiring Chinese writer, though liberated from his chains, was also deprived of the mould into which for so many centuries his predecessors had poured their attempts at self-expression. And the immediate result was a spate of formless and redundant writing. The Octopartite stifled, it stultified (when used to excess), but it also provided a mental discipline, rather like that provided by Latin Prose and Verse Composition in the West.

At first, when translating the scenes involving Octopartite Composition (in chapters 82 and 84), I somewhat tentatively used schoolboy Latin. Then, coming across the last volume of Father Angelo Zottoli's monumental *Cursus Litteraturae Sinicae* (which contains the only detailed study of the subject in any Western language),[3] and seeing how effortlessly the terminology of Octopartite Rhetoric went into Latin, I began to realize that the parallel went much deeper than I had thought. For behind the recent and debased tradition of schoolboy Latin Prose Composition lies the much weightier (and more intimidating) tradition of Latin Rhetoric. And this tradition, though lost to our schools in the early nineteenth century, was kept alive by the Jesuits (like Zottoli) well into the twentieth. The extraordinary ease with which Zottoli used the language of Latin Rhetoric to translate the language of Octopartite Rhetoric emboldened me to take him as my model for the Preceptor.

2. Henry McAleavy, *Wang T'ao*, London, 1953, p. 7.

3. Father Angelo Zottoli, *Cursus Litteraturae Sinicae neo-missionariis accomodatus*, 5 vols., Shanghai, 1879–93.

APPENDIX III

The 'Qin' or Chinese Lute, and Knowing the Sound

The *Qin* is a horizontal zither-like instrument about three and a half feet long, with seven silken strings stretched along a curved board, often made of rare wood and elaborately inlaid with mother-of-pearl. It is the musical instrument most closely associated with the artist and poet, the scholar-gentleman. Its repertoire – exquisite, poignant, and above all suggestive – is the musical counterpart of Chinese landscape painting and lyric verse (*ci*). To play this music, and to hear it and appreciate it properly, one must be in harmony with the Tao. For the sensitive young residents of Prospect Garden, the initiates of the Crab-flower Club, this unspoken understanding, this Knowing the Sound, represents the ideal of True Friendship and True Love.

An old story, known to all Chinese readers, lies behind Dai-yu's remark about 'a Rhapsody of Hills and Streams'.[1] In ancient times, a famous luteplayer, Bo Ya, became friendly with a humble woodcutter, Zhong Ziqi. Zhong was so perfectly in tune with his friend's mind that when Bo 'played about' hills Zhong could see Mount Tai rise before his eyes, and when Bo 'played about' streams he could visualize a headlong torrent. When Zhong died, Bo broke his lute and never played again. Readers wishing to explore the fascinating world of the *Qin* will find it described in loving detail by an accomplished player and connoisseur (and scholar), Robert Van Gulik, in *The Lore of the Chinest Lute* (published in Tokyo in 1940).

1. See Chapter 86, p. 153.

APPENDIX IV

Iron Threshold Temple and Water-moon Priory

In chapter 93, I have had to make a few alterations, in order to straighten out a muddled original text. I hope the result is at least simple to follow, and makes for a consistent plot.

Jia Qin's duties (according to my revised text) are to supervise the twenty-four novices at the Iron Threshold Temple, with additional authority over the Priory, while Xi-feng's shady connection is only with Euergesia, the Prioress at Water-moon Priory (see Vol. 1, pp. 296–301). The two establishments are first introduced in chapter 15, where we are told that Water-moon Priory is situated at no great distance from the Temple of the Iron Threshold (Vol. 1, p. 294). The additional detail, that the Priory is an 'offshoot of Water-moon Abbey', is absent from all manuscripts and seems to have been a last minute addition by Gao E, which far from making things any clearer, only adds to the confusion.

If we imagine the two establishments as loosely affiliated foundations supported by the Jia family, it is then plausible for Jia Qin to try seducing Parfumée at the Priory. To have her living at the Temple would be inconsistent with information contained in chapter 77.

CHARACTERS IN VOL 4

ABBOT ZHANG an old Taoist, chief priest of the Lunar Queen Temple

ADAMANTINA a genteel and eccentric young nun residing in Prospect Garden

AMBER maid of Grandmother Jia

AROMA principal maid of Bao-yu

AUNT XUE widowed sister of Lady Wang and mother of Xue Pan and Bao-chai

AUNT ZHAO concubine of Jia Zheng and mother of Tan-chun and Jia Huan

AUNT ZHOU Jia Zheng's other concubine

AUTUMN concubine given to Jia Lian by his father

BAO-CHAI *see* XUE BAO-CHAI

BAO ER servant employed by Cousin Zhen

BAO-QIN *see* XUE BAO-QIN

BAO YONG Zhen family servant seeking employment with the Jias

BAO-YU *see* JIA BAO-YU

BI ZHI-AN a down-and-out physician

BIG JIAO an old retainer of the Ning-guo Jias

BIJOU stage name of JIANG YU-HAN

BRIGHTIE
BRIGHTIE'S WIFE } couple employed by Jia Lian and Wang Xi-feng

CALTROP Xue Pan's 'chamber wife'; the kidnapped daughter of Zhen Shi-yin

CANDIDA maid of Li Wan

CASTA maid of Li Wan

CHAI *see* XUE BAO-CHAI

CHESS principal maid of Ying-chun

COOK LIU in charge of the kitchen for Prospect Garden; mother of Fivey

COUSIN BAO (1) *see* JIA BAO-YU (2) *see* XUE BAO-CHAI

COUSIN CHAI *see* XUE BAO-CHAI

COUSIN DAI *see* LIN DAI-YU
COUSIN FENG *see* WANG XI-FENG
COUSIN LIAN *see* JIA LIAN
COUSIN LIN *see* LIN DAI-YU
COUSIN PAN *see* XUE PAN
COUSIN QIN *see* XUE BAO-QIN
COUSIN SHI *see* SHI XIANG-YUN
COUSIN TAN *see* JIA TAN-CHUN
COUSIN WAN *see* LI WAN
COUSIN XI *see* JIA XI-CHUN
COUSIN XUE *see* XUE PAN
COUSIN YING *see* JIA YING-CHUN
COUSIN YUN *see* SHI XIANG-YUN
COUSIN ZHEN son of Jia Jing; head of the senior (Ning-guo) branch of the Jia family
CRIMSON maid employed by Xi-feng
CRUCIBLE a young Taoist nun seduced by Jia Qin
DAI *see* LIN DAI-YU
DAI-RU *see* JIA DAI-RU
DAI-YU *see* LIN DAI-YU
DR WANG *see* WANG JI-REN
EARL OF LIN-AN aristocratic friend of the Jias
EBONY maid of Tan-chun
FAITHFUL principal maid of Grandmother Jia
FELICITY maid attendant on Xi-feng
FENG *see* WANG XI-FENG
FENG ZI-YING family friend of the Jias
FIVEY daughter of Cook Liu; taken on as one of Bao-yu's maids
FROWNER *see* LIN DAI-YU
FU QIU-FANG unmarried sister of Fu Shi
FU SHI ambitious protégé of Jia Zheng
GAFFER LI proprietor of Li's Bar
GRANDMOTHER JIA *née* Shi; widow of Bao-yu's paternal grandfather and head of the Rong-guo branch of the Jia family
HER GRACE *see* JIA YUAN-CHUN
HE SAN Zhou Rui's adopted son
HU-SHI Jia Rong's second wife
HUAN *see* JIA HUAN
INKY one of Bao-yu's pages
INTENDANT HU father of Hu-shi
IRON CRUTCH LI a Taoist Immortal

IRON MOUTH LIU a fortune-teller, specializing in word-divining or logomancy

JIA BAO-YU incarnation of the Stone; the eldest surviving son of Jia Zheng and Lady Wang of Rong-guo House

JIA DAI-RU the Preceptor, in charge of the Jia family school

JIA HUAN Bao-yu's half-brother; the son of Jia Zheng and his concubine, 'Aunt' Zhao

JIA LAN Li Wan's son

JIA LIAN son of Jia She and Lady Xing and husband of Wang Xi-feng

JIA QIAO-JIE little daughter of Jia Lian and Wang Xi-feng

JIA QIN junior member of the clan employed by the Rong-guo Jias to look after the nuns from Prospect Garden in the family temple outside the city

JIA RONG son of Cousin Zhen and You-shi

JIA SHE Jia Zheng's elder brother; father of Jia Lian and Ying-chun

JIA TAN-CHUN daughter of Jia Zheng and 'Aunt' Zhao; half-sister of Bao-yu and second of the 'Three Springs'

JIA XI-CHUN daughter of Jia Jing and younger sister of Cousin Zhen; youngest of the 'Three Springs'

JIA YING-CHUN daughter of Jia She by a concubine; eldest of the 'Three Springs'

JIA YU-CUN a careerist claiming relationship with the Jia family

JIA YUAN-CHUN daughter of Jia Zheng and Lady Wang and elder sister of Bao-yu; the Imperial Concubine

JIA YUN poor relation of the Rong-guo Jias, once employed by Xi-feng in Prospect Garden

JIA ZHENG Bao-yu's father; the younger of Grandmother Jia's two sons

JIA ZHU deceased elder brother of Bao-yu; husband of Li Wan and father of her son Jia Lan

JIANG YU-HAN a female impersonator, now turned actor-manager

JIN-GUI *see* XIA JIN-GUI

KINGFISHER Shi Xiang-yun's maid

LADY JIA *see* GRANDMOTHER JIA

LADY WANG wife of Jia Zheng, and mother of Jia Zhu, Yuan-chun and Bao-yu

LADY XING wife of Jia She and mother of Jia Lian

LAI DA Chief Steward of Rong-guo mansion

LAI SHENG Chief Steward of Ning-guo mansion
LANDSCAPE maid of Xi-chun
LI DE a servant at Rong-guo House
LI GUI Nannie Li's son; Bao-yu's foster-brother and chief groom
LI QI Li Wan's cousin; younger sister of Li Wen
LI WAN widow of Bao-yu's deceased elder brother, Jia Zhu, and mother of Jia Lan
LI WEN Li Wan's cousin; elder sister of Li Qi
LI XIANG Xue family servant
LILY name given to Caltrop by Xia Jin-gui
LIN-AN, EARL OF *see* EARL OF LIN-AN
LIN DAI-YU incarnation of the Crimson Pearl Flower; orphaned daughter of Lin Ru-hai and Jia Zheng's sister, Jia Min
LIN ZHI-XIAO, LIN ZHI-XIAO'S WIFE } domestics holding the highest position in the Rong household under the Chief Steward Lai Da
MASTER BAO *see* JIA BAO-YU
MISS BAO *see* XUE BAO-CHAI
MISS LIN *see* LIN DAI-YU
MISS QIAO-JIE *see* JIA QIAO-JIE
MISS SHI *see* SHI XIANG-YUN
MISS XING *see* XING XIU-YAN
MOTHER MA a Wise Woman; Bao-yu's godmother
MR LIAN *see* JIA LIAN
MR QIN *see* JIA QIN
MR SUN *see* SUN SHAO-ZU
MR YUN *see* JIA YUN
MR ZHEN *see* COUSIN ZHEN
MRS LIAN *see* WANG XI-FENG
MRS XUE *see* AUNT XUE
MRS ZHANG *née* Wang; impoverished rustic, mother of Zhang San
MRS ZHAO *see* AUNT ZHAO
MRS ZHEN *see* YOU-SHI
MRS ZHOU *see* ZHOU RUI'S WIFE
MRS ZHU *see* LI WAN
MUSK maid of Bao-yu
NANNIE LI (1) Bao-yu's former wet-nurse (2) Qiao-jie's nurse
NANNIE LIU Another of Qiao-jie's nurses
NANNIE WANG Dai-yu's former wet-nurse
NIGHTINGALE principal maid of Dai-yu

ORIOLE principal maid of Bao-chai
PAN SAN-BAO informant against Mother Ma
PAN YOU-AN cousin and lover of Chess
PARFUMÉE ex-actress, now a nun at Water-moon Priory
PATIENCE chief maid and confidante of Wang Xi-feng
PEARL maid of Grandmother Jia's, elder sister of Simple
PLOUGHBOY one of Bao-yu's pages
PRECEPTOR, THE *see* JIA DAI-RU
PRINCE OF BEI-JING, THE princely connection of the Jias, friendly with Bao-yu
PRINCE OF NAN-AN, THE patron of Jiang Yu-han's theatrical troupe
PROSPER maid to Aunt Xue
QIAO-JIE *see* JIA QIAO-JIE
QIN-ZHONG dead friend of Bao-yu; younger brother of Jia Rong's deceased first wife
RIPPLE maid of Bao-yu
SCRIBE principal maid of Tan-chun
SHI XIANG-YUN orphaned great-niece of Grandmother Jia, niece of Shi Ding, the Marquis of Zhong-jing
SIMPLE a maid in Grandmother Jia's apartment, younger sister of Pearl
SIR SHE *see* JIA SHE
SIR ZHENG *see* JIA ZHENG
SKYBRIGHT one of Bao-yu's maids, now dead
SNOWGOOSE maid of Dai-yu
STEWARD LIN *see* LIN ZHI-XIAO
SUN SHAO-ZU Jia Ying-chun's callous husband
SUNCLOUD, SUNSET } maids of Lady Wang
SUNSHINE page employed by Wang Xi-feng for clerical duties
SWEEPER one of Bao-yu's pages
TAN-CHUN *see* JIA TAN-CHUN
TEALEAF Bao-yu's principal page
THURIBLE a young Buddhist nun, seduced by Jia Qin
WANG ER-TIAO 'Go-between' Wang; one of Jia Zheng's literary gentlemen
WANG JI-REN doctor in regular attendance on Rong-guo Jias
WANG REN Wang Xi-feng's elder brother
WANG XI-FENG wife of Jia Lian and niece of Lady Wang, Aunt Xue and Wang Zi-teng

WANG ZI-SHENG younger brother of Wang Zi-teng
WANG ZI-TENG elder brother of Wang Zi-sheng, Lady Wang and Aunt Xue
WU, EXCELLENCY GOVERNOR high-ranking civil servant, friend of Jia Zheng
WU GUI Skybright's cousin
WU LIANG Xue Pan's fairweather friend
XI-CHUN *see* JIA XI-CHUN
XI-FENG *see* WANG XI-FENG
XIA JIN-GUI wife of Xue Pan; a termagant
XIA SAN adopted brother of Xia Jin-gui
XIANG-YUN *see* SHI XIANG-YUN
XING XIU-YAN Lady Xing's niece; gifted daughter of improvident and sponging parents, betrothed to Xue Ke
XUE BAO-CHAI daughter of Aunt Xue
XUE BAO-QIN niece of Aunt Xue and younger sister of Xue Ke
XUE KE XUE Bao-qin's elder brother, betrothed to Xing Xiu-yan
XUE PAN the 'Oaf King'; son of Aunt Xue and elder brother of Bao-chai
YING *see* JIA YING-CHUN
YING-CHUN *see* JIA YING-CHUN
YOU ER-JIE Jia Lian's mistress, now dead
YOU-SHI wife of Cousin Zhen and mother of Jia Rong
YU-CUN *see* JIA YU-CUN
YUAN-CHUN *see* JIA YUAN-CHUN
YUN (1) *see* SHI XIANG-YUN (2) *see* JIA YUN
ZHAN GUANG one of Jia Zhang's literary gentlemen
ZHANG DE-HUI manager of Xue Pan's largest pawnshop
ZHANG ER brother-in-law of Mrs Zhang, uncle of Zhang San
ZHANG, EXCELLENCY (1) wealthy father of Miss Zhang (2) colleague of Jia Zheng's at the Board of Works (3) a Privy Councillor
ZHANG, MISS only daughter of Excellency Zhang (1), proposed as match for Bao-yu
ZHANG SAN waiter, only surviving son of Mrs Zhang
ZHENS a wealthy Southern family having close ties with the Jias
ZHEN BAO-YU son of Zhen Ying-jia; a 'reformed character'
ZHEN YING-JIA friend of Jia Zheng's; father of Zhen Bao-yu
ZHOU RUI } couple employed on the staff of Rong-
ZHOU RUI'S WIFE } guo House

Genealogy of the Ning-guo and Rong-guo Houses of the Jia Clan

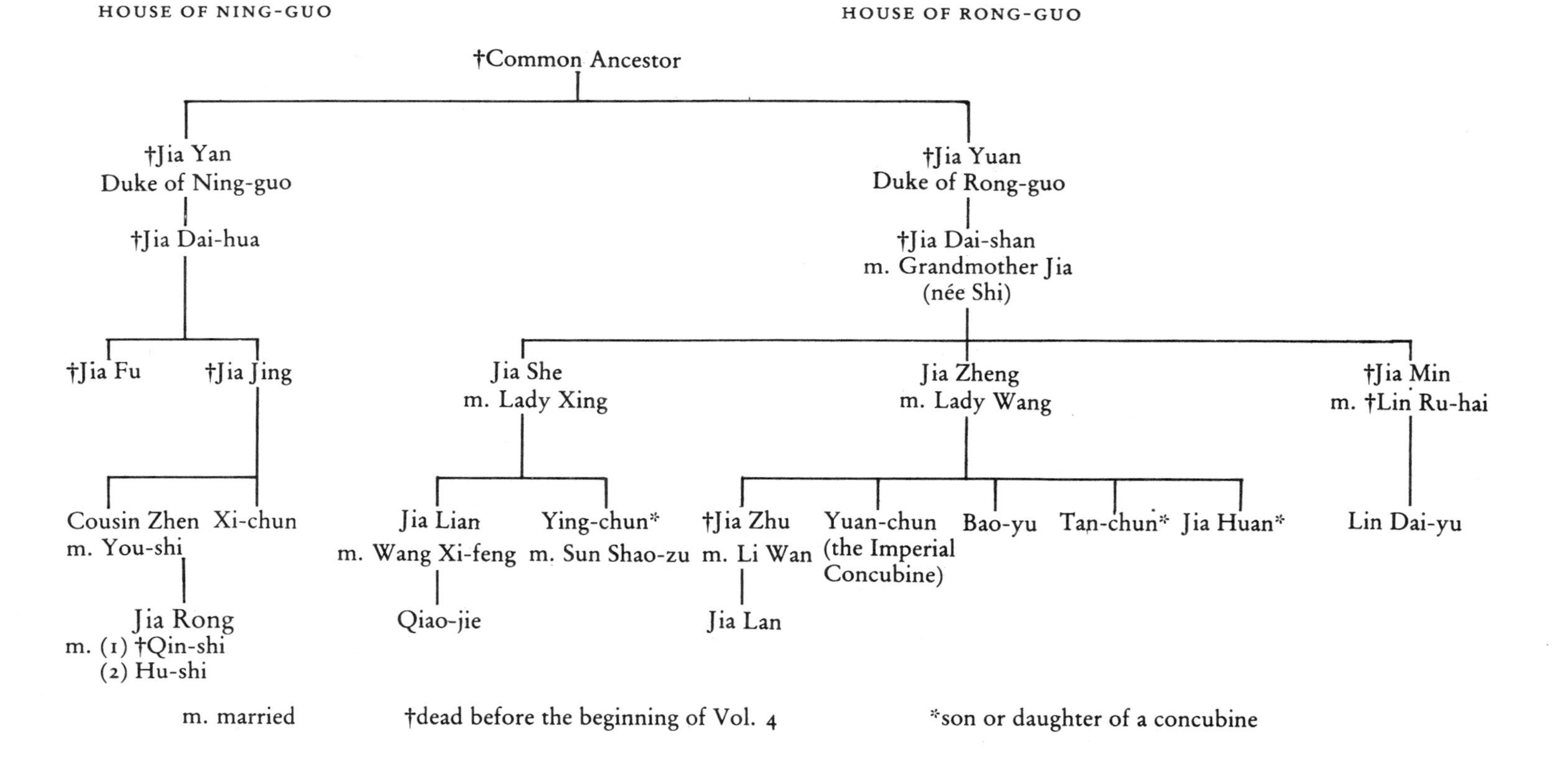

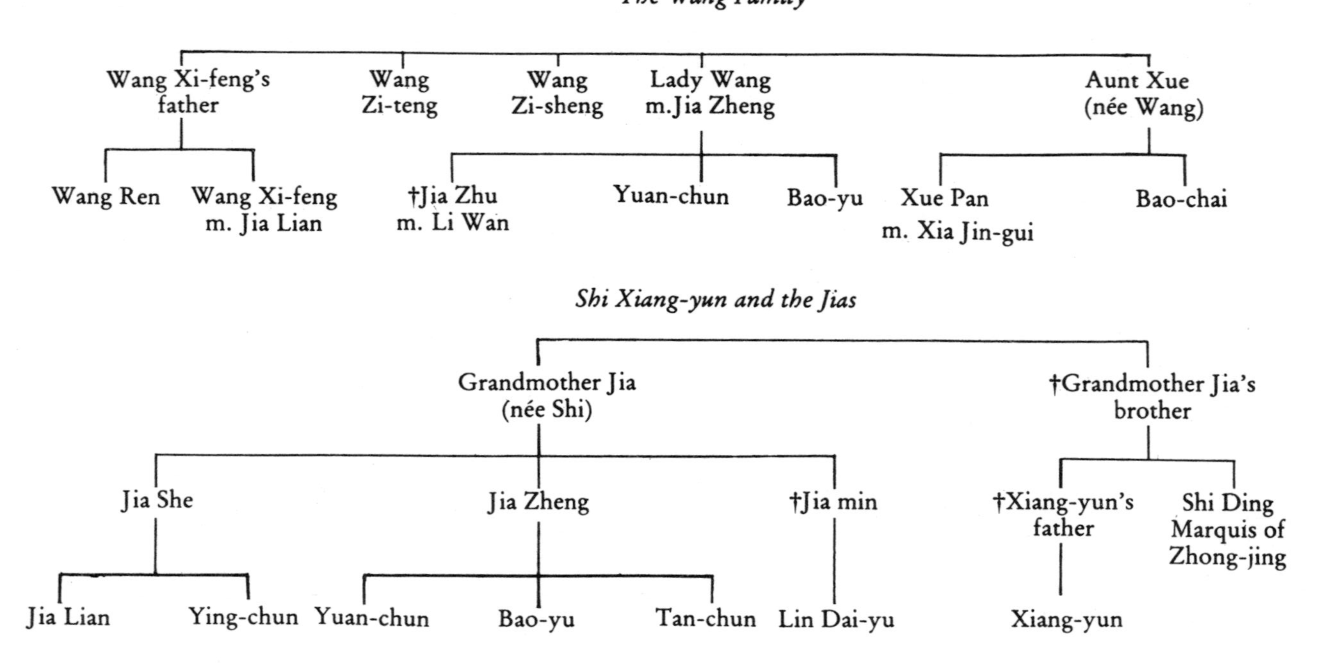
The Wang Family
Wang Xi-feng's father
Wang Zi-teng
Wang Zi-sheng
Lady Wang m.Jia Zheng
Aunt Xue (née Wang)
Wang Ren
Wang Xi-feng m. Jia Lian
†Jia Zhu m. Li Wan
Yuan-chun
Bao-yu
Xue Pan m. Xia Jin-gui
Bao-chai
Shi Xiang-yun and the Jias
Grandmother Jia (née Shi)
†Grandmother Jia's brother
Jia She
Jia Zheng
†Jia min
†Xiang-yun's father
Shi Ding Marquis of Zhong-jing
Jia Lian
Ying-chun
Yuan-chun
Bao-yu
Tan-chun
Lin Dai-yu
Xiang-yun